TERROR in OUR HOMELAND

by DAVID ADAMS

Terror in Our Homeland

David Adams

Published by David Adams, 2022.

Original Copyright 2016 by David Adams. All rights reserved.

Without limiting the rights under copyright reserved above, no part of this publication may be reproduced, stored in or introduced into a retrieval system, or transmitted, in any form, or by means (electronic, mechanical, photocopying, recording, or otherwise) without the prior written permission of the author of this book.

This is a work of fiction.

Names, characters, places, brands, media, and incidents are either the product of the author's imagination or are used fictitiously. Any resemblance to actual events, locales, or persons, living or dead, is coincidental. This Book is licensed for your personal enjoyment only. This eBook may not be re-sold or given away to other people. If you would like to share this book with another person, please purchase another copy for each person you share with. Thank you for respecting the author's work.

Published by: DAVID ADAMS (REVISED VERSION JUNE 2022)

This is a work of fiction. Similarities to real people, places, or events are entirely coincidental.

TERROR IN OUR HOMELAND

First edition. July 12, 2022.

Copyright © 2022 David Adams.

ISBN: 978-0645361124

Written by David Adams.

Also by David Adams

Terror in Our Homeland

I dedicate this book to my long-suffering wife who travels to dangerous parts of the world helping to provide new exciting experiences and locations. As well as this she lives with me being locked in my office and often distracted even if I am with her. Thanks, Broni

A special thanks to my Beta Readers, Marie Watson, and Tanya Tomlinson thank you for your input they help the books quality and my growth as an author.

AUTHOR'S NOTE

This is a revised version of my original eBook.

It is noteworthy that the Australian Federal Police have since arrested Terrorists plotting to carry out one of the attacks found in this book written some years before. As well as this I have received abuse from members of organisations within Australia who would prefer any warning even authentically woven in fiction not exist. I have always treated the Moslem Faith and peaceful believers with respect, some of my friends are devout Moslems.

My books reflect this, Terrorists and their supporters, however, are a different matter.

WHAT READERS HAVE SAID ABOUT TERROR IN OUR HOMELAND

A great read. Seemed to be well researched and current. I hadn't thought about a terrorist attack in Australia.

�����

The book is fast paced, the plot is believable in today's political climate and the characters while flawed are totally likeable and authentic.

�����

I could smell the gun powder when I was reading the battle scenes.

�����

I've found out why people all over the world are loving Steve Wallace, a reluctant but able hero in this fast paced action story. KOBO.

�����

I can't believe this is his first book, can't wait for the next one.

OUT NOW !!!! MY NEXT BOOK, TERROR IN PARADISE

ISIS are funding their evil plans to dominate the world by selling stolen ancient artefacts. The CIA need Australian Agent Steve Wallace to go undercover to collect Intelligence so the organisation can be destroyed. The money gained from these illicit sales is being used to buy missiles, guns, and ammunition as well as fund cells and terrorist attacks including 911. Steve Wallace is ex SAS and one of the best, but this undercover job calls for a James Bond or Jason Bourne. This time he's way out of his depth. Can he succeed out of his comfort zone? Tracking the smugglers all over the world while racking up a body count he sends shock waves through the sophisticated organisation, all the way up to the third generation New York Antique Dealer.

Steve Wallace comes up against Smugglers, Hitmen, Bedouins and ISIS, and they all want him dead. Will his luck run out this time? This mission becomes a real Terror in Paradise when it takes him to exotic places all over the world climaxing aboard a luxury Cruise Liner travelling to New York.

Based on the true story of ISIS funding its operations by selling stolen ancient artefacts. Hawala is an Islamic banking system employing trust between members not requiring the transfer of funds. It was developed over two thousand years ago and thrives to this day.

PROLOGUE

While this is a story set in recent times this Prologue is a dramatisation of a documented true account of the first Terrorist and Moslem Terrorist attack on Australian soil. The people are real Australians who lived and died at that time in our history. This book is pure fiction and I sincerely hope and pray it's in no way prophetic. The topic dictates some details, explanations and political comments, however, there is no agenda other than providing a good yarn that like any such story could be true.

NEW YEAR'S DAY 1915
BROKEN HILL
NEW SOUTH WALES
AUSTRALIA

My name is Jonathan Askew I am a hack reporter on the local rag *The Barrier Miner* here in Broken Hill, usually a busy town too involved in digging up the treasures of lead, zinc and copper that are found in these parts in abundance. I got this job because all the real reporters have been sent over to report on the Great War. For a long time, the war was just a distant story on Page 1. Except for the odd bloke who had gone off to fight and the drop in mineral prices, you wouldn't have known there was a war going on.

The following is my recollection of the events of New Year's Day 1915 and the next couple of days that followed. I can only imagine what will happen in the distant future. This account will all sound like a story of fiction that I have made up to excite and shock the reader but sadly this really did happen. In an attempt to humanise these events my commentary may be creative regarding people's actions at home or their thoughts. However, no facts have been lost through my narration although behind the scene details have been added in a way to weave a fuller picture of the terrible events of that day that should have held so much promise for so many.

Mullah Abdullah was born in Afghanistan in the year 1854, he was a member of the Afridis Tribe, where he had lived and worked. There he and another man Badsha Mohammed Gool who shared his strong religious convictions travelled to Turkey. Gool was the younger having been born in 1874 into the same Tribe. However, he was also a warrior soldier. Gool had enlisted into the Army of the Ottoman Empire (Turks) fighting in four campaigns. He was reportedly a tough trained and dedicated soldier. It is uncertain why, but Abdullah came to Australia in 1898 while Gool moved to Australia sometime after 1900. Being highly experienced working with camels they found employment as Cameleers. While many of their peers were opening up the interior of Australia and helping build Railways, this pair ended up working camels in the developing mines of the Broken Hill Region. They appear to have settled into Australian life in some ways while keeping very strong ties to life back in their homeland.

There is no way of knowing for sure, but it looks like Abdullah was the Religious Zealot of the pair while Gool was the Militant Fundamentalist, a perfect pair completing one an other's views of the world. Possibly brought on by the drop in mineral prices, there was less work for the camels, so they took on other work. Both men lived in the Western Camel Camp outside Broken Hill proper surrounded by their fellow countrymen. Abdullah was seen as an Iman, a Religious Leader of the Camp, he was also the Halal Butcher for all the Moslems in that camp. Gool on the other hand had started up his own business, building an attractive Ice Cream cart that was seen all around the hot mining town. It had become very popular with residents of all ages. It might seem a bit strange to mention some of this but it all ties in as you will soon see. Now it seems that Abdullah's Halal Butcher business attracted more than just flies.

He had been warned and prosecuted on many occasions by the Officers of the Municipal Sanitary Department. Just a few days before the end of 1914 he had been prosecuted and convicted by the Police Court once again for slaughtering sheep at his premises. Abdullah's shop did not hold the necessary licence as it was deemed unsanitary by the Sanitary Inspector Mr Brosnan. I had noticed that Abdullah did not wear the customary Turban that his people wore. As a journalist, I have an enquiring mind and notice such things. When I enquired about this I was told there were reports Abdullah had stopped wearing his tribal headgear after some hooligans had thrown rocks at him and ridiculed him for wearing a towel on his head.

As far as I can tell, except for the sheep slaughtering, neither Abdullah nor Gool did anything to bring any unwanted attention to themselves, at least until that New Year's Day of 1915. At the declaration of war between Turkey and Great Britain Gool being an ex-soldier of the Turkish Army immediately wrote to the Minister of War in Istanbul offering to re-enlist. There is no record or at least a reliable record of any response. However, it is not unbelievable that Gool and his fellow Tribesman Abdullah became some sort of spies or agents for the Turks. The two Afghanis spent a lot of time together. I've been told they often talked about home wondering whether they should head for Turkey or somewhere where they could fight for the faith and the land they loved. I have asked around as much as I could and while there is no way to be sure it seems that late in 1914 they decided on a journey that would take them where they desired, a journey without return.

Seventeen-year-old Alma Cowrie was tired after staying up to see the New Year in with her family. She was standing in front of the mirror brushing her long blond locks and admiring the beautiful blue dress that her mother had just finished the night before. Alma was excited, the Manchester Unity Order of Oddfellows Annual Picnic was pretty much the highlight of the social life in the hard and dusty mining town of Broken Hill. She was looking forward to spending the day with her boyfriend Clarrie O'Brien. Her mind was filled with thoughts of how much she hated the fact that the transport was so crude. But this was life as a miner's daughter and the mines provided nearly everything but clean air. She had heard that this year there was going to be so many people that there would be as many as 40 open ore trucks in the Picnic Train.

The picnic started with a short ride on the Silverton Tramway Company train from Broken Hill to a pretty spot down Penrose Park near Silverton. Once again, she grimaced at the thought of her bright blue dress in an open ore truck. All she could hope was that the men had washed it out successfully. She felt a bit guilty having these thoughts, but she was still excited and grateful for the company picnic being held each year. As Alma and her family arrived at the station she was amazed at how many people were there. The Conductor told her father there were close to twelve hundred men, women and children, the biggest picnic ever.

The air was filled with excited squeals from children and laughter from the adults interspersed with billowing steam from the front of the train and the smell of burning coal. It was truly a beautiful summer's day, the sunshine cascaded down over the happy travellers. The air seemed especially clear which was probably related to the fact that it was one of the few days that the mine and processing plants were shut for the holiday. The passengers moaned loudly as the train jerked away from the station. When the engine finally took up the weight of forty trucks filled with celebrating residents every man, woman and child sent up an almighty cheer. With celebratory toots from the train's whistle, the long centipede of happy picnickers pulled out of the station. Alma was looking around furtively to see if her father was watching and whether she should hold hands with her beau Clarrie O'Brien.

Everyone was talking and joking and laughing. Collectively they were shedding the weight of digging out a hard-living and for a little while putting any thoughts of the war out of their minds. Sometime later as they came around a curve in the track, several people saw the familiar white sign of the Ice Cream cart parked over to the left up on a slight rise. There was a ripple of comments about maybe getting an ice cream which set off the whimpering pleading of the children who couldn't fully see over the steep sides of the ore wagons. Some of the passengers noticed that the Ice Cream men had rifles and assumed they were out hunting rabbits on their day off.

The site was so familiar there could be nothing sinister about the Ice Cream cart as it started down towards the train. The cart was well placed as the train had to all but stop as it attempted to gain its strength to pull up the next hill. As the Afghanis approached the stalled train they raised what appeared to be a flag of some sort, most of the picnickers didn't recognise its origin or its meaning. It was a Turkish flag that the men had made in their home at the Camel Camp. Now only thirty yards away from the happy families, some reaching into their pockets for change to buy ice creams, the two Afghanis started what was to be the only attack on Australian soil of World War One. They raised their Snider and Martini-Henry rifles and opened fire on the highly vulnerable and exposed passengers in the forward trucks. Further down the line, the festive mood continued incorrectly assuming that the gunfire up ahead was part of the celebrations of the New Year with all its promise. Abdullah and Gool were practised shooters.

Taking aim over the metal sights at any available target they showed no mercy or thought to age or gender. They were both wearing full homemade ammunition bandoleers and kept loading and firing until the slow train pulled away. They had cleverly placed themselves slightly higher than the wagons so that they were able to fire down into them.

As the sounds of the first few shots were still echoing off the steel sides of the wagons a large wet red stain appeared on Alma Cowrie's new blue dress. As she was killed instantly she slumped over her boyfriend Clarrie O'Brien and never knew what happened to her. Nine other passengers died under the hail of bullets fired over a very short period. Worth noting was the fact that William John Shaw was killed, and his little daughter Lucy was wounded by some of the first shots. It was no coincidence as Bill

Shaw was a foreman in the Sanitary Department, a note later will explain the relevance of this. The victims included the hapless Pipeline Inspector Alf Millard who was riding his cycle beside the slow-moving train enjoying talking to the laughing passengers inside the Picnic Train. Happy and excited one minute, looking forward to their plans for the New Year and then within a few more minutes dead, wounded or crying, some trying to help the wounded. Amongst the injured; were Mary Kavanagh, George Stokes, Thomas Campbell, Alma Crocker, and Rose Crabb. The two Afghans weren't going to have it all their own way Railway Guard 'Tiger' Dick (Eric Edward) Nyholm was well known in these parts as an exceptional shooter. Tiger always had his rifle nearby and today was no different, so he started returning fire successfully driving back the two assailants and protecting the passengers from further harm as the slow train left the assailants behind.

The attack on the train was over but their murderous desires had not been quenched, Abdullah and Gool headed away from the train towards the Western Camel Camp where they lived. On their way, they killed a man called Alfred Millard who was absolutely no threat to the two killers. Alfred had run into his hut to hide when he saw them coming up the dirt track that swung past his place. The two men knew the area well and headed for a place called White Rocks. Back at the train, there was a stunned silence that only shock and horror can produce. It was occasionally interrupted by a scream of pain either physical from one of the wounded or emotional from one of the survivors who had lost a loved one. The train driver took the sad caravan into a siding. No one is sure who phoned the Police informing them of the atrocity and the direction that the two assailants had taken. The Police Sergeant realising this was much more than just a criminal matter then contacted the local Army Base talking to a young Lieutenant Resch who without hesitation dispatched his men to the area.

After the Police Officers and Soldiers had searched the most likely places they found the killers holed up at the back of the Cable Hotel, behind some white quartz rock for cover. The two Afghanis immediately fired upon the Police and Soldiers wounding Constable Mills. A ninety-minute battle ensued where hundreds of rounds were exchanged especially after the arrival of several angry citizens who had heard about the attack and had armed themselves hoping to stumble upon the killers seeking some rough justice and a lot of revenge. Jim Craig's daughter had been pleading with her father for the last fifteen minutes ever since the shooting at the pub had started.

She tried again. "Father please don't go out there that's a lot more shooting than just a couple of drunk miners having a blue".

In his strong Irish accent, her father's reply did not ease her fears. "Just because I am sixty-nine it doesn't mean I am going to hide under my bed every time I hear a gun go off, and that firewood is not going to chop itself up child".

At this James Craig pushed past his worried daughter took a few steps out his back door towards the waiting wood pile and was shot dead before he got to take up his axe. No one would ever know if the bullet was from one of the two Afghanis, a Soldier, a Police Officer or a civilian but that didn't make poor old Jim any less dead. Nearly an hour and a half after the first shot, the shooting from the pair of murderers had slowed down a lot and had seemed to be getting a lot less accurate. Constable Ward turned to Lieutenant Resch and wondered out loud.

"I'm starting to think they are either running out of ammunition or maybe they are both wounded or one even dead. They seem to have lost their punch what do think Lieutenant?"

"I can't disagree with you Constable Ward, let's keep shooting until one o'clock and then we'll rush them".

And that's exactly what they did, there was some talk later that Gool had a white rag tied to his rifle barrel and was attempting to surrender but who knows?

After everything that had happened and the length of time these two had held off a small army no one was taking any chances, they cut Gool down. Now they found old Abdullah dead as a door nail when they all rushed that rocky outcrop, but I have never been too sure about Gool. I was told by someone who should know that Gool was hit no less than sixteen times. I guess you could believe that with all those men shooting at him. But I was also told that Gool died in hospital a few hours later, it's hard to believe anyone can survive sixteen bullet wounds to die later but who knows? I do know for sure that the locals stopped them from putting Abdullah's body in the ambulance so whether Gool made it to the hospital is anyone's guess.

Well, that was New Year's Day 1915, Broken Hill would never be the same again. To try and quell any public reaction the Police buried the two killer's bodies in a secret location that will probably never be found and that's alright. But the very next day all the mines around Broken Hill fired all employees deemed as aliens quoting the 1914 Commonwealth War Precautions Act. Six Austrians, four

Germans and one lonely Turk were forcibly ordered out of Broken Hill by a public crowd. Shortly after this, all enemy aliens in Australia were interned for the duration of the war. I couldn't see them from where I was, but I heard all the shouting. I found out later that an angry crowd had formed at a local pub and moved off towards the Western Camel Camp. The Police somehow headed them off and talked some sense into them, so they all came back to the pub and promptly forgot all about the Afghanis back in their camp.

That was the only near violence towards the camel drivers and their families. Then someone raised the issue of the other enemy in that far away war, the Germans. The local Germans became the focus of the angry mob. A rumour flew around town that some Germans had agitated the Afghanis into attacking the train. This was never proven and didn't ever line up with common sense as the Germans and Cameleers weren't known didn't to associate with each other. Later, the documents found at White Rocks would also prove this rumour to be unfounded.

A little thing like that wasn't going to worry this mob. They were screaming for blood to avenge the deaths of their fellow workers and neighbours. As one seeking a target, they walked along the main drag Argent Street and then into Delamore Street where the German Club has sat for many a happy year.

After a bit of yelling and rock-throwing, you could see a few of the mob move forward and climb underneath the wooden building, within minutes black smoke poured from the old dry wood billowing out into the street. The Fire Brigade did what all Fire Brigades the world over do and arrived with brass bells ringing loudly. They rolled out all their hoses and began to fight the fire which by now had taken a pretty strong hold. The mob wasn't going to stand there and let their handy work come to aught, so they grabbed axes from the Fire Brigade vehicles and unceremoniously cut the hoses into pieces. The Fire Officers while upset at the damage to their equipment weren't about to fight their friends and neighbours, so everyone relaxed and watched the German Club burn to the ground.

Three days after the horrific attack on so many innocents a miner found some documents hidden at White Rocks. Two revealed the motivation behind the attacks, the other was Gool's application for the Turkish Army.

The contents of the letters quickly spread around town further angering its already annoyed, shocked and grieving residents. Abdullah's letter said he was dying for his faith and obedience to the Order from the Sultan. No copy of any such letter from the Sultan was ever found. Of course, it's possible that Abdullah wanted to assume the same order for himself as his fellow tribesman and assailant Gool had allegedly received. Remember William Shaw the Sanitary Foreman who had been an early target killed in the first volley of shots? It was interesting to note the written evidence found containing Abdullah's comments. 'But owing to my grudge against Chief Sanitary Inspector Brosnan I'd planned to kill him first'.

Perhaps being unable to see Inspector Brosnan, Abdullah settled for his Foreman William Shaw instead. Gool's documents are interesting especially if one believes that these two were some sort of spies or agents working for their Turkish masters. Gool's handwritten suicide note reads.

'I hold the Sultan's order, duly signed and sealed by him. It is in my waist belt now, and if it is not destroyed by cannon shot or rifle bullets, you will find it on me. I must kill your men and give my life for my faith by order of the Sultan (but) I have no enmity against anyone, nor have I consulted with anyone, nor informed anyone.' These documents are very revealing and incredibly interesting and in some ways contradictory to what could be assumed of the two assailants.

The Iman, the religious Leader speaks briefly of obeying an order from the Sultan that may not have even existed and clearly expresses pure hatred and anger at the Municipal Officers.

Abdullah did not attempt to hide the fact that he was seeking personal revenge probably on the

Police as well due to his several appearances in the local Police Court and of course his hatred for the Sanitary Department staff. Interestingly the old soldier of the two talks of obeying an order from the Sultan that he is carrying on his person and talks of professional duty even stating that he has no anger or hatred towards his enemy.

The Office of the Department of War in Turkey denied any knowledge of the order and stated that it must be a forgery. This poses two major questions:

1. Whether Mullah Abdullah and Badsha Mohammed Gool were acting out of a desire to serve their faith or their country, perhaps under orders, will never be known completely?

2. Whether Mullah Abdullah and Badsha Mohammed Gool were acting independently by carrying out their plan as their action against their country's enemies or were they obeying a direct order to kill Australian citizens wherever they were, rather than return to Turkey to fight, once again we will never know?

As a Journalist, I believe all we can do is pray that Terrorism in any form will never come to the shores of this great nation Australia in the future. And as sad as it is that so many innocent Australians were killed or wounded near Broken Hill that New Year's Day, we should be grateful that it was just two men in an isolated unsupported attack.

CHAPTER 1

Afghanistan 2005

Near the town of Tarin Kowt or TK, as we called it, Australia had set up its main base, it was up close and personal being located between the Taliban strongholds of Kandahar and Helmand to the west and Pakistan and the tribal areas to the east. This meant to us as soon as we were outside the wall we were in it deep, anything could happen any time through the last of the checkpoints getting thrown from one side of the vehicle to the other with their chicanes, boom gates and wooden sandbagged guard boxes built up on stilts.

The guards waved us through we knew that if there was any trouble they were well armed with either a MAXIMI Machine Gun in 7.62 or that crowd-pleaser the 50 Cal Machine Gun. The Humvees pushed between the HESCO barriers, the big galvanised mesh cubes filled with dirt blocking any breeze and all light other than from straight above. As we exited the chicane a hot wind blowing from the East filled our vehicles and our senses with the putrid smells of stagnant water, rotting garbage, diesel and raw sewage. It reminds all of us where we were as though that was ever needed.

The first time I was over here in 2002 Char China Valley was a Taliban area, a no-go zone, where no coalition patrols would dare go. Things had improved this tour, things were a little better as a result of various allied forces pushing into the Valley. Although it was not safe at least we could come and go. Some Intel had been picked up from some chatter on ICOM the Taliban Radio Network. Two specialists Talibs were going to be at a compound held by the Taliban in a big open valley west of Deh Rawood. These guys were bad news and were experts in making and teaching about IEDs made from hard graphite rather than steel. This meant our metal detectors couldn't pick up on them. These were skills that we wanted to shut down rather than see multiplied and spread by training others. Our six-man patrol had been tasked to eliminate both the Taliban, designated Tango 1 and Tango 2.

Until recently our Tactics Techniques and Procedures (TTP) were to be flown in fairly close and walk in from there, however, things had changed. After hearing our choppers and noting the direction we were flying the Talib outpost could figure out where we were heading. The outpost would then warn their brothers resulting in them bugging out before we got there. To counteract this, we had adjusted our TTPs by getting the flyboys to fly one way and then another creating misleading directions and confusing the Talib's warning outposts. It meant walking in a lot further, but it paid off in immediate results. These Talibs or their supporters were just about everywhere. Even the locals that hated them were still so oppressed and scared they would report our presence. So just to make sure we hadn't landed right on top of a nest it was standard practice as soon as we landed to lay low for at least fifteen minutes listening hard for any baddies who might be coming our way. As with most Intel tip-offs, the IED Maker and the Teacher were Time Sensitive Targets.

We had been given a certain time and a certain place the targets would be present. This translated into a six-hour walk across a hundred-crumbling shale-covered ridge. We had brought in a hundred litres of water in twenty-litre jerry cans which we now used to fill up our water bottles. We buried two jerry cans so that on the way back we could access it in case we had a wait for the Helo to arrive to evac us. Trying to forget our seventy-kilo packs and our aching legs we walked in a pitch-black night using our Night Vision Goggles (NVGs). We had a simple plan, to hide on top of the ridge overlooking the compound ready for the Talib specialists to show up the next morning.

NVGs were awesome in so many ways but using them on these long walks knocked us around. We were continually falling over rocks that we couldn't see because they were close and low outside the goggle's fields of vision. "

Falling over yet again Smitty my Spotter spat. "Steve, have I ever told you how much I hate these friggin NVGs?"

"I think that's about six times tonight old mate."

As the designated Sniper on this mission, I was more worried about the really bad headache I usually got from the extended use of these vision aides. The other fear we all shared, was shooting your mates as your vision was restricted to a narrow field and everything was green and hard to identify in detail. After slipping, sliding and tripping our way over I don't know how many loose rock ridges, we arrived without any enemy contact or serious injury. At close on 0230 Hours, we climbed onto a narrow rocky ridge around eight hundred yards above the compound.

The boys laid a perimeter while my Spotter Smitty and I settled into working out angles and distances. We had the time so as best as we could we measured off applying these figures to the trigonometric table in my sniper data book.

"Smitty, we've got more time than we usually have, so let's make sure we've got that whole compound marked up."

"Roger that Stevo, no probs. I was just thinking about when I get home. You know how much I love surfing, I just hope all this sand hasn't ruined the beach for me."

"You'll be fine mate a week at home and it'll seem like you never left it."

We always tried to anticipate where targets would be, and where they would run once things got loud. We marked where the targets would hide once the massive .50 Cal projectile sent the first of their brothers to paradise. Sleep was a rare commodity while on patrol, but all of us were trained in 'Field Sleep'. Which in essence meant we were able to sleep but keep a part of our mind alert to danger.

Our body and mind would rest but any movement or sound would result in us becoming instantly alert. The operation was supposed to be easy although no one ever really believed that about any mission, but some Officer said it in any case. There was always a stack of things that could go wrong from weather to goat shepherds stumbling onto our position alerting every Talib for miles.

This op was a little bit different with one of our Afghani members Tariq Hassan going in undercover to tag the targets. The last thing we wanted to do was nail some underling and miss the bomb maker and the teacher. We were using a system developed by the original snipers back in the days of sailing ships.

The snipers would be located up in the crows-nest lookout atop the masts. The sniper's crew would wear a hat or a cap with a Quadraforce sown on top. This would enable the sniper to shoot down on the enemy from above while avoiding his own men identified and protected by the clover-shaped symbol. It was a challenge to brand Hassan's clothes, to ensure we wouldn't shoot him by mistake.

Afghanis and Taliban always dressed to fit into the village crowds mostly in local garb sometimes with the addition of ex-Russian Army vests. Hassan wore such a vest but with a small black square on his back, visible to us but grubby enough to look like some Russian soldier had scribbled the square on the back of his vest in the nineties.

The mission had been progressing well on the walk-in, we had made every checkpoint on schedule and for once we had working Radio Communications (Comms). My Spotter and I had taken a vantage point above the compound and we had settled in and were waiting for our Tangos to show up and for Hassan to tag them. The sun was now high and straight above us in the empty blue sky when we observed a party of males arrive at the compound below our position. There were eight Talibs, some of them were carrying large black canvass bags; all were dressed in drab robes tied around their waist with a black chord.

As usual, they wore scarves covering their heads obscuring most of their faces. There were no weapons sighted initially but looking closer through the scope I could see flashes of metal beneath at least three of the robes as they swaggered into the compound. That confirmed that this was a group of armed Talibs now *all* we had to do was identify our targets Tango 1 the Bomb Maker and Tango 2 the Bomb Making Teacher. Hassan came out of the mud-brick building with a large group of males, we observed a lot of kissing and welcoming and then they all disappeared through the same faded blue door that Hassan and the others had just exited. If you haven't got patience your chances of succeeding as a hunter or a sniper are very slim. We waited, and we waited and then we waited some more. As they had said in training waiting is doing something and once you understand that waiting is no longer passive hopefully you won't get bored because you are active.

We figured because the visitors had arrived close on midday when Al-Zohr (Noon Prayers) was due they all went in and prayed together then they probably shared some Kentucky Fried Goat or some such. Now after nearly three hours the locals and the Talib visitors came back out this time carrying various items that must have been inside those bags. The other obvious change was there were AK47s everywhere carried by the visitors and the locals. They walked away from the house to an area that may have served as a goat pen at some time, but today there were several trestle tables set up in a shaded part of the rectangle. Smitty tapped me lightly on my shoulder, waking me from a light sleep.

"Wake up super sniper time for us to earn our pay buddy."

Instantly alert I ignored his joke. “Thanks, mate, as planned no-frills, let’s have some fun.”

The next phase of the operation was going to be the tricky bit, Hassan needed to tag the Tangos, the plan was Tango 1 first, but it was critical under the circumstances to nail both. I could see Hassan siding his way over towards two of the visitors. I flicked the safety to fire on my Barrett M82A1 50 Cal Sniper Rifle and flexed my trigger finger a few times. In training, they had said a single heartbeat can throw a projectile off by a few feet at the sort of distances we trade-in. Today's tangos were eight hundred and ten metres. So, I took a series of deep breaths and steadied my heart rate, preparing myself to shoot between heartbeats. Hassan moved over to two older-looking men standing a little away from the crowd of Taliban.

He confirmed the targets by pulling down on his vest, a simple yet effective prearranged signal, tugging down once for Tango 1 and twice for Tango 2 we hoped this was virtually undetectable by the enemy. That was good enough for me I caressed the finely set trigger of my rifle sending the fifty-calibre bullet on its way. We had selected Armour Piercing bullets due to the strong possibility the target may be hiding behind some barrier, even a mud concrete wall if necessary.

Smitty whispered. “Tango 1 confirmed as a go.”

I answered. “Affirmative.”

Without hesitation, I took up the final pressure on the trigger and sent the deadly projectile on its way. Tango 1’s head disappeared behind a pink mist of his brain matter covering several Talibs who were standing around him. Tango 2 ducked for cover but not before clubbing Hassan with his AK. I wasn't sure what had happened, but it was clear Tango 2 knew Hassan was a good guy. I was sure the signal had not betrayed him. As much as he should have known better maybe Hassan had been backing away from the first target. This was a normal movement usually that became significant only after the bullet had hit its target. I took out three more Talibs, but the Bomb Making Teacher was too smart to show even an inch of himself, he used Hassan as a shield to re-enter the house.

My Spotter confirmed the target's whereabouts in case I had been busy looking elsewhere.

"Steve, great shot, Tango 2 to back inside the house."

"Roger that Smitty, it looked like Hassan is burnt. Did you see him get smashed?"

"Yeah, we wait and pray hey."

The rear of the house was all flat open ground offering no cover and no high ground, so we had no way of covering that area concentrating our focus on the compound and the front of the two-storey mud building. We had called for a SAS Mounted Patrol to keep the Back Door shut and assist as needed. Thankfully they had held back ready to race in if and when we called them to come closer.

Like nearly all the houses in Afghanistan, this one had a flat roof with a low wall around the sides all around the top. We could see movement on the roof, but the baddies were being super careful having learned the hard way we were there, and any opportunity would bring a bullet their way. There were already two Taliban bodies on the roof to prove this. We heard the three SAS vehicles arrive and saw movement across the roof towards the rear of the house.

After waiting for just such an opportunity a less experienced sniper would have jumped at the offering of some Talibs with an AK47 sticking his head up.

It wasn't Smitty's first rodeo either. "I sure hope your wrong man."

I hoped I was wrong too. However, after waiting for a few moments, we both saw what we were expecting. Two Talibs armed not with AK47s this time but with Rocket Propelled Grenades (RPGs) bobbed up.

I swore. "Mate it's a horrible thought, but it just crossed my mind that the entire Intel that had dragged our sorry asses down here may have been a bait for a Taliban ambush."

They probably knew our Standard Operating Procedures (SOPs). In such circumstances, it was to call in support from either Helos or as we had done Mounted Patrols. They were upping the value of the target. RPGs were great for bringing down choppers or taking out the vehicles and crews with one shot. The shoulder-fired weapons had been and still was a highly effective and widely available killer popular with guerilla-type armies going back decades and all around the world.

"Show time Stevo, on my mark."

"Roger mate, let's make sure of this."

One of the downfalls of using an RPG from a rooftop with a wall such as these houses is in most cases the shooter must stand up to aim and fire the small missile-shaped grenade which only detonates when its nose hits the target squarely on. The first RPG shooter did exactly that. He took aim at something at ground level I couldn't see, probably one of the specially equipped SAS Land Rovers. No time for waiting and seeing now, I eased the Mil-Dot Sight on the Talibs head and gently squeezed the trigger. I was a fraction late but thankfully as my projectile hit its mark the dead man fell backwards pointing the ignited RPG towards the sky. The grenade shot into the air like a lunar mission spinning off harmlessly. Early in my sniper career, I had made the mistake of dwelling on your last shot looking at the body. But this wasn't my first rodeo, I didn't fall for this temptation again searching the roof-line for the second Rocket shooter.

This guy had seen his mate die and figured although he was probably willing to die, he wanted to make it count. Jumping up quickly he too aimed towards the ground and fired. I had shot the instant I had a target, but my bullet had to cover over eight hundred metres so although it killed him instantly it was too late to stop his Rocket. The flare of the rocket and smoke was followed by two explosions the first being the Rocket but sadly the second was the SAS Land Rover.

I had no way of knowing at the time, but it also killed four SAS Troopers and blew off the left arm of a Corporal who was found lying on the ground a few meters from the vehicle. It was a sniper's worst-case scenario. You always evaluated a mission by targets down, but good men had died, was it my fault? I seemed to have done all I could, but had I been so slow I had just let this Talib murder some of my brothers in arms? Could I have done better? Some guys could duck these questions but tell that to these guys' families.

Once we had cleaned up the rest of the Talibs on the roof, we headed down to the compound.

"Smitty even though we scored multiple hits, we missed Tango 2 and I have a sick feeling about Hassan." Smitty didn't respond but nodded and we both sped up as he walked towards the clay buildings. Behind a low wall in the compound, we found Hassan's beheaded body. I added his death to the crushing guilt I carried. Of course, the then Major Walsh and all my mates tried to convince me it was just bad luck or just fate. The Padre had gone out of his way to try to help as well. He was a great bloke, and everyone respected him because he had got through the SAS entry, so he was a real SAS Officer who was also a Padre. It didn't matter I wasn't listening.

ROMA QLD.
MARCH 2014

That was nine years ago, and I was still having nightmares about that sad day in the sandbox like it was yesterday. I had travelled a long way, but I hadn't got anywhere. Except for a miracle or me dying, I knew deep down it didn't matter how much JD I drank or how many pigs or stags I hunted I couldn't run fast enough or far enough to forget. The harsh western Queensland sun broke through the gum tree above my swag waking me from yet another dream that most people would call a nightmare. I was soaking wet from sweat from the heat and the reliving of those twenty-four hours back in 2005. I felt drained and exhausted my heart rate racing as I unzipped my mosquito netting and staggered to my feet. Jake looked at me sorrowfully as I reached blindly for the Jack Daniels bottle I had emptied last night. Disappointed and still thirsty I threw the useless bottle at the base of a nearby tree. Now, even though I was awake I could remember every grain of sand from my nightmare because to me it was all too real, every moment of it.

CHAPTER 2

UNDERWATER WORLD
SUNSHINE COAST
QUEENSLAND

Unbeknown to me, about seven hours East of my rough hunting camp outside Roma things were developing that would eventually change my life forever. At the scream, every head turned expecting to find some terrible accident such as a child dismembered having fallen into the shark tank or perhaps stung by some rare box jellyfish or similar creature.

No, it was nothing so exciting it was just a noisy excited three-year-old racing ahead of her siblings towards the touch pool full of sea shells, anemones and starfish. Another school holiday, another rainy day on the ironically named Sunshine Coast Queensland, Australia's family alternative to the wild and more grown-up Gold Coast. Underwater World was the perfect place for hundreds of children and their weary parents to enjoy the huge aquariums and hands-on displays. This included the spectacular Perspex observation tunnel with its conveyor walkway passing right through the huge aquarium. Every tourist was surrounded by sharks, sting rays, turtles and huge fish, along with an incredible array of colourful tropical fish of every shape, colour and size. The place was packed now the beach was no longer an attractive option in the pouring rain.

Sherif Ibrahim had arrived in Australia amongst thirty-two sad cases who unlike him were escaping their war-torn homes and countries. The trip aboard a leaky wooden boat from Indonesia was at times nothing short of terrifying. But long ago he had decided that if Allah chose to take him there would have been a good reason. In this he found peace. Ibrahim was not tall not short, not overly handsome or memorably unattractive. He had no distinguishing marks such as scars or tattoos. He had been chosen because he was as much as possible just average in every way. There was nothing to cause him to stand out other than possibly being from the Middle East. But every day there were more and more people walking around nearly every Australian city or town with dark skin and eyes just like his.

He had carefully observed and imitated Australian men of his age here on the Sunshine Coast. He had avoided even traditional Western clothes choosing instead an image of a tourist trying to fit in. Once again, he looked at himself in the mirror. Oh, *I am ashamed to have to wear these ridiculous clothes. A grown man in short pants and colourful shirts brighter than a prostitute would wear back in his homeland.* Trained in how to change his appearance without too much trouble he constantly did just that. Each time he left his apartment it changed, beard no beard, glasses no glasses, longer hair shorter hair, different hats and so on. He had successfully achieved being totally unremarkable, nearly invisible. He had always been a devout Moslem and had been recruited while still at school.

School now that was one place he had stood out expressing unswerving faith and hatred for the West, especially America. He was honoured to serve Allah. Ibrahim would have preferred to have been sent on a mission in the USA. But these Australian pigs were close enough.

With all their McDonalds and every other filthy American habit, they seemed to imitate America in every way they could. Music, TV, weak men who allowed their women to parade around nearly naked, children who spoke to parents as equals. From his observations here at Underwater World the whining children seemed to get everything they ever demanded from parents too weak to say no. Australia was a country of no morals and no faith. And of course, following America with fashion or food was only the symptom of America's power over these Infidels. Following the USA into wars that Australia should not have interfered with was the important factor. Every time he thought of that his anger built and his mind raced. *They will pay for invading Islam as they did in Iraq and his home Afghanistan,* this thought brought an evil smile to his dark face. *At least I don't need to fear these Australian Police. They are so easily distracted.* He had often seen them trying to look tough when one of these Australian whore's, even ones with children in tow walked past. He was safe.

Sherif Ibrahim had heard people call Australia the Lucky Country and he would never disagree with this description He was indeed lucky to have come while the back door was wide open, not like now. He remembered the joy that spread through his fellow 'refugees' on his training course preparing to come to Australia when Prime Minister John Howard was kicked out and replaced by that weak wristed people pleaser. Then these corrupt faithless Christians who brag so much about their democracy had removed the elected leader and replaced him with a female Prime Minister who proclaimed she believed in nothing at all. At least she didn't dress like most of these Australian whores although there were times when she looked more like a he than a she.

The important issue was they both opened the flood gates from Indonesia, the boats started flowing again. Ibrahim had been trained in what questions would be asked by the Australian Officials and what answers he needed to give to gain entry. They had welcomed him with open arms. Australians were a soft weak people very friendly and helpful giving him a new set of documents to replace his real ones he had burnt on the beach in Indonesia. They even referred him to a place called Centrelink, welfare for the poor refugee to make sure he had a regular income stream and everything else that he may need. Then they gave him a mobile phone and he was free to go anywhere he wanted and do whatever he pleased. He hated them all for their weakness and their lack of faith, little wonder Allah Al-Hakam (The Impartial Judge) had judged this country. Allah had decided they deserved the punishment that his masters had planned.

When he thought of his training he wondered not for the first time what had become of the others who had been with him through all the different classes. They had been trained in what to say, what to do, how to fit in, and how to change their appearance without really disguising themselves. There had been thirteen others on the course all good men sharing the same faith in Allah and a passion to serve. Ibrahim wasn't sure, but he thought that only seven including himself were assigned to Australia.

He had noticed that in the six weeks of training the first four were more general. He remembered that the last two weeks of the course were much more specifically focused on Australian culture and habits, even some slang terms.

Thinking of his fellow students; *I wonder if they were assigned to another enemy country such as Britain or maybe America, h*e wasn't sure whether the other seven men were nearby or spread out across Australia. He prayed to Allah that they had all made it and that he would bless every one of their Holy Jihads. Ibrahim wondered why the English and the Australians were like this. Their willingness to help America every time the USA invaded some country Vietnam, or Muslim Nations. Maybe it was a debt from another time when America saved these countries. He didn't know the details, but he had some awareness that in the First and Second World Wars that America becoming involved turned the tide of both these wars in favour of England and Australia. He hated America and enjoyed the fact that they could never win worldwide approval. If they didn't help smaller countries that were being invaded or oppressed they would be criticised for not caring or for inactivity. If they did mobilise their huge Military to assist these countries they were called

World Sheriffs like in their cowboy days, or simply world bullies. Likewise, their motivation was always suspect, oil, or some other commercial gain, permission to pass through or build Military Bases they always got *something* for their intervention, didn't they?

He couldn't help himself, as he thought about the word 'Sheriff' Ibrahim smiled and remembered the one thing he liked about America. When he was a child he loved the Cowboy shows and movies usually because there were no women in them and the men were strong and had a moral character. After watching the shows the boys would run around their mud homes and goat pens playing cowboys. He particularly enjoyed the other boys pronouncing his first name the cowboy way of saying Sheriff rather than the Afghani way of *Shereef.* Sherif Ibrahim had no children or family, he liked it that way being able to focus on his calling with no distractions. This was his fifth visit to Under Water World and it had nothing to do with an interest in the creatures of the deep. He had to feign interest in the displays and take some photos. However, his reaction was to shudder when he saw the huge sharks for the first time.

Ibrahim shuddered with the thought; Looking at the shark's dead eyes; I remember you circling the little boat we were in coming *from Indonesia.* He prayed a silent prayer of thanks to Allah.

As he and his fellow students had been trained to do he observed customer numbers and crowd flow for the first week of the school holidays. Ibrahim knew that the next hour was the busiest period of the day. That was the best time to ensure the maximum impact of his mission here at Underwater World. Of course, he still hadn't received the go-ahead so there was every chance that he would miss the school holiday crowds. He had made several trips to the aquarium each time changing his appearance, paying cash, and not going on the same day or same time. Ibrahim was happy with his choice of sites where the most people congregated. His mission instructions were simple.

He had been given his assigned target, and how he carried out his mission was open to his assessment of the local situation.

Ibrahim's personal goal was to make sure as many as possible of these Infidel pigs were there to receive his special gift. Standing on the conveyor-type walkway slowly moving through the huge Perspex tunnel surrounded by millions of gallons of water alive with sea life. He asked himself; *how can I place a bomb into a water-tight clear walkway with a constantly moving floor without it being noticed and removed?* He could not just leave it sitting on the floor as it would instantly be on the move and quite possibly not even be under all that water when it detonated.

A small boy wearing a Brisbane Broncos Football tee-shirt gave him the solution when he threw away a lolly wrapper, as it blew along the floor Ibrahim saw the solution. The solution was to make the device look like a rubbish bin, so it wouldn't be noticed and be small enough and light enough to be affixed to the Perspex wall. Ibrahim was a thorough man, but when you were serving Allah was there any other option but to do even more than your best. He went straight to the merchandise store and purchased eight of the largest Underwater World stickers he could find.

He then found four rubbish bins big enough for the bombs, that were light enough to stick onto the Perspex tunnel wall. He would site the bomb in the middle of the Perspex tunnel, matching another device on the floor directly above the tunnel bomb. When the two devices were detonated the combined explosions going up and down the tunnel would multiply the effect and the outcome. He was staying in a small low-key holiday unit just like similar units hundreds of other tourists had rented near the aquarium. Ibrahim had selected this unit as it was without a view but in a large old block, with no cameras in the lifts or the corridors and no on-site manager. Lots of families with snotty kids and sweating parents not caring enough to take any notice of their fellow tourists. Even though he was only two hundred metres from Underwater World returning from the aquarium always took time. He would look in shop windows in the hope of catching a reflection of a familiar person he had seen earlier. Even when he was satisfied he would enter the block of units next door cutting across to his block. Ibrahim was now sure that he was alone. Before he went through his front door he checked the small piece of electrical tape he had placed on the door and was pleased and relieved to see that it was still in place.

Ibrahim was excited about his new idea, but he was now in a hurry he must prepare for Al-Asr the afternoon prayers. He hated American technology but admitted begrudgingly that Google Maps had enabled him to establish where Mecca was from his unit on the Sunshine Coast. After washing himself in the prescribed manner he commenced the four Rakaahs and then made his personal requests mindful of the calling upon his life and his impending mission. Once he'd finished his prayers he walked over to the small kitchen table and began to prepare for the most wonderful day he could imagine. He carefully placed the stickers onto the four bins instantly turning them into official-looking Underwater World rubbish receptacles. He then went into the en-suite, looking at himself in the bathroom cabinet mirror he smiled. He then took hold of both sides of the medicine cabinet pulling with a slight twisting motion. The whole cabinet came out of the wall revealing a hidden cavity containing four Semtex bombs all the same size. The bombs were based on the model his terrorist brothers had perfected all over the world, detonated by remote control by an agent in the proximity.

Each device held a package of tightly packed nails, screws and ball bearings that when driven by the explosion the shrapnel storm ensured a multiplication factor of death and wounding. In the same way, the Vietcong would spread faeces on their Punji stakes to ensure anyone stepping on the sharpened bamboo would also end up with an infected wound, these bombs too held a secondary weapon. The bomb makers had coated all the shrapnel in their bombs with liquid rat poison so that even their innocent targets receiving relatively minor wounds would often bleed to death. One device contained ample high explosive that would shatter the Perspex tunnel drowning and wounding any tourist within reach. The other three bombs were placed strategically to maximise the casualties based on Ibrahim's reconnaissance and plan.

Ibrahim hoped that he wasn't the only Moslem brother called to such a mission. But he understood that he would probably never know. Unbeknown to him there were bombers just like him who had entered through the same back door to Australia the year he did. They too had gone through all the required hoops and were blending into the Australian society but always with a hidden agenda, a hidden motivation. Just like Ibrahim there was a well-trained and resourced Taliban operative in every state and territory of Australia. All planning a similar mission at specially chosen sites, and just like Ibrahim they were waiting for the green light to execute the mission.

CHAPTER 3

Terrorism for one reason or another had not been seen as a significant threat in Australia. That was reasonable considering that since that fateful New Year's Day in 1915 there had been small almost individual incidents that were labelled often inaccurately as terrorism in the absence of any major attacks. However, nothing sparks a need to create a new anti-terrorist organisation faster than a discovered plot to kill the then Prime Minister Bob Hawke. Australia's attempt to respond to this new type of war started back in early 1979 and was highly dependent on the famous Special Air Services Regiment SAS.

The Regiment developed strategies and techniques to combat potential attacks as they arose. The creation and development of specialist units and individuals and the necessary training were in direct response to each newly identified threat. A 'killing house' was built to train and practice hostage rescue and terrorist cell attack techniques. The Regiment's own funding and expansion were strongly linked. A good example was the identified possibility of oil rigs being hijacked so the Boat Squadron was formed. SAS being based in Western Australia was always a challenge concerning a rapid response to any attack in the east and coordination overall.

Since the infamous terrorist attacks at the 1972 Munich Olympics terrorism was an increasing threat that could not be ignored even in countries far from Europe. When Sydney Australia was announced as the 2000 Olympic venue, security needs rocketed to the top of to-do lists. Every Military and Law Enforcement agency or service started preparing. The protection of the athletes, spectators and of course the dignitaries expected to flood into Australia for months before, during and after the big event became everyone's concern. The event passed without incident however Australia maintained the momentum to some degree in the following years. Eventually, this resulted in the establishment of several different groups being formed, the most recent the Australian National Security Centre (NSC) situated in Canberra. All the required groups were in the capital, the Australian Security Intelligence Organisation (ASIO), all the arms of the Defence Forces, the Australian Federal Police and of course the Defence Minister and Department and the Prime Minister's Office if this were required.

National Security Centre Headquarters
Canberra
March 2014

This year Australia was to host the Commonwealth Heads of Government Meeting (CHOGM) which meant that the same preventative action was required. Once again, every Security, Police and Military organisation at every level was busy gearing up to protect all those world figures.

The entire Australian security community groaned as one when Australia was named as host but like all soldiers of one kind or another after a few confidential grumblings, they all got on with the job. Rob Evans pushed his glasses back up his nose and stretched his back as he stood to get another cup of the strong coffee that he lived on. He had been a Senior Communications Officer at the NSC for three years and he was extremely happy that during this term he had had virtually no serious terrorist incident to deal with. Four other Communication Officers were sharing the open office with Evans.

Sam Jones was the newest to the team and was bored stiff.

"Rob, don't you ever get sick of the lack of action?"

"No Jonesy, the way I look at it the quieter we are the better it is because it means that no one's attacking Australia."

Like every guard without some action, it was only natural to become complacent. The Comms team did a good job. However, they all shared the same attitude that Australia was so far away from everyone there was little real possibility of anything big happening. This, while a little strange for security professionals, was a belief shared by about 99% of the general population of Australia. A complacency that had been bred through the lack of terrorist activity within their shores.

ASIO, Australia's major security service, works closely with its allies around the world. This cooperation in the post-9/11 era saw organisations such as the CIA, FBI, Mossad and M16 routinely monitor and share any terrorism-related Intel. Sadly, this cooperation wasn't uniform between all countries. Some countries were not on board and lacked commitment regarding quality and consistent information sharing. It was usually these same countries that refused to implement effective port and flight security screening. Sitting at the desk opposite Rob Evans, John O'Shea known by his nickname to his colleagues as Rick (O'Shea) was playing Spider Solitaire on his desktop. O'Shea was the team member tasked with monitoring and analysing targeted communications from the Indonesian region. He had been with the service for close to eleven years as his prematurely greying hair attested. He was overweight and possessed the complexion of a vampire because he hadn't seen natural light for a very long time. He looked just like the classic computer geek that he was. And he was a very good one.

Rob Evans could hear Rick win another game of Spider.

"Rick, do you ever do any work? Getting anything from Indo lately?"

Clicking off his computer game he turned to senior. "Nothing international but a bit of chatter in country. Talk of strangers but, interestingly, they're not enemies. They hate us so much I would love to know who they are talking about."

"What do you think it means Rick?" Asking the more experienced man.

"I don't know what the hell it means but I think the Boss ought to know. As usual it might match up with something we don't know yet. You know us mere mortals only see our part of the puzzle". As Rob reached for the phone on his desk and punched in his Team Leader's number he agreed. "Yeah, I think you're right."

The phone was picked up after a single ring. "Gates."

"Sir, it's Rob, have you gotta minute for a catch-up?"

"Sure, Rob give me ten minutes and come up."

As he rested the phone into its cradle, Team Leader Alan Gates wondered what was on the Senior Comms Officer's mind? Gates was in his late fifties, a little over six feet with a ruddy complexion including a large nose covered in freckles, he had moved to foggy Canberra from Queensland and persisted to wear short-sleeved shirts, of course, with the obligatory tie. These short sleeves revealed muscular arms reminiscent of a runner or athlete rather than a wrestler, his arms were pale and like his nose carried a carpet of freckles. Gates appreciated the Senior Comms officer's use of the respectful 'Sir' when others around could hear. This was despite them being close friends outside of work. Ten minutes later Evans knocked on his boss' door and entered.

Dropping the formality Rob got down to business. "Al you know the usual Indo flow never changes much. Both ways between the usual suspects there and our local targets here in Oz. But there's something a bit weird going on. O'Shea picked up several intercepts mentioning strangers but it's clear they are maybe friends to the Indos. Maybe a group of Moslems from somewhere else I suppose."

"Yes, that is strange, something might be cooking or maybe it's just another boat full of illegals. What's your best guess?"

Shaking his head Rob answered his superior. “To be honest I haven’t got a clue, but I have a bad feeling about it, do you think you should kick it upstairs?”

Upstairs referred to the desk of Section Head Clive Millard. He in turn was the conduit to the Australian National Security Centre Committee whose role was to ensure the prevention of Terrorism in Australia and the reaction and deployment of forces against possible threats or events. Gates trusted this experienced officer’s judgement.

“I'll send up a query. I know you guys think you are never told anything but believe me you're not alone. We are all mushrooms, eventually kept in the dark and fed bullshit just varying amounts, that's all.” Rob couldn’t help smiling at Gate's use of such a hackneyed analogy but still appreciated the empathy.

“Rob, I know you would anyway, but you guys keep your ears to the ground. Let me know anything new, OK?”

"Sure Boss, will do."

True to his word Gates finished his cold tea and phoned his Section Head Clive Millard.

Clive Millard was genuinely pleased to hear from Gates, they had worked together for many years and had often played golf together.

“Alan what can I do for you, what's troubling you?”

“Morning Clive, Rob Evans has just left me, it’s about Indonesia. Apparently, there's a group of foreigners up there that are welcomed by the locals. You and I both know that's a bit strange, so I've asked him to keep a close eye on it and let me know what surfaces."

Millard was briefed on a daily basis, so he immediately understood the significance of this report.

“So, it sounds like maybe a mob of Moslems from somewhere, are you thinking they may end up heading our way?”

Gates trusted his team, so he continued. “That was my first thought, but Rob's gut is making him uneasy about them. He seems to have good instincts for trouble”.

"Yeah, Evans was right about that other matter three weeks ago, so there's no argument from me. OK, thanks for letting me know straight away. I'll put it on our Management Agenda for today, let me know if there is any Intel from the cross services angle".

"Roger that Clive, will do, what are you doing Saturday morning, up for a game?"

"Sounds like a plan mate, I'll pick you up around 0630 Hours, loser pays for breakfast hey?"

"Oh, the pressures on already, yeah sure; sounds good, I'll catch you later".

With that Gates hung up his phone and stared at the blank monitor at his workstation pondering what this all meant or if it meant anything at all.

CHAPTER 4

TODAY
NORTHERN TERRITORY
AUSTRALIA

Caerhays Station is 10,500 square miles of Northern Territory cattle country, nearly as big as Jamaica. Its northern boundary consists of 77 miles of coastline looking out on the Arafura Sea. It was rumoured that the cattle station lost over 10,000 acres when the tide came in. The original property was established in the mid- 1800s and has been growing steadily ever since. Like Australian farms everywhere it had seen its share of fires, droughts and flooding rains. It has several private airstrips, numerous cattle yards and hundreds of dams of various sizes. Dirt tracks criss-cross the property enabling access to fix a pump or truck out the cattle to market. As with all the Northern Territory, the entire property was virtually inaccessible during the big wet season. With monsoonal rain, the creeks and rivers would rise covering paddocks and turning the tracks into impassable quagmires.

Until the seventies the property had relied on horses for most of the cattle work, these days helicopters could muster in a day the same huge paddock that might have taken a week employing men and horses. The station made most of its money selling the thousands of beef cattle the property had bred and raised. There were also hundreds of acres populated by scrub or wild cattle that were mustered into one of the big cattle yards and sold every few years. The vast property was home to hundreds of wild horses called Brumbies, these animals were the progeny of stock horses that had escaped in the previous century.

Water Buffalo, huge bad-tempered beasts with wide dangerous horns, originally from Indonesia or Timor. The herds ruined the land by wallowing and moving around in the wet season gouging tracks and eroding huge pieces of land. As well as this they were known to carry terrible diseases dangerous to both man and stock on the station. Caerhays Australia was named after a famous castle and cattle farm in Cornwall England. This huge hunk of the Northern Territory had been owned by the Phillips family for 5 generations. When the last generation of Phillips became too old to keep running the station it had quietly slipped into the hands of a new owner some eighteen months ago. It would take a very clever commercial lawyer a long time to dig through all the layers to attempt to discover who the Directors of the Holding Company were that now appeared on the deeds. If you knew what you were doing, you would apply an old but trusted saying in police work that is 'if all else fails follow the money'. Surprisingly, if anyone could follow that trail they would find it led to a family of successful builders who were originally from Afghanistan now based in Brisbane, Queensland's thriving Capital.

The Al Asiris group were a high-profile family winning government contracts and even putting up a relative to run for State Parliament at the last State election, they seemed integrated into Australian life and business. However, it was not public knowledge that they had funded the building of most of the mosques in the State and had strong ties to their mother country. What they had successfully kept even more secret was that they also had strong links with the Taliban. The family were happy to either finance or act as the local face using their contacts to facilitate any project. Money from some oil-rich Al Qaeda supporter would flow through the brothers hidden within their enterprise. It was no surprise that it was the Al Asiris brothers who had financed with Al Qaeda money and negotiated the purchase of Caerhays Station.

The new managers, a local couple in their mid-thirties who had worked cattle all their lives were experienced cattle property managers. They had adopted the Moslem faith and shown an attitude of anger against the Australian involvement in Iraq and Afghanistan. They seemed motivated towards learning the ways of a fundamentalist rather than that of a moderate, which was noticed by the local Iman. Their anonymous owners employed the Al Asiris Brothers to act as a conduit for communicating their desires to the Australian couple in charge of the immense cattle operation. The first command had been to instruct them to introduce a new system of improving the cattle property's profitability. The managers were not well informed, but they assumed that the purchase of the station and this innovation must be part of the bigger company plan that made real commercial sense. The change was an old idea re-introduced in a modern way using huge road trains transporting the vast numbers of cattle in multi-trailer semis. It was an innovation talked about throughout the beef industry. The famous Kidman who owned huge tracks of Queensland and the Northern Territory in the previous century would employ this strategy. He would move his cattle on huge drives pushing them along with drovers on horseback from one property that was short on water or grass to another that had plenty.

Here the stock would build up ensuring a better market price at times or simply survival in the worst of droughts. The new plan for Caerhays was to move stock down by road trains to a smaller property they owned outside Roma Queensland. Here the cattle would be finished off on better grass adding a bit more weight before sending them off to the Roma Cattle Markets. To the local suppliers and their neighbours, Caerhays operated just like every other Northern Territory property. Having an absent owner was becoming more and more common with many of the bigger places owned either by Australian Corporations or Chinese money which was prevalent in recent times. The station had been carefully chosen for several reasons one of which was the fact that owning your own coastline afforded other much more sinister opportunities.

The Al Asiris brothers had hired the Managers after they had been identified by the local mosque that they were attending in Darwin. While the couple were seen as *friendly* having come to the Moslem faith they were not trusted to be fully informed of the various extracurricular uses the station was purchased for. When directed to, the property managers were required to make sure they sent the station's Jackaroos (cattle workers) away from what was called the beach paddock which included seventy-seven miles of coastline. Every two months or so they would get a very short call telling them what date to dispatch their workers to carry out some function such as checking fences or dams in other parts of the vast property.

They didn't know what went on down at the beach but figured that it was probably something to do with drugs. They were paid good money to manage the place and part of that was to do as they were told. The last thing they wanted to do was upset their owners down in Brisbane. The couple didn't like drugs, but they did like money.

They fully realised that they were being paid a lot more than their peers on other similar stations. After such events when they had eventually returned the beach paddock working either on horseback or Kawasaki Quad Bikes they noticed a few fresh 4WD tracks on the dirt road across the paddock. It was clear that the tracks disappeared into the mud in the direction of the beach.

One minute two well worn tracks and then as they crossed the flotsam line of leaves, sticks and miscellaneous rubbish formed by the high tide the wheel marks disappeared washed away by the huge tides. Over their nightly bottle of wine, they whispered about this. However, after much discussion, it was decided that it was wiser and probably safer to not guess too much about what went on down there on those moonless nights. The truth of the matter was that the Warriors Bikie group based in Darwin was using Caerhays to import huge quantities of drugs and illegal firearms. At times these illegal shipments had a few extras, sometimes people sometimes messages too secret to trust normal communication channels.

CHAPTER 5

On Board Indonesian Freighter
KRI Ratulangi

Captain Budi Tahyadi's looked every bit his 66 years, most of them at sea. His big round face was droopy and cracked from decades of sea air and water and never enough sleep. His hair was long and greasy and was always hidden under a battered Captain's cap so much so that many of the crew had never seen their leader's big coconut head without it. He wore filthy shiny sailor's trousers with a blue jacket that was missing more buttons than were remaining. His shirt of rough cotton had no collar and was stretched across his huge stomach and showed the signs of many a meal's spillages both ancient and recent. As usual, he spent most of his time looking out to sea through his well-worn binoculars, his tired red eyes searching for any sign of other shipping and especially patrol boats.

For the hundredth time, he thought: *I will be so* glad *to get rid of these filthy Afghans they smell like goats and strut around like peacocks. H*e didn't like anything about them. The money was great, but he knew full well that he would be locked up forever if he was caught carrying sixty illegals. You didn't have to be too bright to know they were some type of military, not just ordinary illegals trying to sneak into Australia. He and his crew had been ordered below decks when they first came on board. His curiosity got the better of him and he had sneaked a look at their gear. He was surprised at the quantity and type of weapons and ammunition he discovered.

Even those fat Indo Border Security Officers wouldn't turn a blind eye to that; bribe or no bribe. He had breathed a sigh of relief as they entered open waters. However, he was even more concerned about the Aussies. The Australian Navy were good at what they did, and you couldn't buy them. They had come on board at the Port of Merak Banten. The Captain liked it there. It was so busy with Petrochemical Tankers, and Coal and Gas Carriers making it easy to hide behind these big hulks and move around without being noticed. Other than being away from Djakarta Harbour the other more important feature here was that his nephew was the Customs Officer in charge of the quieter part of the harbour. The loading was done carefully with the men straggling on in twos and threes. Their gear was easier packed in crates marked generator parts. The boats or rafts were a little harder to hide but they had tied them together two at a time and then wrapped them in canvas shrouds breaking up the boat's distinctive shape. After all, it was a cargo ship so unless you were studying this wharf at this time why would anything look out of place. Captain Tahyadi watching the ship's loading was very happy.

Not for the first time he thought it was *good not to have to worry about Customs knowing that his Custom Officer nephew had several girlfriends that required more income than his Government job provided.*

It was always a good feeling to see grubby dock workers lift and throw the freighter's hawsers into the oil and flotsam-covered waters near the wharf. That would mean very few people noticed his rusty old ship slowly leave the harbour. Tahyadi always loved this part of a trip, that burst of fresh sea air flooding the wheelhouse and seeing the filth of the harbour slowly receding, he was a man of the sea. The first morning the Afghanis were on board Captain Budi Tahyadi's thought he may have drunk just one too many bottles of that cheap Indonesian Rum he lived on while at sea. It had just gone 0600 Hours when his red bleary eyes looked up from his charts to see every one of his passengers out on the aft deck. *That arrogant*

Commander Zahir stood there in front of his men. He was saying something the Captain *could not hear. Just the way he stands makes me dislike him even more, he thought.*

Budi Tahyadi was a lazy Moslem, he hadn't gotten out of bed to pray since he was a teenager. Driven by his demanding father he still understood all the requirements and was not surprised when these goat herders were up before dawn all kneeling in rows. But what were they up to now? Happy to have some entertainment the Captain watched Commander Zahir as he was joined by what appeared to be three Sub-Commanders out the front facing the body of men. The four Leaders then began to do star jumps (not that the Captain had any knowledge of exercises). In unison, the men having missed the first one started jumping and from then on kept in time with their leaders. This was followed by push-ups, squats, toe touching, and stretching twenty-five sets five times. The group then jogged around the entire deck to the fore deck, past the superstructure of the bridge and wheelhouse eventually ending up where they had begun.

This circuit was maintained for half an hour when one after another the exhausted Afghanis collapsed onto the grubby wooden deck. The Captain patted his tight filthy overalls stretched over his bulging stomach absent-minded thanking Allah that he didn't have to do these silly things. The men were naturally lean desert fighters. However, Zahir knew that soldiers laying around a ship would soon get fat, lazy and bored. He smiled thinking: *I won't let that happen on the eve of their most important missions.*

Every morning each Leader would assemble his squad and carry out weapons training until Al-Zohr (Noon Prayers) after which they would share lunch. Hour after hour of stripping and assembling their new weapons to the point where Zahir was pleased to see they had started doing it blindfolded.

This training was especially needed as they had been issued the new AK74M, lighter and more reliable than the ancient AK47s that these men were used to carrying back in Afghanistan. The folding butt provided many benefits, enabling the weapon to be concealed easily or extended making the weapon more accurate and controllable. He was very pleased to see many of the AKs had been fitted with the GP30 option an under-barrel 40mm Grenade Launcher. He made a mental note to ensure each smaller group had a share of these guns. The men would also attend lectures where using one of the grey steel walls of the ship Zahir would run through different attack scenarios.

The diagram showed how to establish arcs of fire to ensure the maximum number of the enemy would be killed. One of the grubby ship's crew entered the room.

Zahir didn't need this interruption and he was sick of this captain's whining all the time. As Zahir's boots rang out on each steel step-tread climbing to the wheelhouse he thought: *what's that fat pig of a Captain want now?* Group Commander Abdul Zahir thought how much he hated having to deal with the ship's Captain, a fat dirty person who never seemed to pray. Every second day there seemed to be some minor complaint. Because his men were so bored this had become a pattern over the last week or so. Zahir entered the wheelhouse without knocking with the single purpose of infuriating the ship's Captain. Captain Tahyadi for his part was just as sick of the Commander's arrogance and lack of respect. This might not be the Queen Mary, but you still knocked before you entered a Captain's bridge.

Cursing, he turned away from the chart he was studying and spat on the wheelhouse floor to show he and only he could do that. Nervously, he scratched at an old narrow scar running vertically from just in front of his right ear all the way down to his jawline. For a moment his mind wandered to a simpler time when he had collected the reminder in a bar room brawl over twenty years ago. Glaring he accused his passenger yet again.

"The cook just told me one of your Afghan pricks sneaked into the pantry and stole some bread and jam from the kitchen. I don't like having thieves on my ship".

The Commander's face did not hide his lack of care regarding this accusation. Zahir couldn't decide whether to answer the Captain's complaint or simply ignore him and return to his men. Reluctantly he chose to answer to escape the captain's presence as quickly as possible. With an obvious threat in his tone, he answered.

"You watch your mouth Captain, don't forget that you are being extremely well paid for this little ride. I would think if you want to live to enjoy it a little bread and jam would be nothing to worry about."

Zahir knew this was an empty threat. At least for now. During the planning stages of the mission, he had strongly recommended that as his men left the ship that the ship's crew should be executed and thrown overboard to ensure that no one could talk about their team or identify anyone. However, it was decided that a rusty old freighter sailing along without a crew would attract unwanted attention. The entire operation could be compromised, especially if the empty ship was discovered and boarded before the rafts made it to Australia. Now he despised the Captain and regretted this decision not to kill them all, but orders were orders. Sensing that he had shut the Captain down he growled.

"Tahyadi don't worry, we hate being here as much as you obviously hate us being here. How long before we can get off this filthy rust bucket?"

Not knowing he and his crew were safe a shaky voice betrayed the Captain's fears while attempting to placate the bullying Afghan.

"We should reach the drop point in approximately six hours if not a little sooner". Turning from the map he had been studying, his Navigator turned to him with a smile.

"Captain I figure it's closer to a bit over four hours, about 1400 Hours".

Zahir smiled. "Good, being cooped up is driving us crazy, my men will be ready by 1300 Hours. Have your crew drop the guard rail and have those lifeboat derricks ready for a quick unload and you can rid yourself of us".

Captain Budi Tahyadi attempted to regain some face purposely avoiding using the Afghan Commander's rank or name.

"That is fine with me, the sooner the better".

Wanting to say more the Captain bit his tongue feeling insulted by the way this goat Commander gave orders on his ship. But then he started to think about all the money that would be his in just four hours. More money than he had ever had before, he smiled a toothless smirk and good riddance to these Afghans. Zahir was halfway down the steps when the Captain, looking at the door the Commander had left ajar, turned to his navigator and quietly said.

"And you and all your men can go screw yourselves".

The Navigator didn't miss the fact that the Captain's bravery was always after the Afghani Commander had left the wheelhouse and was always whispered. When the GPS showed Captain Budi Tahyadi that the old coastal freighter had arrived at the planned drop-off point, he ordered all engines stop. There was no fanfare. Except for the ship slowing and continuing forward under inertia to a near standstill no one would have known they had reached their destination. The salty Captain was glad for such a pitch-black night. The inky darkness only intruded upon by the florescent micro-organisms exposed each time the waves hammered against the rust-stained hull of the old freighter. As well as being dark, a rain squall had risen and was whipping the ship, each raindrop stinging the face and hands of every man who was forced to brave the conditions. As arranged the ship's guard rails had already been dropped enabling the ship's crew to deftly lower the rubber boats into the turbulent waters below. Being a freighter who nearly always had some contraband or another to unload cargo without the luxury of a wharf meant that the ship's crew had practised these actions many times before.

Zahir forced a breath through his wet beard relieved that disembarking the ship had been uneventful so far. As he looked down at the occupants of each craft he thought back to how hard he had to argue for them to be travelling in uniform. Finally, it had been decided that the Afghans may as well be in their uniforms. The boats were far too military looking for the passengers to look like boat people or refugees struggling their way to Australia. The last of these brave desert soldiers now terrified by the whipping rain and swelling seas descended the shaky clattering steel ladder and climbed into their designated rafts.

CHAPTER 6

The climb was slow and careful as they carried all their personal gear and weapons, each man thankful to Allah as they clambered into their waiting boats. The ship's crew may have looked like a band of street beggars, but they were adept at unloading cargo of all sizes and shapes in all sorts of conditions. Accordingly, the rubber boats had been placed alongside in the specific order that Commander Zahir had ordered. The disembarking Afghanis knowing their part after having practised as much as they could in the past few months climbed into their boat and took their assigned stations in each boat. To a man the Afghanis struggled against the squalling conditions, their training in the calm Afghani waters hadn't prepared them for this howling horror.

The pilots grasping the controls readied their now fully loaded craft to leave the small amount of shelter that the freighter was offering from the squall. There had been no fond fair-wells between the crew and those departing. Group Commander Abdul Zahir double-checked the deck with a final look around for any missed gear not even glancing up to the stairs where Captain Budi Tahyadi now stood. Once Commander Zahir had jumped into the lead boat the little fleet set off without further hesitation. The Afghans were happy to be off the old ship, but they also knew they had an ordeal ahead of them. Most of them had never even seen the ocean before.

They were desert people not even coast dwellers. To them, the dark seas held so many unknowns that every splash or slap of the waves threatened their low boats terrifying them. Before starting this mission, under the watchful eyes of the Cadre Staff, they had spent three weeks on Lake Haman near the Iranian border.

Here for twelve hours a day, they practised getting in and out of the Zodiac boats from narrow ladders, packing the craft with gear and moving around the lake as a group. The Cadre Staff were all from various SAS Special Boat Service Troops and had initially been enlisted to evaluate and recommend which rubber boats would serve the operation best. Once they had accomplished that, it was abundantly clear that the group of fighters would need to be trained in the use of the water-craft and especially in the finer points of ocean navigation and seamanship. The decision was made to extend their contract and the time the water phase training would require. Brought in to do the impossible in a short time the Cadre Staff did all they could with these totally inexperienced but committed soldiers.

The few men showing any talent for piloting the black rafts were constantly drilled in preparation for the journey and especially the landing once the small flotilla reached Australian shores. It wasn't until the Ex-SAS had begun the training at Lake Haman that they had talked about the specific challenges of trying to land on a Northern Territory beach, a challenge to even experienced sailors. Like the soldiers, the Leadership Group had no experience of anything to do with ocean crossing.

Brought in to do the impossible in a short time the ex-SAS soldiers did all they could with these totally inexperienced but committed Taliban. Those few men showing any talent for piloting the black rafts received extra training. These pilots were constantly drilled in handling the craft with special attention being paid to the beach landing. The Cadre Staff still had their doubts about whether the group would even reach Australia based on present performances. Having a beer after training one day the experienced Ex SAS soldiers sat around the fire discussing this job.

Tall and rangy ex-SAS Sergeant 'Macca' McKenzie laughed and said to no one in particular. "Even if those Afghanis make the Northern Territory beaches those huge tides will destroy them. I give up trying to explain to them dumb asses what a tide is. They've got zero chance of handling a giant tide rising and falling four or five metres in an incredibly short time."

The SAS trainers had attempted to teach them about waves, but it relied a lot on the imagination, it was akin to attempting to describe an elephant to a blind man. Nothing had prepared them for this long journey into the unknown terrifying even the bravest amongst them. However, they had become skilful at navigating and cruising. As soon as they came around the ship they were assaulted by the freezing squalls with slapping water stinging their faces. They were happy to be off the old ship, but they also knew they had an ordeal ahead of them. And if they did make the beaches of the Northern Territory the huge tides might destroy them. They had had it explained to them several times but still, they didn't fully understand what a tide was and especially what a giant fast tide rising and falling metres in an incredibly short time would mean to their safe landing if and when they reached Australia. However, the willing students became skilful at accelerating as quickly as possible when the instructor screamed, simulating riding the tidal waves that they must battle in Australia. It had been eight days since the old Indonesian freighter had dropped the six inflatables into a dark inhospitable ocean just south of the Island of Sawu where the Indian Ocean meets the Timor Sea.

Tonight, there was a small sliver of moon, but it did little to illuminate the oncoming waves, this was a good thing because for many reasons darkness was always their friend. Hiding from the planes and boats of Border Security they were exposed during the day and they may have been even more scared if they could see the circling dorsal fins of the many sharks that followed them hoping for scraps. Zahir was forever grateful that at least these rubber boats were nearly invisible to the Radar of Australian Border Security. At least that was what he'd been assured. Even though every man in the group had toughened skin gained from living under the desert sun they still found the rafts provided no respite from the scorching sun that burnt them all day long, reflected up to them off the sparkling water. Like all craft of this type every time the boat hit a wave it inevitably caused the cold salty water spray to splash high above the inflatable wetting all those riding in the front seats.

Cursing, Group Commander Abdul Zahir once again wiped away the salt water stinging his face and eyes and wished that he was in the desert he loved and missed so much. Zahir had lived and battled in hard conditions going without food, water and sleep before but he had never felt as tired as he now found himself. Nothing but the strength of will kept him going. His thoughts turned to his beautiful desert homeland brought on by a dulled state of long-term fatigue. He wiped a hand over his scalp and face to clear his head. He was amazed that his mind could drift like this when he was constantly being thrown around and splashed by the cold waters. Zahir rechecked his GPS and was glad to see they had made progress against these growing waves. He was honoured to be in command of the mission. He had not been briefed as to what his final mission was. It was obvious that this operation was extremely important requiring so much money being spent on supplies, training and transport. The level of detail regarding the transport and insertion phases suggested something of great significance. Zahir was a faithful Moslem but he was also a soldier he could never be one of those committed yet mindless suicide bomber types. He preferred to apply his intelligence to his training and experience to serve Allah. Zahir was more interested in sending his enemies to their heaven or hell than going there himself. He liked the idea of fighting to live so he could fight again. He was also bright enough to figure out some of the possibilities of what was ahead for his team and himself. They had been issued the latest AK74M. Most of the Taliban soldiers had never seen this lighter calibre 5.45mm x 39mm version. Their homeland was flooded with the old 7.62 Soviet AK47 and 7.62, some of which had seen 30 years or more service. The Taliban looked like everyone else as they went about their business dressed in the same tribal robes and headgear that generations had been wearing for hundreds if not thousands of years. Add a belt of ammunition or sometimes a Russian Vest with all its pockets and loops, but there was no uniform. Group Commander Abdul Zahir once again observed that each soldier on this mission had been issued more conventional camouflage pattern uniforms. He hoped they would suit Australian conditions.

Zahir had limited access to be able to research Australian conditions. He had talked to the SAS Cadre Staff as much as he could about their vegetation, the colours of the dirt, trees and rocks where he was heading. He had been told that much of Australia was very similar to Afghanistan, but he had no way to confirm this other than his boat trainers. He also knew that in a land as big as Australia, as was the case with his homeland, the terrain and environment could change drastically as you travelled from one end to another. He hoped that whoever planned this mission had researched Australian conditions properly and that the uniforms supplied were highly suitable for the Australian climate, vegetation and terrain.

Although Zahir would never admit it, he was as scared as he had ever been not of what the mission held but of this journey across an unknown sea to an unknown land. The Training Staff that put him and his men through all the facets of the boat handling were strange men, clearly hard Military men, being ex-members of SAS Special Boat Squadron. Commander Zahir knew of the Australian SAS. They were the most feared amongst the invaders of his homeland. He respected their knowledge and abilities while being mindful that they were betraying their country and its Allies just for money.

He attempted to lessen his fear of these unknown waters by thinking of what the boat specialists had said. They had told him they had travelled the world and after months of research and testing chose the newer Zodiac Milpro Model FC530 over the previous Model FC470. The FC530 could take twelve people and their gear and had extra speed with a bigger 50-horsepower motor. Room for sixty passengers, their communications, camping gear and weapons on board. One less boat was one less the Australian Navy could detect. To ensure the Australian Border Patrols didn't catch them with all that military hardware they had strict orders to dump everything overboard if the Australian Navy were about to come alongside or board their craft. They realised the boats and the uniforms would cause some suspicion but neither of those facts proved that they were not refugees who had perhaps stolen the Zodiacs.

The Taliban Leadership believed they would be arrested as they attempted to enter Australia illegally but at least they wouldn't alert the authorities to the possibility of an armed force landing on Australian soil. Commander Zahir was to decide on a case-by-case basis whether to follow these orders unless, of course, the Australian Border Security Forces were in a small enough vessel for them to overpower then they would simply kill the Australians and scuttle their boat. A typical soldier, Zahir hated the way the hierarchy took so long to make decisions. If they had made up their collective minds last year when they had the opportunity it would have been much safer. Last year the Australian Border Security was spread thin with so many people smugglers making the best of the then governments' open back door policies. Since the recent election of a new government, they had effectively closed down the people smuggling from Indonesia. It was a lot harder to sneak through. They had timed the journey to suit the moon and the fact that they knew the Patrol Boat's monthly routine but there were no guarantees they would evade all the patrols.

There was always a chance that some fishing boat or surveillance plane would alert the Patrol Boats to the Zodiac fleet heading towards the Northern Territory coastline. They had also discussed travelling singly to make a smaller target to be noticed by a plane or boat. However, they decided that while this made some sense the risk of some of the boats being lost was too high. Having their Commander in the front Zodiac would be the safest way to get all the group into Australia. Twenty-four hours later found Zahir checked his GPS and with great relief found what he had been looking for, a small island like a sentinel guarding the entrance to the Australian mainland. Although the night was pitch black they could see the white spray and hear the waves crashing like cannon fire on the island's rocky coastline. Commander Zahir was relieved to see a coastline that kept going for miles. All they had to do now was to find the part of the coast owned by the Caerhays Cattle Station. The Zodiacs continued travelling east along the rugged coast keeping the beach several hundred metres off to their right. Finally, the GPS coordinate confirmed they had just crossed the western boundary of Caerhays Cattle Station. Although the boat crews had never seen an ocean they had made it to Australia. They had done what the boat soldiers had doubted they could ever do.

The Ex-SAS Cadre Staff had trained and operated in these waters and knew how to traverse the massive tide shifts. They had made it clear that getting to shore would be one of the biggest challenges these desert dwellers would face. As the Zodiacs turned toward the beach they were lifted from underneath by some unseen force that dragged them inland. The Afghani soldiers piloting the Zodiacs had never seen anything like this. Their training carried them as much as the swelling waters beneath them, each raft being driven further away from the sea by the merciless incoming tide like a mini-tsunami. They had never fully understood the endless drills they had endured until this moment. As practised, the rafts flew on the crest of the Northern Territory tides. Each craft had a man holding a rope and pulling the bow high out of the water. Wave after wave they timed their runs twisting the hand throttle on the 50-horse power motors back and forth keeping control and direction.

The other soldiers in the boat hung on for grim life wondering if they had come all this way just to drown this close to their destination. Just when the boat pilots were beginning to think all this would never end the Zodiacs bottomed on the muddy beach that stretched for another mile ahead of them. The passengers knew that once the boat crew gave them the word they were to grab their gear and get off as quickly as possible. Then the two crew would drag the empty raft as far as they could from the water's edge. The soldiers were more than ready to climb out of the cramped rubber boat onto the soft muddy beach. Each soldier feeling very stiff and unsteady after so long at sea made their way up the muddy beach.

CHAPTER 7

Grateful to be on dry land again and without the distraction of battling the tide some of them became mindful of the warnings they had received in their training for this mission. The area was infested with huge saltwater estuarine crocodiles, some as big as six meters long. Although they had seen photos of crocodiles these desert people had no concept of a man-eating dinosaur the size of a truck. What they had missed was the fact that while crocodiles prefer being in the water they are very adept at attacking their prey either on land or near the water's edge.

Once the Zodiacs were fully unloaded they were tied together and the most proficient soldier/pilot towed them out to sea, even with the improved power of the 50-horse power motor it struggled against the incoming tide. While still on the freighter Commander Zahir had directed the soldier to lash together a spear-type weapon for a particular purpose after the boats had landed. Following his detailed orders, the soldier who had towed the little flotilla out to sea untied the rope connecting the other boats to his to ensure that he wasn't dragged to the bottom. He then slowly passed by each raft stabbing the boats several times with the makeshift spear he had made on the freighter. Each Zodiac's remaining fuel tanks and outboard motors served as enough weight to drag each boat down to the black mud bottom.

Keeping the raft, he was in he returned to the beach. He was very happy with himself knowing he had followed his orders and that it had all gone well when suddenly a wave nearly tossed him into the foaming roaring tide. He found that without the extra weight of his fellow soldiers and their gear the Zodiac was thrown around like a cork in the surf. After fighting every wave and cross current the rubber boat finally reached the inland beach. With no weight in it, he gave the throttle one last increase and the raft flew up the beach sliding along the mud eventually skewing to a stop some five metres further up the beach from the wet mud. The soldier's body was full of Adrenalin, his muscles weary and his heart and lungs exploding in his chest. He collapsed still sitting in the Zodiac. Commander Zahir had seen the battle to get in and dispatched two men to assist the exhausted soldier.

After their friend regained enough strength he climbed out of the raft and together they dragged the last remaining Zodiac up the beach and into a patch of mangroves. "What is that clicking sound Al Safi?" asked his friend Corporal Bahij.

"I do not know my friend but keep a good lookout I will concentrate on the raft."

No one knew that the noise was coming from the famous Northern Territory Mud Crab making the sound by clicking their massive claws that were filled with sweet meat. Deflating the raft with the same spear, they placed heavy mangrove branches over the inflatable making it invisible amongst the mud, leaves and mangrove breathers. They all put on brave faces but every one of them was glad to get off that beach and onto dry land re-joining the larger group.

As the three soldiers joined the group that had assembled in a small clearing Commander Zahir carried out a quick assessment of his men and gear. He could see there was nothing that a little exercise and better food wouldn't fix. His men would quickly recover from their time at sea. Mindful of the need to let his troops gain their land legs again he set a slow, steady pace towards their first camp. Passing by what looked like a small tea-tree swamp surrounded by shallow putrid pools at its edge there were loud snorting sounds. Suddenly, something very big crashed through the bush breaking branches and sending a flock of large white birds screaming into the hot air. Crashing into a clear section on their left a herd of five huge water buffaloes appeared.

As they went deeper into the cattle station Zahir's GPS beeped signifying that they had reached their overnight camp. Hidden from sight from above they set up a temporary camp under a large stand of Acacia trees growing by the side of a large tidal stream. Everyone was grateful not to be moving anymore. Eating and resting they waited for the local guide who would take them further. Exhausted after so many days at sea, the stress of the beach landing and the walk after so long cramped up on the Zodiacs each soldier collapsed onto his bedding. Due to the isolation of the place, the Commander decided against posting any guards knowing there was still a very long way to go until they reached their final destination.

Nearly three hours later the only sounds that could be heard were numerous exhausted men snoring loudly and the hoot hoot of an owl. Suddenly the peace of the pitch-black night was shattered by a blood-curdling scream like nothing any of them had ever heard before. Being soldiers most of them reacted quickly grabbing at weapons and trying to see what direction the enemy was attacking their team from. The Commander was screaming orders attempting to get some order and some lighting going cursing himself for making a decision based on his fatigue and that of his men. He had decided that they must sacrifice stealth by illuminating the battle scene, they were clearly compromised in any case.

The Officer needed to be able to see the threat. "Sergeant send up a hand-held flare, now."

A small whoosh was followed by two more and three magnesium flares were suspended on little parachutes in the night sky. The pitch-black camp turned into a garish mix of brightness and corresponding shadows. As the tiny parachutes descended swinging in the breeze they cast a bright yet ghostly flickering light over the entire camp and every person in it. Every soldier looked toward the perimeter of their makeshift camp expecting to see troops advancing against their vulnerable position. From the eastern side of the little camp, a scraping crunching sound could be heard as the flares fizzled out and used casings hit the ground with a soft thud. "More flares, more flares" the Commander shouted in Dari.

Once again, the white light fell from floating parachutes lighting the area between their camp and the bank of the tidal creek. A gigantic crocodile was dragging some poor soldier still in his sleeping bag towards the murky water some fifteen meters away.

The huge crocodile was in total kill mode. The lights, the screams, nothing was going to distract it from its goal of dragging this strange animal it had caught between its stinking jaws into the water. The young soldier was struggling ineffectively against the massive jaws of this six-meter per-historic reptile. He had stopped screaming by now and was whimpering piteously. The crocodile's strategy was instinctive and simple, to drown his victim and probably stash him under a submerged log awaiting a degree of decomposition to assist the croc to dismantle the long-dead soldier.

By now the soldiers had torches going and shuddered as two more monsters slithered into the muddy water. Attracted by all this action, hoping to be as successful as their peer, even an opportunity to steal the victim from the first croc. Rushing forward several soldiers overtook the crocodile who was still dragging their hapless friend closer and closer towards the water. With a mixture of fear and of not knowing where to shoot such a dinosaur for an instant kill, all three soldiers emptied their magazines into the beast, some peppering its fat body but thankfully a few lacing a red dot line across the crocodile's wide head. At the first shots, the two other crocodiles turned rapidly and with a flick of their muscular tails disappeared silently into the green weed-covered creek leaving only claw marks.

Anxiously they approached the huge monster and prised their friend from its jaws. They carefully carried the croc's victim back to camp and got some camp lights going. Removing him from his sleeping bag revealed that he was bleeding profusely from numerous bites on his torso and legs. The crunching noises they had heard earlier had been the incredible crushing power of the crocodile's jaws breaking the young man's legs in several places. The Commander knew there was no choice, no discussion to be had. He also realised even with this group's shared faith and beliefs his decision wouldn't go down well. The whole group had to be ready to go when the guide arrived, this unlucky man could not make the trip. Without hesitation, he commanded two soldiers who were standing nearby.

"You two carry him over to that tree there".

Unbelievably, the young soldier was still conscious his eyes large and white in the camp lights. Commander Zahir willed him to succumb to shock and pass out but the young warrior was strong. Walking over to the wounded soldier the sadness obvious in his voice and his face the Commander whispered to the brave lad.

"Son we cannot take you further and we have no medical support here, so I need to ask for your sacrifice here tonight. The good news is that you know seventy-two virgins are awaiting you and you have served Allah the Merciful and your country well. And..."

The Commander had not planned to say more but was hoping that the unfinished sentence would take the young soldier by surprise as he sunk his pesh-kabz into this young warrior's heart. The Commander had always been proud of his ancient dagger as it had been in his family of warriors since the 1800s. But tonight, there was a tinge of sadness and shame as he cleaned the beautifully curved blade on the blanket he wrapped around the soldier's still body.

Zahir returned to the camp and told his men their brave fellow soldier had just died from his terrible wounds. Talking quietly to his second in charge he commanded. "Don't make a big fuss but take his body down to that horrible water. I realise it is not the normal Moslem way, but we must not leave evidence that we were ever here, and we must leave here in the next hour or so".

Seeing the anguish on his Commander's face the Junior Officer moved away to carry out his grisly orders without comment. He bent beside the dead soldier. Placing his arms under him he extended his legs and effortlessly lifted the lifeless body from the ground. He was a brave Officer who had seen many combat actions. Although he had been too young to fight the Russians he had made up for that by already killing several English, American and Australian invaders. He knew that he was no coward in battle. It didn't help that he was plain terrified as he approached the water's edge to throw his dead comrade's body to those monsters. With every step, he wondered: *would they be in the water and jump up and grab him or were they lying in the dark shadows near the bank ready to grab him and drag him into the water.*

Finally, he got to the bank. Concentrating on not falling in he slid the body of the hapless soldier from his shoulders and pushed the limp body towards the water. He figured that the crocodiles would do the rest for themselves. Besides the fact that he felt like a frightened school girl he just wanted to get back to camp. There was a huge splash. Turning sharply, he ran faster than he had for a long time. He had gone about twenty or so metres when he knew in the depths of his being that the crocodiles had finally won, they had gotten their prey after all.

At 0210 Hours they could hear what sounded like a motorcycle approaching. The men took up defensive positions ready for any potential threat, from the east they could see a faint glow through the trees. A few minutes later the entire bush was lit up by the bike's headlights and spotlights casting ghostly shadows all around the anxious men as the bike went up and down with the rough track. A large red four-wheel Quad Bike and not the two-wheeler they had expected from the engine sound slid into view. To their surprise, the rider stood up on the pegs. Speaking loudly over the roar of his Quad Bike the man welcomed them to Australia in their native tongue

Dari. The use of Dari confirmed that he knew most of these men had all come from the Galcha-Pamir Mountain and surrounding valleys.

Once the Commander was sure this was their guide he ordered his troops to stand down and assemble in front of him ready for travel. The guide requested permission to address the whole group. A nod from the Commander released him to do so and he began to address them in Dari.

"Welcome my brothers Allah Al-Muhaymin (The Preserver of Safety) has blessed your journey with safety and secrecy. Take this as a sign that he is well pleased with your sacrifice and your service."

The group responded as one "Allahu Akbar" God is great.

Some of the soldiers could not help but think: *what does our friend being killed by that monster mean in terms of Allah's blessing or otherwise.* Their thoughts were interrupted by the Australian accented Dari.

The Australian coughed, took a swig from his water bottle and then continued his prepared speech. "You will now walk to a cattle loading yard some five miles away. There you will get onto a truck that will take you to another farm nearly two days south from here. Once you get there you will receive special training that will equip and prepare you for missions that will shake these Infidels in their beds. Each of you will become a razor-sharp weapon of terror that the world has never seen before in such numbers. If it is the will of Allah, you will go to your reward knowing that Allah is greatly pleased with you. Now, with your Commander's approval grab your equipment and follow me. We travel for a little more than an hour, the good news is that after that you don't have to walk for the next part of your journey."

These were well seasoned brave warriors who had been tested again and again coming up against better-equipped Russian, American, British and Australian troops who had all invaded their homeland. Here in this strange land, it was the unknown that caused them to be anxious. They didn't fear dying in battle if that was Allah's will so be it. The vipers and cobras at home were a match for these Australian snakes, but the crocodile attack had shaken all of them. Their country was the inhospitable desert country, full of strange animals and strange sounds. But here any noise caused every head to turn quickly and each heart rate to increase in expectation of another crocodile.

It was hot, not the oven hot they were born to, but a wet heat that crushed your spirit and sapped your energy and soaked you to the bone. Traipsing along after the Quad, this time its engine making very little noise just ticking over, they came to a swampy-looking area where they heard a low bellow and snorting from more than one animal. They had no idea what had made the sounds.

A young soldier turned to his Sergeant. "Do crocodiles sound like that?"

Fear moved through the ranks like a plague but like soldiers everywhere, they kept going, left foot right foot, and left again hoping the noises never became an animal attacking them. Their fear was overpowered by fatigue brought on by arduous long-term travel. After nearly three weeks of minimal sleep and nutrition, they walked as if in a trance, near sleepwalking. Not unlike the goats at home, they marched in two lines stumbling silently along following the quad which continued to maintain a good pace for them to easily keep up in the dark Australian bush.

Without warning, they burst out of a dappled scrubby area of trees as the first hint of dawn lightened. The bush they could see well enough to know that this was a strange and harsh land but not as barren as their home. They became alert, up ahead someone was laughing. The Afghanis didn't know it but, yet another Australian dawn had just been heralded in by a flock of Kookaburras, a bird famous for its song and its ability to catch and kill snakes. As they passed the large birds sitting side by side on a branch of a huge gum tree, a smell unfamiliar to them wafted over the crest of a low ridge. Suddenly those soldiers leading the group could see there was a huge black shape up ahead. Stumbling forward one by one, they got closer and began to realise they had walked up to a high and long truck.

Larger and different to anything they had ever seen back in Afghanistan, in the clearing were three multi-level trailers all attached and being towed by a red Kenworth Prime Mover. The monster trailers were called road trains. The smell of cow manure and urine was overpowering and now they could make out the vague shapes of large horned beasts as they milled around inside the crates. As soon as the last pair arrived a small light on the side of one of the trailers was switched on blinding the men temporarily until their eyes adjusted. The truck driver was an Australian who had agreed to make ten times his usual fee for such a trip. From behind the truck, a broad-shouldered man dressed in blue jeans and a faded blue singlet appeared. Small dust clouds rose and fell as his RM Williams elastic-sided boots cut a path through the grasses. Longish blond hair hung under a black Akubra hat that had several cattle ear tags pinned to it.

Reaching into the cattle crate he drew his muscular arm downwards, there was a loud metallic click and then a grating sound. The men didn't have any idea what was going to happen but they were trained to obey without hesitation and discussion. The guide had dismounted off his Quad bike and now whispered to the Commander who was nodding and looking at the Road Train. The Commander then leapt onto the cattle ramp yelling.

"Everyone get onto the truck". Instantly each man shouldered his weapon and gear and lined up at the base of the ramp and proceeded up the ramp into the road train.

Carrying their equipment and weapons they followed the Australian truck driver up the ramp and into the depths of the cattle truck, the smell was causing some of the soldiers to gag. They noticed they were walking behind the cattle in a hidden sort of corridor into the crate. Anyone looking up from the ground, even a stock inspector would only see cattle and assume the trailer to be full of cattle. Two extra-long cattle trucks swallowed up thirty men and their gear like a giant python. The irony was not lost on Commander Zahir who was prone to deeper than usual thoughts: *in many ways, we soldiers are not unlike cattle. You depended on others for most things and you went where you were told. In many cases, you were sent to the slaughter.* He shrugged dismissing these thoughts as another sign of his ongoing fatigue. The group settled into the truck accepting the soldier's lot as soldiers had done for millenniums all over the world.

Even though the men would never complain it was obvious they were very uncomfortable. They found they were crammed into this secret cavity so tight they could only sit on their gear but not lie down. Each man had his own food and water so that was taken care of and if they needed to relieve themselves just like the cattle the floor was there. The quad guide had said it was a long journey. However, no one ever thought it would take nearly nineteen hundred kilometres and around thirty hours. They encouraged each other by affirming Allah must have his reasons for all hardship and it surely makes paradise sweeter. One by one they settled into a fitful exhausted sleep, some dreamt of the seventy-two virgins awaiting them in the future whilst others dreamt of the crocodile.

CHAPTER 8

ROMA
QUEENSLAND
MARCH 2014

I had been camping and hunting on a friend's cattle property just outside Roma for about nine or ten weeks. I had run out of a few supplies, especially my trusty Jack Daniels, so I headed into town to buy more of the smoky bourbon. Over on my right, the local airport looked more like a parking lot with hundreds of white 4WD Utes that all looked pretty much the same. They were parked awaiting the comings and goings of the large fly-in fly-out gas pipeline workforce. Roma Queensland is one of those thriving Queensland country towns with the ability to adapt to whatever resource was the current action. The town has a history of different types of mining with lots of local agriculture, especially cattle. In more recent times many local businesses supported building the infrastructure required to harvest vast underground gas reserves.

Turning into McDowall Street all I could think about was the sausage rolls I was about to buy, some of which I would demolish before I got back to my Ute. The local bakery made what I reckoned were the best sausage rolls in Queensland maybe the world and I had tried them all around the world, so this was no small claim on my part. I had been hunting and living off what I shot or my Army rations pack for over two weeks so my expectations for something that good were through the roof.

My mouth started watering when I saw the distinctive blue sign of the bakery, there it is just down on the next corner. Sub-consciously my foot increased the pressure on the accelerator of my old Toyota Land Cruiser Utility. It's not as big or as flashy as the American pickups but I could go anywhere I ever wanted. I wasn't worried about looks and I wasn't scared to cross a creek or scratch it chasing a pig through some scrub. The young bucks working on the Gas Pipeline for big money to buy big toys could be seen around town driving American units. GMCs, RAMS, Chevrolets and of course some of those giant Fords were starting to show up more and more. Thoughts of sausage rolls and tomato sauce (I refused to call it ketchup) were fighting something else. It had been so fast that I couldn't recollect what had distracted me. I changed down a gear and looked for a parking spot, *damn what was that up that alley?* It was nearly a subconscious thought; *I am sure I just saw a flash of blue but not just any blue I am sure it was a Queensland Police Service Shirt.*

Swinging the old Land Cruiser Ute around, I slowly idled back towards the gap between two shops. In the city, you would call it an alley I suppose, in Roma, it was just a gap between some buildings. *There I knew I had seen something:* four men standing over something on the ground. I stopped the Ute quietly and stepped out closing the door so as not to make any sound. I approached the group, assessing the men. The angles, the places I wanted to be and where I didn't want to end up. Training and experience had taught me a long time ago to know what to look for and understand what I saw. Lying on the ground in front of these men was a female Police Officer, she had been beaten. She lay on her bare back on the dirty path behind an old laundry. There was blood streaming down her chin onto her bare chest. I could see some rags on the ground a few metres back from where the group now stood. Probably her uniform shirt and bra that had been ripped from her.

She rolled onto her side which was probably what she had been trained to do. Perhaps it was what her instincts told her to do, to curl up as tightly as possible. All four men were of different heights, three were well under the six-foot mark, and the one furthest from me was a bit taller. He appeared to be in good shape and carried a lot more muscle than his friends. I had expected them to be farm hands off the many cattle properties around Roma. To my surprise, they were not all local boys, with three of them being of Middle Eastern origins and the big one was maybe Australian.

All four were wearing jeans over work boots, one was wearing a green John Deere Cap, another was in a red Tee shirt and the other man was in a green bush jacket over a black Tee shirt. The blond guy was dressed in faded jeans, a brown Tee shirt and a green cotton vest covered in pockets, similar to what photographers and fly fishermen wear. By the way, he swaggered around the girl you could tell the blond fancied himself. His big tattooed arms and a chest like a TV wrestler emphasised his V shape leading to his narrow hips. He was standing over the woman on the ground. By his body language, I figured the blond was in charge of the other three in some way or other. I had gotten close enough to be able to hear them now; he was the only one talking. He stepped forward and knelt beside the prone figure. Blondie grabbed her ankles and forced the girl to straighten and spread her legs apart.

He called to the others. "Come on get this slut pig's pants down and we can all have some fun".

Yeah, he's definitely an Aussie, silently I moved a little closer. They were so focused on her that they probably wouldn't have heard me if I was whistling the National Anthem. John Deere had a sick leer on his face and was holding his crotch and rubbing himself, *gross*. You could tell that they were getting hot and bothered sort of shaking like a male dog near a bitch on heat. I knew that would fade as soon as they became aware of me. Still unaware of my presence I decided on my final plan of attack and went in. Redshirt had his back to me. In one smooth motion, I turned my body side onto him, raising my foot and I brought it down hard behind his right knee joint. This was rewarded with a cracking sound accompanied by a curdling scream as he twisted onto the ground holding his destroyed knee. He would play no further part in the confrontation.

Realising what was happening the blond Aussie sprung to his feet and settled into what was clearly a trained Karate stance. I matched this faking in preparation for a roundhouse kick. He began moving in to take advantage of this supposed opportunity that I had created. He closed the gap only to find I hadn't moved in the direction he had expected. I blocked his first kick with my left forearm. Pushing his right foot away, his groin was now open to me, so I punched him hard in the balls feeling them squash beneath my fist. He screamed in agony. But he wasn't going to give in that easy, as he fell he drew a large tactical knife from a sheath mounted horizontally on his belt at his back. In one action he then attempted to stab me with a downward thrust.

Thank God I have always had great reflexes. My arms flew up at the last second catching the man's wrist in the X made by my wrists, I had caught the knife, but this guy was persistent, to say the least. While he was caught in this trap I twisted my arms taking him with me and let his force take the knife away guided by my left forearm. As the knife fell away my right hand was free to deliver an uppercut punch that snapped his jaws together with a loud crack of his teeth. I had had enough of this guy, before he could fall I followed up with an open palm splitting his nose across his face, he fell motionless to the concrete path blood gushing from his bleeding nose and tongue.

I had been wondering where the other two had gone when the guy in the green jacket moved in with a right cross, he was brave but had no idea. He had caught me out, but I was quick enough to duck so it missed my head hitting my shoulder so hard my right arm was immediately numb. He followed up with another right, I stepped to the left blocking this punch upwards and to the right knowing my right arm was still too numb to be any help. This opened him up to a left elbow strike to the side of his head, he staggered then recovered a little swinging around as he fell. The momentum brought him up again where he landed a solid hit to my side knocking me half a step sideways. He then followed up with another right this time finding the side of my head. For a moment darkness fell and so did I. Recovering before I hit the ground I followed his example and came up fast catching him by surprise because he thought it was all over. I slammed my fist hard into his Adam's apple causing him to collapse in a heap gasping and clutching at his throat.

By now John Deere was trying to decide what to do after seeing what had happened to his three friends. He rushed at me flailing his big fists at no specific part of my anatomy. I blocked these as much as I could, left right left right, right again then two lefts. He was what we used to call battle virgins in SAS, they were super trained but not tested in the real deal. Some of these guys handled that well but some overcompensated. Accordingly, we named them EBOA, Eager Beaver Over-Achiever. This untrained random attack was in some ways harder to handle than predictable trained martial arts moves. Hand to hand was not his gift but he was big and strong and scared. This had probably got him by in the past and he was committed based on this confidence. I blocked a right to my face and let it sail past my left shoulder grabbing his fist and forearm I spun under it then I twisted his arm up his back until I heard a sickening crunch as his shoulder tore loose.

I finished him off with a knife-edge hand to the back of his neck; he was unconscious before he hit the ground. I noticed a Police issue Glock sticking out of the waistband of his jeans I grabbed it making sure it was safe, turned and surveyed the scene.

I took a moment to calm my breathing. After a contact or an ambush or even just a bar fight like this one, well-trained men come back to calm by controlling their mental state. The specialist courses I had done had provided me with the skills of knowing when to rush and when to go slow, all managed with trained and practised self-control. This when mixed with experience equipped me throughout the fight I had just had. Looking at the Police Officer I could see she was beginning to come to. I remembered her shirt and bra near the wall, so I walked over and picked them up feeling uncomfortable holding a strange woman's underwear. I tried to subtly wrap the bra in the shirt. As I brought them over to her she began to try to stand up using the short brick wall beside her for support. I helped her to her feet and handed her clothes to her trying not to look in her direction to avoid embarrassing both of us further. While still attempting to get dressed she turned towards the four unconscious men. She drew her right foot back and kicked the nearest one as hard as she could in the balls. I nearly felt sorry for him, nearly. She spat; "the pricks ruined my favourite bra" then fell to her knees sobbing.

I am neither skilled nor experienced in managing crying women, so I avoided her and got busy doing what I hoped needed to be done. Taking the handcuffs from her utility belt now lying on the path I handcuffed the two nearest to me to each other. Then I took red shirt's belt off and tied his hands behind his back threading the belt through the loop in the handcuffs so the three of them were hog-tied and sitting back to back together. The girl began to calm down, and I quietly reassured her. I figured she might like to clean herself up a little before calling it in. I don't know much, but I knew how much ridicule she would get from her male colleagues. Letting four thugs strip her, beat her up and the real biggie for any Police Officer, let them take her gun.

"G' day I'm Steve Wallace just take it slowly for now?"

"Hi, I'm Chris Jackson, everyone around here calls me Jack" sticking her right hand out while being careful to keep her left arm shielding her naked breasts that could be seen through her gaping torn shirt.

Attempting to ease her embarrassment and any residual shock I tried to focus on her eyes, I asked. “You OK, do you think any bones are broken?”

"Thanks for what you did, no I'll be OK, just bruises. I can never repay you for what you did”. She was regrouping but I noticed a tear flow down her left cheek.

Gently dismissing her gratitude with a shrug, I knew it was important for her to move on from the attack. “It’s OK, would you like to slip home and clean up? I can stand guard on these heroes until you get back”.

She was tough, she was regrouping quickly. “No by the time I wash my face” she looked at a tap screwed to the old laundry wall, “and button my shirt a bit better I can call for help and it should all work out. I probably look like I’ve been in a fight hey? Do you want to be involved or disappear before the cavalry arrive?”

This girl might not be able to handle four idiots by herself, but she is tough, sharp, and considerate. I must admit I wasn’t looking forward to all those questions and paperwork.

“I’m happy to be on my way Constable Jackson, whatever story you come up with is totally up to you. Say whatever you want, these scum would never admit a woman could do this to them anyway. So, when they deny it, your mates won’t take any notice anyway. Get yourself some points with your workmates while you have the chance”.

Pointing down at the four prisoners I asked; “Do you know who they are, are they locals?”

“No, I don’t think I’ve seen them before, I’ve noticed there seems to be a few Arab types or whatever they are around town lately. I figured they were something to do with all these gas pipelines that are going in. These pricks will get to sleep in our luxurious Watch House tonight and appear in Court tomorrow morning”.

I smiled. "You sure you're OK?" When she nodded I stepped away a little, "I'm out of here, you take care, and for what it's worth, next time if there is more than one don't be scared to draw your gun and maybe even shoot a leg or two, it's worth the paperwork." Having passed on this profound advice I figured I had more than earned a sausage roll or two.

As I left the alley between the two buildings I was thinking how good-looking Constable Jackson was. *I might look her up one day soon.* Like most men, food and sex can be big distractions for me. Between renewed thoughts of sausage rolls and female Police Officers, I totally missed the two men sitting in a silver Nissan Patrol. From where they were parked they would have seen the whole fight in the alley. As I headed towards the bakery the Nissan slowly left the curb and followed me down the street. In a town where every second vehicle is a 4WD of some make, it was invisible.

Besides that, I was not expecting to be followed in any case. In addition to sausage rolls, I picked up a few bottles of Jack Daniels to keep me warm at night back at camp. I have decided that I hate towns and cities and my little run-in has given me yet another reason. Feeling pretty happy with myself and the thought of seeing my dog Jake soon I headed back out of town. About ten miles out I threw the empty paper bag on the passenger floor of the Ute signalling that I had just finished my third sausage roll and they were awesome. In that fraction of a second, I had looked left, the Nissan from town must have gained on me because right as my eyes re-joined the road there was a shattering of plastic and a crunching of metal as my Ute flew sideways hit from behind by the silver 4WD from town.

Grateful for the seat belt I was wearing and the strength of my old Toyota I held on tight to the steering wheel and kept checking each mirror trying to keep the Nissan in sight. I reacted quickly enough to straighten up again just as my mirrors filled with the silver 4WD. I could see that there were two males in the front seat as the

4WD rocketed toward me again. Just before impact, I swerved to the right dodging the Nissan's onslaught. I was pleased to see the Nissan over-correct and swerve uncontrollably as it hit the dirt shoulder of the road. The driver slammed hard on the breaks sliding to a stop to regain control. The Nissan was a much newer Turbocharged model. It was more powerful than my old diesel Land Cruiser, so I knew outrunning it wasn't an option. I had to pick the spot and try to bait them into over-committing hopefully resulting in disaster for them and escape for me. I had to try to get them off the highway.

Once again, the unknown 4WD caught up to me, this time drawing alongside. Looking over I realised the passenger looked like he could have been a brother to the three rag heads I had run into in Roma. I needed to think about this but not right now. The other worrying matter was the large calibre semi-automatic pistol that was now pointing at my head. I felt like I was back in Afghanistan: *what the hell was going on?* Hitting the brakes, I dropped back pulling hard to the right my bull bar slammed into the Nissan's rear left panel causing the silver 4WD to slew sideways and onto the wrong side of the road. Unbeknown to them or me a shiny white Kenilworth Semi towing a refrigerated trailer coming from the other direction had just crested the hill we were all on. My push had set up the Nissan sideways and still on the wrong side of the highway, right in the path of the semi-trailer, they had nowhere to go.

The Kenilworth's huge bull bar smashed through the silver 4WD; glass, plastic and metal spraying out all over the road like a bomb had gone off. This was accompanied by a sickening metallic screech as the semi-driver braked; his rig still crushing and pushing the Nissan along as he attempted to slow the massive weight and stop. For a fraction of a second, I could see the fear on its occupant's faces and then they were gone driven behind me by forty tons of steel doing nearly a hundred kilometres an hour. I accelerated not wanting to get tangled up with the refrigerated trailer if it jack-knifed. I got over the hill in the other direction and pushed the old Ute as fast as it would go. Whoa, what had just happened, I wanted to pull over. I needed to think. Part of me wanted to check if any of them were still with us but knew that no one could be helped. I didn't want to be pulled into what had just happened. I continued at a steady pace and once again felt the Adrenalin gradually drain from my system.

As it did I began to think things through.

I always like to think when I'm driving, and I think better still if Toby Keith is playing on the stereo, so I did just that. I put on 'Clancy's Tavern' and mentally listed whatever came to mind not discounting anything at this stage:

Question 1: *How did they know I had beaten up their mates in town?*

Answer 1: *Easy, I figured that their driver may have been parked nearby and had seen me.*

Question 2: *If that is true and especially seeing they were armed why didn't they just come over and shoot me and Officer Jackson in the back-saving their friends a beating and being arrested?*

Answer 2: *Maybe they didn't want to attract any more attention than the four already had.*

Question 3: *Was it just a coincidence that in a small western Queensland town like Roma I had had two serious run-ins within two hours of each other?*

Answer 3: *I don't believe in coincidences, especially this type.*

I had a lot to think through.

Question 4: *How come both run-ins were with Afghani-looking characters?*

Answer 4: *Same as 3, I don't believe in coincidences especially this type, even more so.*

Question 5: *How come suddenly there are so many Afghani types around here, I have been hunting in this area for twenty-something years and have never seen a single one before today?*

Answer 5: *No frigging idea, all I know is that wherever they came from there are at least two less than there were an hour ago, and three more locked up in the Roma Watchhouse. And I am extremely happy with that outcome seeing they were trying to kill me.*

I reached the turn-off for the property I hunt on before I could come up with any more profound questions and answers, my brain was tired anyway. My hunting property is about eight miles off the highway and after two deep-sided creek crossings and three cattle grids I made it back to my camp. My border collie-cross Jake looks relieved that I am back. He thinks about getting off my swag bed but thinks better of it and lies down again. Overwhelmed by his excitement I can hardly control myself. "I'm glad to see you too Jake". After I get a fire going and pour a very large Jack into my green plastic Army mug, I sit back and try to relax. This is what it's all about for me a big part of going bush and hunting has always been the camping. The getting away from phones and traffic and the rush of civilisation. Staring into a bush wood fire and looking at all those stars you just can't see in the city. Did I mention that I hate towns and especially cities? Trouble is that tonight these friggin Talibs (that's what we used to call them in Afghanistan amongst other things) had upset my day. I can't stop thinking about all the memories it has stirred up inside me. Tonight, I seem to have more questions than answers; the troubling thing is I am not even sure I have the correct questions. There is an uneasiness that I respect too much to ignore. But usually, I get this gut feeling in some desert or jungle somewhere, not in my little piece of paradise a few hours west of home in Queensland Australia. I have seen Post Traumatic Stress Disorder (PTSD), even though there are still some people who don't believe in it. They're mostly civvies who have never faced anything more dangerous than coming home late to their wife.

It has changed names with different wars but that doesn't change its reality. I had Training Sergeants who had done Vietnam only to struggle through.

Eventually, it was all too much, they went off somewhere and shot themselves with a pistol borrowed from the Armoury. PTSD is real to the guys that have been there. It's not a competition and every war has its horrors. Some handle it some don't. Others handle it when it's happening only to fall apart after the heat is over, no one is qualified to judge another soldier's stuff. I get why mates of mine have come back from Iraq and Afghanistan with problems. Watching friends blown apart mid-sentence, one minute talking about football or their wives or girlfriends. The next minute covered in my mate's blood and brains because of an Improvised Explosive Device (IED) or some rag head prick with an AK. Living on edge for days at a time, seeing how these Talibs treat their fellow Afghanis I get it. I'm grateful that I am OK, at least I think I'm OK. That having been said it only takes a couple of JDs and the slightest thing can take me straight back to some sand pit, another place, another time and some operation where a mate didn't make it back.

My hunting rifle is a Remington 7600 Pump Action in 308 Winchester and there aren't a lot of rifles around that sort out a mob of feral pigs or the occasional Red Deer as well as this unit. My Sniper School Instructors would not have approved of my having a Pump Action and I understood why this would be. Even as a skinny nine-year-old hunting rabbits with a single shot Lithgow 22 calibre Rimfire and of course later all through my sniper training I had learnt and embraced the creed *of one shot one kill.* However, having the ability to go for multiple targets real fast is always a bonus. Of course, I still made my first the best I could but after that shooting quick to get an extra few pigs was a great way to sharpen your reflexes and your shooting. It had to be a Remington; serving as a sniper in Afghanistan I had learnt to respect, even love Remington

Rifles especially the M40 in 7.62 NATO, or civilian equivalent the Win308, and later the 50Cal Barret M 107 Sniper Rifle.

A few JDs later found me staring at the light from the fire flickering off the brass rounds loaded in my ten-shot Remington magazine. Only eight rounds because old habits die hard; it was common knowledge that with a Barret M 107 Sniper Rifle built on a Remington action, the ten shot mags jammed if you loaded ten, most of us went eight to be sure. This wasn't a Barret but, as I said, old habits.

As I sipped my Jack straight because there was no ice within miles, I thought about all these questions about the day's unusual events. At the risk of sounding like Gomer Pyle's "surprise surprise", actually it was more like falling into a mine shaft sort of surprise than winning Lotto sort of surprise, I realised the answer was right in front of me. I started drifting off as all these thoughts took me to another place, a hot sandy place, still with a rifle but for *a very different* purpose.

I had long lost that practised skill and like a tired driver who is close to falling asleep at the wheel, I started to dream of blissful sleep. Unbeknown to me Jake stretched out and his hind leg kicked over the empty billy (saucepan for boiling water on a fire). I was jolted out of the same daydream that had plagued me on so many nights over the past nine years or so. I dropped my mug, the empty sound bringing me back to now. I turned to the JD bottle breaking the spell that had dragged me back to that stony ridge so long ago. "One more to help me sleep Jakey and then we hit the sack. We've got an early start if I want to get onto those Red Deer bucks in the bottom paddock. Some people might think it crazy talking to your dog but out here who else was I going to talk to anyway. The other thing was that the more people I met the more I liked my dog, I think some American President or Politician said that first, but it summed it up for me pretty well.

CHAPTER 9

OUTSIDE PORT ARTHUR
PENAL COLONY
LATE MARCH 2014

Al-Hasan was respected by his cell members, not just because he was their leader, but they knew he had been trained in a Terrorist Camp in Afghanistan. He had that air of authority that came with rank yes but even more strongly with confidence and strength of body, mind and will. Soon after the USB was delivered he had called the six men now sitting around smoking their hookahs to this meeting. They would evaluate and debate the details of the mission long into the night. "Bayhas my old friend, I can understand the attraction to wait the three days to coincide with the eighth anniversary of the famous attack on the same site".

Al-Hasan could see the blank looks on the men around the table; "Do all of you know what we are talking about my brothers?" In response to several shaking heads he went on to explain "on the 28th of April 1996 an infidel named Martin Bryant using several different weapons went berserk at Port Arthur. He single-handedly killed thirty-five tourists and wounded twenty-three others". Abdul a new member of the group spat out the words like he had swallowed a fly; "Who cares! let the infidels rot in hell".

Al-Hasan gently managed the group; "Yes of course who cares about more dead unbelievers. But you all know my only motivation is to maximise the physical and emotional impact of our attacks. What you have forgotten my brothers is that our orders are to attack on ANZAC Day. I do not know if we are alone in this honour my brothers. But, if there are similar groups meeting around Australia

I am sure they too will attack that same day. One can only imagine the power and the message we will send if this nation of faithless infidels is attacked on many fronts. The Government and the people of Australia are just American lackeys, they blindly follow them into every war they fight".

The discussion at times became heated but all knew this was more unity of purpose than discord. "Alright it is settled we go on their ANZAC Day. While they celebrate murdering our Turkish brothers by invading Gallipoli we will give them something they will never forget". As Al-Hasan said this all heads were nodding in better understanding and total agreement. Scouring a map provided by the Tasmanian Tourist Department it still took a lot of time to work out where to place the bomb as the site covers some thirty different buildings across forty hectares of land. Finally, they came to a decision. It came with a sense of irony as it was decided that one of the site's cafes at lunchtime would be perfect. The symbolism added to the value of the target as the Broad Arrow Cafe was now a memorial as a major scene during the Martin Bryant massacre. They were sure that it would be crowded with men and women of all ages and lots of children enjoying their lunch on the National Public Holiday. A perfect target for their bomber.

Melbourne Victoria
Australia
Late March 2014

The third-storey two-bedroom unit smelt of stale body odour, Middle Eastern cooking and smoke. All the windows had been taped over stopping any vision or smell from escaping. The group of men sitting around the lounge floor leaning on colourful cushions were speaking quickly in Pashto. But no one raised their voice just in case a neighbour might hear them. There was a small coffee table in the middle crowded with empty coffee cups and dishes with remnants of the night's dinner everywhere.

Adel (that was the only name he was known by) raised his open hands to quieten his Moslem brothers who were wondering what was going on. "My brothers we live in exciting times and you and I are very honoured to be called by Allah Al-Alim The All-Knowing Himself to be part of this mission". With this they all stood to their feet and as one praised Allah "Alhamdulillah, Alhamdulillah, Alhamdulillah". Each man's face and body language tensed with deep devotion yet still governed by great self-discipline uttering these words quietly so as not to be overheard.

"My brothers please get comfortable for we may be here a while". Adel spoke with authority but in a gentle confident tone. Bakri looking excited asked; "what is this all about what mission?" Making a joke about the meaning of Bakri's name Adel stated; "well you are certainly living up to your name 'one who starts work early', I will explain".

"Does everyone know where the Queen Victoria Markets are and what they are?" Akil who was sitting on the floor to Bakri's left answered for everyone saying.

"Sadly, yes as you know we are all Taxi drivers, so we have all taken the stinking Christians to the markets many times".

Adel was pleased with this response and stated; "that's great it makes everything easier, now let us get down to the plan. The attack will be on ANZAC Day. Akil and Bahij I need you to go there and identify five different bomb locations that will do the most harm, be hard for the Emergency Services to get to and still make the best TV".

The leader asked. "Bahij you look worried, are you concerned about being caught"?

"No, my brother Adel, it is just that most of the stall holders and merchants are our brothers and sisters. They too will die and suffer when we attack this place".

Adel knew he must be careful, "of course you are right Bahij but if we warn them, others will notice, and things may go wrong. Even amongst our brother and sister Moslems, some may betray us.

We must remember just like the Arab Emirates and Turkey; these nations have become nothing but whores to the West. These store holders are not too different. In any case, if they are innocent they will be in paradise before you. As long as they have not sold themselves to the devil. "Are we OK now my brothers?" inquired the leader. All the men nodded in understanding founded on the unity of purpose.

"Now even without your detailed Intelligence about the markets, I have already decided that we will need three separate bombs rather than one large one. There are no walls or floors above to collapse and kill more infidels, we need to kill and maim as many as possible. If we can it would be pleasing to set them in an ambush line so that people running away from the first run into the second and so on."

This brought on a ripple of murmurs and looks, unabashed admiration from the group. Each man was thinking his own version of: *He is so wise, such a warrior we are so fortunate to have him as our leader.*

Ignoring, or more precisely not noticing these looks Adel continued. "When you are looking for places to hide the bombs have that idea in the backs of your minds". The planning continued needing only the exact sites for the devices to be confirmed, however, the linear layout of the markets provided a perfect killing ground. The sequence of events was worked through. The initial explosion would signal the beginning of a series timed to decimate the markets as planned herding and concentrating the targets into the next death trap. Sixty seconds after the first attack the second device would detonate, followed a minute later by the last bomb. Each device would flatten all the stalls, the rows of clothes and other goods turning the place into an inferno. The force driving kilos of ball bearings, bolts and nails would shred any shoppers in a three-hundred-and-sixty-degree blast pattern.

Two days later Akil and Bahij had done their reconnaissance of the markets identifying the best places to locate the three bombs. As ordered they had chosen several alternatives. Adel looked at the printed map of the market and evaluated each of the crosses marked by his two soldiers. He decided on the three locations that would best suit his ambush plan and circled those crosses with a smile. That evening Adel met with the bomb makers.

"My brothers, are our gifts for the infidels ready?" The grey-bearded bomb maker looked at this puppy with unmasked irritation and disgust. Bomb makers used up all their patience making bombs.

Speaking like he was addressing a slow-witted child. "They will be ready when I promised they will be finished, in three days.

Adel smiled, he was not offended by this old man's lack of respect, he couldn't care less, all he wanted was his bombs. Not telling these two specialists the details of his mission was a given but he still had to keep them to a deadline with room for problems.

"Fine, fine I have a date that the gift must be delivered on and I need to be ready."

The bomb maker hissed through closed blackened teeth.

Adel had more. "There is something else, each bomb must have a timer, not a remote detonator, is this possible?"

The old man thought: *If I was younger I would slap this child more than once,* but he was a realist. "Of course, we can go either way. That is how we did every bomb when my beard was not grey and before you were a twinkle in your father's eye. So yes, my young friend we can do that for you."

And in the other three Capital cities; Sydney, Perth and Adelaide it was the same story. Within hours of each other, once the USB was delivered it started a chain reaction, meetings, planning and actions to prepare each cell in readiness to attack their chosen target in the best way possible. Each cell had been formed and slowly mentored by the local Iman or leader. He had carefully recruited potential soldiers for the cause. In the main these were young angry men with no families, little education and no support networks, they would be befriended, drawn in and radicalised. The Iman would fill their minds with stories of the great Moslem heroes, of a paradise full of virgins. He confirmed the enemy by telling them hateful stories of what the Western Nations had done to their motherlands and their faith.

Except at its highest levels, the cell itself was independent of others to minimise the likelihood of infiltration and damage if one cell was compromised and its members captured.

This coming attack had been planned for a long time and many things had to line up for it to progress at this local level. The Iman in each Capital city was asked to establish the cells for an upcoming mission. This must not be rushed. There was a heightened awareness that undercover Federal or Military Police could be recruited. In Australia, there had been cases where people with a mental illness carried out an attack claiming to be part of Islam and serving Allah. Even within the cell, angry young men became angrier when motivated by the Iman's training, or by biased TV stories reporting on the invasions of Moslem countries. There was always a danger they may plan and carry out a one-handed mission that was not supported or approved by the cell. This did more harm than good as it excited the media who in turn brought pressure to bear on the Police and Military to find the terrorists. No group knew of the existence of any other cell. Some of the more thoughtful leaders certainly wondered about this. No one was sure of anything except that the months of waiting for that green light had come to this. The USB delivered by those Bikie pigs demanded that they must attack on ANZAC Day, the place and time were a local decision based on maximising casualties, chaos and media attention.

CHAPTER 10

Terrorist Training Camp
45 Kilometres west of Roma QLD
2130 Hours
15th March 2014

It was now dark and the six-man party that had driven into Roma for supplies was at least four hours overdue. Mobile phones were banned for security reasons as they were notoriously easy to hack sometimes even by accident. Even though Zahir was a confident leader, he knew Aziz his superior was nearly always angry about something. Thankful that the old desert fighter was not in Australia yet. The Commander dreaded having to eventually inform him of this latest event with six more men missing. It was just too much to comprehend. Aziz would be on the warpath.

Zahir could just imagine what he would say in that dangerous arrogant tone of his. "*Commander Zahir I am beginning to suspect that you have been neglecting the men's spiritual needs.* Perhaps you were not the right man for the job after all".

Commander Zahir imagined how he would reply. "*Sir I am a military officer, not an Iman. However, Sir, I have never allowed training to stop a single soldier from going to prayer at the appointed times. I am constantly encouraging them spiritually by re-enforcing their call to service. Reminding them of the great reward that awaits them. The two brothers who disappeared I cannot explain, in training they were amongst our very best." It was* an imagined argument with Aziz that he knew he would never win. One small consolation was that Zahir didn't have to report to Aziz daily. Given time the mystery of the new group of six missing soldiers may be solved.

Commander Zahir thought; What's *happened to our six men today? I cannot believe they have all taken off for freedom or to avoid their mission. There is also a Cadre Staff member with them and there is no way he has run away. And I know soldiers. In a group like that if one did attempt to abscond the others would deal with him in some manner and successfully bring that person back to camp. Those other two were brothers so there was no peer factor in operation other than themselves.*

The Commander continued to think about the challenges that these missing men now presented. Aziz's temper aside, Zahir had been involved in every aspect of this Mission's planning. We have a limited force that we assessed as enough to attack a significant number of targets. Fewer soldiers mean either fewer targets can be assaulted, or less impact on each target. This is highly disappointing, but any battle situation is inherently fluid.

Zahir's thoughts of Aziz's wrath and his missing troops were interrupted by the mercenary, who had to say Zahir's name twice before the Commander returned to the present. "I can see your concern Zahir, there's not much point in worrying too much until we get the Intel we need to understand what has happened.

Shaking his head from side to side, Commander Zahir turned to Major Smith. "What is going on here, last week two men run away to places unknown.

All we can do is sit here hoping they haven't betrayed us. And why would men who were motivated to serve Allah run away? And now six more.

The Major knew the importance of their squads losing members, but he always had a calm approach to such problems. "Now, we don't know they've run away at this stage. But I agree where the hell has one of my best Cadre Staff gone? Maybe they have met some disaster, it must something big. We need solid Intel mate. All this is just guessing until we know as many of the facts as we can collect."

Smith could see Zahir's tension relax a little. "I have dispatched one of *my* men to go into town and have a poke around, I am sure they haven't run off. Corporal Elliot is one of my best men, he has been developing the plan to pick up and transport Aziz; no way he's just disappeared."

Zahir knew what Major Smith was saying was correct. He thought; *Guessing just serves us to become angry and frustrated. We need more information, none of this makes any sense.*

The Australian Officer attempted to cease the conversation. "The NCO I sent into town should be back soon and then we will know more. Why don't you get some rest, I'll get you when he comes in."?

An hour later the lights and engine noise of one of the property's Land Cruiser Utes broke the quiet and darkness of the night. The driver clearly in a hurry, slid to a halt in front of the farmhouse, a cloud of dust catching up and then passing the now stationary vehicle.

Major Smith stood up from the table so quickly that his chair fell backwards onto the floor with a loud clatter, betraying his calm outward appearance. He too was worried about where his man and the Talibs had gone. Smith was concerned on several fronts. He and Zahir had discussed the issue regarding the decreasing number of troops but he was also more worried that the entire operation's security may have in some way been compromised. "How'd ya go, what the hell happened?"

The Cadre Staff Corporal had been in front of enough unhappy superior officers and had delivered enough bad news to know how to react here. He calmly reported the results of his Recce to town, hoping the adage of "don't shoot the messenger" would be applied here. "Sir there is no good news, it took a lot of gentle poking around, but this is what happened. On the way into town, I noticed there was a big oil and radiator fluid stain on the road about twenty-two klicks from here just over a crest of a hill. There were bits of chrome and plastic everywhere so obviously there had been a serious accident, I reckon sometime this afternoon. If it had happened much before that all the debris would be gone or too small to notice".

Zahir couldn't contain himself. "Was it our vehicle?"

The Mercenary Corporal continued. "Well yes it was Sir, I asked around in town and found out where the wreck was being stored. It was a real mess. The rear number plate was about the only recognisable thing, but it was *that* number you told me to look for, Major Smith. There is more to the story, when I was talking to the bloke at the Caltex, he was saying it was a bit freaky how fate works."

"Apparently four of the passengers from that wrecked 4WD hadn't been in it at the time. I asked why they weren't, and he told me that they had been arrested for bashing some female copper." Zahir had understood up to that point. "What is a copper?"

Major Smith quickly explained. "A copper is a Police Officer."

He continued."OK Corporal, what else is there?"

"The guy at the servo was laughing saying it would be the only time in history that people would be grateful to be locked up in the Watch House. Being arrested had saved their lives".

The Major wasn't getting any less concerned. "Did they tell you how many died in the accident?"

The Corporal continued. "Yeah, the word is two dead in what's left of the Nissan".

Major Smith needed more detail. "OK were you able to look into the Police situation, what happens now?"

"Sir I had to be careful, but the town is abuzz with the story, everybody's talking about these strangers who tried to bash and rape some local Policewoman. As far as I can tell, they were arrested and will front Court tomorrow morning. Other than that, I don't know,

I was a bit scared to push my luck showing any more interest than a casual enquiry".

The Major looked grim. "OK good work Rob, you go get something to eat and hit the sack hey?"

"Roger that, thanks Sir. Goodnight Sir". With that, he got back into the 4WD and this time very slowly drove the Ute down to the parking area and headed for the barracks.

Sitting around the table on the verandah, Zahir and Smith discussed this new information.

After draining his coffee Zahir began again. "Major how does all this work in your country?"

Zahir was very annoyed, but he didn't show any sign of his true feelings. There was nothing to be gained now rehashing what had occurred. He preferred to be a solution focused acknowledging local knowledge was required. He knew there would be time for anger later.

Major Smith was far from happy with the report he had received but feeling better that at least now he knew what was going on and so responded confidently.

"Well in one way it will depend on the severity of the charges and whether they are deemed a flight risk if granted bail".

"What we need is a top-class Lawyer under the guise of fairness for these poor refugee types. Their paperwork will hold up so that's how they will be viewed".

"Can we get a Lawyer so quickly?" Commander Zahir asked. While he didn't understand the details, he was always aware of the logistical challenges of being out west of the State Capital, Brisbane. Major Smith had been liaising with the Asiris brothers since the beginning of this operation and especially setting up the training facility.

"I'll call our people back in Brisbane, they have money and contacts. I am sure they will have a Legal Firm on tap. They will understand the urgency of the situation and get someone on a plane tonight" Major Smith responded.

Zahir was suddenly exhausted beyond belief. "Very well Major, that makes sense, all we can do then is wait. We have lost two more men in the road accident, hopefully, we can retrieve these four. If we were at home and if numbers were not as crucial, I would demand that these four were shot for endangering the operation. Such stupidity, assaulting this Police Officer, and of course, getting caught. They deserve punishment".

Nodding angrily. Major Smith agreed. "Yes Sir, of course you are completely correct. We can't afford to shoot them but don't worry they will definitely be punished for their stupidity, that is of course if we get them back".

Neither of the leaders slept well that night or what was left of it, when they regrouped the next morning their shared concern was still evident. Major Smith took a large sip from his coffee mug before reporting. "Some good news our brothers in Brisbane have come through, finance is no problem and I was correct they do have a Legal Firm retained so one of their best Criminal Lawyers accompanied by a Civil Rights expert flew into Roma as we slept. They will visit our men, ascertain the facts and represent them in Court this morning".

Commander Zahir was no happier but at least this sounded promising. "Well done Major, I suppose we don't have any idea how Court will go?"

Smith shook his head and replied. "No, we have done all we can, I won't assume anything, but I am sure that Roma Court has never seen any legal team as powerful as ours, hopefully, it will go well". Zahir still not understanding the Australian legal procedures asked. "What does going well look like Major?"

The Major respected Zahir and answered him in a friendly tone. "I am hoping they will get bail. Bail is money given as security that the offender will return for trial. As I said the brothers have promised money is no object, so the bail will be paid. Then they will leave the jail and disappear back here never to be seen again and free to carry out their assigned task as part of the operation".

The Court appearance was the following morning and the processes went pretty well, exactly as Major Smith had described. The local Magistrate attempted to withstand the legal onslaught, but it was clear to all that she was out of her depth from the start. The Police Prosecutor and his team of Police Officers emphasised that this group had assaulted a member of the Police Service however they were all simply out-gunned by the big city lawyers. Caving in under more pressure than the Roma Court had ever felt, the Magistrate in the end regained some respect for his Court by setting bail at $150,000 per prisoner. The Magistrate had assumed that amount would not be available to refugees and this would keep them in custody. He was wrong. The Lawyers signed all the required paperwork and transferred the $600,000 bail.

Released on Bail the prisoners were escorted around the corner, out of sight of any Court Staff, Police or Media Crews. With stony silence, they were all loaded into yet another white Land Cruiser and headed off towards the Terrorist Camp. The Cadre Staff member and each one of the three Soldiers alike was wondering as they sat silently in the 4WD heading back to the training camp whether they were heading for a worse punishment than any Queensland Court would have administered.

On their return to camp, they were harangued by Major Smith for a good twenty minutes. He screamed and cursed seemingly without the need to take a breath for the entire time. He promised them further punishment for their selfish and thoughtless actions.

He then dismissed them, screaming to get out of his sight before he got any angrier if that was at all possible. The traffic accident required no follow-up or restorative work. All the men at the Camp had been issued high-quality forged documents that under scrutiny would lead the authorities to dead ends. Accordingly, the two men who had died in the road accident had such papers, however, it was not unusual for refugees not to have any kin to advise or to be interested in remains and so on. The Police would concentrate on the dead men and then maybe move onto the vehicle. In any case, the men and the vehicle had no connection to the cattle property come terrorist training camp. All the vehicles used by the Camp had been purchased in Victoria and carried stolen plates, accumulated in three different States so were virtually untraceable.

The outcome of all this disruption was two dead from the vehicle accident. They had their three Taliban soldiers back plus the Cadre Staff member from the Police and as far as they could tell security hadn't been breached or at least it seemed that way.

However, Major Smith had been around too long to believe in coincidences. His mind was busy. *OK, there was a small possibility if these two events had occurred on different days and weeks apart. But no way; for these incidents to happen within hours of each other, there had to be something going on. His alarm bells were just starting to ring; this was just too much for his old soldier's paranoia to ignore. He could sense that something or someone was out there he just didn't know what.*

CHAPTER 11

Early March 2014

Abu Dhabi Airport would have been like a lot of international airports if it wasn't for its incredibly beautiful green and blue-tiled ceiling and the round design of this open space filled with expensive tourist shops, bars and coffee shops. Abdul Aziz saw the beauty and architectural achievement with its Islamic style reminiscent perhaps of one of the magnificent Mosques nearby. His pride was overpowered by anger, fuelled by the fact his beautiful airport was also filled with fat infidel women of every age dressed like whores showing parts of their bodies only a husband should see and men with no testicles. Their women telling them what to do and giving them permission to buy things, women having money of their own.

Even the taxi driver who had driven him to the airport was complaining that it was always the tourist's wife who paid him. "The fat infidel bitch always haggles over the price. Be careful with my bags, do this do that. The husbands they say nothing; Western men have lost all respect and the place of honour Allah has given them".

Aziz was only half listening knowing it was true, he had heard it all before. Abdul Aziz was sitting adjacent to Costa Coffee and even that annoyed him. Damned Greeks! couldn't an Arab buy and run a coffee shop in his own homeland? Finishing his third double espresso, annoyed at being kept waiting, he was exactly what his name meant, Servant of the Powerful, second in charge of one of the largest most successful terrorist groups still operating the Emirati Jihad Cells. Here he sat to be invisible, dressed like most of the Arab men in Abu Dhabi and especially at the airport. His dark complexion highlighted a brilliant white Thobe (robe), a red check

Chutra (head scarf) held in place by a golden Egal (rope or chord) all combined to make him look like royalty or a wealthy oil Sheik. His dark eyes became like chips of coal.

His thoughts turned to a member of his staff whom he was starting to have concerns about regarding commitment and loyalty. He thought of the old wisdom he had been taught long ago and was still true today. *When one is always in a battle for your life you must occasionally take off your helmet otherwise you may miss seeing the enemies at your side.* He made a mental note to get rid of him because in his world where there is doubt there is no doubt. Although he showed no outward sign, he had seen something or someone. He immediately rose from the padded chair he had been occupying and casually placed the travel magazine he had been pretending to read on the coffee table and walked towards the exit.

Ali Al-Abbas arrived dressed in the same manner, he too knew the value of blending in, differing from Aziz only by his Chutra being white and held in place with a double corded black Egal. Abbas was dressed like Aziz but that is where the similarity stalled. He was about the same height but carried a businessman's extra fifty pounds. He also wore many thousands of dollars worth of gold and gems on his fingers and around his neck showing his wealth and success. He had business connections all over the world including in Indonesia.

This was where he was heading tonight being booked on the next direct flight to Djakarta scheduled to depart in about two hours. There was no eye contact, no meeting with usual kisses, without any sign of recognition and any rush Abdul Aziz made his way to the men's room. All the while he watched the shop windows for any sign of a tail. He entered the men's room and waited what would have been too long under normal circumstances in the hope that anybody following would panic and come in to check whether he was still there. No one came in other than an overweight westerner who rushed into the first cubicle. Satisfied but far from relaxed Aziz made his way to the exit. He took a cab to the city first and then walking around the corner jumped in another to take him back towards the airport but turned left to return him to the Shangri-La Hotel. One could not be too careful even in this land of his Moslem brothers. The hotel had been chosen with this in mind. It was one of the best hotels in Abu Dhabi and although some westerners stayed there, not as many as most of the other hotels, it was absolutely wonderful but still out of the hustle and bustle of the city.

In addition to his many successful business activities, Ali Al-Abbas was one of Abdul Aziz's most successful and trusted couriers. Making an act of impromptu decision he sat in the same heavily padded chair that his master had just vacated. As if looking around for something to read he picked up the travel magazine that was on the coffee table in front of him. Carefully he lifted the magazine from the coffee table and appeared to be looking at the articles and pictures. In a smooth unhurried action virtually impossible to detect without filming the action and slowing the frames down Ali palmed a black USB. He believed his successes were founded on his self-discipline, so a full eighteen minutes later he rose and walked to his boarding gate and waited on the call from the Garuda staff for Etihad Flight GA 9044 operated on which would take him from Abu Dhabi to Djakarta. He arrived just a few minutes before boarding and was soon buckling his seat belt. Just over nine hours later Abbas collected his bags and walked outside to the horrific heat of Indonesia. He was used to dry heat flowing across the desert sands, but this humidity was inhumane.

Getting into the first cab at the rank, in perfect English, he asked the driver to head to the Double Tree Hilton. The effort caused him to collapse into the sticky vinyl seat already dreading the ninety-minute journey from the airport to his hotel. Abbas started dreaming of the air-conditioning he knew would be working hard in his room in preparation for his arrival. He felt as though he had just been driven all the way from Abu Dhabi instead of flying. Climbing stiffly out of the taxi and strolled up the marble staircase of the Djakarta Hilton whilst his bags were being loaded onto a trolley by the uniformed attendant. After checking in he took a leisurely hot shower followed by an icy cold slow soak and changed into Western tourist clothes more suitable for the humid heat outside. He then went downstairs to the hotel restaurant where he ate a wonderful seafood meal washed down with the most expensive white wine from the hotel's cellar. There was no one here to care about him enjoying alcohol.

Anyway, it was always good to avoid looking too like a fundamentalist Moslem even in a predominantly Moslem country. The next morning, he arose and enjoyed a breakfast of eggs and toast. As he left the hotel Abbas noted the beginnings of an uneasiness that always preceded this type of handover operation. He got into a taxi that took him downtown weaving through what seemed to be every farm truck in Indonesia. They were all overloaded, full of green unidentifiable things, chickens and children, push bikes and taxi bikes and pedestrians. Abbas had not told the driver a destination other than a vague "downtown". Reaching around the grubby seat he tapped the driver on the shoulder signalling to stop. He paid and got out, immediately the wall of heat hit him in the face. Rushing into the air-conditioned shopping mall, he enjoyed it for only a few minutes. He then walked straight through to the other side entrance and jumped into another taxi. Ali repeated this ploy several times with minor variations until he was happy he wasn't being followed.

He then walked down alleys that smelled worse than toilets towards the handover venue. Though he was a relatively big man, fundamentally he was a businessman. He was always anxious before meeting this contact, he didn't like these rough types. He was not in the habit of socialising with Bikies especially ones from the Warriors who had a well-earned reputation for ruthlessness and merciless violence. However, they served a purpose by providing a secure method of transporting items into Australia. Few Australians realised that several Australian Bikie Gangs had strong contacts in Indonesia, including the Cazador, the Jokers 888 and from Victoria the Diablos MC. While Abbas didn't like associating with his Warrior contact he was the best of that bad bunch and so far, had proven to be very reliable in serving their mutually beneficial relationship. As for the Bikie's business, it was completely compatible with his. While he would never get involved in the distribution of illegal drugs, the damage they did to the already corrupt Australian society was beneficial. As well as the fact that it kept the Australian Navy, Air Force, Custom Service and all the various Police Services busy had to help his cause.

For the Bikie, it wasn't too difficult to take along some packages or perhaps some weapons or a few kilos of Semtex when transporting the shipments of drugs to Australia. And of course, his outrageous fee ensured that he was happy every which way.

Abbas walked several blocks in the Indonesian wet heat passing abandoned warehouses and several boarded-up businesses. He hated dirty places that reeked of failure and despair such as these empty estates. However, they were highly suitable for today's business away from activity and crowds and therefore unlikely to attract any unwanted observers. Abbas didn't know the Bikie's name and he didn't want to know. He didn't even know what he looked like as the exchanges were always done at the side of a road or in some lane behind a factory with the Bikie wearing a full-face helmet. Today would be no different. His heart rate increased when he heard the roar of the Harley Davidson 2013 CVO Breakout not that he knew or was at all interested in what model it was. Abbas was just relieved because he knew, Allah willing, this handover would be over in just a few seconds.

Blade had been a member of the Warrior Outlaw Bikie Club since the club had been formed, he loved the extra work that he was called to do because he had grown bored with the usual drug running and some guns as well. He hated these jobs, but it was only because wearing a full-face helmet on a Harley was just so embarrassing it was just wrong. He could see the fat guy hiding in the shade up ahead, Blade could tell he was scared. It was a skill gained over years of muscling people and collecting debts and just living in his world. He knew it was a bit childish, but he would help this guy's fear along a bit. Abbas took a small step away from the building's eave that he was sheltering under as the roar of the motorcycle grew nearer and nearer. With a crunch of gravel, the huge red bike came into view. With a twist of the throttle, Blade brought the bike hurtling toward Abbas slowing just in time and skidding to the left to shower him in gravel. With a blank face, Abbas thought: *The arrogant Bikie prick had to show off, didn't he.*

The big machine slowed down just close enough for the Bikie to take the envelope from Abba's outstretched hand but without actually stopping. Ali Al-Abbas dusted himself off and smiled happy in the knowledge that he had once again successfully passed on whatever message was needed to serve the faith, his part was complete. As arranged Abbas sent a one-word text SABAA (Tomorrow) to a number he had been given confirming that the green light had been successfully passed on. Abbas then removed the Sim card, bending it he threw it on the filthy pavement grinding it beneath his shoe until it was destroyed. Then he did the same with his phone until it fell apart. He then bent down picked up the pieces and threw them on the road as he walked not breaking his stride or looking at the flying parts as he did so. Two hours later the Bikie courier known only as Blade to most people was boarding a plane destined to land in Darwin later that afternoon.

ABU DHABI

Sitting on his private verandah of the Shangri-La Hotel sipping his mint tea, Aziz was lost in thought. For some reason, he was trying to remember who had famously said "a single death is a tragedy, a million deaths is a statistic". The *ting* interrupted this thought and, as unusual as it was for Abdul Aziz, he found himself rushing to his mobile phone. Smiling with relief after reading the single-word text SABAA (tomorrow), it confirmed that his best courier had successfully completed his mission. The green light and mission details were on its way to Australia. He praised Allah and returned to the verandah with his phone. Aziz then put in a number he had committed to memory into the same phone and sent another one-word text. He then removed its Sim card and sprayed it with lighter fluid before setting it alight in the hotel ashtray. He then entered the beautifully decorated bathroom dominated by its black marble, gold fittings and of course the obligatory bidet as well as the toilet in which he now flushed the evidence to oblivion. After wrapping the burned phone in a towel, he then stepped on it until it was in little pieces, destroyed. As he walked back out onto the verandah he finally remembered who said that thing about a million deaths. It was Joseph Stalin. 'One death is a tragedy, a million deaths a statistic.'.

Happy to have finally trawled that up from his vast memory he poured another mint tea and looked across the shimmering sand and deep blue water at the beautiful Mosque.

In Djakarta Aziz's one-word text caused a vibration in the pocket of a young Indonesian. On seeing the word, he involuntarily put his hand inside his jacket pocket and walked to the corner of the street. There he waited looking like a hundred other young men on a hundred other corners of the city just killing time.

Ali Al-Abbas turned to head back to the Double Tree Hilton filled with success and thoughts of rewarding himself with another seafood lunch. Perhaps even a bottle or two of Champagne and definitely that girl that seemed to live on a corner stool of the Bamboo Bar next to his Hotel. He was very glad to be leaving this depressing, filthy part of the city where he never really felt completely safe. He turned the corner of the last warehouse before re-entering a busy street full of thriving enterprises and choked with trucks and bikes and crowds of urchins carrying bundles.

There was a sudden flash of steel and Ali's thoughts of Champagne left him as he smelled copper of all things as he silently fell to the filthy footpath. His final thought was the realisation that the coppery smell was his own blood flowing freely from a long deep gash across his ample stomach. The young assassin took Abbas's wallet, watch and jewellery which was probably worth more than his fee for killing this fat stranger. He couldn't believe his luck. His contact had ordered him to take everything to make it look like just another mugging of a foreigner who should not have strayed away from the tourist areas.

Gazing out at the beautiful Mosque across the water Aziz gave his best courier lasting all of three seconds of thought. Yes, he had been a great courier, but this mission demanded a higher level of security than usual, removing Ali Al-Abbas was necessary. Aziz made a mental note to replace him when he got the chance. Once the Green Light message arrived in Australia it would be sent on to the operators who had been preparing for their mission over the past months. He thought of all those Australians that had supported the satanic Coalition to invade his country and impose their values on his people. They would be sleeping peacefully while his Nation's people slept in fear and hardship. *Well not for much longer, not long at all, and the good part is that this is only the beginning,* he said out loud to himself. Feeling good he smiled widely with his mouth, but his flinty eyes showed no mirth or any other emotion other than hatred.

In this modern world of high-tech communications, Aziz liked to sidestep the high-tech monitoring and eavesdropping that they all assumed the Infidel Security Services maintained daily. While physically moving a USB by a courier still had some risks, by employing this old-style communication he avoided all the technology. Even posting the USB could have been disastrous. With everything being X-rayed these days some sort of overzealous Postal worker might think it was porn and try to look at it. And besides, it was good management to be able to know exactly where the package was at any given time. So, using his own couriers made Aziz about as comfortable as he ever got.

In fear rather than respect, it would always be behind his back, but he knew younger operators would have ridiculed this Low-Tech approach. But Abdul Aziz had not survived and personally orchestrated as many devastating attacks on the West as he had by caring what over ambitious underlings had to say.

Thinking of the young bucks clawing their way up the Taliban ladder an old Christian scripture came to mind. As much as he hated all things Christian he also believed you must study your enemies to be able to understand their ways and defeat them. From the Christian Bible, Old Testament came wisdom that had appealed to Aziz when he had read it; "one who puts on his armour should not boast like the one who takes it off", this thought brought another smile to his usually serious face. From the moment that USB had left Abu Dhabi the mission go ahead would not, could not be stopped or recalled. Once again, he thought about how much he hated Australia and sarcastically wished them all a good night's sleep. Abdul Aziz was enjoying his stay at the Shangri-La; he had specially asked for Room 341, so he could look out over the pool and the private resort beach towards the spectacularly beautiful Sheikh Zayed Mosque. He loved the view day or night when out on his individual verandah smoking his Hookah (water-cooled pipe) or enjoying a refreshing drink. Once more he was enjoying a mint tea and with the inspiration the famous Mosque offered, he silently thanked Al-Baasit (Allah The Extender of Generosity) for his provision of such luxury. Aziz stayed here because it allowed him a little taste of Europe while still having the foundations and language of home. Although he had never visited Sodom and Gomorrah in America they called Vegas he had been told that the stupid Americans had created a fake Europe experience. Here at the Shangri-La they too had imitated Europe, but he had been led to believe here at the Hotel was a much classier more subtle experience. Instead of the garish glittering Vegas with its naked dancing whores and its imitations of the Eiffel Tower, of the canals of Venice and who knows what else, here things were subdued and peaceful.

These thoughts filled his mind as he enjoyed the Gondola ride to the restaurant area of the Shangri-La. He had decided on French cuisine this evening and had a table overlooking the moonlit water safely in the corner of the Bordeaux Restaurant. Aziz did love it here. Staying in such a hotel he was using an old trade-craft technique; "when everybody is looking for you they will expect you are hiding in shadows and be looking there, so the best place to hide is in the sun". He thought: *Yes, that's a wonderful idea. Tomorrow I will spend some time in front of my room swimming.* He knew from past experience he would enjoy the service lying on the hotel's cabana lounges partaking in snacks and cold drinks on the Hotel's private beach. That would be his last treat before checking out. Very fitting, as it was all good preparation for the long journey that Allah had ordained.

Lying on the fluffy white towel atop the cabana lounge on one end of the private hotel beach sipping an ice-cold Three Horses Beer, Aziz was annoyed yet again. Was he destined to always have his enjoyment intruded upon? This time he wasn't annoyed by Western tourists intruding. An early morning phone call had come from his superior telling him to stay where he was and await contact with further instructions. He seldom took any leave but just occasionally when it worked into an operation he would grab an opportunity such as he had this time. He needed, at least a few days to pretend his life was different to what reality was. Aziz saw this break as maintaining himself to ensure longevity and service quality.

He resented some underling's presence endangering his security and deep down in a secondary sense intruding on his break. With incredible self-control, he resisted the impulse to reach under his towel and grab the SIG Sauer P226 9mm and shoot whoever had just cast that shadow over him. Seeing who it was he immediately regretted not shooting him. Aziz didn't know his real name, he was known by the name Ayham Arif which translated meant Brave Corporal. He had ambition and a reputation to be much, much more than a Corporal. However, he showed no respect for history or his elders, and even in the company he kept lacked any morals.

"As-salaam 'Alaykum (upon you be peace) Ashraf Ashim the mighty Amid sends his greetings".

Purposely not returning his peace blessing and establishing the subordinate's place from the start Aziz answered.

"Thank you Arif *you* calling me Most Honoured Defender and bringing greetings from the General confirms that your message must be of great importance and be time urgent as well".

The younger man was shaken by his superior's assertive address. "Thank you, you are correct Ashraf Amid is concerned about your planned trip to Australia and asks if it can be avoided, is there any alternative?" Aziz was nearly speechless. He could not believe this fool's failure to maintain even basic security. A junior like this idiot knowing his plans was bad enough. However, mentioning Aziz's travel arrangements and actually specifying his destination was unforgivable. Aziz made a mental note that this ambitious underling must go and go permanently because along with every other bad characteristic he was a threat to security. Security to the mission and Aziz himself. He nearly vomited at the thought of having to justify himself and his decisions to this underling.

The only way Aziz coped with the situation was to accept in essence that he was speaking directly to his superior. He gently spoke in sincere tones that could not be overheard "Please inform him that I understand his concern and convey that if this trip was avoidable that is what I would have done. But more importantly, phase two of the operation is so important and so complicated I believe I must be there to motivate the brothers. I will be there to launch and maintain the entire operation and share with our local Commander to ensure overall supervision and decision-making as needed. Please inform our Leader unless he forbids me to travel I will text him as arranged on my departure and arrival. Of course, he will know of our success if Allah the merciful wills it by what appears in the news. Now it would be best if you disappeared from here before someone starts wondering who you are."

The young man was amazed that Aziz had spoken so strongly and appeared relieved to be dismissed. He stuttered, "Ma'a as-salaam". "Goodbye Abdul Aziz", and he was gone.

The Arab sun had claimed the Three Horses Beer, left too long it was already too warm to drink. He nearly wished he drank alcohol to wash himself of the annoyance of that ambitious nothing, but as a Senior Leader, he must remain pure.

Aziz ordered another non-alcoholic beer from the white-jacketed waiter and thought about what had just occurred. Was the young fool ordered to compromise his operation, or cause his capture or was the upstart attempting to get rid of Aziz by his own initiative? Aziz lived in a world that had little or no trust in any direction, so he could not dismiss any of those theories one hundred per cent. However, so much work and money had already been poured into the Australian operation it was impossible to believe that his superiors wanted it to fail now.

That left only two real options, firstly; that our 'brave Corporal' Ayham Arif was showing initiative and trying to remove Aziz without anyone else's knowledge or blessing. Or secondly; was he, as Aziz had thought when the young man had displayed no trade-craft whatsoever, simply an inept fool. Aziz couldn't believe that Arif had a creative thought or an original idea, it had never happened before. Possibly, his ambition may be becoming confused with his ability by attempting to eliminate or destabilise Aziz. No. Aziz returned to his original assessment the man had camel shit for brains as they say. Aziz picked up yet another untraceable phone and dialled.

He put on a friendly near fatherly tone. "Ayham my son I have been thinking and I have been neglectful, we are both staying in this city tonight alone. Why don't you come back and have dinner with me here at the Shangri-La?"

Aziz could just imagine the underling's confusion at this call let alone this invitation. the older man was playing to Ayham Arif's biggest weakness his ambitious ego.

"Oh", the Oh was drawn out like a child would say it in front of a sweet shop. "Sir that would be wonderful, thank you Sir for thinking of me".

Aziz couldn't help smiling at the young man's swooning. "No problem my son, meet me at 2100 Hours down where they load the Gondolas one floor below Reception. Now don't forget we still need to keep a low profile".

"Certainly, Sir you know how conscious I am of security matters, and how discreet I can be, I will see you tonight Sir, and once again thank you".

Yes, indeed Aziz did know how discreet and security-conscious the young man was, yes indeed. Aziz then phoned another contact he had used many times when the need arose in or around Abu

Dhabi. The conversation was brief, the man taking the call understanding that Aziz only phoned when his particular skills were required. A location, a time and a description were all that were needed. Aziz had felt burdened before he had made this decision. He now felt much better. He needed to lift his spirits another way. For a man such as Aziz his choices were limited; no alcohol or drugs or even women.

He decided on the Italian Restaurant this evening for this special dinner and this expectation began to buoy him. With thoughts of his plans for Australia, he closed his eyes in bliss.

He started to smile because he always enjoyed twisting a thought or a Bible verse back against the Christians he hated so much. He had read somewhere that the greatest trick the devil had succeeded in carrying out was making the world believe he didn't exist. All over the world including in Australia, the Moslem faith had successfully pulled off a similar trick. That of making all those naive Westerners believe that the Moslem faith was one of peace that could live side by side with other religions. Any violence being assigned to radical believers. He thanked Allah for all those Australian TV stations, Politicians and Moslems that continued to work so hard together to convince the world of this huge lie. They were right not all Moslems are terrorists, but his belief was to be a "real" Moslem, you could not have peace with the Infidels. Many places in the world demonstrated that Moslem people could live and work in peace with Infidels. Morocco came to mind, where Moslems, Christians and Jews lived in peace for centuries. But they were weak compromising Moslems that had sold out like some of the ones living in places like New York or London. He got even angrier when he thought of Morocco because there was even a population of Jews living successfully beside Moslem families.

After waiting at the hotel's entrance since 2045 Hours at precisely 2100 Hours, Ayham Arif arrived at the Hotel reception. He quickly walked to the right of the main doors and down the stairs to the Gondola waiting area next to the well-lit canal. He had taken his time dressing for tonight, he knew that a man of Aziz's age would be in traditional robes and had dressed accordingly. He studied himself in one of the large windows and was impressed. Ayham liked what he saw even though these clothes were the old way, in flowing white robes any man became a warrior, a man of power. *Who knows* he thought to himself: *tonight's dinner may be the break I have been praying for.*

Aziz is finally recognising my qualities and my potential. Then he thought; *I have been standing in this well-lit area too long. I will impress Aziz when he comes down by making a grand entrance from the shadows like the spy I can be.* With that the young man stepped into the dark area adjacent to the staircase, facing out he began to imagine his conversations over dinner, the opportunities to show Aziz that he was well informed and had contacts in the Leadership circles.

The wire was so thin that Arif didn't see it as the loop was placed silently around his throat, it was also so thin that when the assassin tightened the Garrotte it sliced all the way through to the young man's spine. With a deft motion, the Garrotte was unwound and removed, once the weight was removed the lifeless body fell quietly to the marble floor. Due to the neck being nearly severed completely, the head lolled to one side. With the last few beats of his heart, blood spurted onto the large pot plant eventually making its way as a small river flowing toward the canal.

There was no need for any calls or texting, Aziz looked at his watch and knew without any doubt the young man would have arrived early in some lame way to impress Aziz. It was now dead on 2100 Hours, and Aziz knew that the annoyance was no more, it would have been done. The waiter attending his table placed the tray of Cannoli before him, returning to the bar to pick up someone's order. A celebratory dessert was a fine way to complete a magnificent

Italian meal. Returning to the harsh realities he wondered if he was getting old or getting soft, these thoughts seemed to be becoming more frequent.

He decided this was him getting as close to relaxing as he ever could. Although he understood it would be dangerous to do this too often he knew it was a medicine that he occasionally needed.

CHAPTER 12

Darwin
Northern Territory
March 2014

Knocking back his third Jack Daniels while looking out towards East Point on Darwin Harbour, Mick Edwards swirled his glass enjoying the sound of the melting ice cubes clinking on the side of the heavy crystal. He had lived here for just over two years and yet he still appreciated the view from his unit one more time. Turning to his old friend Blade who had just arrived on a Jetstar flight from Djakarta, Edwards smiled remembering some of the fun and just as much trouble the two bikies had been through together. His Warrior brother had originally been called Blade because he did resemble Wesley Snipes in those vampire movies. But in more recent years it was just as much because when he was in Australia he had developed the habit of always carrying at least five different knives on him including a set of three beautiful throwing blades.

"I guess seeing you're here all went well in Indo?" Edwards asked.

Blade grinned with a smile that didn't reach all the way from his mouth to his eyes. "Yeah, I couldn't help myself with that fat Arab courier, he was hiding near a building playing James Bond or something. When I arrived man, you could tell he was just about wetting himself he was so scared".

"Blade these raggies are paying our bills mate, I hope you didn't do anything he will complain about?"

"No mate I just sprayed the fat pig with a bit of gravel, he'll be fine, he'd be too scared to complain about me anyway". Not much worried Mick Edwards but he didn't want anything to upset these customers. He didn't know what they were into and he didn't give a stuff in any case. He just didn't want the money to stop, especially for some stupid ego trip from someone like Blade.

He visibly relaxed as Blade handed him the USB that was worth as much as several drug runs to him. Edwards inserted the USB that Blade had brought over from Indonesia into his laptop and began to make the necessary copies. He was not real geeky, but he was impressed they could set a stick-up that couldn't be opened without the proper code or codes but allowed copying. He had followed the set protocol many times before. He still wondered what was on the USBs, he had always figured it was probably child porn out of Asia somewhere or Indonesia, but he was never totally convinced about this. In any case, he had no choice he couldn't open the USB as the original was always encrypted.

As Edwards copied the USBs it crossed his mind: *why each State got their own USB*. He had no idea that each cell leader had a different code that would only access their State's files. In any case, he didn't want to endanger this income stream. Plus, the fact that if they even thought that he knew what was on the sticks he figured that he would be a little too dead to enjoy spending it. It was always safer not to know, not to ask and not to care.

The Bikie President completed the seven copies and pocketed them plus the original, nodding to Blade they both stood and walked to the lift punching the button for the car park. Edwards and Blade jumped on their bikes and riding side by side roared out of the underground garage heading down to the Warrior Club House. There were Harleys parked off to one side of the locked clubhouse gates. Their riders were all standing around in a circle smoking and laughing, both of which ceased when they saw Edwards and Blade arrive. The clubhouse was empty today on orders from Edwards who wanted some privacy; he had work to do. He unlocked the gates and the seven couriers followed him to the large steel entry door into the

Club House. These guys had done this type of courier work before, so Edwards handed out the USBs to each of the Warrior Bikies.

Mick Edwards stood in front of the seven men who had been tasked to distribute the USBs. The leather-clad men looked at the floor and shuffled their boots as Edwards eye-balled each one of them. Often Bikie's work was pretty casual, usually kept simple, take this package here, hammer that person there and so on. But the way Edwards was the couriers could tell this was all business. His body language and tone shouted that this work was totally serious and to approach their task casually would result in their death. He reminded anyone going to or through Queensland not to wear their club colours due to the introduction of anti-Bikie laws forbidding the wearing of club colours and more than two Bikies being together in a public place.

With a non-negotiable firmness in his voice, Edwards told them all, "hand over everything you're carrying boys, put 'em on that side table".

This command was met with moans and curses summarised best by a comment from an older Bikie named Spider. He had a shaved head with a red tattoo of a spider's web covering his shiny scalp, large gold earrings in both ears and a long thick grey beard.

"Oh, Mick we feel naked with no clubs or knives or nuthin, it ain't right for us to travel unprotected".

"No problem, and you don't have to make all that money either, come on you'll be right. You all carry on every time, but the rules are the same on every job we do for this mob, no weapons."

This was standard procedure each time there was one of these runs. As well as this the couriers were not permitted to carry drugs for personal use, weapons or anything else that gave the Police a reason to arrest them if they happened to be pulled over. This was a focused operation the package being too valuable to endanger or stall over some local law. Cops always targeted Bikies everywhere so if the local pigs noticed some strange Bikie passing through town they would find some excuse to pull them over. Then they would always search the Bikies and their bikes for drugs and weapons, that all made sense.

But they weren't looking for anything as small and as boring as a USB stick that was easy to secrete somewhere in a leather jacket or a boot. It was for this reason the customer had also demanded that the Bikies were not to carry any drug deliveries on the same run. They were never to attempt to serve two masters at one time.

Edwards talked to them like children going off for the first time. "Now boys same as usual stay within the speed limits and laws. Let's try to avoid the local Police taking more than the usual interest in our presence. OK, hit the road and I'll see you all soon."

With a long way to go the seven Bikies roared off heading for their respective States or Territories. One had a short run to a local address, all the other couriers had individual addresses to deliver to. For a while, the Queensland, New South Wales and Australian Capital Territory couriers would travel together splitting up when they crossed the Queensland border.

The South Australian and Victorian riders would stay in loose contact travelling through Alice Springs and then South to Cooper Pedy until they reached Port Augusta where the Victorian courier would branch east, and the South Australian courier continued on it, Adelaide. For some of them, it would take days before they would reach their destinations and deliver their packages. But that was the price to be paid to avoid being detected by High Tech hacking and conscientious Mail Workers if they were to use snail mail. With a fifty-hour plus trip from Darwin to Perth, some of the Bikies wouldn't make it back for over a week. The Tassie courier's bike would go on the Spirit of Tasmania Vehicular Ferry to cross the Bass Strait. It all took time and effort, but its simplicity made it safe. And while the money kept coming none of the Warriors were complaining. Once the couriers had been dispatched Mick Edwards turned to the grumbling Bikies hovering outside the clubhouse. "Ok you miserable bunch come in and I'll shout you all a drink for being good little boys." This was welcomed with a cheer as they all moved towards the bar.

After a drink at the club, Edwards elbowed Blade, "old mate it's time to '**PARTAY**' let's head home for a while."

Now the work was done the pair kicked over their bikes left the clubhouse and headed back to Edward's unit. The two men raced each other home enjoying the freedom and the feeling their work had been done and done well. They were both ready for a lot of drinks and some fun. Two hours later and finishing their second bottle of Bourbon, Edwards fell back away from his friend when Blade in one rapid movement produced an evil-looking knife from somewhere. Its blade serrated with sharp teeth along the top and a shiny fillet edge on the bottom, Edwards did not see where it had come from and he was right there looking at Blade as he did it. He made a quick mental note not to ever assume Blade was not a dangerous man to have nearby.

With the razor-sharp knife in his right-hand Blade reached towards Edwards the Bikie leader. Though he was in trouble he was busily working out what he would do. Oblivious to Edward's concerns, Blade picked up a new bottle of JD cutting the plastic wrap on the screw cap and flicking it onto the table between them.

Edwards did his best not to let his breath out too quickly without his friend noticing. Blade unscrewed the plastic cap and poured the smoky liquid into two glasses sliding one to his friend. Blade hadn't noticed his friend tense up a moment ago, perhaps he may have missed it because of his long relationship with Edwards. It might have been being relaxed in a secure environment, or maybe the copious amount of Jack he had swilled was slowing him down. If he had been sharp, he may have wondered what was troubling his friend or what was on his mind. After a while, Edwards produced an ivory box the size of a good hardback novel, placing it on the table he raised the hinged lid on the beautifully carved container. Picking out of the box a small silver spoon which he filled and clearer a space by brushing a Playboy Magazine off the glass table. He then carefully emptied the contents of the spoon onto the glass surface in two fairly straight lines.

Edwards took a credit card from the black leather wallet sitting on the table and proceeded to work the white powder back and forth, back and forth until each grain was completely free of its peer. He then reassembled the two lines using the card as a little plough pushing the Cocaine into two snowy uniform ridges. Taking a hundred-dollar note from his wallet he rolled it into a small straw, now everything was ready. Edwards lowered his head to the glass table placing the note in his left nostril like some big-time Californian Drug Dealer. He moved along one of the lines of coke noisily inhaling as he went.

He came up smiling then turned to his mate Blade and swept his hand across the remaining line and said, "help yourself buddy, and then we might go out for a feed of seafood, pick up some tourists and then back here and do it all again hey?" Blade nodded and said, "that would be great I'm starving, they don't feed you on those Jetstar flights. I could eat the leg off a low flying duck."

Edwards handed Blade the money straw, and even though they were mates made a big show of reversing it so as not to share the nostril end. Blade then leaned forward towards the table and the line of snow that Edwards had prepared for them. As he did this Edwards silently moved a little closer and placed the silenced Walther PPK/S 22 Rimfire Pistol just off the back of Blade's bent neck and fired twice so fast that it was nearly hard to distinguish one shot from the other. Edwards looked at his dead friend through eyes as compassionate as those of a Great White Shark.

With just as much coldness in his voice whispered. "It's a girl's gun old mate but it did the job, better than any knife hey? Nothin personal Blado just a metric ton of money if I did a bit of tidying up of some loose ends". With that Edwards left for town to carry out his original social plans of seafood probably out on the Wharf followed by some tourists for dessert.

The restaurants were all owned and staffed by Asian women willing to work the crap hours where the locals wouldn't, the food was great and thinking about *dessert* the tourists flocked there as well. He hoped he would bring home more than just one tourist. Those English girls always liked the bad boy stuff, leather jackets and tatts.

Edwards knew by the time he returned home everything would be cleaned up by his housekeeper and what was left of Blade would have been taken out on a one-way deep-sea fishing trip. All this bullshit the media pushed about Bikie loyalty was only true when it came to coming against outsiders like Politicians and Police or some ordinary punter who may have cut one of them off in traffic. Everyone knew *that it was all about the money in the long run,* the Bikie leader thought as he approached two backpackers sitting at the bar.

Edwards dreamed briefly about the extra money he was picking up on this deal, his cut naturally, getting Blade's cut was only fair, plus all the money that the couriers were due. Yes, he had plans for his seven Warrior Brothers. On their return from their courier runs one by one he would end them and send them on their own deep-sea trips. It all added up to a small fortune, maybe it was time to pull out of Darwin it was too hot and too wet here anyway. Buy a little bar or shagging shop in Bangkok or Bali, maybe become an exporter instead of an importer.

When you were talking drugs, it was a lot simpler to just send the shit to Australia; all that retail distribution was the hard work in a way. If you wanted some cream you could go retail selling to all those stupid tourists from Australia.

Who else would be so dumb as to pay good money to get VD, bad drugs, poisoned drinks and food, mugged and even arrested, not to mention getting bombed occasionally in a hole like Bali, sounds like paradise hey? He thought to himself; yeah, I think I can live with all that and at least they will be giving their money over to an Aussie, very patriotic. The Warrior Leader Mick Edwards had no idea what his management of the distribution of those USBs meant to Australia and nor would he care, he had done it all before.

He had no way of knowing that the delivery of those USBs would start an action not seen in Australia since New Year's Day 1915 and certainly not of this magnitude Nationwide. Sadly, it would cause the innocence of this nation to be lost forever, with life in Australia never to be the same again. Even if he had known he couldn't have cared unless of course if the fallout affected his business drastically.

Sunshine Coast Queensland
Australia

When March was nearly over the green light still hadn't been given in time for the school holidays Sherif Ibrahim was disappointed. He knew that now without the holidays, the crowds may not be as big as they had been. But he was also a servant who understood there must have been a reason. He had wondered about where his brothers were, had they been given the go-ahead or were they waiting like him. Ibrahim didn't mind being by himself in some ways, but he was lonely for the company of brothers with the same language, values and beliefs. He had been having dinner when there was a loud knocking on his front door. Ibrahim had many escape routes but they all depended on him being outside his unit because like most holiday units there was only one way in and the same way out. That was the front door where someone was knocking. There was a peep-hole in the door, but Ibrahim knew there was a good chance if he looked through it he would be shot in the eye. There was another more insistent knocking now, he had to do something. This knocking terrified him because no one knew he was there or he even existed.

He knew the hiding place behind the bathroom cupboard would keep any 'honest criminals' breaking in to burgle the place from finding the bombs. But if the Police or any other security services searched the unit they would be far more thorough and use technology. They would have metal detectors or bomb-sniffing dogs and it wouldn't take them long to discover all the bombs and close his operation down. All these thoughts paralysed Ibrahim, he hadn't moved. He wasn't even sure if he had actually breathed since the knocking had started. Ibrahim had no choice. He stood up from the small dining table and slowly walked towards the front door. His voice betrayed how scared he was and was so shaky it was unrecognisable. "Who is there?" he stammered. Back in camp, a code word had been established. Without this word, any contact or communication was highly suspect. His mind so filled with fear struggled to remember what the man outside should say.

A deep angry voice from the other side of the door responded harshly. "Who do you think camel brain, open the friggin door?"

Ibrahim was still very scared and now he was totally confused, to make things worse he didn't understand what this man had just said. He knew the man sounded very angry and the last thing he wanted to do was open the door.

"You must have the wrong unit go away", Ibrahim said as strongly as he could. He wondered: *Would this intrusion harm the security of his mission he had worked so hard to maintain*. Fear was replaced with shock when the voice from the other side of the door became much quieter and thankfully sounded less angry.

Finally, the code word he had been trained to expect before any official communication came, "Malibu, Malibu". He fell against the hallway wall, he couldn't believe his ears.

But now his training kicked in and he responded to the strange word. He wasn't sure, but it had to do with surfing which was very popular here on the Sunshine Coast. Ibrahim responded to the word "Malibu" saying, "Board". As he said this word he unhooked the safety chain and unlocked the deadlock in the door, and as he turned the key he opened the door. Ibrahim was a little taken aback when he saw his visitor was a huge man with long greasy-looking red hair pulled behind his head in a ponytail tied with a leather thong. The man he saw had enormous arms that were covered with tattoos of animals, skeletons, knives and swords. His biceps were banded by a tattoo of dark-coloured barb wire. He was wearing faded jeans, a black tee-shirt covered by a sleeveless black leather vest that was devoid of any patches or badges of any kind.

His eyes were hidden behind mirror sunglasses making him look even more ferocious. The Bikie's hairy chest poked over the top of the tee-shirt and around his neck was a heavy link silver chain carrying a silver pentagram.

"I'm glad you finally got brave enough to open the door, I was getting a bit lonely out here".

There was no way Ibrahim was going to invite this gorilla into his unit. But he did want to get him out of sight. He only hoped none of his neighbours had heard all that noise or seen this unforgettable giant of a man.

Ibrahim's only alternative was to get the information from the tattooed man and send him on his way.

"You have something for me?" With a hand, the size of a leg of ham the Bikie retrieved something from a small pocket in his vest. He produced a blue standard-size USB which he handed to Ibrahim. As soon as he had handed the USB to Ibrahim the man turned and walked two paces. Then without a backward glance began descending the stairs two at a time, his decorated riding boots banging loudly with each step. Ibrahim could hardly contain himself. He had been waiting, preparing and hoping for this moment for so long. He booted up his Acer laptop and entered the password to access the computer. Once the programmes were loaded he inserted the blue USB. He then opened the first stage of the stick. A red screen appeared demanding a further password to fully open the device. Ibrahim had memorised these two fourteen-character alpha-numeric passwords in the last few days of his training.

Once he had entered the last digit of the series the encryption stood down, the screen changed to green, and a word, a date and a blessing appeared.

1. GO

2. 25/04/2014

ALLAHU AKBAR (god is great)

Sheriff Ibrahim had his green light.

Until he had received this USB he had often wondered whether the operation would ever occur. Ibrahim had been a vocal Moslem since his youth.

He had always taken an avid interest in all things related to the war between Moslems and the Infidels. He also understood that symbolism was one of the most powerful tools in terrorism, second only to fear at least. This multiplying factor came in many forms all-powerful. Attacking some nation at a certain location of significance, for example, the White House or Buckingham Palace. Similarly assassinating a person of special importance, or especially loved or admired by that nation, increased the psychological impact of the physical act. As did carrying out an attack on a special date or occasion to that nation. His mission was the latter.

Symbolism was easily understood by the victim nation or group. If you were fighting capitalism you may attack banks or the stock market. If it was a Military action you might attack a Military symbol like an Army Unit, a sentimental Military Statue, or a Naval Ship in port. Even just a few Soldiers out on leave, the IRA used this very successfully.

Smiling the lecturer continued, "imagine killing the US President and his family on Thanksgiving Day when he is at church", all the students laughed but it taught the lesson well.

Ibrahim had taken close to a month to decide on the Queensland target, it was his choice and he had worked through some of those symbolic criteria. There were lots of places that meant something to these Australians, and there were a few Army bases in Brisbane and Townsville but nothing significant. He had thought about war memorials, and churches but nothing set them apart. Nothing stood out Ibrahim had travelled around the State looking for a suitable target. Sitting in a few internet cafes he worked his way through hundreds of potential sites. He had prayed for wisdom and had eventually come upon the idea of a tourist attraction, maybe a Theme Park. He liked the symbolism. It would be terrifying because from that day on families would wonder if the Fun Park they were visiting would be targeted next. It would also hit hard because of the demographics of the victims, every age and gender. It struck at the heart of the very thing that Australians seemed to worship, their casual pampered lifestyle.

The women and children of his homeland scratched for survival in a harsh environment. Hiding under the bed every time a Helo flew over or the sound of a Humvee was heard, their homes being searched, their friends murdered. Here the women and children sat back and received a King's luxuries. The children complained if they didn't get an ice cream and the women moaned if they broke a fingernail. YES, he had found his target and now his controllers had added to his quest for symbolism by choosing a date that was so significant and so relevant to their fight. ANZAC Day 25th April. The operation was to be executed on the 25th of April, Ibrahim wasn't highly educated but he did have an interest in history when it involved Moslems. ANZAC Day celebrated a failed invasion of his Moslem brothers in Turkey by Australian and New Zealand troops, on that day back in 1915. He had to concede that it was a brilliant invasion. The attack was equalled by the Turks resisting the Australian attack with an incredibly brave and determined holding of the ground won over a protracted period. This was followed by a very clever military withdrawal by the Australians and New Zealanders. Every year on the 25th of April the Australians had parades and services starting at dawn all over the country.

From what he had read men and women who had served in every war marched and participated in these activities and the rest of the population supported these activities in their thousands. He had a fleeting thought that if he had known the date his superiors had chosen he may have swung towards an ANZAC target. He had previously discounted this because he had figured that security would be much higher at one of those venues and other symbolic values may have been lost.

It was also a Public Holiday which meant everyone would either be at the Anzac events or treat it as a holiday and go to theme parks and shopping and movies wherever people relax and have fun. Well, Ibrahim was happy to add to their fun this ANZAC Day, he was ready.

Within forty-eight hours of Ibrahim receiving his Green Light, five other operatives that had been on the same training course had similar interactions with Bikie couriers. Seven Taliban operatives in seven different States and Territories had been primed to go, they were now human-ticking time bombs. Each had decided on a local target, using the criteria they had learnt while sitting side by side in a lecture room near Lake Haman. Like all students, these zealots had talked over lunch about what it all meant. Were they destined to be used by Allah to attack the Infidels where they lived? Or was this training just generic training making them thoughtful understanding soldiers of the faith, just useful swords for the future. As the course went on and training became more specific, especially in the last few weeks they had their answer. It became clear they were to be deployed as sharpened attack weapons and they thanked Allah for this privileged opportunity. Some of their training provided hints as to what they might be assigned to do and where in the world they may be deployed. Now each man was like an excited gun dog waiting for the hunter to fire so they could go into action. To do what they were trained to do, what they existed for, each waiting to receive their individual Green Light that had finally arrived. Suspected but unknown to each operative was the fact they were all out there primed to deliver their package of death. Of course, for security reasons they were also unaware that their missions were to be synchronised to the same day a special day here in Australia.

CHAPTER 13

National Security Centre Headquarters
Canberra Australia
0900Hrs
25th April 2014
ANZAC Day

Colonel Peter Goodrich loved his new posting with the National Security Centre, he was settling in well and liked his high-powered superiors. It felt a bit strange to be talking to Brigadiers and Major Generals on a near-daily basis, but he was getting used to it. Pete Goodrich and his wife Bronwyn had been planning a long and well-deserved holiday to Darwin and the Northern Territory in April to avoid the crippling heat of the North. However, there was no way Goodrich could grab the six weeks he had accumulated now his transfer had come through and he had his feet under an NSC desk in foggy old Canberra. That was why his wife Bronwyn, and his twin daughters, now five years old going on twenty, were enjoying their holiday in Darwin without him. Goodrich was tired and was allowing himself to daydream a little wondering what his family was up to this Anzac Day. He had happily drawn Duty Officer because he was around and unlike most of his fellow Officers had no family to spend the Public Holiday with. It was dead quiet and as he took a sip from his coffee mug with 'Best Dad' on the side his phone chirped causing him to jump a little but not enough to spill the steaming brew. He was surprised to hear his wife's voice after just thinking about her.

"Hi, hon. Pete, I hate to make you feel worse, but it is so beautiful here, the harbour is incredible and it's all so tropical. You would go crazy with all the World War 2 stuff and the Military Museum. There are underground tunnels in the middle of town where they stored fuel oil to protect it from the Japanese bombers, everywhere you turn there is something."

Colonel Goodrich smiled to hear his wife so excited. "It's good just to hear your voice and I wish I was there. But I'm really happy you like the place, I've flown in and out of there many times but never had a good look around. Maybe we will get back there when we retire?" he said with a sigh in his voice.

Bronwyn sounded rested already. "The girls love where we are staying, it's a lovely unit looking out over the bay and has a big park directly opposite us".

Feeling lonely suddenly Goodrich asked. "Are you going to the march? Of course, ANZAC Day is huge down here with the War Memorial and so on, but every Capital City of Australia has one, I'm sure Darwin will have a big march past".

Bronwyn sounded guilty because she had been to every ANZAC march for the last thirty-something years said. "You know without you and us being on holiday I'm not sure, but we might see some of it. I'm planning to take the kids to have lunch on that big jetty full of cafes and restaurants, I think it's called Stokes Hill Wharf".

Pete Goodrich sighed loudly and said; "I so wish I was there with you, that place is famous for the scenery and the seafood and I am already missing you. You girls enjoy yourselves, hey".

Bronwyn felt the same way but committed to making the best of the holiday and tried to cheer Goodrich up a bit. "You'll be right Pete, we'll be back in no time now. We're only having the week up here, I suppose I better get going, love you".

"You too, my Hon, I'll call you tomorrow, have heaps of fun, take plenty of photos, Broni love you and give the girls a hug". He hung up the phone on his desk and woke up his computer.

Underwater World

Sunshine Coast Queensland Australia
1000Hrs.
25th April 2014
ANZAC Day

Just over an hour after Colonel Goodrich spoke to his wife Bronwyn in Darwin Sheriff Ibrahim opened the door of his small unit and stuck his head out of the doorway just enough to see if there was anyone around. Satisfied no one was waiting for him he entered the fire escape and descended to the ground floor. Walking into the cool sunny day he moved anonymously along the familiar footpath. He was thinking to himself: *how many times he had gone this way, but today this is my last time*. He slowed his pace a little as he wanted to be there around lunch. He also wanted one last coffee. He was sure that the coffee in paradise would be better than in the cafes on the esplanade at Mooloolaba, but it was like a final treat for his journey. There was a large A-frame at the base of the steps up to the entrance to Underwater World, it read:

FREE ENTRY as a thank you to all serving past and presently for Australian Servicemen and Women on this Anzac Day.

Ibrahim's face showed a reptilian smile on reading this sign. As he waited to purchase his entry ticket he prayed that some military personnel or their families would take up this offer and be visiting today. He was standing in the queue when he felt someone tug his sleeve. Terrified, his first thought was that it was a Police Officer or Security guard alerted by some mistake he had inadvertently made. Ibrahim spun around and looked to see who it was. Initially, he found no one behind him, until he looked down to see a small boy who looked up and said.

"Are you scared of sharks Mr, I sure am?"

Ibrahim shook his head and mumbled that he wasn't. as he walked slowly up the steps to the ticket counter. He silently prayed to Allah that his heart rate would soon return to normal and no one would notice the beads of sweat that had formed on his forehead. He was carrying a large blue bag, one that could easily be holding items for the beach, towels, buckets and spades, flippers. But, today it held the rubbish bin bombs he had carefully prepared. Once inside he wandered around looking at the different displays. He wanted the crowds to build a little more before giving them his gift.

He had thought it through and had decided it would be foolhardy to place them too soon in case they were discovered by cleaning or general facility staff. After about half an hour the place was buzzing with the public holiday crowd. Ibrahim placed his other two rubbish bin bombs on the floor above the large aquarium in the identified high-traffic areas of Underwater World. He then affixed the last two special bins on the Perspex wall of the large aquarium one-third and two-thirds of the way down the walking conveyor in the observation tunnel. Sherif Ibrahim was very happy because the tunnel and the entire attraction above the tunnel were crowded with tourists of every age.

Ibrahim noticed a large group of Moslem children go past on the conveyor walkway giggling and pointing to the sharks and fish all around them. Not for a moment did he consider waiting for them to be safe as this mercy might endanger his mission. Anyway, if Allah the Merciful chose to save these children that was up to him. He was ready to find out when he met Allah face to face and he knew he wouldn't have to wait long.

National Security Centre Headquarters
Canberra Australia
Anzac Day

Alan Gate pushed the lift button to go upstairs to the NSC analyst section and for the hundredth time wondered why he had a crushing sense that something was wrong. He knew something was happening and it had started in Indonesia but what it was none of the team had been able to get a fix on. This made him uneasy it was the same feeling that he used to get in Vietnam just before the V.C. attacked.

Underwater World

Sunshine Coast Queensland Australia

1000Hrs

25th of April 2014

Anzac Day

At the precise instant Gates had pushed the lift button Sherif Ibrahim started Screaming "Allahu Akbar (God is Great), Allahu Akbar, Allahu Akbar."

On the third cry, he too pushed a button, this one on the small remote control in his hand setting off all four of the bombs.

The bombs detonated together in an ear-splitting explosion that rocked the very foundations of the tourist venue. Acrid smoke filled the entire building. This was especially thick on the upper levels where wounded, terrified screaming adults and crying children staggered around in the dark building trying to escape this hell. Unusually, there was virtually no fire on the bottom level. This was because of the incredible amount of water that had cascaded down after the Perspex tunnel was ruptured by the Semtex exploding. Many of the victims were either drowned because of their weakened bleeding state or driven against walls and brick pillars so hard by the tons of water from the destroyed aquarium that their bodies were crushed. The thousands of sharks and other marine creatures became missiles, some flying, some falling, some dead, but some very much alive landing amongst the dead and wounded causing further chaos.

The floor above the huge aquarium and observatory walk totally collapsed onto the destroyed floor below. It had been built with very few supports to facilitate the aquarium and openness of the people-moving walkway. The contents of hundreds of small aquariums housing individual displays along with the limbs and torsos of the victims adorned the tons of twisted concrete and steel. In many places, there was a writhing mess of live sharks and other marine creatures now stranded from the thousands of gallons of water that had escaped after the bombing.

Many were dead before they hit the floor below them. Others drowned, some were bitten by sharks in pain or terror while others were electrocuted by the live wires that had fallen into the water. The shrapnel had worked incredibly well with the large bags of poisoned nails and ball bearings driven by the explosions tearing through flesh and walls and everything else within range. Not that Sherif Ibrahim heard or saw any of the results of his handy work because he had been vaporised a moment after he pushed that remote button. The damage and the incredible weight were too much for the structure to bear, the entire building seemed to shudder and scream as the aquarium walls and observation tunnel slid sideways off the frame that was now a twisted wet mess. The screams of the dying building were matched by those who were terribly wounded by the bombs or others who were realising how lucky they had been to escape any real harm.

Museum Coffee Shop,
Port Arthur Historic Site
25th of April 2014
Anzac Day

Around lunchtime, the entire historical precinct was full of families and couples enjoying the Public holiday and the historical displays. It was a beautiful day, sunny yet cool. There was a salty breeze blowing from the nearby bay. In the clear country atmosphere, the entire convict site looked pristine with manicured lawns and sandstone buildings laid out hundreds of years before to punish and confine British citizens, some deservedly, others perhaps unfairly. Sarah Jones was thinking how lucky she was to arrive just as that German couple were standing up to leave their table and had instructed her husband and two children to hold the picnic table as there were people everywhere trying to get some shade and a place to eat their lunch. Sarah was also annoyed as Karen, her three-year-old, was acting up and had refused to say what she would like to eat.

Sarah knew that she would throw a tantrum whatever was brought back for her. These thoughts filled Sarah's mind as she pushed open the screen door into the café and headed toward the serving counter.

It was twelve thirty-three as the door closed behind her with a bang. It was the last sound she ever heard. The bomb detonated with such force that her body was thrown back through the closed door shredding her now lifeless torso. This was a single explosion from a bomb that had been placed under a table moments before by Bayhas who walked slowly away from the busy cafes and museum area. He had chosen a table in the near centre of the cafes inside the eating area and had patiently waited for the table to become available.

There was a minor disagreement when a couple of American tourists attempted to claim the table but Bayhas had asserted himself. He wasn't sure, but he thought he had heard the male mutter something about a rag head as they walked away. Bayhas had smiled to himself as he exited the cafe thinking that the presence of two American pigs was truly a gift from Allah the Generous. The bomb was large and designed to explode in all directions and it worked perfectly. At hundreds of miles an hour, the ball bearings and shrapnel followed the initial percussion vaporising those in the immediate vicinity and ripping limbs from bodies in a three-hundred-and-sixty-degree pattern. Out of the two hundred and twenty-one tourists and staff present at the time of detonation, there was one survivor. A young kitchen hand had entered the industrial-size freezer to get some chicken pieces. The strength of the freezer saved him from any injury at all. Although immediate shock and long-term psychological damage had probably changed his life forever.

Queen Victoria Markets
Melbourne Victoria
25th of April 2014
ANZAC Day

When the 25th of April 2014 came, the day was just like so many other days in Melbourne. Grey, cold and wet with a wind driving the freezing rain horizontally. Just like Port Arthur, here too it was time for lunch. Adel smiled. He knew that the inclement weather would not deter the crowds coming to the Markets. The citizens of that fair city were so used to its weather and besides, if they stayed home because of a bit of cold or rain they would hardly ever leave their beds. Adel, the leader of the Victorian Cell arrived by tram along with hundreds of shoppers. The stop was straight outside the entrance to the Queen Victoria Markets and next to a line of coffee and food shops.

He bought a triple espresso and sat down to watch the alley he knew his team would be coming down in the next half an hour. The Cell Leader shook his head in wonder when he saw one man leading a sheep around on a lead like a dog. An aspiring politician drumming up votes for the upcoming election moved through the Markets smiling widely and shaking hands. Adel silently prayed: *Allah please keep him here until it's time.*

Bahij, Akil and Bakri drove their own taxis to the Markets. In the trunk of each cab was a backpack, the type that was sold at these very Markets in their hundreds. Even though they were focused on their mission they couldn't help but enjoy driving to the Markets. It felt good to totally ignore all the Australian unbelievers waving and getting annoyed as they attempted to flag their taxis down. Their travel and arrival were carefully staggered and although each knew he must enter through the food entrance they parked their vehicles in different locations to each other. Akil walked down the wet cement path leading between the food and coffee shops and the covered area where there were tables and chairs.

He was encouraged to see many shoppers dressed formally wearing their Service Medals. He knew they had come from the ANZAC Marches or some other ANZAC Services held throughout Melbourne that morning. His thoughts were; *I hope my bomb kills you like you have killed my brothers when you invaded their homeland.* This was especially so when he saw a group of younger men wearing medals. He immediately thought they may well have been to Iraq or Afghanistan.

Adel slowly sipping his third rich sweet coffee had seen him go by of course. There was not even a flicker of acknowledgement by either man. Sticking to the plan perfectly, he saw the other two cell members enter one at a time. Bahij and Bakri blended in with many of the other shoppers, Adel noted that a lot of them carried similar Australian Football backpacks as did his men. With the volume of people arriving and walking up and down the shopping lanes there was no need to stagger his cell members by more than a two-minute gap. Each man meandered around looking at goods as if they were interested to end up at their designated target site.

At exactly twelve forty-five each man was to casually place his backpack on the ground under one of the trestle tables covered in merchandise in three separate areas. They would then kneel down as if to tie their shoelace, set the timer and walk slowly away ensuring they looked at items on sale as they went. No rush, no urgency. They had plenty of time to leave the area and each bomb was set to go off two minutes apart maximising fatalities as people moved away from the initial blast centre. Each man carried out these tasks without a hitch. Thankfully no do-gooder noticed they had left their packs amongst a crowd of thousands many of which came from the Middle East making these three devotees virtually invisible. They went in three different directions and without any sense of urgency unlocked their Taxis and drove away from the area. Adel had instructed each of them to avoid attracting attention by picking up fairs once they were well away from the Markets.

Adel stood and went out into the cold Melbourne rain. Crossing Elizabeth Street, he walked up to the fenced tram stop section in the middle of the road.

He knew a tram was due at 1258 Hours and it arrived exactly as scheduled. He climbed the steps, grateful to be out of the wind and rain. The Cell Leader chose a seat that had him facing backwards and was on the Market side of the tram. Just as he departed the stop there was an incredibly loud explosion from deep within the Markets, dust and smoke rapidly spilled out of the ends of the shopping lanes. He resisted two very strong urges. The first was to loudly praise Allah and the second was to check his watch counting down for the next bomb to detonate.

The tram had its own timetable. Nothing, weather or even a bomb, would change that so although the shock of the first explosion had rattled the carriage it still proceeded up the road. The crowds of shoppers who had just embarked were screaming and crying but the tram driver did his job and the vehicle continued on its way. When the second device detonated no vibration was felt on the tram. This time however the sound was like thunder and echoed up and down the streets feeding into Elizabeth Street. Adel couldn't even smile but he was very proud of what he and his cell had achieved. He gave Allah the glory, he was still very pleased.

CHAPTER 14

National Security Centre Headquarters
Canberra
Australia
1300 Hours
25th of April 2014
ANZAC Day

The Data Analysts had listened to Alan Gate's report yesterday afternoon and although there wasn't much to go on they often started with less. They all knew it was this sort of 'out of the ordinary' observation that could at times mean much more than initially thought. The men and women in this Section were all serving the Military and had, if it was at all possible, already participated in the day's ANZAC Parades or dawn Services. However, now they were on duty, their service in a small way honouring the past. As with every morning, they were systematically dissecting all the information that had come in during the night.

Alan Gates exited the secure lift on the fourth floor and was walking through the glass doors into the area housing the twenty Data Analysts. All the phones started ringing at once and every computer signalled incoming emails. Simultaneously the news hit every section of the National Security Centre and any Anti-Terrorist agency in Australia. Reports poured in, State after State. *It couldn't be happening! No, not here in Australia, but it already had.*

Within twenty minutes every Director or Commander in the National Security Centre was sitting in the situation room. Somehow the Senior Advisor for the Defence, Minister Rhonda Davis, had raced over from Parliament House and was looking like she was about to have a stroke. She was talking quietly to Felix Norman who looked worse than her. Major General William Watson the Special Action Adviser to the Chief of the Defence Force started proceedings. "OK, what do we have so far?"

Section Head Clive Millard briefed the meeting. "At approximately 1100 Hours Queensland time, remember they don't have Daylight Saving, several explosions occurred in or under the observation tunnel at Underwater World Mooloolaba Sunshine Coast. Details are still light on at this stage with over two hundred dead and seventy-seven wounded, all demographics but sadly, as you'd expect, most of them children".

Commissioner Doug Wilson from the Australian Federal Police asked. "Has anyone claimed ownership?"

"Not at this stage" replied Millard.

MAJGEN Watson demanded "I want us to sit tight here until we know what this is all about, it sounds to me that we aren't even sure whether it's an industrial accident or our problem. Having said that, still get onto your FBI and CIA contacts. See what they have heard, what they know. Happy to get some advice. It's not like we have a heap of experience with this sort of thing if it is terrorists".

Felix Norman looked at Rhonda Davis seeking agreement; as the only two political representatives in the room. He was well known for being critical, demanding by nature and in possession of an overinflated idea of his power. Having said that he did represent the Prime Minister.

Felix stated. "You're kidding, right, it has to be some half-arsed accident up there at Sea World or Underwater World or whatever. I want any thought of this being a terrorist attack to stay in this room".

Ms Davis didn't know where to look so she looked down at the empty table in front of her. Everyone in the room was trying to decide whether to correct his confusion between Sea World and

Underwater World, with everyone coming to the same conclusion they all knew Felix didn't like being corrected.

At least Felix was nothing if not consistent he stated. "Let's face it what you don't know can't hurt you right?"

Section Head Clive Millard couldn't contain himself. "I'm sorry Felix but that has always been a ridiculous saying because in my experience it's nearly always the things you don't know that hurt you most".

The other members of the group put on their best poker faces to hide their gratitude for one of their number's honesty. Excluding Davis and Norman, the group were men of action, decisive in the face of dealing with any potential conflict. Of course, there was no way anyone knew it, but a number of those around the table couldn't help but compare the Prime Minister's Advisor with a movie character. He was reminding them of the Mayor of Amity Point where JAWS was eating people and the Mayor kept denying the shark's presence which eventually cost more lives. It was still early days but politically if this turned out to be a terrorist act the dangers of attempting to minimise it was immeasurable.

As they quietly discussed these matters, unbeknown to them, the phones in the Intel room started ringing again. Then something happened that the group as well trained and experienced as it was had never considered possible. Aides from every department and section knocked and came rushing in, an unprecedented act interrupting any meeting, especially one with every high-ranking Officer attending. MAJGEN Watson clearly bewildered by this break in protocol began to speak. "What the hell is going on! Why are these people interrupting this highly important meeting?"

His Second in Charge (2IC) Brigadier Dodds responded as he had overheard the reports being provided on either side of his chair. "Sir I'm not sure what it means but it looks like Australia is under attack. Underwater World was only the beginning".

As he said this his face seemed to age before their eyes.

MAJGEN Watson realised something horrendous must be going on. "OK let's all wait a moment until the Intel is in, each report will appear on that screen as we receive the data". Nodding to Dodds, the 2IC flicked the projector to life. As the first information showed on the huge digital screen MAJGEN Watson commanded "All phones off as of now, sadly it seems we have enough to start".

The Digital Screen lit up with the heading:

Terrorists Attack Australia

- **Underwater World Mooloolaba Queensland**

CASUALTIES 414 UNCONFIRMED

- **Port Arthur Convict Site Tasmania**

CASUALTIES 242 UNCONFIRMED

- **Queen Victoria Markets Melbourne**

CASUALTIES 568 UNCONFIRMED

- **Art Gallery of South Australia Adelaide**

CASUALTIES 189 UNCONFIRMED

- **Perth Mint Perth**

CASUALTIES 95 UNCONFIRMED

- **Sydney Opera House Sydney**

CASUALTIES 312 UNCONFIRMED

MAJGEN Watson clearly shaken by this screen addressed the group "SITREP (Situation Report) now."

Section Head Clive Millard took the lead. "All these locations have been attacked by an unknown individual or group. The attacks were in the form of bombs. Casualties are unconfirmed at this stage, but the timing appears to have been specifically coordinated to maximise the number of victims in the proximity. High volume visiting time at a venue, a concert at the Opera House and so on."

Angered by the impact of this report, MAJGEN Watson said what they were all thinking. "Any stupid thoughts of these being accidents are gone as this is clearly a well-planned, well-coordinated attack. Full of symbolism, attacking our lifestyle, our history, our economy and our culture. I don't want to jump to any conclusions before all the facts are in, but I think we are all coming to the same conclusion about which gutless mongrels are responsible for these cowardly acts. I don't need to emphasise that we have lived in a sanctuary that as of today no longer exists."

The Major General thumped the table and continued. "We used to believe and say these things couldn't happen in Australia then after Bali and 9/11 those in the know started saying it's only a matter of time."

"Well sadly, our time has come and come with a vengeance, we are under attack. Australia has trained and practised and listened and analysed for over thirty years. We have watched our enemies and allies and learnt from both. We have even stopped the odd angry Moslem or anti-government red neck. But this has just gone up a thousand gears. Stating the bleeding obvious this doesn't get any bigger". As the Major General continued in his deep gravelly tone a new entry was added to the digital screen

Stokes Wharf Darwin Harbour

CASUALTIES 393 UNCONFIRMED

Colonel Peter Goodrich screamed. It was a tearing of the heart sort of a scream, not a word or a curse but a cry of extreme pain. He stood so fast that his chair flew backwards clattering against the wall behind him. He rushed out of the room knocking aside a steward who was replenishing the water carafes distributed along with the board table.

MAJGEN Watson was the first to recover from this unexpected spectacle and in a voice of authority developed over many years of commanding men, he looked around the group of senior security specialists and asked. "What the devil was that all about?"

Peter Goodrich didn't hear him and if he had he would have ignored him. As Goodrich ran to his office to grab his mobile phone he prayed this hadn't happened. It was some sort of horrible hoax or mistake. His only thoughts were that his wife and daughters were having lunch on Stokes Wharf today as part of their holiday in Darwin.

He hit the contact on his mobile, the call went unanswered. Its tone ridiculed him with every ring, his heart breaking again and again. Uncontrollably his hand contracted around his mobile so hard the battery holder sprung open, his heart exploding in his chest, his eyes filled with tears as he re-dialled. On hearing the familiar ringtone, he let out a painful sob.

"Pete, oh Pete, I have been phoning you for over an hour I knew you would be so worried".

The hardened Army Officer's voice cracked into sobs. "You're alive, you're OK, the girls?" Another heart-wrenching sob muffles his question; "The girls are they alright?"

Peter Goodrich's wife heard her husband's pain and fought to control her own voice while tears began to well in her eyes; "yes honey we're all OK, the girls woke up grumpy and tired, so we decided to stay home and watch the Parade on TV and relax around the pool, we're all fine".

"Oh, Broni I was so scared I thought I had lost you". "Pete you probably know but it's terrible up here the TV is running the story non-stop, so many dead and ambulances are just going back and forth with the wounded, all of Darwin is in shock".

"Listen hon, I can't explain how relieved I am but keep it to yourself, but this has happened in every State. I've gotta get back to work, I'm sorry, talk tonight hey?"

Bronwyn Goodrich was relieved to hear her husband's voice was much more normal. I understand, you take care, love you". The call terminated as he walked back towards the meeting room. He was so thankful. Broni was a wonderful wife and an experienced Army wife to boot and he thanked God she and the girls were alive.

Now the initial shock and gut-wrenching fear had gone Goodrich realised the scene he had just made exiting that high-powered meeting as he had. He wasn't regretting it, but he would have to explain and that would be it. He knocked confidently on the glass doors leading into the boardroom and entered without waiting for a reply.

The Major General looked up with a warm welcoming look and a tone to match, "Welcome back Colonel, are you OK?" MAJGEN Watson clearly understood that something extremely important must be the only explanation for a fine young Officer like Goodrich to scream and run out of the room as he had.

"I am very sorry Sir. I was talking with my wife this morning as she and the girls are up in Darwin at present. She was saying that they were planning to go to Stokes Wharf today for lunch. So, when I saw the info come up on the screen I'm afraid I thought the worst. It turns out they didn't go and are all safe, thank God".

"Pete we totally understand and all of us are happy to hear they are safe". With that everyone in the room nodded and as a group returned to the work at hand.

The reports continued to flow in painting a picture already pre-empted by the Major General's comments. He was right on the money. Four hours after the first attack they could confirm through forensic testing that some branch or cell of Al Qaeda was involved. There had been no communication in any way, no one claiming the credit or making any demands. The very concept of terrorism is to keep the victim nation or group wondering if or when and where the next action was to occur. Australia as a nation had been forced to start living under that threat. However, the very power of terrorism is the fact that once an act of aggression has occurred all those wondering questions are virtually recurrent. Australia was now experiencing this for the first time; with a sector of the population literally hiding under their beds figuring and not incorrectly that another atrocity could happen any time anywhere.

The State Police were doing their best to manage the collateral damage such as traffic or infrastructure damage. Chaos had resulted within the blast areas and on the evacuation, routes now choked with emergency vehicles and terrified civilians. The Police had another problem. Some of the citizens of Australia woken from their slumber of apathy by these attacks decided the Government needed their assistance. This was mixed with anger that knew no bounds especially when TV News showed images of children's bodies torn apart by these bombs. Some just wanted an excuse to vent their pre-existing anger or racist red-neck values and get away with it as vigilantes.

One week later the experts at the NSC had more forensic evidence than at any time in Australia's history. Although there wasn't much left of some of the bombers themselves, hard work and training had paid off after reviewing hours of CCTV footage enabling the Security Forces to identify some of the terrorists. They were able to cross-reference that with their refugee files and Centrelink accounts and come up with names and addresses.

Still, there was no known group claiming credit. No cell or organisation seemed to have links with these bombers. Except for the fact they had all arrived within a three-month window, there was not a thing connecting anyone with another.

MAJGEN Watson had called another meeting of the Senior Committee. "Gentlemen I thought it wise to get together and review the past week or so. Clearly, we have an absolute ton of information, general, forensic, and follow-up, but will that information tell us who is responsible for these attacks? Will it help us stop a repetition of these horrendous events? I am sorry gentlemen, but I am not convinced that I can confidently answer those questions in the affirmative."

Sighing deeply, the Major General continued. "Sadly, we have learned from our colleagues from America that Post 9/11 they were in the same boat as we are. They knew a lot about what *had* happened, *how* it happened and so on. But that still didn't catch everyone involved. We especially need to know the organisers, the coordinators. If we know this, then we can smash any future efforts."

Clearly, the devastation was weighing heavily upon the Major General who seemed to be looking for understanding as well as answers. "Obviously, the Americans knew their enemies, I am beginning to think, as the Intel flows in, that all we will know is that they were Moslems. It is very strange to say at least no one has bragged about giving Australia a black eye. It appears that we must live with never knowing who the cowardly dogs were that convinced these men to die for their cause and kill and wound so many innocents. I need all of you to continue doing your work, something will break it's got to and I need you to be on the ball when it does".

Australia returned to normal as best it could. As a nation it was never going to be the same, its innocence was lost but its spirit was strong. The Nation's need for retribution, revenge and even the beginning of the healing process was more difficult because of the lack of an identified attack architect. All Security and Military

Forces were kept at high alert along with every Police Force or Service whether Federal or State. Airport Security had become similar to the USA, less friendly, with more technology and a more rigid criterion. This annoyed some travellers but most understood.

CHAPTER 15

ABU DHABI
UNITED ARAB EMIRATES
APRIL 2014

Riding in the back of the taxi Aziz had some initial annoyance that his driver was an Indian, but he let it go and looked out the window enjoying his last moments in Abu Dhabi. He loved the look of this place, the green grass with lots of palms and trees along the road to the airport. Even though there is a lot of building going on, he was pleased to see it was more low-set houses and keeping with Arab traditions of style and colours. Unlike the city's big brother Dubai just down the road; a city of Western designs of concrete, glass and chrome each competing to reach the sun first. He was already sad to be leaving the luxury of the hotel. He had enjoyed every moment and could not fault the excellent service. He smiled thinking of the report the maid had. "That was a terrible business, that poor man, apparently nearly decapitated so my friend told me. They found his body in the canal. Probably a thief who took on the wrong wealthy Arab who had a bodyguard, who knows?" the young servant reported.

The Police allowed his leaving because he had numerous witnesses from the Italian restaurant who provided his alibi. Luxury was fine, but he was first and foremost a soldier. He had started life with six siblings in a poor dusty brown compound herding goats and carrying water from a well that seemed miles away from his mud-brick home where he shared a room and a bed with his four elder brothers. Then becoming a soldier of the Taliban, he lived in caves and ate whatever they could take from the local families. So, he had tasted both harsh privation and now having earned his place, a little luxury.

But he was still fundamentally a soldier, and like every soldier, in the world, you make the best of what's going on at the time. The old saying is if you can sit then sit if you can lie down lie down, if you have time to eat or sleep you do that because there is no guarantee you will have another opportunity in the near future. As the taxi pulled into the drop-off zone for departures Abdul Aziz once again found himself at the Abu Dhabi Airport. He was already dreading the queues and the crowds. Although he had come by his own taxi the Shangri-La had once again lived up to its reputation for incredibly good service. Obviously, the hotel's concierge had noted the number of the taxi as it picked Aziz up at the grand courtyard and entrance to the hotel and had phoned ahead. Aziz was initially concerned when a short man immaculately clothed in Arab garb that looked as though he could have been just another passenger approached the taxi.

As he opened the taxi's door for Aziz to alight he bowed, "As-salām 'Alaykum (hello) and Ahlan wa sahlan (welcome). I am from the Shangri-La Hotel my only purpose in life is to assist you, Sir".

He then loaded the bags onto a trolley he had brought with him as Aziz paid the sleepy-looking Indian driver. Then respectfully requesting Aziz to follow him he entered the chaos and noise of the Airport Departure area. Understanding that he was a servant unworthy of introductions the unnamed employee stopped.

Turning to Aziz he asked; "Sir if you would be so kind as to give me your travel papers and passport I will get all that done for you. After that, I will assist you to check in your bags. Aziz was in a near state of shock, amazed at this unexpected service. He handed over his air ticket an aide had purchased online and his Passport showing him as a citizen of Balaban, Turkey. The man thanked him with the customary "shukran" and headed off towards the counters.

Aziz sat down heavily, sighing with gratitude, knowing this man was saving him from having to stand in queues with smelly infidel women and sticky crying children and then adding further insult, having to answer intrusive questions from Passport Officials, even worse usually from some Arab woman without shame showing her face to all the men in the world. The Shangri-La man walked to the barrier before the X-ray and passenger scanners where he unloaded the carry-on bags from the trolley as no trolleys passed this point. Aziz waited for the eye contact or a gentle movement of his hand ready to receive his well-earned tip, neither was evident. Aziz having to move through into the 'passenger only' area took a large denomination note from his wallet and went to hand it to the man; "Oh no shukran (thank you) Sir it has been our pleasure to assist you today.

He hated not travelling on Etihad Airlines as the staff could speak his language and the food while still aeroplane style and quality was at least not Western or Asian. However, for security reasons, he felt he should travel with Singapore Airlines breaking his trip at Singapore and entering Australia without the added Middle Eastern inference of flying Etihad or Emirates. This was probably a bit paranoid but having such thoughts and making such decisions had kept him free and alive so far. The plane bounced on the tarmac of Singapore Changi International and Aziz braced himself for the humidity that was about to crush him. How could people live in such wet heat was beyond him. He planned to stay in his hotel, surviving in the air-conditioning. He would either eat in the buffet restaurant where he was sure to find something he could eat both regarding law and taste or have room service. One night and fly out tomorrow. It was annoying wasting time here, but he had stayed in worse places that's for sure.

After leaving Abu Dhabi his break was over and this transit was part of the mission. Checking out of the hotel was uneventful as he had expected and entering the taxi he was grateful to feel the cold air inside the cabin after escaping the oppressive humid atmosphere of the street. Getting through Changi Airport like some poor beast trudging towards the slaughterhouse floor he went through all the necessary queues. While tedious, these processes allowed Aziz to carefully observe there was no reaction on the officer's part when he handed over his passport. He could also keep an eye on the surrounding areas to ensure he wasn't being followed.

He had travelled enough to know what the standard procedure was. He knew what the normal questions were and was alert to any change. Any unusual reaction or some official reaching under counters to press buttons and he would attempt to disappear. Walking through all the duty frees, past the highly expensive retail shops, bars and coffee shops, Aziz thought some exercise would be good after being cooped up on the plane. The airport was huge. He estimated he had walked several hundred meters before seeing his assigned Gate 34. All seemed clear, but he would not sit in Gate 34's waiting area with his fellow passengers. The cameras in both of the waiting room's corners placed him under too much scrutiny and, most importantly showed others where he was expected to be. He chose to sit in the Gate 33 area across the wide crowded thoroughfare where he could sit but still see when it was time to board. He was sure the cameras in that area would only be functioning when a plane was scheduled through that particular gate.

While he waited he thought about the coming month or so. He believed it would be a defining period in his life. He planned to take charge of the entire operation, ensuring that everything was in place and everyone was battle-ready. He had faith in the people that had been appointed but that didn't mean he wouldn't take over. His leadership style was not "off you go and do your best". Aziz's style was "I'll make sure you are ready, equip you in every way and failure is not an option". It seemed to take forever but eventually they started boarding the plane and Aziz moved seamlessly onto a queue waiting for their tickets to be processed and to board. Once on the plane, he took up where he had left his thoughts to get on the plane and was once again wondering what he would find in Australia. Abdul Aziz was finally on his way to Australia and whatever Allah had in store for him. His thoughts were interrupted by some mundane announcement from the co-pilot on the intercom that he could not hear properly or understand. At last, the huge aircraft increased its speed as it accelerated towards the end of the runway. By the time it levelled off he was asleep.

The timing of the trip was decided after much thought. Aziz devoid of any emotion had worked it all through. After those wonderful bombings all around Australia last week the security forces would be thinly spread, concentrating on identifying suspects, analysing data and attempting to catch the terrorists involved. Aziz had figured that although Border Security would be increased it would be focused on passengers trying to flee the country not so much as those entering through the front door. By now the authorities would know that most of the bombers died a magnificent death worthy of a martyr at the time of the bombings. However, just as certainly they would also have worked out that some of the terrorists had detonated their bombs from a distance and had escaped into the resulting chaos. The security forces would have assumed that any bombers or their associates still alive would be trying to flee Australia as soon as possible. Hence, he believed the expected increased security would be facing inwards at every port or airport throughout Australia not outwards as it would be normally. That was the main reason he had dispatched Commander Zahir and his men some months ago, and also to provide them ample time to be thoroughly trained.

What Aziz didn't realise was that even though he was meticulously careful, ASIO Officers based at Singapore Airport were alerted by a Red Flag not from the Turkish name and Passport even though the forgery was absolutely first class.

They had picked up Aziz from the Facial Recognition Programme (FRP) from Abdul Aziz's passport photo and the photo they took of him while he was standing in front of the Singaporean Passport counter. The ASIO Officers immediately contacted their Commander in Canberra Australia to enquire as to how to proceed. They had about forty minutes to arrest Aziz before he boarded Flight S246 to Sydney Australia. Alternatively, they could let him board and their counterparts arrest him as he disembarked at Mascot International Airport Sydney. They had placed an Asian Officer amongst the passengers waiting at Gate 34. He reported their suspect was avoiding his plane's waiting area which suggested he was hiding something. Accordingly, ASIO HQ in Canberra decided that in the current atmosphere the Australian National Security Centre should be informed of such a significant target attempting to enter Australia.

NATIONAL SECURITY CENTRE CANBERRA

ASIO Director-General of Security, Clive Millard, was informed of the situation in Singapore and immediately rushed to inform Major General Watson, the Special Action Adviser to the Chief of the Defence Force whose office was on the same floor as his. He couldn't help but notice he had knocked on the Major General's door a little too loudly. Obviously, the excitement of picking up a terrorist of this significance had excited even this experienced agent.

"Come in" the MAJGEN called.

"Good morning Sir".

"How's it going Clive, you seem to have a burr under your saddle about something?"

"Well Sir, some great news out of Changi Airport, a hit on target Aziz."

Watson looked up and a smile started to make his manicured moustache twitch. "I assume it has been confirmed by your boys he's heading our way, how long before he arrives in Australia?"

Millard couldn't stop smiling. "About eight and half hours Sir, but the time pressure is on. Do we let him get on that flight or arrest him there? We have thirty-four minutes to decide that."

The Major General stood up to respond. "Clive, nearly all of me wants to say grab him now, but a part of me wonders what we can learn if we let him come our way. What are your thoughts?"

The Section Head had been weighing up the same quandary. "Well Sir, I must admit I am thinking the same way as you are".

The Senior Officer decided. "OK, this is what we'll do. Let him, board. I won't tell you your job but a short leash. Now that will give us time to get everybody together and nut out a plan for his welcome party. That seems reasonable to you?"

Millard was in sincere agreement with MAJGEN Watson. "Sounds good Sir, gives us plenty of time and we'll secure this end tighter than a fish's backside".

A high-priority meeting of all the Department Heads was called immediately. Major General Watson didn't waste any time updating the Senior Officers sitting around the boardroom table. Clive Millard completed the update by saying, "The target has been under close surveillance at the boarding gate".

He looked at his watch. "He boarded six minutes ago, and of course, we have a man on board keeping an eye on him. So probably Aziz's flight is now taxiing up the runway on its way to us".

Commissioner Doug Wilson of the Australian Federal Police took a predictable Police approach, wanting to make the arrest on his home turf.

He attempted to claim the big prize. "Great call Sir not grabbing him in Singapore too many things can go wrong. It would probably become a media circus trying to get him out of there in any case. We should let him off the plane and arrest this guy as he walks down the ramp. Take control when he's still in the tunnel, where the area is manageable instead of the entire airport."

2IC of the National Security Centre Brigadier Dodds nodded appreciatively. "I like the risk management facet of your plan Doug, but what do we end up with? A high-priority prisoner who may not tell us anything. You know these tough old warriors they would rather die than betray their cause. I think we need to get more from our mate Aziz." The normally calm ASIO Director-General of Security Clive Millard had been shaving his head for over a decade. Today his skull was so red that it might explode like an over-ripe tomato at any minute.

Millard's voice reflected his elevated levels, of both volume and assertiveness. "Let's pick him up but not until after he has had time to meet up with his local contacts. We could end up closing down a large group or a heap of cells instead of putting away just one man and I agree he may not give us any Intel, especially local stuff. No one is saying he doesn't deserve to pay for all the things we know he's done, but let's see if we can use him to catch even more baddies".

Major General Watson considered these comments. "Take it easy you guys, we are all on the same side here. Look I know, with those cowardly bombings everything has changed, but it is important that we don't lose sight of the bigger picture. None of the proposed plans is bad. It's just that in this heightened alert we must maximise every shot we get. The last thing we want is some shoot out in the middle of the airport with a crew of his mob sent to pick him up."

Voicing everybody's loss of certainty they once had, he continued.

"Obviously, although after last week's bombings I suppose nothing is *obvious* anymore. Because he's gone through security checks to board the plane Aziz shouldn't be armed when he lands but his contacts may be. I think I back Clive's idea for that reason as well as the possibility of the extra Intel. He is so important that he must be here for something big. Get him off the plane, out of the airport and then let's see where our rabbit runs hey? Clive, you let your boys know they have done a great job spotting this mongrel."

Everyone around the table had been shaken by the terrorists' bombings of the previous week. Some felt guilty for not seeing it coming or for not heading it off. The passion displayed in the discussion was founded on a need for retribution and a desire to avoid any further attacks. They were all good men, good at their jobs and angry at seeing their beloved Australia under attack with hundreds of innocent men, women and children murdered. They were all united in stopping it from happening again, now there were no egos, no competition, and no buck-passing. These were top echelon leaders that knew part of being a great leader was the ability to follow orders and take responsibility for their decisions and actions. They all nodded and then began the detailed planning of the operation to track Aziz including the follow-up actions required to maximise the outcomes of any Intel collected. They named the operation Code Name Rabbit after what the Major General had called Aziz.

In a sign of acceptance and commitment, in a calm voice, Doug Wilson said. "OK, we have just under eight hours twenty minutes flight time before the Rabbit arrives so let's get cracking".

The planning meeting took an hour and a half covering every aspect of surveillance at the airport and after Aziz left the airport. They all hoped he would be picked up by car rather than jump on the Airport Link Train into Sydney. Having a series of nondescript cars coming and going on a busy motorway was a lot easier than having officers on a relatively small train close to their target especially as the train trip was only twelve minutes long.

Chapter 16

Descending into Mascot Airport
Sydney
Australia

Aziz finished his coffee in time for the Flight attendant to remove the cup in preparation for the descent into Sydney. The landing was uneventful, and Aziz could feel the anticipation causing a flood of Adrenalin through his stiff body. Believing the Australian Authorities would be busy elsewhere, it was with an amount of confidence Aziz stood and stretched his back. He then removed his carry-on bag from the overhead locker and proceeded to disembark blending in with the other passengers as much as possible.

He had changed from his traditional robes and as uncomfortable as they were, he was dressed in a mid-priced Western business suit in a charcoal tone just like twenty other businessmen now disembarking. He was very careful not to leave his robes on the plane to be discovered and cause some overzealous cleaner to mention it to a superior. They were now safely in his carry-on bag, so he could wear them again once he got to the camp. He didn't believe they were looking for him but if they were they would be looking for a single man travelling by himself. With this in mind throughout the flight, he had struck up a conversation with a young woman in the window seat beside him. He had hidden his feelings perfectly but inwardly he was disgusted with the fact the woman had breastfed her baby many times over the last eight hours as though he was blind or not there. The harlot had actually removed her breast from her underwear and fed the baby while she was speaking with him, a woman of no shame.

After he had gotten his bag down Aziz helped the woman get her bags and baby's needs down from the overhead locker. Then gallantly he volunteered to carry these off the plane. It was impossible to comprehend a dangerous terrorist carrying such domestic items. The bags were colourfully decorated with all manner of ducks and kittens and ribbons and the final humiliation for a devout Moslem was several pink pigs. Aziz was confident that Allah would forgive him. As he traversed the moving walkway to Arrivals he felt the little spark of excitement that always signalled the real start of a mission, the anticipation, the little bit of uncertainty. He was a seasoned old battle warrior, but he still enjoyed serving Allah Al-Mutakabbir (Allah the Dominant One) in the way of his calling. Aziz continued towards the baggage carousel looking relaxed and joking with the woman, making faces at the baby as if he could be his father or grandfather perhaps.

But behind this act, he was on high alert looking once again for any gesture or hesitation by the passport or Customs officials. He searched for any military types standing near exits or hanging around the baggage collection talking into their sleeves or their collars. But once again he saw nothing, Allah surely was merciful to his servants.

He kept up the pretence with the woman and the baby, helping her with her bigger bags and getting trolleys for them both. Once they got to Passport Control they would separate, she joining the Australian citizen's queue, he the other nationalities. He did not want to highlight this separation so without a goodbye or a second glance he was gone. Heading to the shorter queue he left the woman and child to go their way. Aziz went through all the checks and procedures eventually coming to the exit out of Arrivals. Aziz observed all the family and friends laughing and crying as they met their loved ones. He thought to himself that they would soon have more to cry about Allah willing.

When Aziz and his superiors were planning this part of his arrival they had noted that whenever a plane arrived there were always drivers and chauffeurs from hotels and resorts picking up their customers. They all held up signs with hotel names or individual names. This system had created the perfect cover for him to meet someone he had never met before. Hiding out in the open. A blend of field craft of never using just one method, one minute in the shadows then in the light, being fluid, ready to change as things around him changed. There it was. He was relieved to see a sign with his Turkish name and yes, they followed his instructions avoiding a driver of Middle Eastern appearance. The man holding the sign was a young blond Australian-looking man. He wore a Chauffeur's uniform and peak cap in matching colours a nice professional dark blue. The Chauffeur took Aziz's baggage trolley and in a broad Australian accent loud enough for everyone around them to hear said, “Welcome to Australia, please follow me”. Aziz asked, “Is everything in place for our trip?” The Chauffeur nodded and moved off with the trolley of bags.

For a moment Aziz's mind reeled realising he was actually standing in Australia and close enough to touch the people that he hated so much. He felt justified in this hatred because of their willingness to support America and invade his country. He thought to himself; *well now I have invaded your country, now let's see how you like it you infidel pigs*. This was a country with no faith, no morals or values. He thought of the woman on the plane again, fancy taking out your breast in front of a strange man and that little piglet making filthy suckling noises. They all deserve what we will deliver, correction of what Allah Al-Mumeet (The Inflictor of Death) will deliver.

They had reached the limousine; the Chauffeur placed all the bags in the boot that these Australians called a trunk. Aziz looked around one last time, not seeing anything that concerned him, he climbed through the rear door settling into the tinted darkened interior. He let his travel-weary body sink into the rich black leather seat. He closed his eyes and dreamt of the havoc he was about to wreak.

ROMA
QUEENSLAND
MAY 2014

It was still dark when I started up my Honda 4WD Quad Bike and headed out of camp, Jake was grumpy because I had told him to stay in camp. He was fine if I was after pigs or bunnies and even foxes. But deer could smell a dog a hundred miles away and be so spooked I wouldn't even get a glimpse of the herd let alone a shot at a decent stag. Half an hour later I parked the Quad under some trees that should offer some shade once the sun came up. Grabbing my day pack and rifle I started the hike into the back country where I had seen deer in the past.

I quietly followed under ridge lines keeping down to ensure my silhouette wasn't poking out over a hilltop or around some rock feature.

I tried as much as possible to stay in the shady broken areas and stopped frequently to use my binoculars to search the country ahead of me for any sign of my quarry. I came across a large valley surrounded by heavily wooded sides in three directions. By now it was hot and sunny, and I knew the deer would be lying under trees in the shade chewing their cud and sleeping after a night of eating and foraging. Using my Bushnell Fusion Matrix Range-Finder binoculars I glassed the far ridge line for any sign of deer. I have been hunting this property for years and there was a small herd of red deer that passed through from time to time. I always walk with the wind in my face and a gentle breeze confirmed I didn't have any worries about the buck smelling my scent. I slowly moved from shadow to shadow stopping checking ridge lines with my binos.

He was about eight years old and in his prime, the huge buck's antlers were even bigger this year than last season. He was king of all he surveyed having avoided hunters many times while many of his peers had fallen to a hunter's rifle. He was the last mature buck left which suited him when rutting season came. It was good to only have young rivals vying for his little harem of does. He lay there, his rump out in the sun, breaking up the shape of his body with the rest shaded and dark. A single flick of an ear was all it took to betray the majestic stag's incredible camouflage. The buck's brown dappled coat makes him nearly invisible in the fallen timber interspersed with long grass and the ever-changing shadows cast by the hundred-plus-year-old ghost gums around him.

I was doing what dad had taught me as a kid and later on, that prick of a sniper sergeant who, although I hated him, taught me as much about being a soldier and a man as sniping skills. Several things would betray a man's or group of men's presences, Shape, Size, Silhouette and Spacing and of course, the one just demonstrated so well by this buck movement. To avoid making the same mistake as the buck had just made I hadn't moved anything but my fingers for the last twenty minutes at this stop. Making sure the wind continued taking my scent away from my quarry I slowly started to stalk in closer.

Moving a few metres at a time, getting behind cover when I could, my Ghillie sniper suit broke up every human shape as I moved. When I had seen his ear flicker the range finder binoculars had read just over seven hundred and fifty metres, now I had closed the distance to three hundred and ten metres. The buck hadn't got that big being stupid. Although I was confident he hadn't seen me the wind had begun to swirl a little as it does when you climb out of a valley like this. Whatever the reason, through the binos I could see that the buck had become even more alert and I knew it was only seconds before he would stand and disappear over the ridge.

Deciding to settle in for the shot placed the illuminated cross-hairs on his chest and took a good breath and let a little out as I began to take up some of the pressure on the trigger. I held my breath and took up the final trigger travel, a millisecond before the report of my rifle there was a shot to the east from the next-door property behind the ridge that the buck lay on. As a sniper, I am trained not to be distracted so the shot didn't worry me. But it did worry the buck. Usually, my shot would still have been perfect, but the flight time didn't allow for the instantaneous reaction to another hunter's shot next. The highly nervous creature launched to his front causing my projectile to enter his stomach region rather than the instant death of the planned heart shot.

As predicted he was spooked and continued forward without breaking stride, without hesitation the buck raced up and over the ridge.

Like any hunter, this whole scenario broke my heart. The last thing any ethical hunter wants is a painful wounding shot instead of an instantaneous one shot one kill. I ran after the buck and crested the ridge in time to see him jump a three-strand barbed wire fence as though it was not there. He landed on the narrow dirt road that divided our property from another cattle property to the north. This track provided access to four other cattle farms that fed off this public road. The beautiful buck stumbled as his hooves landed on the gravel surface, obviously troubled by his gunshot wound. He retained that royal majestic look as he gathered himself from his near fall and in two steps crossed the dirt road and disappeared into the thick scrub of my neighbour's property.

Two minutes later climbing through the boundary fence he had just jumped I followed the wounded buck across the dirt road into the adjoining cattle property. I knew that they would be OK with me doing this, as no farmer likes to see animals suffer. As well as this I knew the property entrance and homestead were east of here on the main Roma road. I picked up the blood trail straight away and followed the stricken animal across the small grassy paddock to an area covered in thick foliage, a mix of gums, casuarinas and wattles. As I entered the darkness of the heavily wooded wind break my eyes adjusted to the gloom and once again I began tracking my buck. The blood trail seemed to have disappeared and I was starting to think the deer had finally died and was hidden in one of the many thickets.

Suddenly, I smelled smoke not from a fire but cigarette smoke and even more specifically middle eastern tobacco. My senses took it in and analysed it, I had smelled it before a million times in Iraq and Afghanistan, and I was sure of it. But all logic told me I was in a cow paddock in the middle of Queensland Australia. I had to be wrong. Without choice or being mindful of any thought or decision I hit the deck, and my training kicked in against my logic. Was I finally having the breakdown of all breakdowns, here in front of me were two men? No, not just two men but Talibs just like in Afghanistan, they were dressed differently in an Army-type uniform which was strange. But here they were, or were they? They seemed so real I started to wonder if was I back in Afghanistan, and that the deer hunt had been a dream evoked by missing home.

Lying in the undergrowth I was invisible, still camed up, and whether or not this was a dream or flashback, I was trained and smart enough not to move. I could hear their boots on the gravel track as they approached my position although they were extremely quiet. Automatically I silently flicked the safety on my pump action to fire and waited. It took on a dreamlike feel. I kept questioning what was happening but never got any answers. Second, guessing my mental health was not a common experience. Well, to be more honest, yes it was a common occurrence but nothing like this. This was pushing all my boundaries and the crunching gravel wasn't making it better. Was this real?

From the sound of their footsteps, I thought they had made it past me without stopping until I heard a harsh sort of bark followed by a loud sigh somewhere nearby. I have heard enough things die both animals and men to know exactly what that sound was. The poor old buck had come to the end of his race, he had lain down with a last sigh and breathed a final ragged breath. The two soldiers spoke quietly to each other.

Dari is the language spoken more in the north and west of Afghanistan, while Pashto is used in the rest of that country. I speak a fair bit of Pashto, but I recognised what I was pretty sure was Dari.

I heard someone ask the question; "Sunny what was that?"

Was I dreaming, or had I totally lost it, what the hell was going on here? No way, this had to be real. I could smell the grass, I could feel the warmth of the sunbeam that had forced its way through the wattles warming my legs, this had to be happening but how?'

Sunny and Hammad were dressed in combat camouflage uniforms and each one of them carried on their belts, water bottles, spare ammo and a large combat knife.

At first, they had felt strange dressed like the enemy soldiers instead of their tribal robes but now they strutted like soldiers all over the world. An attitude that comes from training and the fact you have so many like-minded and equipped friends beside you. Sunny and Hammad had been on guard duty patrolling around this boundary for the last three hours. They had performed this duty off and on for the last two months. Nothing had ever happened before. Sure, the occasional rustle in the leaves would stop them. But so far on investigation, it was always nothing, they hadn't even seen much wildlife.

Today, on hearing this strange sound, the two soldiers became excited. Months of repetitive training and countless hot dusty miles of sentry marches had become tedious, finally some real action.

So, speaking in their native Dari, Hammad asked his partner "Sunny what was that?" "I do not know, could it be a crocodile Hammad?"

Fear showing on his face his eyes large and white against his dark skin. "Don't be stupid Sunny. They said there were no crocodiles this far south and besides there is no water".

Sunny hadn't forgotten the crunching sound of the crocodile breaking his friend's bones and seeing the huge reptile dragging the soldier around. He wasn't about to relax. "Do they have tigers or wolves here?"

None of the group had fully gotten over their first brush with Australian wildlife. They were all trained and brave for their mission but being eaten by some huge lizard had shaken them all. Hammad raised his hand to still his nervous friend. "I don't think so my friend".

As I said I know a bit of Pashto but couldn't make much sense of what I had just heard. There were several words in there I had never heard before. Once again, I wondered if this was some incredibly real dream as nothing made sense. I heard them move off the track. They were very quiet now; no talking and their footfalls were nearly non-existent. Unlike wet jungle, the dry Aussie bush works both ways. It can betray your movement or that of your enemies. I was stationary so this time it was on my side. I could hear them pushing through the grass and fallen tree branches pushed over in this area by a bulldozer when clearing the track. Five more steps and even if they didn't see me they would walk on top of me. I might have been lucky enough for one to walk past me. But with two, one of them was sure to trip over me.

I heard them take their weapons off safe with a quiet click. I made my decision it didn't matter whether this was a dream or real. I would shoot them before they shot me, I sat up. My first shot took off the head of the soldier on the right as per my training I always shot right to left. I pumped the Remington 308 and squeezed the trigger in one fluid action hitting the second one in the throat before his friend had hit the ground. Two shots, two kills, without them getting a shot away.

I knew better than to take a long time to think this through. I could smell the metallic scent of blood and realised I had some warm splatter on my cheek, reaching out I touched the nearest soldier just to make sure he was real. HE WAS REAL I WASN'T CRAZY AFTER ALL. Well, at least not that sort of crazy. Although I had just killed two strangers because they looked, sounded and even smelt like Taliban near Roma Queensland Australia, that was crazy.

I knew I needed to clean this up. Just leaving two bodies would eventually return to bite me on the arse somehow. It was doubtful that whoever had sent the two heavily armed soldiers out would go to the Police. It was doubtful that either a report of them missing or the discovery of their bodies report would ever be made. I had no idea what was going on but usually, two armed soldiers meant more armed soldiers nearby. And once they knew I had killed two of their mates they would solve their problems by avoiding, at all costs, involving the authorities. I had a heap of questions but most of them would have to wait. I began to wonder if there were more of these soldiers already on the way, so the urgent question was did they just stumble onto me after hearing the deer or was it just by fate. Were there cameras, or maybe listening devices or sensor plates buried along the property boundary? The answer to these questions would dictate what direction I could take. What I had to do right now was work out how long I had to complete my planned action.

CHAPTER 17

Thinking it all through, firstly the contact with the soldiers had happened long enough ago that if there were hidden cameras the place would be crawling with more troops as soon as they had seen me end these two. Secondly, if there were hidden microphones, the same would apply and surely at the sound of the first shot, more soldiers would have rushed to the scene. All this same logic applied if there were sensor plates buried just below the surface. If they existed and were set off by the stag or myself, someone would be here by now. I guess there are times when things just happen if they had passed five minutes earlier or I had decided to sleep in. Whatever it was, however it works, it was bad luck bringing us all together, but especially bad for them.

It took no time at all to come to some hard truths. I had no regrets or doubts about my having any choice, but I had killed two men. The local Police would take a dim view of that and I would end up in more trouble than I could explain or escape from. All the other questions rattling around my brain would take time to figure out, but none of it felt good. When it came to the bodies, when farms are so big there are a lot of places a body or two could be hidden. Another alternative was to rely on the local feral pigs who could eat a fully-grown cow in a night leaving virtually nothing but a stain on the dirt. With that in mind, I began carrying the soldiers, one at a time back across the dirt road back to my home property.

Once I had gotten both bodies and their weapons hidden on my side of the track I ran back to the place they had died. I systematically searched the area for anything not natural, I found one of my spent rounds but not the second. I searched for anything one of us may have dropped, a freshly broken twig and so on, once satisfied that the area was back to the way it was before any of us arrived I moved to the track. I was pleased to see the stag's prints and a small patch of pink frothy blood indicating a lung shot. Immediately after the stag's prints, I could see my own distinctive pattern left by my Army Issue Boots (General Purpose) GP.

The way the two soldiers had moved quietly and then spread out a little when they began their search told me someone must have been training these Talibs in field craft, someone who knew what they were doing. So, the chances were that on discovering two of his soldiers were missing they would check the sentry route and then fan out to look for any signs of the missing men. Well, at least that's what I would do. I brushed out my footprints being careful not to erase the Stag's trail and also not to create a smooth path crossing the gravel road. That would account for the sound of the shot if it was heard and the stag's body once it began to smell and was discovered. All I could hope was whoever these guys were when they realised they were two down and then couldn't find any sign of them they would conclude the two had decided to take off to better places.

With that done I ran back to where I had parked the quad bike before walking in early this morning. Man, that seemed like days ago already. I rode my quad down to where I had hidden both bodies earlier and lifted their corpses, one onto the front rack of the quad, the other on the rear. The trip away from that side of the property was painfully slow with all that weight but still much better than having to carry them.

I had decided the wild pig idea was the best option to make sure they were gone for good. Burying had its problems you never knew when a new dam or a new fence-line would be dug, accidentally digging up the remains, or exposed when some flood washes off the topsoil if I buried them too near a creek. I placed them side by side in a gully where I had always found pigs around, and after stripping them of their equipment and uniforms I left them unceremoniously to the elements. I knew the pigs would be attracted by the smell of blood and decomposition in these hot conditions and I would return to the spot in the next few days and make sure the pigs had done their job on the bodies. After stripping the two dead Talibs I opened them up with my hunting knife to speed up the pigs finding their next feast.

I took their uniforms and underwear and any other equipment about five miles away and burnt it all except for one pair of the Talib-type boots. Once it had all burnt down and cooled I collected any buttons or buckles. These I buried, but high on a hill and under a tree, so nothing would dig them up. I knew I couldn't dump the AK74s. Hey what can I say, I'm a sniper, I love guns I would just hide them well and keep them for a rainy day. Once I had disposed of the bodies and gear I headed back to camp my mind shuffling and analysing and filing in some order all the questions that had been raised by this morning's bizarre events.

People say talking to yourself is a sign of madness. However, when you spend a lot of time alone or with a dog who doesn't talk much, it becomes a way of working things through. Out loud I said in my most studious voice, "let's try to make sense of what had just happened". So, what did I have so far?

Two Talibs in uniform, with weapons and equipment and in camouflage uniforms, uncommon to most of the Talibs, that I have seen on more like us or maybe Russians.

1. The only trouble is that this was Roma Queensland, not Afghanistan.
2. I knew without a doubt they would have killed me if I hadn't killed them first, the safety was off on both their weapons.
3. This was Australia, not Afghanistan and killing your neighbours was somewhat illegal.
4. What were two Talibs with the latest AK74M chambered in the lighter 5.45×39mm doing on a cattle farm?

5. What were trained soldiers (I could tell they were inexperienced but well trained by the way they moved along the track and then began to search) doing guarding a cattle farm?
6. Why guard a cattle farm with armed soldiers?
7. What was I going to do, call the Police? No, it was too late after hiding the bodies, maybe the Army?

I still had a lot of questions I couldn't answer but I had gotten rid of the bodies and the gear. I still had the two AK74Ms, but they couldn't be tied to anything. I knew how these things went. It would be hard to convince anyone anything was going on out here because it made absolutely no sense. I was there, and it had still taken time for me to come to grips with it being real. But I had a knot in my stomach that I trusted too much to ignore. I had to try to do something, the more I thought about all this the more alarms started ringing in my head. But even that decision gave me yet another set of questions. I couldn't bring in the local Police, but the Feds might be OK. Or would I be better talking to the National Security Centre? I knew how that would go without any credentials or someone introducing me as OK. It was like trying to report a possible crime unless you were a cop, all these institutions treated you like a nut-job.

All through my specialist training, it was drilled into us that if you had a lot of questions or even just one big one that you couldn't figure out, the solution was often found by breaking it down into smaller pieces. OK, the way I saw it I had two choices and neither of them was named good or better. But I had tried to look at the smaller pieces which is why I had decided to phone my old Company Commander. I had served with him during one tour of Iraq and two in Afghanistan. He had worked closely with me and I knew he would have my back and hopefully, he would listen to me. Well, he used to back in the day. He had been promoted to full Colonel since we had last spoken.

I looked up his number and punched it in; two rings later an aide, a Lieutenant Fox, answered in the usual formal Army manner. I explained who I was and asked to speak to Colonel Jim Walsh. The aide attempted to put me through the third degree to decide whether or not to put me through. He was just doing his job, but it was still damned annoying. As an ex-Officer I and member of that Unit it was strange to be treated like a stranger. I suppose it is true what they say. 'When you are in you are a guest but when you're out you are a pest'. Anyway, I was already sick of being on hold when an old, rough and very familiar voice shouted into the phone. "What do you want, to re-enlist, no chance".

Smiling at his style I replied. "It's nice to hear your sweet voice again Sir." Even though we are friends and brothers in arms, and I'm no longer Army but it's always hard to stop calling superior ranks Sir. It's just like breathing.

The gruff voice again. "You to son. How's civvy life treating you, goin OK?"

"Yeah, I'm OK, can't sleep in, can't see any jobs that I could stand longer than a day. Can't keep a girlfriend longer than a month and my best friend is still my old border collie" I said frankly.

The Colonel laughed. "That sounds normal from what I hear for a fella like you, you hitting that JD?"

My turn to laugh. "Na, I'm OK," I lied, "Hey I need to talk to you about something that could be important".

"OK shoot, if I can help, you know I am there for you".

Knowing that this would draw a quick response I kept going. "Well, Sir I was out Roma way deer hunting and to cut a long story short I had a run-in with a couple of Talibs."

The laugh had been replaced with concern. "Sorry to interrupt Steve, but are you sure about my booze question. What on earth would the Taliban be doing running around the bush outside Roma Queensland?"

I smiled, "I know, I know I keep asking myself the very same question. But I have the two AK74Ms I took off them. They are definitely Talibs. They were dressed in Russian-style cams but still Afghanis for sure".

Probably thinking I had lost it, you could hear the Colonel take on as near a counselling tone for him as he asked, "OK, son what were they doing, tell me what happened?"

I began the account of what had happened. "The abridged version is I was on the neighbouring property looking for a wounded stag and these guys turned up all gung ho and all geared up, AKs ready and looking for me. I assumed they were after me. I figured they must have noise sensors, or perhaps pressure sensors but no one has followed up on me and if they had cameras they would have caught me then or maybe since".

Talking like he was addressing an elderly parent Walsh continued. "Steve if we didn't go back as far and as deep as you and I do, I would be suggesting you talk to Psych, and maybe you should old mate. OK just to help me what are your thoughts on all this?"

Understanding the old man's concerns after hearing such a wild story I responded as logically as I could. "Sir I have tossed it all every which way and without going back in there I don't know. They were well equipped and armed, and they moved like they were well trained. It just raises more questions and doesn't give me any answers. I suppose they may be guarding some sort of drug set-up, but it seems a bit over the top for that".

He was trying to believe my outlandish story. "Son I feel like we're all saddled up but are we ready to ride?"

Even though I was frustrated by the tone of this conversation I had to smile remembering my old Company Commander loved Colonel Potter from MASH. He always used a lot of horsey sayings as naturally as any cowboy. "Let me think on it and get back to you. Maybe I'll bounce it off a guy I graduated with who scored a posting with the NSC. No promises but I'll see what I can do, sometimes they know stuff and are just waiting for another piece of the jigsaw before acting on it, who knows hey?"

I gave it one more try. "Thank you, Sir, I know it sounds crazy, but my gut tells me something big is going on. I'll stand down until I hear back from you, thanks again Sir".

The Colonel ended the call. "OK talk soon son and you take care".

I hung up wondering if the strength of a relationship built on bullets and blood would be enough to encourage the Colonel to pass on my report. Colonel Walsh was a very experienced Army Officer who although he was savvy in the politics of power had chosen to remain operational rather than the alternative postings in Canberra or even overseas. Unbeknown to me, it was for that reason after a sleepless night Colonel Jim Walsh sat staring out his window on a grey rainy morning overlooking Enoggera Barracks Parade Ground Brisbane. His face betrayed the quandary he now found himself in; play it safe and sit on Steve Wallace's report or pass it on? Should he keep a promise to a brother who in all honesty he would trust with his life and have trusted with his life on many occasions previously?

But being realistic his confidence sat at maybe a little less than the 100% of the old days now due to the lack of contact over the last two years. Steve Wallace had sounded OK and in the past, Steve's gut feeling had been more than reliable. However, he would be sticking his neck out by passing on Steve's report, you couldn't call it Intel. He was potentially endangering his future promotion prospects founded on his highly credible reputation as a straight shooter everyone could depend on. A reputation that had not been accrued without great effort and at times danger. He was a battle-hardened Army Officer used to and practised making big decisions fast and often under fire.

So, it rattled him to find himself oscillating between phoning his contact in the National Security Centre (NSC) and not passing on Steve Wallace's story. The other problem was if he decided not to pass on the information he would then have to give Steve Wallace a brush-off. Steve would recognise any explanation as just that before the end of that call. For the third time in an hour, the Colonel's hand moved toward the phone this time picking it up and dialling his old friend's mobile phone.

Walsh chose to use the mobile to ensure the call would not be recorded as per NSC Standard Operating Procedure (SOP). As the phone rang Jim Walsh wondered again whether he was endangering his old Duntroon College roommate's reputation as well as his own by involving him. Wild stories can spread and cause damage like a bush fire.

Colonel Peter Goodrich answered the phone casually, obviously recognising the call was from his old friend. "G'day Jim, how's sunny Brisbane today?"

The stress could be heard in Walsh's voice. "Hey mate, not too sunny just at present but we can do with the rain. Pete, I know I am heading your way for that briefing next week, we catch up more then? For now, I need to talk to you about something".

"Sure, Canberra won't know what hit it hey, two old diggers like us, what on your mind?"

Jim Walsh commenced his promised report. "Firstly, I want to start by making it clear that all I am doing is passing on just a bit of info".

His friend in Canberra was instantly concerned. "Jim you're starting to worry me. Are you OK mate?"

With a bit of hesitation, Colonel Walsh replied. "Yeah, yeah, I'm fine. Now listen up buddy; I back the source but the information is very vague and pretty weird. The last thing I want to be accused of is Pareidolia".

Goodrich tried to help his mate with some humour. “Hang on mate you're the world scrabble champ using all those big words, I’m just a dumb grunt remember”.

Walsh replied. “It means seeing something that is meaningless as being meaningful. Having said that let me tell you what I know. No, more accurately what I was told. It came from one of my best Officers, now retired. Although it sounds weird, I figure that's up to your experts to check and analyse and do all that spooky stuff you guys do down there in the castle”.

Goodrich could hear the tension in his friend's voice. “Alright you've got my attention and if you vouch for this guy that's good enough for me”.

Colonel Walsh went on to explain everything that Steve Wallace had said including having the AKs as solid evidence.

Goodrich listened not interrupting his friend again until he was finished. “Well Jim you were right both times, this is a bit vague and weird as bat shit, but you were right to phone it in. We have a saying around here; *the absence of evidence is not the evidence of absence.* There might just be something there. Jim, I hate to sound like this but how about I keep this to myself for the time being. I'll look around to see if there are any warnings in place or any other reports re Roma area and I will look at any Sat photos we have of the area".

This call was going exactly as Jim Walsh had expected. "I'd appreciate that Pete, Steve's a good man who has seen and done it all. I must admit my guts twinging a bit as well after talking to him".

Colonel Goodrich was as sharp as ever. "And I purposely avoided asking you how he came to have those AKs. I figured on a non-secured line that would be best and it's probably the reason he didn't go to the local coppers. OK mate, I'll get onto it and be back to you ASAP”.

"Thanks again Pete my shout at that Chinese restaurant near the office".

Goodrich tried again to lighten the call. "Sounds good, any time I can get you to pay I'm there, see you then Jim".

"Very not funny Pete, see ya". Colonel Walsh gently replaced the receiver as though he may break it if he was not overly careful. Well, it was done, let's see where this wagon took them all.

CHAPTER 18

NATIONAL SECURITY CENTRE
CANBERRA
AUSTRALIAN CAPITAL TERRITORY
EARLY MAY 2014

Sitting in his office high above the green quadrangle he watched as National Security Centre staff took their lunch break. Colonel Peter Goodrich was good to his word. He had searched every database that was available to the extensive resources of the NSC. Goodrich had also looked at twelve months' worth of satellite passes over the Roma and surrounding districts. He looked closely at any photos that caught his attention of any of the properties around the grid reference Jim Walsh had given him, pawing over hundreds of stills, looking for anything that showed new earthworks or some significant building.

Something caught his eye he thought: *Hang on, what was that, that's an awful lot of different colour dirt, it was a huge fresh scar in the middle of the cattle property.* But then under the magnifier, he saw it was a huge dam dug at the base of some high ground to catch runoff water.

Goodrich was in Intelligence because he was thorough and had a gift for noticing things that were out of place. He continued to flip through the glossy photos on his desk. There's the same shot four months later confirming yes, it is definitely a dam now about a third full. He continued searching until he knew he was neglecting his designated tasks too long, he found nothing that looked out of place.

He then stuck his neck out as much as he felt he could. He trusted Jim Walsh's judgement. However, he couldn't allocate any more resources without it becoming NSC official and he just couldn't see anything to support such a request. Despite that, he figured he owed Jim Walsh and this ex-Captain a little more effort. He figured bouncing off someone who had a ton of experience interpreting reports would make sense. Colonel Goodrich went to his immediate Superior Officer who oversaw the Intelligence Attachment at the NSC.

This very Senior Officer was extremely experienced in Intel analysis and data collection but was still highly approachable, Brigadier Roy Dodds. Although now in his fifties he had that look about him that suggested he carried too much weight while still retaining a muscular physique his blonde hair was thinning a little and matched his regulation moustache that he had started growing on recruit course some thirty-eight years ago. One look at this Officer and you knew he was a no-nonsense type of man. Or at least that is what he projected as his work image, however, he was a very funny sociable bloke when enjoying the bar at the Officer's mess or home.

Colonel Goodrich had only been at the NSC for a little over seven months and believed he had a good working relationship with his boss. He certainly respected the Brigadier acknowledging he had already learned a lot under his command.

Knocking on the boss's thick wooden door he immediately heard the Brigadier's deep voice call. "Come in".

Colonel Goodrich took a deep breath and entered the office. "Morning Sir, I was wondering if I could take five minutes of your time?"

"Good morning Pete, of course, come in, how's that database of potential explosives sources going?"

"Pretty well Sir, I have all the fertiliser manufacturers nailed down from the first of next month, they will submit monthly reports on any unusual sales". "I'm working on an idea I've had for a model that should identify any unusual spikes in fertiliser sales down as low as at the produce store level. I have another team working on mining companies and their suppliers for the more sophisticated explosives. That's coming along fine as well because they are very highly regulated in the first place".

The Brigadier smiled, "Sounds interesting, let me know how you get on. OK now, what did you want to talk about Pete?"

Peter Goodrich carefully and without stretching his neck out too far started from the beginning. He was careful to state his respect for both his source and the fact Colonel Walsh had vouched for his Ex-Platoon Commander. Goodrich could see mentioning some rank and some history of service supported his story, or at least to some degree.

"Sir he reports he had a serious run-in with two men who had the appearance of Taliban, remembering this Ex did two Afghan tours. The report was very detailed Sir, as you would expect from an Ex-SAS Captain. He stated they were dead-set Afghani possibly speaking Dari rather than straight Pashto, they even smoked Afghani tobacco. He reported they were dressed in what could have been Russian camos and were armed with brand new AK74Ms, I thought that was interesting. He also stated they struck him as well trained but probably inexperienced". Goodrich passed his completed report verbally and handed the Brigadier a hard copy.

The Brigadier had listened carefully until Goodrich was finished. "This is interesting stuff, Pete. Have you got any hard evidence; photos, or local Police reports?"

Goodrich shook his head. "No Sir, just what this retired Captain claims he has seen and that he has the two AKs in his possession of course".

He had decided that alluding to a possible double murder to the Brigadier would erode any respect or trust the ex-Captain's past Military history had so recently established.

"What do you think it all means Pete?" The older Officer asked.

Goodrich had known the 'Old Man' would get to this question and he had prepared his answer. Attempting to be fair while at the same time carefully covering his own butt.

"Sir because of the sources there is probably something there, but I don't think there is enough to go on at the moment for us to get involved".

The Brig exhaled through his closed teeth. "Normally, I might be able to give you some resources to investigate this a bit more, but not with the Commonwealth Heads shindig on our doorstep. Thank God it's only every two years hey?" the Brigadier stated sarcastically.

Goodrich could tell the Brigadier had already moved on. "Pete, I need you to focus on *your* project because that is strongly related to the security preparations for CHOGM. We've only got eight months before all those Commonwealth Leaders flood in here and I've just been informed Obama is going to make a speech at the Opera House of all places, it only gets better".

Colonel Goodrich had heard the Brigadier loud and clear, and you couldn't fight a battle on such a shaky platform in any case. Standing, Goodrich knew he had kept his promise. "Roger that, thank you, Sir, I'll file the report just in case anything else comes in later and cross matches, thanks again Sir".

The Brig closed the meeting. "No worries Pete I'll catch up in the mess and buy you a beer after work hey?"

Goodrich liked and respected the old warrior sitting in front of him. "Look forward to that Sir, thanks again".

Colonel Goodrich returned to his desk sensing a growing uneasiness, but he was unsure of its origin. Was it the Roma report that had initiated a twinge in his gut as well? Maybe there was something to this Taliban stuff. Or was it that he would now be calling his friend and telling him he was going to file it under 'C' for crap or at least that's how it would sound. He was pretty sure the

Brigadier had been fine with his looking into the report without it being official. Intel work was all about initiative and you never knew what you would uncover especially with data sharing across Australia and indeed the World.

The Brigadier had made himself available to Colonel Goodrich because he had to be over everything but that five minutes was all there was today. He had bigger fish to fry that he couldn't share with Colonel Goodrich. Upstairs the whole place was abuzz because of Operation Rabbit. And today some deer hunter out in the back blocks thought he had seen something, somewhere which wasn't going to interest anyone today.

Brigadier Dodds looked at his watch again noting the Rabbit's plane was due any minute now. A mix of anxiety and pleasure at the possibility of catching such a prize raced around the Brig's thoughts. No one had had time to report to the Brigadier that the plane had been fifteen minutes early and the operation was already in full swing while he was meeting with Pete Goodrich. The Brigadier checked his emails and saw the Situation Report (SITREP) and that Operation Rabbit had started without him. He pushed a small black button on a device in front of him and increased the volume on his desk-mounted radio monitor tuned into the car chase.

Agents had a visual on the Rabbit as soon as he got off the plane. They had dressed like passengers and had carry-on type luggage. Now they carefully changed places with each other tracking him through the exit processes until he exited into the public waiting area. One agent beside the Rabbit was pulling a large black bag behind him looking around with bleary eyes for perhaps a family member or friend. Black bag saw the Rabbit go to a tall blond man dressed in a Chauffeur's uniform and turned the other way speaking into his throat mike handing over to the mobile chasers.

"All call signs this is Zulu 2 Rabbit has met Chauffeur, looks like the road is a go I say again looks like the road is a go. Over".

Zulu 1 was well trained and experienced and knew lengthy communications were trouble, so he confirmed the mode of transport, first allowing all teams to settle. Team Rail while not standing down completely collectively breathed a sigh of relief due to the hardships of keeping a subject under surveillance on a small train. Back at NSC HQ, every Senior Officer monitoring the radio comms joined them understanding that following a vehicle was a much more manageable situation.

"All Alpha Teams this is Zulu 2 Over". Zulu 2 go-ahead Over". Alphas be advised Chauffeur is six-foot, longish blond hair, blue Chauffeur's uniform, looks like ex- Military heading for Exit 3. I say again heading for Exit 3, Over". "Roger that Zulu 2, good work will take it from here. Alpha 1 Out".

With that, all Zulu Team members headed for a pre-arranged Rendezvous (RV) to regroup and head back to base. In their planning meetings, they had discussed the possibility of any number of scenarios that required the accurate identification of the target vehicle. It was discussed whether the person on foot could accomplish that by following the target and then returning to the chase car. It was decided this may be impossible in a multi-level car park set-up, so they deployed three agents on foot to cover the exits whose role was to tag the targets and then their vehicle. They were given the title Walker to ensure everyone knew who was on task and when. Having heard Zulu 2's report Walker 1 made his way to exit 3 and waited for the targets to arrive. He already knew what the Rabbit looked like and now thanks to the updated info had the description of the Chauffeur.

Inside the Rabbit and the uniformed Chauffeur had stopped.

"What's wrong did you see something?" A look of concern flashed across his face as Aziz asked his Chauffeur.

The Chauffeur, with an Australian accent, responded calmly. "No but out here on our own, I felt like we were sticking out like dog's balls".

Aziz had no idea what he had just said, but then looking around immediately understood the young driver's strategy. They waited for several other passengers and their drivers to catch up to them. Using the uniforms and common appearance Aziz and his driver were swallowed up by this swarm of Chauffeurs, luggage porters and their clients. When the bigger group passed by, they moved on surrounded and protected by similar-looking pairs, like two wildebeests hiding in a herd of wildebeests. Even so, the Australian agent spotted the blond driver amongst the crowd. Then to confirm he had the right pair, he noted beside the Chauffeur was a well-dressed businessman with dark features, a match to the photos each agent was carrying. They had their target the Rabbit.

The herd of drivers and customers moved as one through exit 3 across the two small airport roads, the first fed the lanes for traffic picking up arrivals, the other the two lanes that ran into the multi-level car park. The human herd proceeded into the car park. Acting as though he was looking for his car Walker 1 slung his day pack over his shoulder. While he looked around never losing sight of the Rabbit, he noted the target pair break away from the group. This was the tricky part where it would be harder to stay out of sight. Rabbit and Chauffeur turned left and moved towards a black Limousine parked in bay 2235. Walker 1 immediately noted the registration number.

"Walker 1 to Team Alpha, Walker 1 to Team Alpha Over".

Walker 1 this is Alpha 1 Over".

"Alpha 2 Over".

"Alpha 3 Over".

Once the Walker knew that all three Alphas were listening he responded. "All Alphas, Rabbit is mobile, I say again Rabbit is mobile. Rego Papa Delta Sierra two niner four, say back Over".

Once all three Alphas had repeated the limo's registration number correctly. "Control have you copied Over?"

"Walker 1 offline, Out".

"Roger that all Units proceed as planned, Out".

The target limo that had picked up the Rabbit from the Sydney Airport moved steadily towards Sydney's famous Harbour Bridge.

For about twenty minutes Car Alpha 1 had been following three cars back from the limo and was ready to swap with Alpha 2 for the third time. As arranged Alpha 2 pulled out and passed the limo and then turned off. Charlie merged from the on-ramp and joined in the routine that appeared random but was being coordinated by central command. Alpha 2 would re-join further down and the whole charade would be repeated as many times as necessary. Leaving the airport, the followers had to be very careful to ensure they were following the correct limo as there was a convoy of nearly identical black limousines all heading away from the airport and all at the same time. They had the registration number but lagging back two or three cars, the number plate wasn't visible, so this didn't help all the time.

It became like the old pea hidden under one of three identical cups game. The only way to get it right was to never take your eyes off the pea or more precisely the limo carrying the Rabbit. As soon as Control had been given the registration she had identified it on the Airport CCTV and had immediately noticed that danger as all the other limos appeared on the feed from the airport security cameras. She warned all the Alpha Team followers who had already realised the challenge for themselves. Whether Aziz or his driver had banked on this as a ploy to avoid being tailed no one would ever know. But to them even if they didn't realise it, it was a bonus. As the target limo approached the harbour it appeared that the driver was going to head over the iconic Sydney Harbour Bridge as he moved into that designated lane. The black limousine was proceeding past the turnoff to the tunnel that took you under the harbour instead of over the bridge.

At the very last possible moment, the driver threw the limo sideways. The severe change in direction caused the vehicle to slew to the left leaving behind a cacophony of screeching tyres, blaring horns and the sound of metal and plastic crunching. Tyres squealed under full brakes and echoed as two lanes were blocked simultaneously by several nose-to-tail accidents. Somehow the limo made the turn, a credit to the Chauffeur's ability, Aziz was thrown hard against the door and cursed in Arabic. The manoeuvre was of far greater concern to Control who had switched to the Harbour Bridge Security CCTV system. She yelled, "all cars SITREP (Situation Report) now, Over".

"Control this is Alpha 2 I'm way back, can't see a way through at this time, Over".

"Control, Alpha 1, I'm still with Tango Rabbit, Alpha 3 is alongside so we are GO Over".

Alpha 3 didn't take up any air time as his location had been confirmed by Alpha 1.

" 1 and 3 great, do the best you can with just the two of you. I will try to get some add-ons on the other side of the harbour out".

"Roger Control, Alpha 1 Out".

"Roger Control, Alpha 3 Out".

Control was sounding a little better because at least two of her chasers were still in the race. She switched to the CCTV coverage inside the tunnel and immediately picked up the visual on the target limo. She said to herself: *"OK there you are my Rabbit. Thought you would get away from us, did you?"*

"Control to Alpha 1 and Alpha 2. I have visual on one plus two vehicles, all proceeding as planned, Over".

Those listening at the National Security Centre (NSC) started breathing again after having thought the prize Rabbit had escaped. They were all thinking they were glad the chasers were so well trained. The two cars didn't need to respond and besides, they were a little busy keeping up with Michael Schumacher up ahead. While driving within the road rules the Chauffeur pushed every boundary of that law, zipping in and out of lanes like he was driving a Porsche, not a limo. He was very aware that he had no desire to be pulled over by some traffic cop, but he had also followed enough limos to know they often behaved like they were royalty in a hurry. No one had any doubt about the special passenger being in that specific limo, but the Chauffeur's driving continued to confirm it. The Operation seemed to be going well but Control had a sinking feeling as it became obvious the Rabbit knew or at the very least was driving like he had assumed he was being followed. Although the driver was pushing it a bit it was clear he was just keeping ahead of the hounds and he wasn't trying to get away. This worried Control, what was he up to, what was coming next?

Control was pondering why this could be when all hell broke loose in the tunnel. The limo had just gone through a smooth left-hand curve when two of the civilian cars travelling immediately behind the black luxury car went drastically sideways. Then another two joined those and then another in the adjacent lane. In a matter of seconds, there were a dozen or more cars sliding and braking, skidding. Some doing one hundred and eighty degree turns or more, but most were being ploughed into by following cars before they fully turned around. Control could see Alpha 1 had dodged the start of the chaos but had now been T-boned by a large yellow courier van, one down.

"Alpha 3 are you still rolling I can't see you?"

"Control this is 3 I got around the pile-up, but the tunnel is completely stopped, no cars moving at all, I repeat no cars moving from crash site forward Over".

"3 does that include the Rabbit Over?" Hope sounding through the controller's voice.

Alpha 3 had to shout over the incredible noise that had filled the tunnel when he answered. "Control, Rabbit has run he started the chaos somehow and just kept rolling as it all happened behind him, Rabbit has gone, I repeat Rabbit is gone Over".

Control hoped in all the noise she had misheard 3 but deep down she knew the operation had just turned to shit with a capital "S". She then started to wonder if she still had a job.

Control had been warned that anyone that counted in Australian Security was sitting and listening to the communications in any number of offices in both Sydney and Canberra. Senior Security and Intelligence Officers probably right up to the top had been following every step of the way and were now wondering what had gone so terribly wrong. She had no way to know but she was confident there was a unanimous and deathly silence from each one of the agents who were listening. Just as she was the Controller, she figured they were now staring at their monitors in a state of temporary shock and amazement.

The tunnel CCTV was already being played and replayed and frozen and analysed by five different specialists at the NSC. A young red-headed Scottish girl called Maureen was the first to see what had happened, she let out a scream.

This was followed quickly by a thick accented "It's like a fookin James Bond movie. The limousine sprayed something, probably oil, out of the back of the car making the road as slippery as the ice back home. Then everyone following loses it in every direction, instant chaos".

The Team Leader didn't approve of such behaviour, screaming and then swearing loudly but he knew she was good at her job and young and lively. "Maureen, what have you got?" Maureen brushed her wavy red hair off her forehead and played the video on slomo pausing it at the instant the limo driver sprayed the road and initiated the resulting carnage.

Ten minutes later Major General (MAJGEN) Watson was chairing an emergency meeting of the various Heads serving on the Australian National Security Centre Committee. "OK there are no words to express how we all feel at present, but whatever we say won't put Aziz in a cage. So, we need to admit they were smarter than us this time and figure out what we are going to do next. We have CHOGM coming up and now we have one of the world's worst terrorists on the loose in Australia".

The MAJGEN paused sucking a breath through his teeth. I hate making assumptions, as the saying goes. "Assumptions are the mother of all stuff ups", however, things probably couldn't get much worse. I am concerned Aziz must be here for CHOGM."

Turning to his 2IC Brigadier Dodds; "Roy what have you got so far?"

"Sir, you pretty well summed it up in your opening statement. One of the analysts has figured out how he escaped our surveillance team. Apparently, some device was triggered by the driver spraying some slippery product probably oil on the road behind the limousine".

Dodds continued. "The rest as they say is history. It was very clever reducing the number of chaser cars by employing two different strategies. We still don't know if they even knew we were there, in any case, they played it as though we were and got away from us. We got road blocks up as soon as possible but they may well have kept going anticipating that move. We are viewing every CCTV system the limo may have passed through after the tunnel, maybe we will catch a break and see them turn or stop. What they are driving by now is a mystery. They seem smart enough to have changed vehicles several times. They certainly know about the Traffic Cameras, but they can't know where every camera is. I am not too optimistic they will make a mistake, but we have to be there to see it if they do. Still waiting for any result Sir".

Commissioner Doug Wilson chimed in; "Of course, I have the Federal Police out looking anywhere they think he might head. My men are shaking informants. We have the State Police in every State and Territory looking for the limousine but as the Brigadier said they would have ditched it soon after they ditched us. We've upped the security alert at every airport, railway and bus depot in the country. We don't want the media to know there is a wanted terrorist in the country who made us look like amateurs by escaping from us."

The senior Police Officer continued. "They will absolutely crucify us without mercy. We have labelled him as a big-time drug smuggler, and we've been circulating his picture through all these agencies and media outlets. We are damned if we do and damned if we don't, we can't keep the story low-key and still expect them to be wanting to run the story, first item page one. Whether the media shove it in their news will depend on what else is happening on that news cycle, how many cats are caught up a tree".

Brigadier Dodds chimed in; "We have our people watching all the usuals, we've increased coverage on anyone known to be even just a little bit sympathetic to terrorist organisations. Or organisations we think might have links with them and of course all the Fundamentalist Moslem groups".

MAJGEN Watson had had enough. "OK, we are better off chasing our people and keeping fires under them than sitting here anymore. Situation Reports every hour or before for anything urgent. I want this mongrel on a chain ASAP. He is here for a reason and that reason is scarier than just his presence in this country, thanks everyone".

Brigadier Dodds returned to his office and collapsed into his large black chair. He had backed the plan to follow Aziz and see what bonus Intel or other contacts they could harvest from this senior Terrorist. This was a high-value target and as with all things of high return, the risks were high as well. That justification did nothing to help the acid feeling that was growing worse in the Brigadier's stomach. He had a fleeting thought about the constant argument regarding refugees having the potential of being terrorists. These thoughts were not racist or without purpose. These principles contributed to the foundations on which this Nation's Government made decisions. How they directed the Armed Forces had a massive impact on his area of responsibility, anti-terrorism intelligence and action.

He had often thought about all this before; he was not an old war horse hoping for an enemy. He loved peace, he loved Australia. With such a high-level terrorist threat closer than ever before he thought he should think through these issues another time. He needed to see whether they were getting it wrong and maybe to see where Australia and policy were heading. Terrorist activity overseas was building every day with bombings, shootings and assassinations becoming a near-daily occurrence. And now we were under attack, that horrific series of bombings on ANZAC Day and now Aziz coming to Australia, what did it all mean? He sat back his sad eyes closed and hoped and prayed that his organisation could stop whatever was coming. Sadly, they were already off to a terrible start.

CHAPTER 19

Aziz had remained very still and very calm all through his ride from the airport. He had been warned of the plan but seeing it happen was an enjoyable if not frightening experience. They still weren't sure they were being followed but if there were infidels set on arresting or killing him they were certainly being made fools of. He was disappointed there had only been five deaths in the tunnel accidents but to Aziz that was like an entrée. Five fewer Australians was a nice starting bonus. If they did know he was there he would have been surprised. It meant that somehow his security had failed because he had expected to slip into the country without anyone noticing. When planning Aziz always thought about what could go wrong. He lived by the rule, that he would hope for the best but always plan for the worst.

He was also deeply committed to the fact Allah Ar-Rahmaan (He Who Wills Goodness and Mercy) was with him as he served Allah in his diverse role. Aziz had faith in this, and to some degree believed that he just couldn't lose. This wasn't a faith that allowed him to be slack or reckless. He believed that Allah gave him wisdom, Allah gave him the strength to continue and Allah gave him answers when he asked for solutions. He was in what the Westerners called a Win/Win situation. If he lived through another mission he was blessed, if he died serving Allah he would go to his great reward, whatever that meant.

They had changed vehicles four times and the latest vehicle was interesting, once again employing the technique of hiding out in the open. They were now rolling down the highway north in an RV Sunliner Motorhome. The irony of the model name of the Motorhome 'HOLIDAY' had not escaped Aziz. He noted the name emblazoned on the side of the shiny white vehicle. This could not have been further from a holiday for him.

He didn't know for sure, but he had been told by the Chauffeur the roads and highways of Australia were full of motorhomes and caravans driven by 'Grey Nomads'. Aziz didn't understand it, but it was a name for retirees who travelled around Australia. Aziz had to admit his Australian agents were sharp at reading the local culture and blending into it. Since he left Sydney there did seem to be a lot of caravans and motorhomes going in both directions. It was also a good security move because Aziz could stay out of sight in transit or during any stops. To avoid nosy tourists and fellow travellers they would not be staying at any Holiday Parks instead they would camp up a country road or behind the bitumen piles of an old Main Road's Maintenance Department camp-site.

The Sunliner Holiday was equipped with its kitchen, toilet and shower so there was little reason for Aziz to ever endanger himself, being seen by having to go to a public bathroom. He felt like an infant depending on a parent for everything and Aziz was well and truly out of his comfort zone. He was unused to being away from familiar surroundings and he was not used to depending on others. Strangers deciding when he did this or did that. The Chauffeur set the schedule for everything, so Aziz felt as if he was a voluntary kidnap victim. He trusted *no one* but Allah and himself. Yet here he was sitting in the four-seater dining area of this Sunliner motorhome not knowing where he was going and not knowing what they would find around each bend of the road. At least he was able to read his beloved Koran.

Aziz could even pray at the appointed times. Although kneeling in a moving vehicle was a challenge, as was facing Mecca when you were constantly changing direction, he had faith that Allah the Merciful knew a man's heart and would forgive these circumstances.

The Chauffeur, Aziz thought to himself; *wait, calling him that didn't seem right anymore, driving a twenty-three-foot motorhome.* The driver was the same man who had picked Aziz up from the airport.

Initially, Aziz questioned the wisdom of having the same driver. Surely his face must now be on the files of the Australian Security Forces and still travelling together must increase the risk of some local Police Officer recognising them. However, the driver had surprised Aziz yet again. He came out of the well-appointed en suite at the rear of the motorhome and was unrecognisable when compared to the young blond man in the blue Chauffeur's peak cap and uniform. He had shaved his head completely and now had a big cowboy-type moustache. Believing most fake moustaches look exactly that, fake, he had started growing it three days before picking up Aziz and although it was still new it was gaining colour and thickness. Aziz was amazed this was enough to change his facial features and his age making him look at least ten years older. Aziz also appreciated the fact the driver was not talkative he had spoken very few words since they had met at the airport. Although Aziz did not know his way to their final destination he had noticed the driver was careful to avoid the cities and bigger towns. Once again, the camouflage of travelling in the Motorhome worked well because this is a common practice for the retired Grey Nomads. Meandering around Australia without an agenda or time constraints. Aziz noted the windows were heavily tinted ensuring his privacy and letting him look out as they drove along and even in a Service Station when the driver was refuelling. Aziz felt like those big fat Americans salivating in front of a hotel buffet. Looking out he could see Australians going about everyday life. The whores going shopping wearing nearly nothing, the weak men following along. This is surely a land of no morals, no faith and no restraint, doomed for judgement but blissfully ignorant of how soon that would be.

At one such stop at a Service Station, the driver was refuelling the Motorhome when a couple came up on the other side of the RV and started peering in the window and kneeling to look underneath the Motorhome. Aziz forgetting, that they could not see through the tinted windows threw himself on the floor thinking the couple were Police of some sort.

Wearing a big smile, the driver walked over to the man and woman. “G'day can I help you?”

The young woman turned towards the driver, “Oh, we are so sorry we didn't mean to intrude. We have always wanted a Motorhome and when we saw yours we both just couldn't stop ourselves from taking a closer look. It sure is a good size”.

The driver smiled again and responded, “Not too big to handle but still with all the comforts of home”.

The husband looking hopeful asked, “I know it's a bit rude mate, but do you think we could have a look inside?”

The driver knew he didn't want to leave a lasting impression on the couple who would remember if questioned by Police by him insulting them or being aggressive. Yet he knew they could never get past that door. “Look I am so sorry my wife has been sick, and she is actually in bed”.

Without hesitation, the interested woman stepped forward a little in front of her husband, “We are so sorry, hope your wife is feeling better soon”. With that the couple returned to their Toyota sedan, still glancing back at the RV and gesturing.

Aziz was still prone on the floor when the driver re-entered the Motorhome. The driver to his credit hid his surprise and showed no smirk or ridicule of the older man's embarrassment at cowering on the blue carpet. Aziz took some reassurance that the couple were not undercover Police. The driver stated he had researched Motorhome life by reading the Australian Motorhome Owner's Club Magazine. He explained people looking and even approaching a Motorhome as this couple had done was a common experience.

Aziz was continually impressed with this Australian driver's casual yet highly skilled approach to everything he did. Once they had entered Queensland he had noticed the thick bush gave way to more sparse woods and eventually just a bit of dry grass. Aziz saw they crossed creek after creek even large rivers with high bridges that were nothing but sandy gullies and ravines. Preparing for this trip Aziz had studied many photos of Australia and had been expecting terrain very similar to home. But so far even the dryer country still must have had some water source because they supported huge grey and white trees and vast fields of crops. He did not realise that further west all this gave way to big sky country and eventually deserts. This country was riddled with the strangest names, some seemed English while others were some other language, full of long words with lots of double RRs and double OOs and MM's. However, it was interesting, but not enough for Aziz to bother to ask the driver for an explanation.

The old desert warrior looked out at the empty flat land, some of it growing watermelons that were the main crop of the area. Other fields were empty except for a few straggly-looking sheep and some bony cattle. He knew where he was heading had some very dry rocky areas mixed with stands of trees that followed the water courses even though they were dry most of the time. The road noise changed and bumped as they crossed yet another bridge and dry creek. Then he saw the large green road sign showing Chinchilla five kilometres, Roma one hundred and eighty-six kilometres. He started feeling a mixture of relief and excitement that he was nearly there. Aziz knew his fate was about to roll out like a beautiful Persian carpet. The thought crossed his mind that he had been born for a time such as this.

The driver had not explained the strategy to Aziz, but he had been maintaining a steady speed of ten kilometres under the speed limit. He knew this frustrated other travellers, but it was standard for these Grey Nomads apparently to save fuel or demonstrate they were in no rush and so made up part of their cover. The other advantage was there was no chance that some Traffic Police would catch the

Motorhome speeding and stumble onto their identity. Accordingly, one hundred and eighty-six kilometres would take nearly two and half hours. Aziz feeling the Motorhome stop put down his well-worn Koran and looked out the heavily tinted window. He saw they had been stopped by a red light, they were in the town of Roma. They were surrounded by a thriving business community of tyre services, mechanical workshops and stores selling everything anyone could ever want. Aziz looked to his left, seething at the symbol of America spreading all over the world like a stain or a virus. There before his eyes was a McDonald's beside their vehicle. Further up there was a Kentucky Fried Chicken.

Roma had sold out just like the rest of the world. The driver refuelled the Motorhome and bought two bottles of Iced Tea. He climbed back into the driver's seat handing one of the drinks through to Aziz in the back and started the engine. Aziz knew he had about another half an hour or so and he would be very close to the cattle property his team had occupied for a little over a year. Aziz was used to travelling long distances, but this last leg of the journey seemed to drag on forever. He was anxious to see the set-up of the Base and the level of preparation the team had so far achieved. As the kilometres rolled by, they entered an area of low rolling hills now well grassed and wooded and with much larger flocks of sheep. There were also groups of some strange-looking grey animals. Aziz was fascinated as the kangaroos sat back on two large back legs and scratched their furry white chests.

The Motorhome slowed after coming over a rise. The driver took a small track off the highway that led down to a dry creek that had thick undergrowth which would eventually hide the track and the Motorhome from the highway. Once out of sight the driver expertly reversed the Motorhome around, so the nose faced the direction they would leave in the morning. Once again, the driver's security awareness impressed the Taliban veteran. Still a man of few words the driver turned to Aziz. "We wait until dark before heading down to the camp, we're nearly there. Get some rest hey?"

Four hours later and about two hours after dark the driver started up the Motorhome and without turning on the lights drove slowly back to the highway. He made sure no vehicles were coming either way before re-entering the highway and switching his headlights on. A few kilometres up the road a sheep paddock spread out on the other side of the highway. It had a small dam shining in the bright full moon. The driver changed down a couple of gears and took a left turn once again making sure there was no one in front or behind to see them turn off. On the right corner of the road, there was a small bus shelter on a cleared area where all the local children were picked up and dropped off by the local school bus. All this was lost on Aziz who was on alert like a gun dog who senses his master is about to shoot a duck or quail.

Aziz's state was broken by the Australian twangy accent of the driver. "The Motorhome can't get right into the place because there are two steep creek crossings, they'll pull this rig's arse off. Someone will meet you this side in a Four-Wheel Drive (4WD)".

Aziz didn't understand the first part of what the driver had said but understood enough to gather his personal belongings. The Motorhome's lights pierced the darkness up ahead showing the road falling away steeply about one hundred metres in front of the vehicle. The driver gently stopped the Motorhome just before the road fell away to the creek crossing. Within a minute or two the darkness was assaulted by lights, at first shining through the tree tops as a 4WD arrived on the other side of the crossing. The small diesel engine of a Land Cruiser could be heard climbing in and out of the creek bed. Turning off the pair of spotlights as it crested the rise a white 4WD slowed. It then continued past the stationary Motorhome before doing a U-turn and pulling in behind the RV. Aziz mumbled a blessing to the driver and hefting his bags walked towards the idling 4WD. He had arrived.

Aziz awoke the next morning, rising before dawn as he always did. He was pleased to see Commander Zahir had located and marked the Qibla with a red dot on the lounge room wall signifying the direction of Mecca. He rolled out his Baluchi Prayer Rug made by the Baloch people of the southwest of his homeland. The older man knelt beside Zahir who had his forehead touching the floor and together commenced Al-Fayr (Dawn Prayers). Aziz thought it's good to be amongst devout people again, this is where our strength comes from. After completing the two obligatory Rakaahs, Aziz asked Allah to further bless this camp, the soldiers and staff and most importantly the mission.

Out on the verandah, they had a traditional but simple Afghani breakfast which Aziz enjoyed immensely after all the other food he had encountered on his long journey.

Aziz took another sip of coffee and turning to Zahir asked. "Zahir, my driver who was he?"

Zahir looking up from his plate smiled. "He is one of the Cadre Staff here. He is a bit strange. You hardly hear a word from him. He doesn't have the appearance of a seasoned warrior, but he is very smart, good with the men, and is an expert in the use of small arms".

Aziz nodded wisely. "He was very impressive in his duties as a driver evading any followers we may have had. And he never ceased in maintaining security by employing numerous strategies that were very clever".

Zahir knew he needed to impress his newly arrived superior. "Ah yes he is a good man, Major Smith and I sat at this very table for many hours thinking through the entire exercise of your transport to here. I must say Smith and his team are first class. Of course, they are still Infidels but seem committed to our plans."

Aziz sneered at this, "Or at least the money we are paying them hey?

Aziz was looking forward to a tour of the Training Camp, so far if the driver was any indication these Australian Cadre Staff were very good at what they did. When he had arrived at the camp last night after leaving the Motorhome, Aziz had met with Group Commander Abdul Zahir. They had shared coffee on the verandah of the old farmhouse which was their HQ and accommodation. Aziz had been the one who had selected Zahir for this mission after he had found out about Zahir's battle history and had spoken to several Taliban Leaders that Aziz had known for many years. So far Zahir's selection looked to be a good decision, Aziz would confirm this after he had inspected the training facility. It sounded like the training had progressed well, but Aziz would only believe that when he saw the soldiers in action.

Major Smith an Ex-Australian Army Officer was coordinating the training, but he would be away for a few days as he was carrying out further reconnaissance of several potential attack sites. Once all this recon had been carried out and the plans confirmed, the operation would be launched in full. A day he eagerly awaited more than any other day of his life. As light started to fill the Eastern sky the two men began their tour of the training camp.

Zahir explained. “We are very conscious of being observed by satellite, fortunately, Major Smith knows the satellite pass times, so we make sure no outside training is occurring when the satellite is overhead”.

As he said this they arrived at their first stop; the rifle range was built into the wall of the large dam in the paddock south of the farmhouse. You had to stand where the shooters stood before realising the function of the site. The dam wall was just like every dam wall and had very little vegetation. The dirt backdrop to the range appeared to be a normal dam surrounded chopped up by cattle moving in and out. The vertical targets were nearly impossible to detect from above, set close to each other and in a straight line. From the satellite, these would appear to be a small fence of some sort probably placed there by the farmer attempting to reduce erosion damage by re-directing the stock to another area of the dam. This successfully achieved the appearance of the usual day-to-day actions carried out on farms everywhere. Even though completely out in the open there was no chance a satellite photo would pick it up. As they drove along Zahir waved across the windscreen. "As you can see the property is still stocked with red and black Angus cattle to make sure curious neighbours or suppliers in town didn't start asking questions. Of course, the cattle would appear on any satellite photos adding to our cover".

When they stopped at the next training venue Aziz could not see what they were supposed to be inspecting. Until Zahir began to show him the features many of the sites were virtually invisible.

It was an obstacle course built from natural barriers such as fallen trees, a small creek, ant mounds and a series of boulders set out randomly. These were combined with the most normal-looking things you would expect to see lying out in a paddock, things like piles of barbed wire and stacked-up fence posts, once again from the air or a satellite all but invisible. Back near the house, there were several outbuildings and sheds, Zahir pulled the Land Cruiser up outside the first building of grey galvanised steel sheet construction on its walls and roof. There was an old tractor parked near one wall and some rusty forty-four-gallon drums on the other side of the entrance. As Zahir pulled back the iron door to the shed it complained bitterly at having to move. Zahir then ushered Aziz over the threshold. Aziz was amazed to find himself looking at another doorway ahead of him that strongly resembled either the airport or a shopping mall entrance.

Zahir seeing the puzzlement on Aziz's face started to explain. "We built these facades to provide the soldiers with real experiences. We thought this was especially important considering all these men have never seen an airport or a shopping centre. We were concerned they would be overwhelmed or maybe couldn't even find the automatic doors. They are good servants of Allah but goat herders when all is said and done."

Aziz, a man not easily impressed, once again was so pleased to be surrounded by thoughtful practical men such as these. Later sipping mint tea, the two leaders sat on the cool wide verandah that in the past had seen the previous owners relax the same way. However, instead of discussing the weather and beef prices these new owners discussed death and destruction on a scale never seen in Australian history.

The terrorist leader had conceived the initial plan and although he had never been a husband or a father he thought it must be similar to awaiting the arrival of a baby. His plan was near to birth. Aziz and Zahir used the wall of the verandah where they set up a chart. The basics maths were that they had sixty men, no, fifty-seven men who they would divide into twelve attack teams. These small teams would simultaneously hit twelve key targets around Australia. After the bombings last month Australia was already reeling and the shock that terrorism had finally come to this 'lucky country' was beginning to sink in on every level.

Aziz would record and distribute to all the media groups a video message claiming responsibility and making demands for the Prime Minister to order all Australian troops to be withdrawn from all Moslem countries, especially Afghanistan. It didn't matter how strong a leader he was, he and his Cabinet would quickly buckle when he saw the pictures of the carnage. The dead and wounded would cause the people of Australia to demand that he accept their demands. Aziz was very happy with what he had seen so far. The camp was better than he had dared to dream, but he hadn't seen his soldiers in action yet. However, Commander Zahir had said a special demonstration was planned for that afternoon. They would enjoy sharing Al-Zohr (midday prayers) and then some more simple but wonderful Afghan dishes.

After lunch, the two leaders sat on the verandah smoking their Hookah (a pipe using water to cool the smoke) and drinking strong sweet black coffee.

Zahir turned to Aziz who was just putting the mouthpiece of the Hookah back on the table "Major Smith will be back this afternoon, he's expected in around 1500 Hours and once he gets here we will get the men out and you can see them in action".

The older man was still at a loss as to where the sixty or, so men were. He had been in the training camp for over twenty hours and seen no one except Zahir and the household staff. He had assumed that there must be a barracks hidden away somewhere away from the main camp. Aziz had asked Zahir several times and was very aware he had never received a proper answer. Somehow Zahir had changed the subject or re-directed Aziz each time. Back in Afghanistan, he would not have tolerated this for a moment, but the Commander had impressed him so much that he was prepared to wait, hoping there was a good reason for this ploy. Aziz was very interested in this Major Smith. Smith, even Aziz knew that name in the West usually meant it wasn't his real name. He didn't care in any case, so far this Smith or whoever he was had done a good job converting a cattle property into a quality training centre. A working terrorist training camp that appeared to be undetectable from the air or satellite and to some degree when you stood in front of it was a great achievement.

The old desert fighter was pragmatic about his attitude towards Smith. It was unusual to use a non-believer, but you hired the skills you needed where you could find them. But Aziz still saw Major Smith as nothing more than a traitor betraying his faith, his country and his Army. He like all mercenaries served one thing and that was money, American Dollars he didn't even want his own country's currency. It had been decided that an Ex Australian Army Officer was needed as a local expert. However, he had also shown himself as invaluable in his contribution to the establishment of this facility and from what Commander Zahir had told Aziz about the realism and effectiveness of the training.

Zahir was nowhere to be found, so Aziz knelt on the prayer rug for Al-Asr (afternoon prayers) and after the obligatory four Rakaahs (set prayers), he again humbly beseeched Allah the Merciful to give this mission victory over the unbelieving infidels and to give him wisdom in all things. Aziz finished his prayer time happy that he could get back into his usual spiritual routine that travel had disrupted.

Zahir arrived back and joined Aziz for another smoke and several sweet coffees. Their conversations were never social or menial, Aziz's nature was all business, and he had no desire for friendship. Even with a good man and servant such as Zahir, he was still his Leader and he must maintain a distance from him and fuel a type of fear that commands respect and obedience. As often as possible they discussed different targets, different scenarios, and escape plans and identified possible Rendezvous (RVs). They may have discussed escape plans, RVs and transport arrangements for their soldiers after their missions but they both knew there would be no escape. It was highly unlikely that any of these brave young martyrs would survive their missions or ever return to their homeland. These attack teams knew no more than what Aziz was prepared to let the Australian authorities access. They were mindless weapons nothing more. As these thoughts crossed Aziz's mind there was a sound of a vehicle approaching the house. Aziz noted, that Zahir who never went anywhere without his sidearm in a shoulder holster and an AK nearby, reached for his rifle and subtly drew it a little closer.

CHAPTER 20

Yet another white Land Cruiser came into view, this one a utility, sliding sideways around the last little bend in the gravel road leading up to the house.

Zahir visibly relaxed; "That would be Major Smith. He loves to drive fast and arrive with a touch of drama".

Aziz fought the urge to stand. He chose to sit and wait to make Major Smith approach him rather than meeting him like some returning hero. Zahir was glad to see Major Smith. They had grown close over the last two months working closely to drag Zahir's soldiers into the twenty-first century. He also liked the Major, he didn't know his first name as the Major preferred to be called Smithy by his peers and Sir or Major by anyone else. With that in mind, Zahir introduced Aziz to Major Smith and sensed the initial pressure in the atmosphere. It wasn't a social occasion and neither man wanted the other as a new friend, so no one gave the other permission to make the titles more casual.

Aziz, ever the one to try to take and maintain the initiative addressed the Major first; "Major I must compliment you on your contribution here, impressive to say the least".

The Major was too experienced to put a lot of store in such compliments. Turning towards the older man, he asked "Were you happy with the driver who brought you here? He is Ex-Special Air Services (SAS) and has been my aide since getting out, he's been with me in a lot of scrapes".

Aziz for all his old-world feel and seniority was also good at getting people to drop their guard. Uncharacteristically, he responded using humour to establish rapport with Major Smith. "He was wonderful Major except that he talks so much". Smith knew his aide well enough to know he was a man of few words and realised that Aziz was making a joke. Both men laughed breaking the stiffness of the meeting and reducing the pressure by at least half.

Major Smith smiled at this fellow warrior, "Have you worked out where the men are?"

Aziz looked puzzled. "No, I haven't, I assumed they must be barracked somewhere else on the property".

The Major was enjoying having the initiative. "Watch this". As he spoke he pressed a remote control he had in his pocket. There was a loud metallic click followed by the whirring sound of an electric motor.

Aziz followed Smith's and Zahir's expectant gaze but all he could see was a very large stump that was perhaps a metre high and at least the same in diameter. It was in the very centre of the turnaround area that fed the house, cattle yards and surrounding sheds. He had walked around it several times stretching his legs and getting some country air. Located in a bare area of probably half a football field it was the only thing left standing, Aziz assumed that it was so big it was easier just to leave it there. It stood out on the small man-made gravel plain but being a stump seemed perfectly natural. Aziz was astounded to see the top of the stump open like the lid of a box hinged at the far side from where they were now standing.

As soon as the door of the stump opened a man appeared fully kitted out in the familiar Russian battle fatigues. He was wearing a tactical vest and carried an AK74M.

Aziz was no stranger to hiding in caves and burying weapons and explosives and other stores in caches, but he was stunned by this display. He couldn't believe his eyes, the first man climbed higher then sprung to the ground and ran to his right where he stood at attention looking directly to his front, weapon across his chest in the high port position. Aziz was not used to Taliban soldiers displaying such military discipline. They were voluntary guerrilla fighters recruited from the villages, they fought like tigers, but they weren't trained military. As this assessment of the first man flew through Aziz's mind a second, then a third soldier appeared followed by more and more, the same actions repeated.

One at a time they climbed up, jumped down to the ground and formed three ranks around the first man. In just a few minutes there were two platoons of three ranks of ten men standing in parade formation in front of the three Leaders. When Aziz was young he had trained with the Iraqi Army, so he understood Army practices. He could see that the men in front of him were well trained, well equipped and motivated. They had moved on from goat herders with guns to real soldiers.

Aziz nodded appreciatively turning to Zahir and Smith smiling, "Congratulations are in order and the proof is in the eating as they say. I can see these men have changed. You have transformed them into weapons of destruction, well done".

Major Smith responded; "Thank you, Sir, if it is OK, we don't like to stand on parade in the daytime too long, so I will send them off to their assigned training areas".

It was more a statement than a request but done respectfully and of course, Aziz understood that sixty-plus armed men including the Cadre Staff would make an interesting satellite photo if they were caught standing out in the open. Aziz had noticed there were four Westerners standing off to one side, one of them his driver.

Smith saw the direction of his gaze. "They are Senior Cadre Staff, my own handpicked men, those four specialists have been doing a lot of the hands-on training. With a nod from Major Smith, the Cadre moved the soldiers off in formation, not like some reviewing parade but efficiently just the same.

Commander Zahir looked like a proud father whose son had just scored the winning goal; "Would you like to see the barracks? they are quite interesting?"

Aziz simply nodded. He had never considered going to Disneyland or some such place, but he nearly had that childlike twinkle in his eyes as he moved off towards the stump. He appreciated intelligence, security and creativity and this camp seemed to have that as its consistent theme. Major Smith had disappeared again as was his style, always checking something. Aziz once again thought what a fine Officer Smith must have been before he betrayed his country. Someone had placed a small step ladder in front of the stump in preparation for Aziz's inspection.

Zahir stepped aside and with a sweep of his hand ushered Aziz up the short ladder. "As you get to the top you will see handrails, grab them, turn and climb down".

The two Leaders climbed down twenty or so steps into a well-lit white cement-lined cave. Zahir explained. "One of the reasons we selected this particular cattle property was the presence of underground caves. We have turned this one into an invisible, bomb-proof barracks that can accommodate sixty men comfortably and one hundred for a short time if needed."

Zahir continued. "The beauty of the stump entrance is there are no tracks or trampled areas, no obvious diggings or changes to surroundings to be compared with last month's satellite photos from above or if someone drove in say by mistake they would see nothing out of the ordinary.

Even the truck that comes every few months to pick up a load of steers simply sees a hundred-year-old dirt road leading into a turning area used by trucks and vehicles every day."

The Commander proudly explained to Aziz. "As you see the barracks are basic but you and I, and all of these men have lived in far worse conditions back home. Besides, we are not running a resort".

Aziz smiled in agreement. He was committed to looking after his men but always believed if you pampered soldiers they grew soft, so he liked what he heard from Zahir.

The Commander sensing that he was impressing his Leader, continued. “They train up top and live down here. Mess (dining room), kitchen, bunks and prayer rooms, everything they need. There is a huge ventilation system to remove stale air and smells through large fans hidden on the surface”.

The old fighter asked.” Zahir, is the stump the only way in or out?”

Zahir just shook his head in equal amounts of gratefulness and approval that his Leader, who he must trust with everything including his life, was so astute as to ask this question.

Any facility with only one door is highly vulnerable to attack as the enemy must only block one door and the fort, the strongroom, or in this case the barracks becomes a trap. Then all the enemy has to do is starve you out. Zahir smiled “pointing towards the rear of the second Prayer Room, there is a hidden exit behind that carpet hanging on the wall. No one is allowed to use it without being commanded to do so, and that command will only be made if we are under attack. We have done this as the tunnel from it leads to an area of grassed bushland on the northern side of the house paddock. If we used the rear exit regularly the grass would become worn down and it would be an obvious scar on a satellite photo”.

On hearing the answer to his question Aziz thought to himself surely Allah the Merciful had blessed me with good men and this he saw as a sign of the mission is just as blessed. “Very good Commander, this facility is exceptional”.

Commander Zahir and Aziz climbed the ladder back to the surface, the bright sunshine causing them both to squint until their eyes fully adjusted to the glare. They then proceeded to the Land Cruiser and headed out of the house paddock down to the training areas. Sitting in the 4WD Aziz witnessed the men of one of the Platoons going through the obstacle course. Zahir pointed to the course saying. “The men do this course at least twice a day. The run is designed so that the soldier can approach each obstacle in several different ways and therefore to some degree still be challenged by it even after completing an alternative way".

Aziz could see that the men were exceptionally fit, highly mobile and oozing confidence. There was no hesitation and there was also a sense that they would overcome any obstacle. The terrorist leader was pleased to see how well the soldiers worked together in the parts of the course that required teamwork to get the entire section of ten men through or over some barrier. He noted that creative solutions were being employed to get the group through.

Zahir then drove the 4WD down to the Rifle Range. Aziz noticed and understood immediately that this was not a usual Army Training Range where soldiers were trained and practised how to shoot at ranges up to a thousand metres plus. With the mission at hand, there was no need to train the soldiers to shoot from long distances.

Their targets were going to be no more than fifty metres or so away from the shooters.

Each soldier would be using an AK74 on full auto looking to maximise the killing and wounding of as many targets as possible. They would not even take the time to aim properly. The targets were set up at random distances and rigged so they would turn around or pop up, some would move left to right while others right to left. Aziz did not miss the fact that the targets were not the usual cutouts of soldiers but of civilian men, women and children, solid preparation for the mission to come. In addition to training the soldiers to engage moving, standing and sitting civilian targets, the other training objectives on the range were for other purposes namely, each soldier had become comfortable with loading, firing and fixing any jams that may occur. They had been trained for a specific mission and appeared to be ready.

Next, the two men drove to the Reality Training Shed where Aziz had visited earlier. Aziz was ushered into the building to a safe observation point where he saw squad after squad come through self-opening glass doors similar to those entering a shopping mall of a large department store.

Commander Zahir spoke quietly. "We have seen them on the range. This is a type of simulator to practice them in how it may look, where to stand and so on".

Once inside, the small teams of soldiers took their places without duplication or any confusion. Each knew where they were to stand to maximise their arcs of fire. From these positions, they would fire one magazine of blank cartridges while aiming at a variety of targets within their designated kill zone. Once that mag was empty they would immediately put in a fresh mag and resume firing. Being inside a building there was far more smoke, and the noise was incredible preparing each man for the task they would be called upon to complete.

Proudly Zahir stated. "They were unbelievably slow at this when we first started but as you see they are now very smooth and fast."

This training coupled with the live firing at the range had made these soldiers into near robots. Programmed to enter, spread out across the shops, remove their weapon hidden under a coat or perhaps in a large carry bag and fire. Aziz observed that without any communication these attacks were beautifully coordinated with no one firing until all shooters were in place and ready to unleash hell. Acknowledging they could not build sets for every scenario there was also a lecture room with whiteboards and magnet boards used for working through set movements and firing for other target areas. The groups discussed things they would encounter in shopping centres or train stations, specifics such as lifts and escalators. There were pictures of such target sites showing the layout of large department or clothing stores, railway entrances and platforms, as well as airport check-in areas. The cadre staff slowly and systematically went through these blown-up pictures and photos showing each location and explaining the item's function and characteristics. Aziz was now confident his men had received exceptional training and mission-specific preparation. Specially vital for good men from a primitive country that didn't have city trains and shopping centres and all the technology that comes with such civilisation. The training would continue right up to mission time. For now, he and Zahir with Major Smith's input would plan each mission in detail. Once that was done the twelve teams would be transported to the target area and at the same time, on the same date, Australia would feel the wrath of Allah and the Taliban for invading Afghanistan and killing its fathers and sons. It would be a glorious day. From his initial ideas had come the seed for the wonderful work Zahir, Smith, his team and the Taliban Warriors had achieved. Allah Al-Fattah (The Victory Giver) was with them and with Allah's blessing who could stand against them.

CHAPTER 21

ENOGGERA ARMY BARRACKS
BRISBANE
QUEENSLAND

Colonel Jim Walsh was up to his neck in paperwork. He sometimes wondered if promotion was really worth it. It seemed that the 80/20% ratio of action/paperwork had steadily reversed the higher in rank that he got. He was glad to have an excuse to stop when his phone rang. But his happiness was short-lived when he saw the call was from his friend at the NSC, Colonel Peter Goodrich. This was because he expected it to mean the information was rejected as useless and don't call us we'll call you speech.

Goodrich sounded happy enough. "Hi Jim, weather any better today, mate?"

Walsh on the other hand sounded very pissed off. "Yeah, it's friggin great, not that I get to see or feel it I'm stuck inside doing yearly personnel reports. And you know what it's like in these days of political correctness, you have to sound encouraging, can't hurt any of my little princess's feelings can we".

From his Canberra office at the NSC HQ, the Colonel continued. "Well you sound like you are having a bad day so I'm sorry I am probably not going to make it any better mate".

"Pete if this is about Captain Wallace's Roma report I know you would have done the right thing, how did it go?"

"Jim the boss listened and was keen but there just wasn't enough to go on. I'll keep an eye out for anything that comes through. But with CHOGM coming up in a few months you can imagine how crazy it is around here".

This was no surprise to Walsh, he had expected even less interest. "Mate, I totally understand. Pete, I appreciate you trying.

Goodrich attempted to make his friend feel a little better. "I hope it rains in Brisbane when you come down next week, let me know the details and I'll meet your plane, talk soon Jim".

With that, the call ended. Jim Walsh looked out his window briefly and then turned and dialled Steve Wallace's mobile. There was no answer, but he didn't leave a message, that wouldn't be fair.

CATTLE PROPERTY
OUTSIDE ROMA QLD.

I'd been looking after a mate's cattle property while they were overseas for three months. One of my duties was to check on some dams and pumps way out the back of the property. Soon after dawn, Jake my dog and I had headed out there on my quad and by eleven o'clock I'd had enough. Jake had just irrigated another tank stand marking his territory the best way he knew how.

I tapped the carry tray of my quad bike. Jake jumped up and settled in for the trip back to camp. Up ahead I saw a large boar running parallel to the track about a hundred metres off to the right.

I took my Remington Pump out of the rifle bucket on my quad and stopped as the huge pig slowed to go under a barbed-wire fence. The rifle bucked into my shoulder sending the 308WIN projectile on its way catching the old pig just behind the left foreleg and entering his chest area destroying his heart and lungs, he cartwheeled into a log, twitched twice and never moved again. This gave me a sense of satisfaction. On my rounds, I had passed through the adjacent paddock where we were running some sheep that were lambing. I had found heartbreaking evidence that a large pig had killed and eaten several lambs and part of one unfortunate adult sheep that couldn't get up after delivering her twin lambs. This marauder would never harm another sheep or calf again. My mind was filled with thoughts of a coffee and some late breakfast as I got close to camp. Slowing, I parked the bike next to a big old blood-wood tree and dismounted. Jake jumped off and looked for his water bowl.

Checking the time on my phone I saw there was a missed call from Colonel Jim. I was anxious to find out how my report had gone so I phoned the Colonel before anything else. Once again, I struck his aide, thankfully my credentials must have been OK now as he didn't ask any questions and put me through after a short wait. The Colonel was used to controlling meetings and conversations however, I could hear in his voice that he was uncomfortable taking this call and I figured he was about to pass on to me the thanks but no thanks message.

"Hey Steve boy I am flat out like a one-legged man in a butt-kicking contest, so I'll come straight to the point. Now, this is going to sound like a brush-off, but it isn't that we didn't try. My mate at the National Security Centre (NSC) took it up to the Brigadier but there is too much going on there. They are up to their armpits in getting ready for CHOGM and just couldn't do anything with the info you passed through".

Colonel Walsh continued. "Can't tell you what to do anymore Steve but just like the old days if one of your boys came to you with enough Intel to prick your interest but not enough to act on, what would you do? We both know you'd send 'em right back out there to get some more info, maybe answer some questions, collect some evidence like photos or something solid".

I felt a bit sorry for the Colonel. Uncharacteristically, he was talking very fast and not letting me say anything. I could tell he thought I would blame him for my report being ignored. "Sir I knew when I gave you that Intel it was a bit weird and light on. I wasn't even sure if I believed it so anything you've done is a bonus to me and I really appreciate your help with it. I just hope trying hasn't harmed you or your mate in any way".

With a loud sigh, I could sense the Colonel relax a little. "Oh Steve, I'm glad you see it that way and understand how things work".

"Sir you might be right about not being able to give me orders anymore but as usual you are right on target about what I need to do."

There was little point in prolonging this call. "Leave it all with me, Sir, and I'll keep in touch. I might end up going back over there and taking a second look. I'll give it some thought, Colonel. Talk to you then".

The Colonel knew Steve was too good an officer not to investigate these strange occurrences. "OK son, you take care, if you are thinking of going in again remember working without backup or evac or bloody anything could get a bit hairy. If you do take a second look and there is something more to it, let me know how you get on".

With that, the call was terminated. I sat on my camp chair looking at the cold fire from last night. I had a lot on my mind, one thing was trying to figure out why I had such an uneasy feeling. I had done my time in the Military and now I could finally enjoy some hunting, some drinking and doing absolutely nothing if that's what I choose to do so why was I complicating my life with all this. OK, that was my pity party and the party was over, so let's move on. I began to think about what I was about to do. Making the decision that I was going to do something made me feel better than I had for a long time. Jake was worrying the bag of dog food, so I went over and fed him, reminding myself that I was still hungry. I built the fire up again and got it going well enough to cook a good feed of sausages and eggs. I would have loved it all on toast, but I had run out of bread a week ago. It still hit the spot as I washed it down with a strong black coffee and all was well with the world again. It was 1600 Hours, but I knew I had a long night ahead of me, so I hit the sack. All through my time in the Military, I was always able to set my internal alarm clock, I decided what time I would wake to give myself time to get my gear organised. Tonight, I would once again cross that dirt road and then Recce the property that was so well guarded. Then I would try to find out what was really going on across at the neighbours.

At 2100 Hours I awoke, had another coffee and systematically set up my gear ready for the Recce of the cattle property where I had encountered the two Talibs. I put on my darkest camouflage paint, even though I was sure there would be virtually no moon tonight, it is spectacular how a white face shines at night. I waited until 2300 Hours and moved slowly across the gravel road. One of the guys I had killed had kindly donated a pair of Talib boots that fitted me, I had kept these with such a patrol in mind. I was still unsure whether they had sensor plates dug in along the boundary, but I was sure they wouldn't have any on the dirt tracks that crisscrossed the whole property because the normal comings and goings would set them off all day long.

Wearing the Talib boots I would leave boot prints on the tracks but I was banking on them thinking they had been made by their own sentries or patrols at some time. I had decided not to use my Night Vision Goggles (NVGs) because I wanted to be quiet. With all these low bushes and fallen timber, I was sure to fall over some branch and make a heap of noise due to the restricted field of vision the goggles provided. Without the moon, I was able to travel along the dirt tracks which were also quieter and quicker. Moving along the gravel path I opened my mouth slightly as this aids hearing.

I was taking three or four steps at a time stopping and listening, staying to the side of the track ready to jump off into a shadow if anything spooked me.

I knew where the farmhouse was having been there a couple of years back when the old owners lived there. Following the dirt road, I travelled past the spot where my stag and the two Taliban had died. The deer was well and truly decomposing, the stench hanging like a blanket as I walked the track near it. Having crossed the first open paddock, I disturbed a herd of grazing kangaroos who certainly didn't expect any humans walking around in the middle of the night. However, they only moved about fifty metres and settled back to eating the grass again. I was glad to get across the clearing and pulled up in the darkness offered by a stand of trees. I stood at the side of the track and looked around and waited to see if I had been detected.

All was quiet. From what I could remember the farmhouse was just around the next bend, about another kilometre or so further on. So, I left the track and very slowly made my way through the bush towards the house. I took the chance that most of the sensors if they were installed, would all be near the boundaries not this close to the farmhouse.

Coming around a thick stand of eucalyptus I could see a halo of light off to my left but still in the distance, I closed my left eye preserving my night vision. Your eye contains chemicals called visual purple that enable us to see to some degree with limited light. These chemicals are affected by light which is why you can't see if you are in total darkness and a light is shone in your eyes. The soldiers learned in Vietnam to walk on night patrols with one eye shut so that if a trip flare went off they could still see to shoot and move to a safe position. Otherwise like a deer in the headlights they couldn't see a thing until the eye chemicals got their act together. Slowly I continued towards where I thought the house should be. As I climbed a small rise I saw that all the lights were on in the house.

Over to the right was what most farms call the tractor and implement shed which is a high pole tin-roofed structure with a dirt floor and no walls. Strangely, instead of tractors and slashers and post-hole diggers in this shed, there were at least twenty Quad Bikes painted in a camouflage pattern. I could see that each Quad had two rifle buckets one on either side. Every farm has a handful of Quads these days, sadly in some ways, they have replaced the horse in most cases. So, having a few quads wasn't unusual, but having twenty plus all set up with rifle buckets that's different, especially two rifle buckets.

A Jackaroo (male cattle worker), probably wouldn't have one, let alone be set up for an armed passenger as well. I slowly took out my Canon Power Shot G7 a great little camera. Back at camp, I had removed the flash battery to ensure that nothing could illuminate me accidentally as I took photos. I couldn't drag around my favourite Canon EOS Digital SLR, it was great for taking long shots of wildlife and scenery but was just too bulky and heavy for this sort of work.

I hadn't expected so much light. Surely if you were up to no good you wouldn't have lights on all night. Farmers haven't changed, early to rise and so on.

I moved into a perfect spot to observe the gravel turning circle in front of the old weatherboard farmhouse. Old farms had big cleared areas, plenty of turning room for cattle trucks and tractors with hay trailers and so on. I hadn't been inside, but the home probably consisted of three or four small bedrooms, a big kitchen, a small dining room and a lounge. And like nearly all Australian farm houses the roof extended past the sides of the house making a wide verandah providing shade for all the doors and windows plus a place to spend time during the heat of the day. Sometimes families would even sleep out on the hardwood verandah when it was hot at night trying to benefit from any breeze that might arise. I surveyed the rest of the layout; there were the cattle yards, the fence standing nearly seven feet high to ensure some terrified steer didn't jump the rails and injure itself or some farm worker. The original hardwood yards had now been replaced with shiny galvanised steel. It all looked pretty standard, complete with a crush for holding a beast when carrying out some function such as spraying for parasites or fitting identifying ear tags and so on.

There was the usual loading ramp pointing up to meet the gate height of trucks that came to take the cattle to market. Except for the number of Quads, I started to feel a little letdown, I wasn't sure what I had expected to find but it all looked pretty much like any well-established cattle property around here. I knew concentrating and searching especially at night was taxing on your mind and your eyes, so as I had been trained to do I closed my eyes and steadied my breathing and then heart rate. After a minute or two a whirring sound started, opening my eyes I turned my head towards the direction of the sound. I slowly moved towards the noise, taking two or three steps at a time I moved without a sound. The whirring was getting louder as I approached its source. I knew by the noise I must be near it but in the dark, I tripped over whatever was making the whirring sound. I was annoyed at myself for being so clumsy. It was so dark you couldn't see your hand if you held it up to your face, but I wasn't about to use my torch even though it had the usual red tactical lens. I had learnt long ago that even this glowed incredibly, especially on a night like tonight. I held out my hand trying to touch the object and interpret what I was feeling in the pitch black. It seemed to be a curved metallic surface and warm to my fingertips sticking out from my black tactical gloves. It was maybe half a metre or two feet high in the old money.

I decided to run my hand around the circumference of it to get some idea of the size, I did this and guessed it was about the size of the average household spa pool. Carefully I moved my hand up the vertical part of the mystery object finding a wire mesh shield of some sort I could feel hot air blowing quite strongly from below my position. *Of course,* it was some sort of ventilator shaft with a massive extraction fan. OK, a little more information without any explanation. I didn't bother taking any photos it was just too dark, I would draw a diagram back at camp. I decided to return to my original Observation Post (OP) above the house yard. When you are moving around the bush at night going slowly is the only way to keep the noise down.

If you move too quickly you will make more noise and probably fall over, in any case, making it worse, injury or detection resulting. Hopefully, that wouldn't happen tonight, I took it very slowly. It was so dark you felt like it was pressing into your body.

That was OK. Darkness was exactly what I needed on a mission like this. As though someone had read my mind about the lights blazing so late into the night, with a loud click the shed housing the Quads was thrown into total darkness. The yellow verandah lights from the house were still on but the Quad shed was shaded from them by a row of bushy fruit trees along the small wire fence surrounding the house yard. Then all the lights on the verandah were extinguished leaving just one bulb glowing in the home, throwing the gravel turning circle in front of the house and yards into darkness.

Once again, a loud metallic clunk shattered the peace of the inky night. There was a faint movement that seemed to appear like a shadow from nowhere. This then became a ghostly shape of a man. As I watched, one figure became two and then three and in no time at all, there were at least ten or twelve men standing in two ragged lines in the dark. No one was speaking, no one was smoking, and no one was moving, they were just standing there. I've seen enough soldiers in the dark to recognise what I was looking at. These were men in bush uniforms. Occasionally a small reflection from the house lights revealed the unmistakable curved magazine of an AK machine gun.

Hiding in the shadow of a large gum tree I lay motionless for some time. It was heading towards dawn and as usual the last couple of hours before sunrise got colder and colder. With the soldiers so close and facing where I was lying, I had to trust my camouflage and my choice of hiding spot. It seemed to be OK, so far. However, just like that stag, movement can be a lethal enemy whether you are the sniper or the target. If you move you will probably be seen, so I remained perfectly still.

As cold as I was I had been trained to stay motionless for hours and to direct warmth to certain areas of my body. So, I waited, and I waited. About twenty minutes later I heard a noise over my left shoulder and saw a squad of soldiers walking in. Not marching but maintaining some order, and, except for the occasional scuffing on the gravel road, making virtually no noise.

They appeared tired and could not be described as sharp or alert, but they were showing that their fatigue had not translated into slackness. I had seen this happen many times in the first Infantry Unit I had been posted to as a brand-new Second Lieutenant after graduating from Officer Cadet School Portsea, Victoria. I figured out the tired squad were the night shift sentries and the squad standing before me was there to relieve them and start patrolling the property. As I watched I felt a strange sensation across the back of my calves, a weight was resting on the backs of my legs and a pulling rubbing feeling moved from my left to my right leg. To my horror, I realised it was a snake and by the weight a very large snake, probably a Brown, one of the most venomous snakes in the world.

With the arrival of the second squad, I now had twenty or so well-armed soldiers in front of me, ten looking my way but so far not seeing me. My moving away from the snake wasn't an option. In any case, if the snake sensed my legs moving it would attack interpreting such close movement as an assault on itself. I could only concentrate even more on not moving and held my breath so even my rib cage was still. Thankfully I felt the large snake's weight disappear from my legs as his pointy tail flicked over my right leg. I breathed in a cold breath and wondered how long I would have to stay hidden with so many enemy troops so close to my position.

I had seen a thousand sentry or guard changes, the fresh squad replacing the soldiers who had just completed their shift, and this one was taking longer than most. Once the group that had come down the road to the area in front of the house got closer, the squad waiting became more animated. With the coming light of dawn, I was starting to feel vulnerable, to say the least, if these guys could swap over quickly I would have just enough darkness to slither back into the bush and return to my camp. Sadly, they kept taking their time and as with all dawns it seemed to gain some sort of momentum like a rock rolling down a hillside, it was nearly too late to move. The old sentries had what we might call a hand-over meeting, which normally shouldn't take very long. Once that was completed the new sentries headed off down the track. I assumed they would drop off two soldiers at a time to take their assigned positions and patrol their areas of operation (AO) until the end of their shift. I was watching the soldiers walking away from the turning area using my eyes, not daring to move my head even slowly. I was concentrating on the new guard as they would be passing very close to my position.

Suddenly, there was a loud metallic clunk causing me to flick my eyes back to the large open area wondering what had caused the noise. I could not understand what I was seeing as one of the soldiers handed his weapon to his colleague and bent to the sandy ground near a large stump. He appeared to dig a little with his hands shaking something while still on the ground then he stood. In his hands, he was holding a short ladder of some kind. In the growing light, I could not see what was before me. He then leaned this ladder against an old stump in the middle of the turnaround in front of the house. I then realised the top of the stump had opened like the top of a can of spaghetti bending back. To my astonishment, one by one the soldiers wearily climbed down the little ladder. Once they reached the top, they turned and reaching down as a submariner would when entering the cabin, disappeared into the stump.

I then realised that was how the relief squad had seemed to appear from nowhere in the pre-dawn darkness. They too had come up and out of this stump.

I took as many photos as I could as they entered the stump. I was thinking: *as soon as the last man disappears down that stump I can withdraw into the bush.* I had no concerns about snakes because if you are moving you are making vibrations they sense and will in most cases keep out of your way. In any case, after a lifetime spent in the Australian bush you get used to all the snakes and lizards and scorpions. Just as the last man descended into the stump the front door of the farmhouse flew open flooding a yellow light into the thin dawn glow. Two men walked onto the verandah both dressed in Army fatigues, each had the bearing of a Leader, an Officer, one man appeared to be somewhat older than the other.

Thinking my Recce had finished I had stowed my camera away, so I slowly undid my cargo pocket button and withdrew it. I took four quick photos of the men, zooming in as far as the Canon would go. The men then went back inside, and I saw them kneel down. I then realised they were commencing their Al-Fayr (Dawn Prayers). Looking back at the door my view of the men praying was blocked by a tall man with broad shoulders and close-cropped dark hair who stood in the doorway with the light behind him. I saw the flare of a match as he lit a cigarette and took another photo. Simultaneously, as the match illuminated his face shock hit me like a well-delivered punch to my face. There before me in what I had now assessed as some type of Military Camp was my ex-Platoon Commander SAS Captain Dave Fitzpatrick. What was he doing here with all these Talibs? He had fought beside me in Afghanistan, he had lost the same friends and brothers as I had. Fitzy and I had been friends for a long time and although I had lost contact with him when you've been there for each other and through hell together, the friendship lasts forever.

Even so, it was clear that he was on the inside, he had turned and was helping the enemy. I knew straight away that explained how these Taliban were much better trained and organised than the usual Afghani. I could feel the rage building inside me, he was my friend and brother how could he be there like that? It took all my self-control not to withdraw, and move around to the house to get a little closer. All I had was my sidearm. I could put two in his head and be gone before his lifeless body hit the wooden floor of the verandah. Fitzpatrick would never know just how close he was to death that cold morning, but I made a promise, it was only a postponement, not a cancelled mission. One day soon I would kill him.

Once Fitzpatrick had gone back inside I slowly moved backwards out of my observation post and being careful to avoid the sentries I made my way in the ever-growing light. I quickly crossed the cleared paddock happy to make the sanctuary of the surrounding trees and after waiting a little while began to move off towards the dirt road. I knew this area would be where they were patrolling the most using the road as the boundary for their patrols. Thankfully I made it to the road without incident. Like a child crossing a city street, I carefully looked both ways and then did it again before running across the gravel road. I then made my way through my home paddocks eventually returning to my camp. I was exhausted after going all night and felt drained by the amount of Adrenalin that had flowed through me operating so deep into enemy territory.

CHAPTER 22

LATE MAY 2014

I was seriously weighing up between a Jack Daniels and a coffee before phoning the Colonel. Coffee it was otherwise I might not make any sense because nothing else did. After getting the fire going I sat down to review the photos I had taken. Considering the changing quantities and qualities of light that was available they weren't too bad. The two men on the verandah were unknown to me and sadly their faces were not clear. I still wasn't sure what I had seen but I was very sure that what I had seen was very important. I didn't want to wait another moment before sending through my report. I phoned Colonel Walsh this time on his mobile phone, so I could avoid his aide but also, so he would be ready for me to send through the photos and see what he made of them.

The Colonel's voice sounded gravelly but alert. "Hi Steve, do you realise it's 0600 Hours on Sunday morning?"

"Sorry Sir, so how long have you been up?"

"Yeah, you are right old soldiers can't sleep in, can we?" The Colonel admitted.

I continued.. I wanted to get on with this call. "Sir to be honest with you I have been in the scrub so long I have lost track of what time or day it is. Colonel I went back in, you knew I would, didn't you?"

You could hear the trepidation in the old soldier's question. "Did you find anything worthwhile son? I really need something good if I'm to go back to the NSC, friend or no friend".

Feeling for him I spoke quietly yet confidently. "Sir now I've seen enough to be sure there is definitely some sort of Military Camp set up across the road. It's full of armed and well-trained soldiers, probably Taliban. And there's something else that will probably upset your Sunday morning, Fitzy's there". There was a long silence.

"Fitzy, you mean as in Ex-SAS Captain Dave Fitzpatrick. You've got to be kidding me, what the hell would Fitzy be doing with all those rag heads?"

I could tell that had rattled the Colonel. I don't think I had ever heard him use that or any similar term before. I had to continue. "I'm not sure but even after my first contact with them I knew someone half decent had been training these soldiers, maybe that's what he's there for. I did the best I could with the photos Sir, I'll send them through ASAP".

He recovered quickly. "Steve from what you've told me, I'm sure someone from the NSC will need to get a full report directly from you. I'll pass on a summary and then leave it to them".

"Roger that Sir, as soon as we end this call I'll shoot those photos through. Thanks again for your help with this. I have a feeling it's about to go pear shaped real soon."

Terminating the call, I went to messages and did as I had promised sending through the photos to the Colonel's mobile. I could only send a few at a time but I was sure they had all got through.

I was exhausted from the night's activities and the concentration that I had needed to speak coherently to the Colonel. I cooked up a feed washed down by some more coffee and hit my swag. Jake came over, licked my face once and lay down next to me leaning against my back to gain some warmth.

Colonel Walsh had no reservation or hesitation this time. He was pleased that his confidence in his ex-Platoon Commander appeared to have been justified. However, until the Intel was fully analysed by the experts there was no way to know what Steve Wallace had discovered and its importance to Australian security. The

Colonel doubted Steve was wrong with his assessment of what he had seen. However, the fact they had been identified as Afghani Soldiers, that was definitely way out there. But one way or another what Steve had stumbled upon was worrying to say the least. Taliban types in Queensland Australia set off alarms to the Colonel's very core.

From Steve's report it didn't sound like some red neck training camp, or some wannabe civvies playing soldier. No, Steve Wallace was too switched on for that. Within a minute of finishing the call with Steve Wallace,

Walsh made the call to his friend at the NSC Colonel Goodrich. "Don't mean to be rude mate but can't it wait 'til next week at the Conference Jim?"

Walsh understood his friend's initial reaction. "Nice to be so welcomed by one's old friends. No this can't wait until we catch up next week. Remember that vague report from my Ex-Captain out at Roma?"

Sighing Goodrich responded. "Of course, I do, deep down I thought there was something to it, but we just couldn't spare the time".

"Well Pete, I don't think you'll have a choice this time mate. He went back in for a better look. You're going to want to talk with him, maybe even face to face, and to save you asking I have a heap of photos he took from in close, I'll send them on for you to analyse".

Colonel Goodrich asked. "OK Jim give me the short version of what he saw?"

Walsh proceeded to give Steve Wallace's Recce report. Goodrich listened carefully without interruption until Walsh finished.

The importance of the report evoked a strong reaction from the usually calm Intel Officer. "You weren't joking Jim when you said I might want to talk with him. I will, but not until the photos are analysed so they can be included in the detailed Recce brief. Jim, am I able to contact this Steve Wallace, does he have phone service where he is at the moment?"

Walsh could sense his NSC friend's excitement. "It seems he does, I had to wait for him to get back to me, but I think that was because he was away from his base camp out hunting. With all this happening I'd be surprised if he wasn't sitting on his phone waiting for you to call".

"Alright mate, I'll let you know how it's all going, talk soon". Deep inside an old soldier's gut, Colonel Jim Walsh felt that little twist that meant only one thing and that was that something big had just happened or was about to.

Walsh felt he owed Steve to keep him informed of the status of the situation, he had hated brushing Steve off last time. He felt a little encouragement for his old brother in arms was a good idea. He wasn't big on texting, firstly because he preferred to talk to people. Secondly because he was aware they were less secure than talking because they were filed, but he figured a short text would be best. It read: "Story and photos passed onto my old friend, he may contact you, enjoy rest of holiday. Dad".

The Colonel couldn't help but smile at the inclusion of Dad. He knew Steve could do with a little humour to lighten the load.

Aziz now sat rather uncomfortably with Major Smith and Commander Zahir around the Western style kitchen table. Major Smith had insisted that all the farm furniture remained the same in case of some visitor calling by. Smith had also been training Zahir in Australian customs, not in any structured way, more incidentally with topics presenting themselves as they lived in the farm house over the past few months. The Major was concerned about how Zahir would handle the situation if a neighbour or some farm supplies representative called at the farm while he was away. It was often the simple things that let the game down. Smith had explained that something as simple as not inviting them to come out of the sun and offering a 'cuppa' could cause trouble. That person would have gone away wondering and more importantly they would probably talk about how strange the new owners were.

That was another of the Major's secondary functions. He was to act as if he was the Australian owner of this cattle property in the unlikely event of someone visiting. Visitors may notice a few dark-skinned house staff but with an "Aussie" owner they wouldn't worry unduly. The three Leaders all believed that once the mission was over they would be forced to abandon the place assuming the security would be compromised. Aziz could see Smith's role made a lot of sense, and everyone did their part in the overall security of the facility, and although he had travelled the world, he and Zahir both preferred to recline on cushions with a low table and not sit up on hard chairs across the farm house table. Major Smith had not accepted Islam, but Aziz had noticed that he did show respect to his employers by not buying or bringing onto the property any pork products because even smelling it cooking would be offensive to Aziz and Zahir.

Once again, they sat at the table, however they were not sharing a meal they were planning the operation. Their shared objective being a final plan, they had agreed to stick at it until this was achieved. The wooden lining of the old kitchen/dining room, what the Australians called tongue and groove, was perfect for pinning the twelve A4 sheets of paper. Each sheet had a heading which was the Mission Location and under that the names of the Soldiers in that particular squad. The Mission would be executed by seven groups of five assailants and five groups which only had four names. The original plan had brought over sixty soldiers for this Mission, twelve targets with five soldiers per location.

The reduced groups were thanks to the loss of five Soldiers; the first soldier's encounter with the crocodile, the two missing men assumed to be Absent Without Leave (AWOL s), and two dead in the car versus truck accident. Aziz stood up so fast his light wooden chair flew backwards clattering onto the floor. "I had planned this operation with sixty men and now we only have fifty-five".

Commander Zahir didn't want to cross his Leader but he felt he had to settle the situation. "Sir, losing a man to a huge crocodile could not be foreseen. We are in a new and strange country with dangers beyond our experience".

Aziz wasn't about to let his subordinate off the hook that easily; "Zahir could you have not camped further away from the water?"

Zahir held his tongue and just shook his head in an ambiguous gesture that could have meant anything. Zahir being reminded of that first night in Australia, it seemed such a long time ago now, inwardly shuddered as he remembered that dreadful crunching sound and the poor brother's screams.

Aziz started in again. "I know you say you supported your troops spiritually and motivationally, but *you* were responsible for their selection before leaving Afghanistan, yet two more ran away".

Zahir knew he could not win this battle so he decided he would let Aziz rant. He was embarrassed that Major Smith was present and who was looking like he wished he was somewhere else.

On the other hand, Major Smith felt he didn't really have a lot at stake here, so he waded in to take some heat from his peer. "With all due respect, Aziz, some of these things may be true and in hindsight may have been avoidable, but we will never know for sure. Let's have a real good look at what we can do with what we have and go from there, shall we? On investigation it was discovered the two sentries that have disappeared were brothers and came from another area of Afghanistan to the other soldiers. There were also reports that they had never really fitted in and had also talked about having relatives that had come through Indonesia and had happily settled in Sydney. Accordingly, the evidence suggests they have taken off to Sydney together."

While it made sense, the old soldier in him still worried about it. They wouldn't have risked carrying their weapons but the two AKs had never been found. It just didn't feel right.

Building on Major Smith's attempt to get back on track, Zahir started in again. "I believe we are ready to attack, all twelve targets are covered. Granted some have one less man but we have chosen these and the absence of the fifth shooter will have minimal impact.

Zahir was looking for support. "What are your thoughts Major Smith?"

Aziz had quickly noticed Zahir had distanced himself from Smith since Aziz had arrived. He was uncertain whether this was sincere or to disguise they had become friends. The Commander was astute enough to know Aziz would be particularly sensitive to any suggestion that in a debate Zahir would side with this infidel traitor against him. Maybe he was reading too much into it. Perhaps Zahir simply saw that the training was coming to an end and therefore so was the need for such close working relations.

With the carefulness of a politician Smith stated, "They have certainly come a long way. I believe we understand their strengths and weaknesses to a level that will enable us to confirm the squad leader we have identified during the training. We can also match certain squads to the most compatible target to maximise our successes".

Aziz took this opportunity to put Smith in his place emphasising the word OUR. "*Our* successes are really Allah's (The Victory Giver) Major Smith".

Major Smith knew when he was being admonished by a superior Officer and with an exaggerated nod of his head he responded. "Of course, Sir, of course". Smith thought to himself: *Aziz is certainly in a fine old mood this morning.*

Zahir ever the soldier focused on outcomes rather than point scoring attempted to get the meeting back on track. "Let's get down to the small details and scenarios. We will look at each target and discuss the squad allocation first".

Aziz having asserted his position was still not finished with Commander Zahir. He slighted him further by praising the mercenary Officer. "Major you have done an excellent job training these martyrs. I am sure your reconnaissance of the targets has been carried out in just the same manner. Please lead this part of the planning".

And so, it went, three men with the same goal but different motivations discussed and dissected squads and targets for the next four hours. The house staff had been told not to interrupt so on about the three-hour mark Smith rose stiffly from the table and called the kitchen staff, ordering food and tea for all. They knew to serve Australian tea for him and mint tea for the other two men. Aziz had made a big deal of it one night. He didn't like anything about the West including the horrible weak excuse for tea these Australians seemed to consume non-stop. The discussion ceased when the staff arrived with trays of food and steaming carafes and pots. The staff could see the charts pinned to the walls but none of the three were highly concerned regarding the house staff as it had already been decided they would be executed just before the squads left the cattle property for their assigned missions.

Now refreshed the three men's discussion moved on to logistics, supply and transport. Usually there would be a big focus on communication however it had been decided that once the squads were on their way no further communication would occur between base camp and the mobile teams and certainly never from team to team. The deployment of Taliban Soldiers here in Australia was designed to send shock waves throughout every level of this Infidel corrupt society. One of the down sides of using these soldiers was that they had not been exposed to everything a First World Country has including highways, motorways, toll roads and all the other things found on modern road systems. These soldiers had literally come off the dirt roads and simple highways of Afghanistan. Some of them had not experienced anything much better than dirt tracks.

There was no way they could drive and navigate themselves from the Training Camp to their assigned targets without getting lost or attracting unwanted attention. Major Smith had been thinking about this for the last couple of months and had a solution.

Smith stated. "We are confident that they will do what they have been trained to do once they are in place, but we have to get these squads on site".

Aziz demanded, "Have you got a solution to this Major Smith?"

The Ex SAS Officer was ready for this agro Afghan and was not used to being drilled like this. "Yes, Sir I have. I can have twelve good men of mine all trained, all switched on, that will drive each squad to their mission site. I trust them, but they don't need to know anything but where to deliver each of their packages. There is no need for them to ever know about this camp or where it is. We will transport the entire group to a staging area, then dispatch the twelve groups to their assigned locations. All these Land Cruisers that we have here on the property will be fine. No one will notice them moving around".

It was starting to get dark by the time that they felt they had covered everything. The advantage of working together in a set-up such as this camp was that if anyone thought of any additional issue it was easy to re-convene and work through the new item. This was a lot easier and more efficient than some paranoid clandestine meeting in some hotel room, forever wondering who saw them arrive and who was listening. Here they were providing central control and command with minimum risk.

They got to the end and, in a reverent voice lacking all his usual power but full of zeal and purpose Aziz said, "My brothers, I believe Allah has been with us the entire journey of this mission, from the first thoughts he placed in my head to this moment, let us now pray to Al-Mumeet The Inflictor of Death.

Not being a Christian or a Moslem, Major Smith felt like a third person on a honeymoon. However, he was compliant closing his eyes and remaining still, Zahir, of course fully supported the suggestion that was really an order. Once Aziz had finished his prayer the group went their different ways seeking some peace and quiet after so many hours of talking and concentration. While Aziz was angered that the Major had not adopted their faith, he showed nothing, quickly thinking to himself what would one expect from a traitorous infidel who served only one god with a very small 'g' and that was money. As they walked out onto the verandah the cool of the evening embraced them. The staleness of so many hours cooped up in the kitchen was washed away.

"Sir, when do you see my men and I moving out and of course being paid?" Smith asked. It was a reasonable question, but Aziz was so excited by the mission planning to be brought down to earth by this Australian pig was annoying. He believed he could feel the full of power straight from Allah himself. Aziz looked forward to no longer needing Smith or whatever his name was. Mentally he patted himself on the back for placing Zahir close enough to accumulate Smith's knowledge and training and his methods. Aziz thought how much he hated traitors, but he understood Smith's value. But even that would be ending abruptly, sooner rather than later. With this pleasant thought in mind, Aziz turned to Smith with a smile on his face. Smith saw it and relaxed. Aziz inwardly laughed at what had made him smile. These Australians really were stupid.

"Major Smith I believe you and your team can head off as soon as the last squads leave us. And Major, as you have done such a wonderful job for us, I have instructed Commander Zahir to pay you a bonus of fifty thousand American Dollars". Aziz saw the man's greed shine in his eyes and couldn't resist toying with him further.

"Major it is totally up to you whether you tell your men of this extra thank you gift". Aziz's game was rewarded by the pig Major actually licking his lips confirming, that as Aziz had assumed, Smith would keep all the bonus for himself.

The only thing to do now was to decide on a date for the mission to be executed. The men would keep practising in preparation for the big day. Now there would be a slight shift of emphasis to training in their mission. They would train in their assigned squads with the Squad Leaders being mentored by the Cadre Staff. These men were chosen to take on the responsibilities of that role and the Squad Members had to learn to operate in their roles with their new Squad Leader.

A Christian day of significance would be good, but they had missed Easter. Aziz was thinking: *we are in May, thinking about the months to come maybe the Christian's Christmas would make an impact.* However, he decided that it was too far off. His soldiers were ready and although there had been no communications he knew he must return to Afghanistan and resume his role, driving the invaders from his homeland. Security, even great security, started to fray the longer it had to hold. The other issue was that the soldiers would become stale. They were ready now and would be OK for a while but not indefinitely.

It came to him from a different direction, forget these unbelieving infidels, Christmas was more and more a commercial holiday these days. His Moslem brothers and sisters living in this "lucky country" had cried that they were offended by decorations and carols. Spectacularly, teachers no longer taught Christmas Carols or read stories, shops played non-Christian carols and displayed decorations and lights without any meaning. The gutless media and people pleasing politicians didn't even have the courage to say Merry Christmas any more it was now Happy Holidays. He smiled when he thought; imagine what would happen in his homeland if a few Christians did not want Ramadan mentioned.

Like a little jolt of electricity there it was, Ramadan was next month, in fact the first day of Ramadan was just fifteen days away. "We have our date", Aziz said out loud. Even though he was by himself he had been reading his well-worn Koran in the shade of the verandah. They would *really* celebrate the first day of Ramadan on June 14 this year. It will be a day with a wonderful sacrifice to Allah with many martyr brothers reaching paradise and the rewards waiting for them. What a fitting way to celebrate.

CHAPTER 23

JUNE 2014

Colonel Goodrich got off the phone from his friend up in Brisbane, Jim Walsh and sat for a good five minutes. Working through this new information in his head and thanking God that he had not dismissed that first call. It would have been easy to do; with its vague information from some Ex-Captain fellow. Goodrich needed the information from the first report, so he could marry it up with this new Intel.

He then turned to one of his staff who had appeared at his door. "Corporal Baldwin, pull everything we have on Roma. I filed it last week in the Archive filing cabinet. Bring it all to me ASAP".

"Yes Sir", Baldwin turned and disappeared around the corner heading towards the archive room.

Corporal Baldwin arrived back a few minutes later with a thin Manila folder that designated it as No Further Action.

Taking the file he handed the Corporal a stick."Corporal I have downloaded some images onto this USB, get it to the photo boys to see what they can do with them. The shots are a bit dark to see clearly. If they turn anything up that's interesting send it up to the brig's office, I'll be there."

Goodrich thought to himself: this new Intel *has just earned itself a Red Folder that was for sure.* Re-reading the file he took another five minutes to confirm that he had recollected the details correctly. He knew he must be what they called 'full bottle', fully informed before he took this to the Brigadier again.

Goodrich phoned the Brig trying to hide his excitement: “Sir, sorry to bother you. I have some very interesting follow-up Intel re that Roma report we discussed last week”.

Not bothering to hide his irritation Brigadier Dodds challenged the Colonel. “Pete, what could be happening out in the back blocks of Queensland that could be more important than what we are working on now?”

By now everyone at the NSC knew about Aziz being in-country and on the run, so Goodrich could fully understand the Senior Officer's comment. "Well Sir I didn't think I had any choice. I’m sure you’ll agree once you see what our Ex-SAS Captain has come up with now”.

“Alright Pete, you have my attention, come on in”.

Goodrich looked serious. “Sir, may I close your door?”

Dodds nodded his permission and lent forward expectantly. “It must be interesting if you want to close my door”.

Colonel Goodrich sat down in the chair that the Brig waved him, the armchair opposite to him. He began to remind the Brigadier of the information they had discussed last week and then proceeded to update the report. Brigadier Dodds said nothing, his blonde moustache trimmed exactly to the corners of his mouth twitched several times. Goodrich had learned that this was signifying he wanted to ask questions but stayed himself until Goodrich had finished.

Sighing loudly the brig commented. “Pete, firstly great work that you saw something in the first report enough to discuss it and file it. You know in this game, we have to work on facts and data. However, great Intelligence gathering often starts with seeing something when others don't or remembering some minute detail that later becomes vital. Pete, I want you to head this up, get your entire Section onto it until further notice. Have you given any thought about getting Captain Wallace down here for a face-to-face debrief?”

Colonel Goodrich answered thoughtfully. “Um, yes Sir I think that would be a good move, he's Ex-SAS. From his reports, I'd say his observations and deductions should be pretty well as good as anyone under this roof so let's make the most of it."

The Brig started to say something and then didn’t, so Goodrich continued. "It's too early to know, but if we decide to go in in force he would be invaluable in the planning stages, the execution phase as a guide, everything.”

“I totally agree, your assessment of him, seems sound and Colonel Walsh up in Brissy backs him. If we must go with this we will, but it couldn't be worse timing with Aziz still on the run and CHOGM getting closer every day”.

Goodrich was about to stand when the office door flew open and banged into the wall behind it; Corporal Baldwin burst into the office.

Colonel Goodrich sprung to his feet yelling. “Where are your manners Corporal. Is that how you enter a Brigadier’s office, especially when the door is shut?”.

“I am so sorry Brigadier, Colonel I.. I.. I..” stuttered the Non-com.

“Come on man. What is it?” the Brigadier demanded.

Baldwin held up a photo that Colonel Goodrich immediately recognised as one of the bundle Jim Walsh had sent through. “Sir! I am sorry, Sir! It’s him, it's the bloody Rabbit! It’s him Sir, Aziz as bold as brass standing on that verandah”.

Goodrich exclaimed “No way; how could that be, who or how was this confirmed?”

The Brigadier speaking softly as though a raised voice might cause all this revelation to evaporate said, “Corporal have the analyst from the photo section that worked on this in front of me in the next sixty seconds.”

"Sir"! With that Corporal, Baldwin came to attention performed a parade ground quality 'about turn' and was gone as though he was never actually there.

The Brig jumped to his feet. "If this turns out to be true; thank the Lord Almighty, Pete, if it's him all my prayers have been answered. I haven't had a good night's sleep since Aziz slipped his leash in that tunnel. I can't stop thinking and wondering why the hell a Terrorist Leader such as him would stick his neck out by leaving Afghanistan and showing up here?"

The Brigadier continued, nearly talking to himself. "It has to be something massive and that scares me no end, and I have to tell you, his arriving so soon after those bombings make me wonder if he's behind them. It would certainly make sense."

The atmosphere in the room was like someone had hit the pause or the mute button on a DVD of the Brigadier and Goodrich. Neither Officer said anything, each stunned, sitting with his own thoughts of what this Intel may mean and what actions it would demand. Goodrich was truly stunned. He had progressed from seeing the first Roma report as the possible rantings of a good Ex-Officer sadly affected by Post Traumatic Stress Disorder (PTSD) to this.

He had initially listened to Wallace's report because he was supported by Jim Walsh. But now based on what he had in front of him he had been justified. He had done the right thing. Trying to make sense of the reported run-in with the two supposed Taliban, he had wondered if they were just some local Arab-type red-neck gas workers that bit off more than they could chew when they went hunting Steve Wallace. These thoughts filled Goodrich's mind as he sat on the edge of his chair in front of the Senior Officer. The Brigadier was hardly breathing and was constantly shaking his head from left to right and back again. For the twentieth time, he grasped the photos so tightly that they bent over then relaxed his grip. He held them under his desk lamp hoping that he could see the faces of the men on the old farmhouse verandah.

Both Officers jumped when they heard a loud knocking. Corporal Baldwin stood at the door with a Sergeant standing a pace behind him and slightly to his right. "Enter" commanded the Brigadier with a wave to the area in front of the working table at which the Brigadier and Colonel now sat.

Baldwin introduced the NCO. "Sir, this is Sergeant Kane. He is a specialist trained in Photo Enhancing and Interpretation".

"Sir, Sergeant Kane at your service Sir". He was a small man but fit and muscular considering his speciality. His uniform was just OK. He wasn't used to senior Officers talking to him. He was clearly nervous.

The Brigadier controlled his emotions to help the NCO settle. "Thank you, Sergeant. Son this may be the most important discovery of your career. Now I want you to relax. And carefully explain what you used, what you think you have found and what methods you used to confirm your findings? Can you do that for me, son?" The Brigadier had led men for thirty-eight years and understood the fear that would be in the heart of a young Sergeant summoned to the Brigadier's Office for a face-to-face. He had done a good job trying to calm the young man.

Sergeant Kane commenced his report, growing in confidence as he was immersed in his speciality. "Sir our Section received a USB with twenty-two photos electronically transmitted to Colonel Goodrich who then passed them to us. The Photo Section Commander split the photos up as best as he could, grouping them by reference, the subject of the photos, so if it was soldiers, locations etc."

In a soothing tone. "Yes, yes son, I get that, please move on". The Brigadier as impatient as he was, was attempting to avoid making the young soldier even more anxious.

The young Sergeant continued. “Sorry Sir, anyway I was given what I named the Verandah group of photos. They were shockers Sir, whoever took them was certainly no photographer. Anyway, the exposure was terrible and most of them were very dark. A couple had so much light behind them you could hardly see any details anyway.”

The Brigadier had turned red with the strain. “Sergeant, I need the details so we can be confident of your findings, but please get to the guts of it all”.

The Photo Analyst continued. “Well Sir, as we got them digitally I was able to Photo-Shop them, that’s a programme that enhances photos, fixes up any problems and so on."

He saw the Brig was about to explode and started to speak more quickly. "Once I had done that the faces could be seen clearly and straight away. Sir. I recognised the Rabbit. We have all been alerted to watch for him, Sir. I was so excited, Sir; I, sorry Sir. Anyway, I ran his mug through the Facial Recognition Programme (FRP) it identifies marks and high points such as cheekbones etc.”

Looking like he was about to have a stroke or explode the Brig now totally frustrated yelled. "Son I know what FRP is."

Sergeant Kane was near the finish line and the Brig’s raised voice was not going to stop him. "Anyway, Sir the verandah photo scored 100%. It's him, Sir. No doubts, it's definitely Aziz.”

“That is great work Sergeant, well-done son”.

“Well thank you Sir, but there's more Sir”.

“How could there be more Sergeant Kane he's the top terrorist target in Australia”. The Brigadier amazed at the discovery couldn't imagine any other value target could be present in the same location.

“Yes Sir, but another face was identified by the FRP; this time from his Officer Cadet School Portsea Graduation Photo. A picture of a very young Second Lieutenant Fitzpatrick confirmed that he was with Aziz on that verandah on that night”.

"Outstanding, thank you, Sergeant Kane. That is disturbing news but once again great work, thank you too Corporal Baldwin. You two return to your desks but don't go anywhere outside the building and do not discuss this Intel with anyone outside your Sections. Thank you, you're dismissed".

The Brigadier didn't know whether to smile or jump up and down like an excited school boy. "Pete, what on earth is going on? Last week we didn't have enough to take a second look and now this has just become one of the most important pieces of Anti-Terrorist Intel maybe this decade and we still don't know what any of it means. I am going to call a meeting of all the Department Heads. I would like you beside me to add any detail I may not have grabbed and your opinions seeing as you have been involved with this since that first call."

The Brig stood. "I think bringing Wallace down here is now obligatory, get onto him and have him here ASAP".

Colonel Goodrich replied. "Will do Sir, I'll get Admin to make up sets of this file for everyone attending, I'll get going Sir if that's OK?"

"Pete, I need to bring Major General Watson up to speed with all this. I'm sure he will agree to bring the Commanding Officer and his staff of the Anti-Terrorist Unit 2 Commando Company over for the meeting. We'll start as soon as they arrive from Sydney and Wallace gets down from Roma. We'll need everyone's help but without pre-empting the meeting I think this has just become a full-on assault scenario if I am not mistaken. You take off and do what's needed. I'll see you at the meeting, thanks again, Pete. Your gut feeling was certainly spot on with this one. Oh, and Pete, I need to know everything about this Lieutenant Fitzpatrick ASAP."

"Thank you, Sir, will do." With that Goodrich scooped up the file and headed for his office. As he went Goodrich was thinking: *I bet the sparks will fly when the Brigadier briefs the Commanding*

Officer of the NSC, Brigadier General Watson. With that, Colonel Goodrich returned to his office. Calling his staff together he ordered twenty sets of the file now to be placed in a red folder and designated Top Secret. He also gave a warning order for Movement Control to be ready for a pick up at Roma Airport ASAP. He then cleared the office and immediately phoned Steve Wallace.

Being unsure of the phone reception where he was, Goodrich was happy to hear Wallace answer on the third ring. "Captain Wallace this is Colonel Peter Goodrich at the NSC, I am the old mate of Jim Walsh's, the one who he passed your two reports on to. We can talk later Captain, but right now your Intel has caused a great deal of action and concern down this way. We want you here ASAP. If you can get mobile as a matter of urgency, how long before you can be at Roma airport?"

Roma
Queensland

Sitting on my old camping chair I was wondering: *when I had joined up again and started being Captain Wallace again, being told what to do, when and where to go*. But then I remembered that this was all my doing. A Colonel Goodrich had phoned and asked me to come to Canberra to discuss my reports.

I fell into line like a rookie Private. "I can be there in an hour, max".

Goodrich sounded happy with my reply. "Great just wait in the lounge and we will come and get you." Feeling a bit like something out of an old spy movie I asked, "how will I recognise the pilot?"

"Good point I'll get back to you".

I replied automatically. "Rodger that, see you in Canberra Sir." With that, I hung up and started to get ready. Friends in town would look after Jake, I needed a shower and some decent clothes, I didn't have either when I was hunting.

By the time Colonel Goodrich got onto the Movement Control Officer, he had worked out a signal for Wallace to identify the Pilot. Goodrich explained what he needed, a Brisbane Bronco's Cap. He had gone the Bronco's way because the pick-up was in Queensland. He knew several of the NSC Staff were from there and someone would have a cap. It was a quick plan, but he was sure it would be fine.

"Corporal Baldwin, confirm that the Bronco cap is a go as soon as you have one, thanks." Downstairs Lieutenant Brian Hayward of Movement Control had already captured the data for Roma Airport when the Colonel had given him a vague Warning Order an hour ago. Good news, there, the runway was a lot longer than the 2,488 feet the NSC Cessna Citation CJ1 required. All going well they would be wheels up in the next fifteen minutes. They could have taken off immediately as the Pilots were already on standby at the airport, however, they had to wait for the Bronco cap to be delivered.

Baldwin had found a Bronco's Cap which was now being sped out to the pilots as they did their pre-flight checks. The estimated flight time was around one hour forty-two minutes with a bit of time finding Wallace, whoever that was, and they should be back at Canberra Airport (CBR) in a little under four hours. Lieutenant Hayward emailed Colonel Goodrich with this information and then went back to what he had been arranging before Colonel Goodrich's call. He had been arranging for some Sergeant's person and gear to be transported to Townsville Barracks the following week.

Goodrich saw the Roma travel arrangements email arrive and thought to himself: *OK four hours to ponder what was going on at that cattle property so far away from where he sat.* An experienced Army

Officer, he knew keeping information flowing both up and down saved a lot of trouble in the long run. Accordingly, he emailed the Brigadier confirming Captain Wallace should be in the building by close on 1800 Hours.

The Intel Colonel phoned Brigadier Dodds. "Sir it's Pete Goodrich, I was wondering what you thought about getting the local Coppers to block the highway in either direction of the farm. We could give them some excuse and have them watch for a certain type of traveller. I'm a bit concerned that we have no idea who these Afghanis are or what they are planning to do, or where or when. I'd hate to sit down here, plan a party and then arrive after they have all bugged out. What do you think Sir?"

Once again the Brigadier was glad Goodrich had joined the team. "It's a good thought, Pete, do some more work on what you want the local Police to be saying and set the criteria for their filter. I suppose locals and others who can prove who they are would be OK and fit through the screen. You know what I mean, say two adults and three fighting crying kids are probably just on a holiday if you know what I mean?"

"Roger that Sir, I'll let you know the outcome".

Colonel Goodrich got his aide to connect him with the Officer-in-Charge of Roma Police. "Senior Sergeant Townsend, this is Colonel Peter Goodrich at the National Security Centre Canberra, how are you going up there?"

"Pretty good Colonel, still dry as a bone but otherwise we're alright, what can I do for you?"

Goodrich went on to explain who he was and that there were concerns that the drug importer on the bulletin they received last week may be coming through their area. He may well be in the company of other men of Middle Eastern appearance. Goodrich made it clear that anyone fitting that flyer even remotely and looking Middle Eastern should be taken into custody under the National

Security Act. He assured the Senior Police Officer that anyone they arrested would be taken off their hands within hours. The Colonel did not want to give too close a location of the Target Property to the Senior Sergeant, so he asked that roadblocks be located at Injune, north of Roma and on the Injune/Roma Highway at Roma.

The seasoned Police Sergeant had to smile, all this excitement on his turf. "That will be fine Colonel, I'll set blocks at the border of my area of operations on the Injune end and just north of town this end".

"Firstly, if you can manage it, please call me Pete. Secondly, now I know it might be near impossible but if the media get onto these roadblocks can you spin them a yarn that you're looking for a fugitive on the run from Brisbane. It's the truth in a way in any case".

"Sure, you're right about the media, it's pretty quiet out here so a roadblock near town will be big news but we'll keep it low-key, we'll be right, Colonel, I mean Pete".

Goodrich felt good about this man's ability to do what he had promised. "Thanks for your cooperation Sergeant. I really appreciate it".

"It's Rob, my pleasure. It was a long time ago, but I did a tour of Nam, so I still have a little green blood in me. Just let me know if there is anything else you need. I'm not asking what's going on but if you need more help please ask?"

"Thanks again Rob will do. Make sure your guys know that these people could be armed and dangerous, stay safe".

"Roger that, talk soon". With that, the connection broke.

For the next few hours, the NSC resembled a hotel with drivers leaving to go to the airport to pick up the various teams and individuals and return them to the NSC Head Quarters (HQ). The first to arrive was the Officers of 2 Commando Company (Coy), then the Australian Federal Police Commissioner Doug Wilson who had been at a meeting in Melbourne when he was summoned.

Members who were spread all around the country came home like homing pigeons to roost.

CHAPTER 24

With nothing much to pack I got going fast and raced to Roma. As I got closer to town on the northern side of the Airport, I noticed up ahead there were barriers across the road and Police blue and red lights flashing. Man, I didn't have time for this. They were probably looking for drunk drivers or doing licence checks or some bullshit reason. I pulled up just short of the roadblock and waited as a big bull of a cop came strutting over and I knew straight away this wouldn't be fast. He looked at me and explained that they were looking for an escaped fugitive and could he look in the back of my old Ute. Of course, I gave him permission. He had a look and as he was walking around to the driver's side window a female Police Officer walked into view.

It was Chris Jackson; the cop I had helped last time I was in Roma. She saw me and came over, her partner arriving at the same time. The male Officer said: "You're right to go, Sir, have a good day".

Constable Jackson came over to talk, but I just didn't have time. "Sorry, Chris. Gotta fly I'll catch up with you when I get back, promise".

With that, I accelerated away from the roadblock wondering if the *roadblock was a result of my report.* Looking in the rear-view mirror I could tell by her body language that Constable Jackson was put out by my not talking to her, but that was bad luck.

Being a person who doesn't believe in coincidences I had already answered that question before I turned left into town. Canberra must have requested that the locals seal off that farm from a distance so as not to let anyone get out while still being careful not to alert them. I was headed to a mate's place and dropped off poor old Jake who is so smart he knew I was leaving him as soon as he saw me packing my overnight bag.

As I was driving into Roma, I received a call from Colonel Goodrich. "Captain Wallace I don't want this to become over-complicated. To minimise any interest in a private jet arriving at Roma Airport, a pilot in civilian clothes wearing a Broncos Football Cap will arrive at the lounge from the airstrip side. He will walk to the reception counter and then leave, you are to follow him back to the Cessna Citation".

"Roger that Sir sounds good". Call ended.

As planned I had been waiting in the lounge area for about fifteen minutes when a guy came through from the airstrip side wearing a red Bronco's Cap. He didn't look Military in any way, dressed casually he was fit with short dark hair. After following him to the bottom step of the Citation I ascended the fold upstairs behind him and into the plane. The pilot went left towards the cockpit gesturing to me that I was to go to the right into the cabin area, talking over his shoulder.

"Take any seat you want, you're the only passenger".

No introductions or pats on the back from this guy so I took a window seat. I fastened my seat belt and was asleep before we got to the end of the runway. It's a gift that soldiers develop grabbing rest whenever and wherever you can.

At 1820 Hours we arrived at Canberra Airport (CBR), one of the plane's crew escorted me to the terminal. The crewman signalled a soldier standing near the entrance door.

I read his name tag as Corporal Freeman grabbed my bag and took me to a waiting 4WD.

He then drove through Canberra's leafy streets stopping outside an office block that could have been a bank or insurance company's HQ, however, it was this Nation's security hub, the HQ of the National Security Centre.

Goodrich had just made himself a strong coffee that he was sure wouldn't be strong enough to boost his weariness when his phone rang.

"Pete, Felix (who was the Prime Minister's Advisor on Security matters). I just wanted to touch base with you before the meeting".

Goodrich hated this, Felix pulled this stunt every time there was an important meeting. It was such a political bullshit strategy that Soldiers did not need and liked even less. 'A meeting before the meeting', people like Felix Norman were so insecure they needed to count votes and try to form alliances before everyone was sitting around a table in case they couldn't get their own way through communication and debate.

Putting his tiredness aside and his immense dislike for this weak bureaucratic link in an otherwise strong chain, he replied "Yes, Felix what can I do for you?"

"Well I have a few concerns, I got the invite and summary from the Brig. Come on Pete you don't really believe there is a large number of Terrorists at some sort of camp, and in all places to choose from, near a hole like Roma?" Goodrich really couldn't stand this arrogant prick. He let the slight at beautiful Roma slide.

"Seriously Felix, you are like some friggin OWL, the more light gets shined on something the less you see".

Goodrich would never talk to Felix this way at a meeting, but if he was silly enough to call him, he could cop a private response.

Felix had the skin of a Rhino. "We had one initial report that you didn't take seriously, now we have a second report and we have a few poor-quality photos of some fuzzy bloke that might sell cars in western Sydney for all I know".

"With all due respect, those photos have been cleaned up and run through data banks as good as the CIA and FBI have. I know that because that's who we share them with".

Felix attempted to calm the Colonel he had just infuriated. “Alright, alright don't get all excited, tell me about this Wally guy who reported all this stuff. How do we know he's not with them and this is all some sort of a diversion or a distraction?”

Attempting to hide his frustration and getting close to not caring if he failed Goodrich tried again. “His name is Wallace and he's as good as it gets when it comes to a witness or doing a covert Recce. He’s an Ex-SAS Captain. Felix even you couldn't ask for better than that”.

Felix wasn't military and therefore had no respect for training and experience. “Well I suppose even a blind pig finds the odd truffle. I just remembered isn't there another Ex-SAS Officer in those photos, they are probably in this together”.

Goodrich came close to losing it with this time waster civilian with a powerful master. “Captain Wallace has a Military Record that I would be proud of and has kept in contact with trusted Officers I know personally. Fitzpatrick, on the other hand, disappeared off the grid as soon as he resigned from the Regiment and as you know that usually translates to one word, mercenary. Anyway, Felix gotta go, another call waiting, see you at the meeting”. The Colonel hung up on Felix. Goodrich sagged in his chair exhausted but glad in one way that he had handled all that bullshit before the meeting.

Felix Norman was so friggin up himself he didn't even realise when you had a go at him. He was perfect for his job. Goodrich looked up to see a dirty-looking civvy standing in his doorway or more precisely filling his doorway. The man looked to be just under six feet, his broad shoulders and large arms sticking out of his rolled-up sleeves. All this emphasised his barrel chest and V shape that lead to his narrow hips. His hair was long, especially around a building staffed by the Military. Long wavy blond curls fell all around his round head like some dirty surfer. He had a moustache that was far too long for Military standards, his eyes were brown but very dark and hard to see under thick eyebrows that hid them. A sloping scar over his left eye framed the sun-darkened face. The man was dressed in faded blue jeans, a black Tee shirt and a red checked flannel shirt all of which had seen better days and looked dirty.

"Sorry I didn't mean to eavesdrop. I don't know who that was Sir and I couldn't hear what he was saying but from what you said, thank you. I may end up punching his lights out if I get half a chance".

"Captain Wallace I presume".

"Just Steve Wallace now Sir, and, for you Sir, just Steve is fine".

"Thanks, Steve. Come in. I could talk to you all night, but the meeting is scheduled for forty-three minutes from now.

Goodrich maintained eye contact with me continued. "Now I have never believed that clothes maketh the man, but this is the Army, I'm sure you wouldn't have forgotten how important uniforms are when people are judging what you are selling. Now as far as being just Steve, I would like to re-enlist you back to full rank plus promotion and conditions. That is as a Major acknowledging that you were a Captain when you retired, correct?".

"Yes Sir."

He went on before I could add anything further.

Goodrich was on a roll. "I have several reasons for wanting you back in the Green Machine; one of them is to help you deal with a dickhead like you just overheard on that phone call. What do you think about coming back, you know I can't force you?"

"That comes as a bit of shock Colonel, it was hard enough to leave the first time but to come back, well?

As though I hadn't spoken, the Colonel continued. "Another much more important reason is that it is more than obvious that you are still loyal to your oath and this country. As a Regular Army Officer, you would also, or your family be entitled to any compensation, medical expenses etc. well if anything goes wrong".

I wasn't used to being rushed. "Hang on, hang on. Did I just hear a clear invitation to attend this bun fight? I assume you guys are planning to go up there and kick them out?"

Colonel Goodrich was good. "Steve you've seen more action than most of the people in this building. Nothing's firm but if we do go it will be with an attack force of specialist-trained, hardened Commandos. We were going to bring in some of your old mates but they're a bit thin on the ground for a few different reasons. So, I figured why not get the next best thing and that's you. You help them plan the op and lead them in, in a scout role. What do you think, nothing's in stone mate, not yet, but time is running fast?"

"Sir with all due respect (in the military if anyone ever started a statement with this you knew that something completely disrespectful was about to follow); you could have been a used car salesman. Sorry Sir, but you did lay it on pretty thick, give me a couple of minutes, please. It's a big step coming back and jumping straight back into the pan or the fire".

I knew the Colonel was passionate about the importance of what was going on. And I also knew that the Colonel in front of me was responsible for my report being taken seriously. I had thoroughly assessed the situation; and don't worry I had already wondered how I would feel if they had dumped me in Roma. Heading off to fight the war across the road from my home property without me. How would I feel? The answer, Bloody Annoyed. I knew how demanding an op was on a young body, let alone my old retired one. I wasn't too bad; between hunting, drinking and not eating much junk I had kept fit. Yeah, I could keep up with the young bucks from 2 Commando at least for an op that shouldn't take too long.

"OK Sir I am in. I wasn't stringing you along Sir, I know what it takes and the last thing I want to be is some old bloke who screws up because he is unfit. Sir I'm in full, plan anything you want".

"Major Wallace welcome back, I knew you'd understood what was needed and don't worry I appreciate your frank self-assessment because no one knows what's out there. And you know the old saying; the best of plans usually flies out the window the moment the first shot is fired. Now I will have my Corporal get you kitted up for the meeting. I am afraid the best we can do is parade class camos with slide on Major's Crowns, but you'll look the part. At least in camos for now you can get away without any unit ID or anything else. I also have a man to shave that fungus and give you a haircut, welcome back again. I'll see you at the meeting ASAP."

With that, the Colonel buzzed on his phone and a smart-looking Corporal appeared coming to attention as he acknowledged his Officer it sounded more like Sar. "Sir".

"Thanks, Corporal Baldwin as discussed, can you take Captain Wallace, correction Major Wallace, downstairs and get him all kitted out?"

The Corporal reacted. "Sar, please follow me Sir", turning he was off with me following.

"Thanks, Colonel" was all I had time to say over my shoulder as I went through the office doorway. The next thirty-five minutes were like one of those dreadful makeover shows on TV; grungy deer hunter walks in and reasonably starched Major Wallace walks out.

I had done it all before because in SAS we often grew beards and looked pretty bad when we returned from extended patrols. This was especially the case when you are living out of a water bottle in the deserts of Afghanistan. The only difference this time was I had helped to clean up and I was wearing another man's uniform and another man's face, a much older face back in uniform, looked back at me from the mirror.

CHAPTER 25

With three minutes to spare I was delivered by Corporal Baldwin to the meeting room. I had about thirty seconds tops to gather my thoughts, and turn back all those years, and walk through those doors as a current Army Officer. It was a big ask, however Military life is ingrained so deeply into every part of one's being, like calling Superior Officers, Sir, when you no longer have to, or just the way you stand. I was fine, well I felt fine until I walked into the room and saw more brass than a friggin antique store in London. Thank God Colonel Goodrich saw my shaky entrance and came over guiding me to a big padded chair next to his. Glancing in front of the Colonel's chair I noticed the table was covered in printed copies of the photos I had taken last week. Was that only two days ago?

A Major General stood up and it took all my self-control not to stand in the presence of a Superior Officer. Looking carefully to my right I followed Colonel Goodrich's lead and remained seated.

"Welcome everyone you all know the importance of what the new Intel contains. Speaking of Intel, I welcome Major Wallace, proper introductions will have to wait, but good work on your part. You have found someone we had lost and for that alone we are all eternally grateful. Without pre-empting this meeting, I can't see any outcome other than some plan of action to clear out this rat hole. We are unsure of who they are, why they are in the bush near Roma and probably more importantly why they are there at all, and of course what their plans are. If nothing else we want Aziz code-named Rabbit captured at best, eliminated if there is no choice. But gentlemen let me be clear the Rabbit is not to leave that cattle property unless he is wearing handcuffs or a toe tag."

The MAJGEN continued. "Now Brigadier Dodds and I will leave you to thrash out the nuts and bolts. In my experience meetings like this always go better without the 'brass" sitting in on it. Of course, give us a call when you have a final plan that we can look at. We are all aware that time is of the essence and that we can't completely rely on the local Police to contain such a force, especially when there are so many unknowns. Thank you, gentlemen,".

At this the two Senior Officers stood in unison and left the room in step exactly one pace between them, you had to love Army training.

Once they were gone, as the Brig had predicted, everyone seemed to relax to varying degrees. Colonel Goodrich took the lead as was his designated role, introducing everyone to me obviously, I was the only new boy in the class. When he got to Felix Norman, I knew just looking at him that he was the political rep at the table. And yes, he looked like the dickhead that had already upset me on the Colonel's phone by proxy. Colonel Goodrich's strategy was spot on; my rank and being SAS immediately broke down all the barriers that may have come up from the Officers of 2nd Commando Coy and the other various Officers around the large white table.

Colonel Goodrich got the meeting going. "OK there is tea and coffee and sandwiches at the side there, let's get cracking."

For the next hour or so I was interrogated by all and sundry. I had expected this and would have been disappointed and more than a little concerned if I hadn't been. As a soldier, you know Intel is always shonky. Yeah, they do their best, but often you are given half the picture and there are little things missing like the enemy has double the troops that the Intel report included. They had me as a bonus, they could ask questions to clarify, double-check and ask my assessment of what I had seen and what seemed to be happening.

I couldn't guarantee troop strengths, but I could talk about equipment, weapons and training skills. These were all a Christmas present to any Officer deciding whether to send in friendlies and if so how to do it. The more we talked the more I grew to respect the high quality around this table these were a group of specialists, not just General-Purpose Grunt (Infantry) Officers. I had been fortunate enough to have done several Anti-Terrorist courses, so we were all on the same page quickly talking the same language. There were a couple of times the PM's man, not having a Military background, couldn't keep up but credit where credit is due he asked reasonable questions and understood the answers quickly. He had either decided I was on their side or at least lacked the courage to imply I was a spy again, either way, it saved me having to hit him in front of all these witnesses. As you would expect the 2nd Commando Officers asked the real hard questions. They knew this was their opportunity to get as much Intel as they could, and it was more important to them than anyone else because it was going to be them and their men who would be in the thick of it.

The longer the meeting went on the Brig's prophesy/order to clear out the camp became a certainty. There was a lot of discussion about that stump. I described its location, the strange clunk as the action opened and the ladder system both ways. The stump was named 'Ant Nest'. From that point on the need to start creating detailed maps and designated objectives for the teams to be responsible for became a natural planning progression. Initially, the use of Black Hawk Helos was mooted but I raised the concern that in that open country a squadron of choppers would be heard a long way off. We all studied the maps and came up with a plan that would enable the choppers use without warning the rats we were coming. The cattle property was a challenge to cordon off because of the size and its lengthy secluded boundaries across all sorts of terrain.

Another threat to eliminate was if the enemy mobilised quickly enough to utilise all those Quad Bikes they could launch a mobile assault on ground troops, which could be a disaster, especially on the enemy's home turf.

Colonel Black, the Company Commander of 2 Commando, asked, "what weapons are we likely to encounter?"

I answered as best I could from what I had seen. “The grunts are armed with the new 5.56mm x 39mm AK74Ms, none of the AKs I saw had been fitted with the grenade option but who knows. I didn't see anything else except that the Commander had some sort of sidearm but in the dark, I couldn't see it to identify it.”

Understanding how vital this information could be I continued. “I’m sure you guys are the same; I’ve never seen a group of more than three or four Talibs go anywhere without at least one old Russian Duska Heavy Machine Gun but like I said I didn't actually see one.”

Nodding his head Colonel Black agreed. “You might not have seen one, but my experience agrees with yours and the absence of evidence does not equal the evidence of absence, we will expect to have at least four or five minimum to overcome. You would have mentioned them if you had seen any, but they probably have some RPGs as well”.

The more these guys talked the quicker my confidence in them grew. “Yes, you are right Sir. I saw none, but these Talibs love RPGs so I agree we might see some come out”. I didn't see anything else but who knows what they have in that ‘Ant Nest’ or stashed away someplace else. I wish I had seen more but clearly, they do their training away from the farmhouse area.”

Colonel Colin Black was a small wiry man with piercing black eyes and a face that suggested he tolerated no bullshit and always wanted the truth even if it wasn't pleasant. I noticed that even though he and his Adjutant Captain Pat Thompson had come to the ‘big smoke’, knowing that they would be in the presence of senior brass they were dressed the same as I was, parade class camos, except they had their unit insignia and the Australian shoulder cloth flash. This spoke volumes to me that they weren't here to impress anyone with spit and polish. They meant business. That and the way they worked in the meeting gave me no choice but to respect and like them in a short time.

Colonel Black turned to face me with a look of concentration radiating from his facial expression, his voice was strong and steady. "Steve you saw all these soldiers come out of the 'Ant Nest' and return via this stump thing. At any time did you see them use another entrance, a Back Door?"

I leaned forward and picked up my coffee. "Colonel, the answer is no. However, I've been giving everything I saw a great deal of thought, and not just what I saw, but what I didn't see as well. The troops are well trained, but my guess is they are probably inexperienced. The gear looks nearly new, the gear and the weapons I took from the two sentries were in first-class battle order, and lightly oiled. I mean right down to being clean but not over-oiled, just as we are trained to operate in sandy conditions. OK, the whole set-up is too smart, too savvy to have their entire force bottled up under one cork, that stump. Let's face it one man with an M60 machine gun could keep them down there until he ran out of ammo".

Captain Thompson unwound his lanky body like a python waking and asked, "So what you're saying Sir is that you believe there has to be a Back Door?"

I answered, "Exactly, and the trouble is that the whole area is riddled with underground caves. I think we need to work on the assumption that there must be a back exit. With your permission, we should name it Objective Back Door and be mindful it could be miles away from that stump and farmhouse."

"In one way I wouldn't have it that far away because I would like my troops close by to circle round and use if we were under attack, but it could be anywhere between those two options."

Black replied, "OK that's a pretty good answer and assessment of that threat. I agree we need to designate that as another objective and Back Door is as good as any other name. Let's all keep thinking that one through. We need to plug up that rat hole so none of those rats can get away".

Clive Millard a Spook with ASIO added. "Now there are a few other targets we need to discuss, not that any of us needed the Brigadier's motivation.

We all know that Jihad Rabbit needs catching or killing, and some of us feel we owe him one for slipping the leash when he came into Australia so he's the main game here gentlemen. I suggest we assign at least one team with that as their only objective. By doing that it should reduce the risk of the Rabbit slipping out while we are all concentrating on the minor troops and objectives. What are your thoughts?" The Military Officers around the table nodded signalling they all agreed.

The Australian Federal Police Commissioner Doug Wilson had been silent so far, understanding that the plan was a Military Plan. "I'm unsure whether we're at the point to raise this but I see that putting a tight net around this operation should be twofold. You Military guys want to put cordons or ambush sites to contain them on the property which is your area of operation. However, in the unlikely possibility that some of the enemy do slip through, it might make sense for my boys to control an outer perimeter. Thanks to Colonel Goodrich who realised that possibility from the get-go the local Police have sealed off the place from both directions but at a distance and under a civilian cover story."

The Commissioner paused and took a sip of water. "Once the assault starts I was thinking of having roadblocks and checkpoints in closer to the target property than the present roadblocks, these manned by my people. This would ensure security both ways because we don't know what enemy resources are available. The last thing you would want is enemy reinforcements coming in from outside the property and arriving at your backs to find you guys in the middle of it".

Goodrich enjoyed collaborative planning, especially with such high calibre personnel. "Great thinking Doug, you know the movies and the media always make out that the Military and Civilian Authorities can't work together. That our egos can't fit in the same meeting room but surprise, surprise that's just bullshit. Doug, we'll do just that. Let's mark out this map placing the cordon for us and then probable locations for your roadblocks and checkpoints."

Until then Colonel Goodrich had been quiet preferring instead to release the experts, the ones who would be boots on the ground to ask the questions and create the necessary strategies.

The Colonel continued. "Steve, something just crossed my mind, was there any chance these guys had any air? A lot of cattle properties have their own airstrip or a chopper for mustering cattle?

Shaking my head, I responded. "Thankfully the properties around Roma aren't as big as those up in the Northern Territory. It's pretty rare for a farmer around Roma to have his plane. It's possible but in all my time hunting on my property I haven't noticed a small fixed-wing around, so I would think it's unlikely and the same goes with choppers."

Goodrich looked relieved. "That's good, following our assault the Black Hawks can be there as a backup within a few minutes if we need them".

Colonel Black still looked like he had something else on his mind. "One thing we haven't thrown around is the presence of the two other men on the verandah with the Rabbit. The unnamed other Talib we figure is probably the Commander of the soldiers on the farm.

Goodrich chimed in. "There were no matches when we ran him through the Facial Recognition Program (FRP). The other man though is very well known to us. He is Ex-Captain Fitzpatrick of SAS Regiment. Disappeared after he resigned his commission after he screwed up and ordered his Patrol to open fire on a group of unarmed civvies in the sunny sandpit. We heard rumours he was making it big as a mercenary, a contractor as they prefer to be called these days. Operating mostly in Africa, which is why we hadn't thought of him in a long time. Most security services had assumed that he was either on a beach in Majorca or dead in a jungle grave somewhere.

Well, neither was true, he is here, and I think we all agree he is probably the reason these soldiers look so damned good. Everything Steve has seen and assessed reeks of SAS, approaches to training and higher quality demands, with all due respect to the present company. Remember gentlemen, we still don't know who these guys are or what they are here for. Are they a group of boat people that are now trained soldiers or were they soldiers somewhere else? We won't know the answers to some of these questions until we are inside that farm house, collect some Intel and we get to interrogate our prisoners".

Captain Thompson asked. "Major Wallace, do you know Fitzpatrick? You seem to have served in a few of the same hot spots as recently as 2009. Did you ever bump into him?"

I wondered if there was more to that question than the obvious but decided to ignore my paranoia for now. "He was always anti-authority but in a controlled way that is nearly a SAS requirement. Operating independently, and making big decisions without the constraints of worrying too much about the repercussions is all part of that game.

He was very good at what he did and was in the training wing for about a year if I remember correctly. He had a lot to do with sniper training, so I guess that's something to consider. We all worked on Tactics Techniques and Procedures (TTPs), virtually a more sophisticated version of Standard Operating Procedures (SOPs) that all of the Army integrated a hundred years ago. Anyway, this guy actually developed a lot of them. The other thing he had a lot to do with was the establishment of the 'House'. This was a fully functional house that our guys would assault learning breaching and search techniques in real-life environments".

"Sounds like we are up against a high-quality Officer who sold out. We can't take anything for granted." Thompson surmised.

Being a Military Operation on Australian soil the 2nd Commando Officers understandably wanted very clear Rules of Engagement (ROE). The Brigadier had made it clear that a goal to score a few prisoners was vital and the management of the Rabbit had been established as a High Priority Target. Capture would be outstanding, but his elimination was Green Lighted if capture was not an option. The overall plan was what we called in the SAS a Standard Strike to Develop Action (SSDA) where we carried out our planned actions to force the enemy to do something we wanted, say to break cover. The simpler the plan usually meant the bigger chance of success. For me, the SSDA was like breathing because even as a child I had often thrown a rock into some brush to scare out a real rabbit. We were all hoping that this would work just as effectively for a different type of Rabbit.

Just over three hours after the Brigadiers had excused themselves Colonel Goodrich looked around the room and asked: "OK gentlemen how are we going? If the Brigadier & the Major General approve this plan, we'll all need to have a few fine-tuning get-togethers, but I think we have enough right now to talk them through it."

While I agreed with the Colonel's statement I was still very aware we had no idea why this camp existed and what their plans were.

The most worrying part was regarding how much or how little time we had before they were going to do whatever they were planning. Little wonder that the Brig and the MAJGEN had set us a time limit for the next forty-eight hours. The room was full of very experienced highly trained soldiers. They all knew what needed to be done and they also knew the potential risks of letting a major terrorist, like the Rabbit and a team of over fifty enemy soldiers, be free to do whatever they chose. Colonel Goodrich picked up the only phone in the room, punched in three numbers, and spoke softly into the mouthpiece.

Less than two minutes later the two Senior Officers returned to the room, this time no one remained seated even our civilian member. Major General Watson took charge, "Stand easy gentlemen, how did you go?"

Colonel Goodrich responded first, outlining the plan and directing each senior person to add detail as needed. Major General Watson sat patiently for the full plan to be provided without interruption.

"Gentlemen, it is of no surprise to either of us I'm sure," gesturing to Brigadier Dodds sitting at his right, "that a high-level group of Officers, such as yourselves, could come up with such a workable plan in such a short time. One massive consideration that I chose not to burden you with earlier is the fact that you will be launching a Company size attack on Australian soil. This is unheard of; didn't even get to do it when it looked like the Japs were going to take over. However, that is for Mr Norman there, the PM and sadly myself to iron out. By the time you are wheels up, we will have our part done. My guess is that you will go in unannounced, do the job and get out unannounced. No one will know it ever happened or at least not until we are all gone to a better place. You do the dirty work and I'll get the political work done making sure your backs are covered when you return. That is why I wear all this stuff on my shoulders."

With that, the Brigadier and MAJGEN started to ask some questions. They were good questions, not nit-picking, not inferring failure, things we hadn't thought of and not to justify their inclusion in the meeting.

These were experienced senior warriors as well and they were about to send brave Australian men into harm's way. They knew that some would not be coming home alive. They were responsible, and they were interested in making sure this was the best plan we could go with.

MAJGEN Watson looked at Brigadier Dodds who nodded. "OK boys it's a GO; wheels up in twenty-four hours, over the top ASAP after. Good luck and God bless you all. Major Wallace, can you hang back after they all go?" That was a Brigadier's subtle way of saying, clear the room. The high-powered group stood gathering their papers and left in small groups still discussing the plan in smaller pieces.

The two Senior Officers remained seated. Watson started. "First of all, I just wanted to meet you properly, and thank you for your dedication to this whole thing. If you hadn't persisted with the Intel who knows what would have happened."

I responded. "Sir I couldn't have done this without Colonel Walsh in Brisbane and your Colonel Goodrich. It must have been pretty scary having some hunter in Roma saying there was an army of Taliban next door. I probably wouldn't have believed it if I was them".

Nodding, the MAJGEN continued. "Son you don't surprise me showing such personal loyalty. It's what you're made of." He continued. "Anyway, as I said I wanted to meet you properly before the balloon goes up, do you think we are on the right track?"

Inwardly, I smiled at the use of the term "when the balloon goes up", it referred to the old-World War One method of starting an attack. Several balloons would be launched signalling the troops to leave their trenches and advance toward the enemy lines.

"Sir I think we are pretty right, I've been sent out with a lot less Intel than we now have. It would be great to know more; who they were and what this is all about but like I said we have heaps to go on. I am sure what we have planned needs to be done and after what I saw in this room we have the right team to get it done". I said.

"Well said Major, see you at the airport". With that, the Brigadier and MAJGEN left me sitting alone wondering again how the hell I had gone from hunting and drinking with my dog Jake to being back in all this and about to get busy again.

CHAPTER 26

JUNE 2014

After that historic meeting at NSC HQ, the 2nd Commando Company Officers met with the Commanding Officer of the 6th Aviation Regiment, Colonel Jeff Cockburn, and the 171st Squadron Leader, Major John Jones, along with his Second in Command (2IC). They were based at Luscombe Army Airfield Holsworthy which would be the stepping-off point for the operation in a matter of hours. There was a lot to discuss to give Aviation time to do their own planning. Working backwards the Commando Officers needed to know where their men would be dropped prior to the assault on the Terrorist Camp.

The first question was how close they thought they could get without the noise giving away the show? It was one of those questions that had a lot of variables affecting the answer but with their expert advice, a safe distance was established. Flying in low to avoid being heard or seen was a given but pilots only ever worried about two things, Landing Zones (L.Z.s) and the weather. One big bonus for the Fly Boys, which always made them happy, was they would not have to worry about the enemy having any radar capability. That didn't mean the Talibs might not have RPGs. In fact, it was highly possible that they may have some Surface to Air Missiles (SAMs) which thankfully while this couldn't be dismissed was less likely. But at least with these weapons, they would have to rely on a soldier seeing a Helo to aim at. And if he could do that, so could the Blackhawk's Crew Chief/Gunners and Pilots could see the shooter and eliminate him.

Working together they identified several Landing Zone possibilities, eventually deciding on a suitable one. They named it LZ Echo. It was located on a cattle property south of the Terrorist Camp. It was far enough away that there was no chance any of the Talibs would hear the Helos fly in. With the number of enemy troops unconfirmed, all they could do was base their plans on my Recce. Their best guess was maybe sixty-plus Talibs. So, an attack force of one hundred Commandos and Officers with Air Support and Police assistance was decided to be sufficient. Uplifting one hundred plus and gear would require at least ten UH-60s Black Hawks carrying about ten or eleven in each sortie.

The Fly Boys decided on allocating twelve UH-60s just to have a little wiggle room if needed. The 171St Aviation Squadron was based there at Luscombe Army Airfield, Holsworthy and would transport the entire attack force from Holsworthy to Oakey, Queensland. There, they would refuel and continue on the second leg of the journey of a bit less than three hundred kilometres to Roma. This LZ needed to be confirmed but for planning purposes, this all seemed to fit well. In an open rural area, Landing Zones were a lot easier to find than in a built-up area. If for any reason the planned LZ didn't pan out there were other contingent areas to utilise.

Colonel Cockburn turned to Major Jones. "John, get on the blower to Oakey and have them dispatch a couple of Lieutenants, young ones, John. We want to make this look low-key, not really important, you with me? Get them to that cattle property to check out our first choice LZ, what did you name it, Echo?

We need them to confirm if it is a suitable location as per our boy's flying needs. And John ask them to check out the surrounds for our ground troops."

Colonel Black nodded his appreciation. "We need to make sure it is away from the highway, so no travellers would see the Helos landing and there must be access to load the friendlies onto wheeled vehicles of some sort to travel via the highway to the Target cattle property".

The Brigadier added, "Obviously get these Officers to gain permission from the property owner. Remind them to use that new paperwork we all got last month. They'll need to spin a yarn along the lines that we need permission to use the LZ for a Training Exercise". These Oakey Flying Officers didn't muck around; by lunchtime that day the Lieutenants had been to the property and LZ Echo had been confirmed as suitable. All done. The property owner had a copy of his signed permission form under his favourite teapot sitting on his kitchen table. Air transport was sorted.

It was decided that once the raid had commenced, having some air support would be advantageous. Covering escape routes and using the Black Hawks would use various weapons to support the ground forces. Two more Landing Zones near the farmhouse of the Terrorist Camp were assigned LZ Delta for Casualty Evacuation and LZ Foxtrot as the main Rendezvous (RV) if it all went bad. All going well the large turning area in front of the farmhouse would be used to pick up all parties after the operation and return home. The allocation of the Black Hawks in the hunting role was left to the Fly Boys as the sky would be a bit crowded if all twelve Helos were prowling around. Moving over one hundred men plus equipment from the nearby property by wheeled transport unnoticed would be enough of a challenge.

The Commando Officers pondered how they would get that many Army trucks or even 4WDs in location in time and keep them out of sight?

Sitting back in Canberra, I was thinking about this next transport phase when the 4WD solution hit me in the face like a wet fish.

I phoned Colonel Black. He wasn't available, so they put me through to his Adjutant Captain, Tim Thompson. "It's Steve Wallace, Hey how you goin?"

"Busier than a one-armed bricklayer in Beirut, Sir".

I'd forgotten he was a Captain and I wasn't Steve but Major Wallace now. "Hey I just had an idea about the road transport from LZ Echo to the Forming Up Area (FUP), I'd be interested in what you guys think about it".

"I hope it works Sir. We've been wracking our brains on that part". Thompson sounded a little dejected.

"OK, now at the Roma Airport there would be at least two hundred white Land Cruiser seven-seater Sedans and Utes parked there. They are used by the Fly in Fly out Contractors building that Gas Pipeline."

I paused then continued. "Number One, I can't see why we can't borrow the required number of 4WDs to transport men and gear. I'm sure we can tell the Gas Company something that makes sense. Number Two the reason I mentioned their colour is that everyone around the Roma region is used to seeing these vehicles coming and going on every part of the highway and side roads. Some even have company signs or logos on the doors".

Dejection was replaced with enthusiasm. "I think you've nailed it, Sir. That sounds like good camouflage. The fact that everyone is used to seeing them, I like it. A heap of Army vehicles would have caused a stir. I'll talk to the Colonel as soon as he gets back, but I'm sure he'll love that idea. I'll come back to you ASAP."

With that Captain Thompson ended the call. As promised Thompson presented this idea to his Colonel as soon as he got back to the office. And as predicted Colonel Black thought it was a great solution to the logistical problem of quietly moving all those men into the Forming Up Place. "Tim we're sure lucky to have Steve

Wallace on our side. Having all that local knowledge plus being Army he's a major asset".

The Colonel said with a smile. "I agree. Get onto someone at that Gas Company and arrange to borrow those 4WDs. Spin them the same yarn about a training exercise. And Tim, see if you can get them for a week to keep the attack date secure, it'll give us some flexibility too."

Colonel Goodrich sat at his NSC desk and mentally ticked off the two logistical biggies: *OK Air Transport under control, Road Transport under control.* The Target property was roughly triangular in shape. It had been decided Alpha Platoon, about one-third of the Commando Company would mount the boundary cordon. The size of the cattle property meant it would take the entire Commando Company to cover the whole boundary fence in case the enemy simply dispersed to the boundaries in all directions. However, it was decided the Talibs were unlikely to do that, at least in the early stages of contact. They would stand and fight. It was also believed that if the enemy did withdraw it would be driven by our forces' assault and therefore be restricted to a certain direction and location. Commissioner Doug Wilson had dispatched his Federal Police early to give them plenty of time to liaise with the local Police. Because roadblocks were already in place it was relatively simple to use local maps to ensure any farm track or minor road couldn't be used as an escape route. A few were identified and immediately plugged up.

The local Police Inspector was more than happy to have the extra manpower and although he realised something important was going on if the Feds were here, one way or another he was happy for his team to play a part. He didn't have the details but if that fella they were looking for was still in his area he was happy to catch him, get some kudos and then get back to normal. The plan was to fly from Oakey by Helos to the LZ Echo, then travel by 4WDs drive to the cattle property I was camped on. We would use my home paddock as a FUP and from there move towards the Terrorist Camp across the small dirt road.

There is an old adage, 'To impose order on potential chaos, ensure simplicity'. The more complex the plans, the more they can and usually do go wrong. Thinking through just the transport side of this Op it all sounded simple, but stuff always goes wrong. I'm an optimist but I've been there and done that in places you don't go back to. Real battles and make no mistake this would be a battle. With fifty or sixty trained and armed men believing they were serving their god, they were not about to roll over just because the cavalry rides in. I was always taught to hope for the best and plan for the worst and it had been proven a sound platform on many occasions. Don't get me wrong. I love it but the real Army even SAS is not some Swiss-made precision instrument. It's hardly ever like in the movies where choppers fly in on the dot of an arranged time. Most times we can't even get trucks on time.

As a soldier, you spend a lot of your life waiting. Waiting for something, for orders, for resupply of ammo or water or rations and you definitely spend time waiting for transport of some sort. The Army is famous for repeating the same action as though the outcome will change without anything else changing as well. The choppers or trucks will *actually* be waiting for you and not the other way around. Hurry up and wait is the system and it has probably been that way since wars began and the horses and wagons arrived late. Having said all that and knowing it is all true, Officers still must make plans and believe in their plans. In the original planning meetings at NSC HQ, we had identified an unacceptable threat; that shed full of Quad Bikes set up with Weapon Buckets on both sides clearly equipped for two soldiers at a time. Having chased pigs all over my property on a Quad I knew how lethal they could be with me operating by myself. They would be especially dangerous with one soldier controlling the Quad and the other shooting.

Colonel Black took me aside. "Steve you have already done more than your fair share in all this." He paused. "But I need to ask if you would be willing to sneak back in and plant some explosives amongst the Quad Bikes? The charges will be detonated by remote as the assault is launched. I have plenty of good men to go with you if you want some company".

I gave this some thought and decided it was doable but only under the cover of darkness. "Sir I'm OK to do it but I'll go in alone, two men means twice the noise, twice the bodies that have to hide someplace".

Black smiled. "Thanks, Steve. I'm not surprised you want to go it alone, I'll have my Engineers make up a pack of explosive devices ready for you to deliver".

My other role was to guide the main party into the Terrorist Camp to ensure the two Assault Platoons' pincer formation caught the farmhouse right in the middle. We still had no idea if there was a Back Door to the underground barracks and if there was, where it was. We had studied every satellite photo we could find. I had asked Colonel Goodrich to get his expert photo analysis guys to take a second look as well. We had got onto some geological charts. These revealed the numerous cave systems in the area and while this wasn't definitive, it gave us some possible parameters to contain.

As discussed, there was a Section of Commandos assigned to this task. They were to infiltrate the modified stump entry and systematically search for any sign of a possible exit from the Ant Nest. Not knowing where the Back Door to the Ant Nest was, worried us all. The Helos would patrol for any escapees just appearing in the middle of farmland to the rear of the house paddock. Twenty-four hours and counting down we filed into the Helos at Luscombe Army Airfield. We climbed in and sat on either side of the cabin like kids on a bus ride to school. It was not like the old days of Iroquois where the unlucky sap carrying the

General-Purpose Machine Gun (GPMG M60) sat on the floor with his legs dangling out. The UH-60s went so much faster. If you tried that in a Black Hawk you would get sucked right out.

The pilots had been tasked to avoid going over or near Roma township, to keep the local population from thinking they were being invaded. Well before they reached the Roma region the Helos swung west around and past the town before heading towards Landing Zone Echo. Each chopper arrived with the pilot letting inertia take the machine a little past the LZ. Standing on its tail, the Helo hovered momentarily and then touched down in an absolute storm of dirt, leaves and twigs. We had all been trained to jump out, run three steps and hit the ground.

This was probably unnecessary in a secure Landing Zone. However, if you don't do things like that automatically you are likely to not do it when it's needed. Once the choppers left, each man stood up and formed into a defensive Section group off to one side. Three Sections to a Platoon and three Platoons to a Company. Officers check on the Non-Commissioned Officers (NCO s) and the Sergeants and Corporals check on their men. A good system tried and true. OK all down, we now loaded into the anonymous fleet of Gas Pipeline 4WDs and headed off to the Forming Up Place that used to be my hunting camp. The Road Transport phase was uneventful with the white Land Cruisers travelling in pairs, taking no chances and keeping a low profile. We did well, all personnel and equipment were in place by 1645 Hours, no accidents, no injuries, and no one lost.

We had decided that having over one hundred men a few klicks away from the enemy camp for an extended period was asking for trouble. We were on a tight timeframe, in any case, attempting to isolate and destroy the camp before anyone could leave. Obviously, we did all we could to minimise the noise of our convoy of 4WDs bringing the men into the Forming Up Place from the LZ. However, late at night camp sounds are magnified significantly and travel for miles. We had decided all troops were to be in the FUP just before dark, and thankfully that stage of the Op was completed on schedule.

They would cold camp (no smoking, no fires) at the FUP from then until they all moved off in readiness for the assault just before dawn the following morning. Each NCO had his Section set up a defensive perimeter in their sector and send out pickets (sentries) while the rest of the Commandos settled in for the night.

I walked among the troops. Smiling, a young Corporal looked up from his ration pack. "Evening Sir, do you know what's the most dangerous thing in the bush?"

It was a very old joke, but I played along. "No idea what?"

With a good-humoured laugh, he responded. "An Officer with a compass." With that, the three other men within earshot all laughed at my expense.

"Very funny Corporal, that frigging joke is older than you. You guys are doing great, keep your heads down later hey?" With that, I moved on.

From what I had seen of the enemy they were focused on guarding their boundary, keeping people out, and it made no sense to advertise their presence by sending out roving patrols that went outside their own property. Based on this assessment we believed that so as long as we kept the noise down the chances of being discovered were minimal. Soldiers everywhere were all the same. As I continued my walk around the camp I saw that some of these guys had already hit the sack. The way these Commandos snored I was surprised the Talibs hadn't heard them already.

About half an hour before dark I started to get ready to return to the enemy base. I had got away with it last time and wondered: *am I pushing my luck going back in tonight?* One of the Commando Demolition Engineers filled up a backpack with explosive devices that would detonate by remote control. Not unlike a garage roller door remote except with a little antenna you raised before pushing the button. My task tonight was to place these devices throughout the Quad shed ready to be set off during the raid tomorrow neutralising the Quads as either an offensive weapon or as an escape vehicle. I had decided to only carry my 9mm semi-auto pistol for this task as trying to move quietly between the bikes and equipment with a rifle slung over your shoulder is asking for trouble.

To avoid warning the Talibs of our impending raid it was vital my visit was not detected. Tonight, even if I had to kill a sentry quietly with a knife or my hands, my mission would be a failure. I waited for what I hoped was long enough for the Talibs to return to the Ant Nest for the night. I hadn't forgotten the Talib sentries, but I was counting on them being away from the house area keeping to the surrounding tracks and bush. I hoped they would make the same mistake most guards and sentries made, always looking outward and never inward, never behind themselves.

All armies go to bed early because they usually get up early, so I figured that by 2000 Hours they would all be tucked up dreaming of seventy-something virgins or their favourite hillside back home. As I stood up I surveyed my usually secluded hunting camp that was now surrounded by a full Company of Commandos and ancillary extras. My life was upside down and was still tumbling.

CHAPTER 27

Over the years, heading off into different jungles and deserts I had always liked to daydream for the first few minutes, it seemed to relax me. As I picked up the backpack and moved off I thought: *I'd much rather be hunting wild pigs and was glad Jake wasn't here, he didn't like crowds either.* I know it's a bit weird with everything going on in my mind, but it hit me just how much I missed him. He's a good mate, never talks back and doesn't like JD, perfect. On the way through the Platoon lines, I dropped into Company Headquarters (Coy HQ) where Colonel Black and Captain Thompson were going over the attack plan for the hundredth time.

"Colonel, anything new I should know before going on my visit to the neighbours?"

"Nothing that comes to mind, Steve, the Code Word for tonight is SPEAR. Don't forget it. I would hate to see you get shot by our picket (sentry) when you come back" he said laughing.

"Well I have to agree with you there that's for sure."

The Colonel shook my hand. "Good luck Steve and thanks for doing this, one of my men could have tried it but it makes sense with you knowing your way around".

We all realised that this was the beginning of the unknown and that men would be injured or die in just a few hours so just like soldiers all through history.

I attempted to take some of the pressure off with some lame humour. "No worries Sir I wasn't busy anyway".

With a quick smile, I melted into the darkness. Twenty metres on, a sentry I didn't see bailed me up but then relaxed when I whispered the word "Spear".

Good work so far, but only what you would expect from Commandos. I had done the walk to the dirt road between the two properties a thousand times, so I was able to move silently and quickly down the slope towards the gravel track. I could feel the Adrenalin kick in thinking about what was ahead of me and, trusting my bush skills, I was happy to be going alone.

There was a sliver of moon tonight and it reflected off the quartz in the gravel road. I moved across this ribbon of light quickly and quietly blended into the darkness caused by the trees growing close to the access track into the property. Reaching the sanctuary of the scrub I stopped for a full ten minutes listening for any sign I had been seen or heard by one of the Talib sentries. Nothing but an owl calling to its mate. Tonight, I would repeat the same route I used the last time I sneaked in for a Recce. With the extra moonlight tonight, I was super careful to move from shadow to shadow, listening at each pause. Instead of moving off the track to the right and heading to where I had hidden on my last Recce this time I broke left off the track. To get to the Quad shed I had to circle around the farmhouse to arrive at the rear of the big shed staying out of sight from the house and without crossing any open ground.

This was new country to me, but I was in no hurry and that sliver of moon was helpful from time to time, getting around the odd fallen timber or a wash away. I went wide to make sure I didn't bump into someone getting some air or sitting on the verandah. I was just about to move again when over to my left a match flared illuminating a sentry's bearded face. So much for my theory that all the sentries would be a long way from the house. It was probably another example of Fitzpatrick's Military mind at work. Trust him to think of protecting his king as it were. Anyway, at least I now knew where the sentry was, and I made a mental note to avoid him on my way back.

Knowing I had plenty of time, I took nearly two hours to get to the rear of the Quad shed. Giving the house a wide birth stretched out the distance. Once I arrived I swung the pack onto the ground and unpacked the explosives. Thankfully the bright lights that were on the other night were off and only one small bulb flickered on a long electric chord swinging in the gentle breeze at the very front of the shed. There was a single bare bulb on the verandah shining with a yellow light bulb with a sort of halo around it. There were no other lights on in the farmhouse hopefully suggesting all the occupants had gone to bed. I stepped out of the darkness and up onto the rough concrete slab. Systematically, I started to weave my way around the rows of Quad Bikes. I then went about depositing and setting the remote-controlled explosive devices ensuring all the shed was covered. Satisfied the explosions would destroy all or most of the bikes, I once again quietly withdrew to the welcoming darkness.

It was crucial that I returned to the Forming Up Place undetected, as any contact now even if I escaped unharmed could well warn the camp of the impending attack. This would be especially so if I was to be captured or killed as Fitzpatrick would immediately know what my presence in that uniform meant; other Australian soldiers had to be nearby. Backing away from the Quad shed I stopped and waited again just to make sure no one was coming toward me. Looking up towards the house I saw the door open framing Fitzpatrick and another man as they stepped into the ring of golden light cast onto the verandah. I am normally pretty calm, but any traitor makes me sick and especially one I called a friend like Fitzy. He had betrayed his country and was also a traitor to the Regiment. To anyone from SAS that means a whole lot. I was so angry at seeing him again and in such company, my fists clenched involuntarily.

I could taste the bile rising in my throat. It would be so easy for me to ease back up to the house and put a couple of nine millimetres in Fitzpatrick's head right where he stood. Depending on his reactions I figured I could probably get the other guy too. I remembered that we wanted to capture the second man if possible. As much as I would have loved to end Fitzpatrick's life, the bigger picture was far more important. I calmed myself, silently making a promise. *Tomorrow, I'll look for you on the battlefield.* I slowly headed back to the track silently moving along its darkened fringe. About where I expected the sentry to be I could smell smouldering tobacco pinpointing the new location of the Talib I had seen light up earlier. Once past him, I made my way towards the gravel road that separated my hunting property from the enemy camp. By now the little light from the moon had gone.

As I placed my right boot on the gravel road I suddenly heard a vehicle starter motor turn over and a diesel engine kick in. Headlights and a bank of spotlights assaulted the dark night all around where I had been entering the road. Hearing the engine crank gave me the instant I needed to spring back into the darkness beside the road. I couldn't see a thing, my night vision destroyed by the incredibly bright lights after such darkness. The driver engaged first gear and the vehicle slowly headed my way. I was somewhat relieved as I figured if they had seen me they would be rushing towards my location. Thankfully they were maintaining the slow pace they had begun with. I stayed in the shadows off the side of the road praying they were not going to sweep search with a hand-held spotlight. They drove on slowly turning onto the narrow track I had just left that took them back down towards the farmhouse. Once they were well down the track I got up and quickly crossed the gravel road and made my way back to camp.

Our sentry was a lot more switched on than his Talib counterpart across the road and was alert to my return. He still challenged me, only allowing me to pass after I had whispered "Spear" in reply. I walked through the rows of dispersed sleeping Commandos and grabbed a bottle of Jack Daniels from my kit. I then headed back down the small hill returning to Coy HQ because

I knew the Commando Officers would not be asleep. "Colonel just thought I'd let you know I was back and that all went as planned. Share a drink with you two?"

Pouring three Jacks for us all I reported how the mission had gone in a bit more detail and we quietly talked about tomorrow and the day to come. I refilled each of our coffee mugs with some more smoky whiskey, enjoying the quiet, three old Soldiers sharing our thoughts of what might happen in the coming battle. Once we had run out of Jack Daniels we called it a night. I climbed the hill again and hit the sack. Usually, I can sleep standing up, however, I wasn't so sure that I would sleep tonight. My mind was double-checking and trying to play a video in my head of what tomorrow's assault on the Terror Camp might look like. It would come soon enough.

CHAPTER 28

Forming Up Area
Cattle Property
Roma

There is an unmistakable sound that a group of soldiers make when a new day starts. It doesn't matter how careful, how quiet and strangely enough even how many soldiers. There are always little clicks as buckles are engaged. The sound that army webbing belts and packs rubbing against one another and the slosh of water bottles all combine. It was to these subtle sounds that I awoke as I had so many times before in very similar circumstances. The soldiers around me were consuming their tubed rations cold and like all soldiers immediately before a battle, they all had routines.

With experience, you can pick the different types, the ones who pray or hold religious medals. The quiet ones looking out at nothing, the incessant talkers, the jokers, the ones that are constantly checking and re-checking their gear. Some get touchy usually irritated by the jokers or the talkers. Me, I just get up itching to get going.

If I had been out on a sniping job I could wait patiently forever, but the actual leaving to start a patrol, I wanted it done and over. I had seen plenty of soldiers in my time and these Commandos were way better than I had ever realised. They were well disciplined. They knew what to do and when to do it and they looked after their weapons and gear as good as anyone I had seen. I made my way down to the Company HQ again. Captain Thompson and Colonel Black welcomed me into their command tent. They had set up a trestle table and had a large topographical map spread out on it displaying the two cattle properties, my hunting property and the

Target Property. We had marked this up back at NSC HQ. The detail and the scale made it look nearly as good as an aerial photo.

Using satellite photos, the Forming Up Point, the farmhouse, the Ant Nest, the Quad Shed and all the other outbuildings were all located accurately. It was also planned that two flat areas adjacent to the RVs would serve as both a Casualty Evacuation Landing Zone known as Delta and an R.V. LZ Foxtrot serving as a place to load up under fire if we were in trouble and had to bug out quickly. As planned if the attack was successful we would use the clearing in front of the Quad shed and cattle yards for routine Evac for the flight back to Sydney after it was all over. All the LZ had a designated code name of their own.

They had also marked a blind end gully to serve as a secure area to hold prisoners who would be flown out from the Casualty Evacuation Landing Zone just off to the north of the farmhouse. Prisoners would be transported back to Sydney for interrogation. Part of the plan was that if the farmhouse was not destroyed it would be used as an aide post to treat any wounded. This map had been used the previous night for the Orders Group where the Colonel briefed his Officers in full detail for the last time. All the Platoon responsibilities had been discussed before leaving Canberra giving the Platoon Commanders time to plan and bring the NCOs into the plan as well.

Alpha Platoon had to get into position to cordon off any escape through the rear of the property. Transported in the white Land Cruisers that had brought them into the Forming Up Place the night before, they had left two hours before the other two platoons moved off. The vehicles dropped off pairs of Commandos at regular intervals until the perimeter was covered. There was to be no radio communication until after the commencement of the assault. Only the use of pre-arranged squelch messages, which is when the microphone button is compressed silencing the squelching static type sound on radios.

The Platoon Commander squelched twice confirming that they had the cordon in place. On receiving the confirmation from Alpha, Bravo, and Charlie Platoons with the HQ Group, the centre moved off down the hill towards the enemy camp. I was assigned to HQ Group as the guide. We moved off as quietly as seventy-odd soldiers can move and to be fair did a great job. As planned the two Platoons halted just before the boundary road and fanned out in one line; Bravo on the left flank Charlie on the right, HQ where the two Platoons met. Colonel Black using hand signals ordered the wings of Bravo and Charlie forward holding the HQ Group back to create a V-shaped assault line.

In the V-shaped formation, the two Commando Platoons with their HQ in the centre moved across the road and into the scrub, advancing slowly but steadily. We continued this way until about a hundred metres before the farmhouse clearing. Coming over a small rise, which left the HQ group a little behind and lower than the Platoons, two heavy machine guns opened up on us from the right and left flanks. They were well-sited, firing straight ahead and not at each other in a cross-fire situation. By the sound of it, they were probably DushkM, a Russian-made Heavy Machine Gun often called Dushkas. They had originally been made in World War Two but the 'M' represented Modernised. They were still as deadly as ever.

The Commandos reacted quickly and exactly as they had been trained to do. The wings moved wider to outflank their respective machine guns while everyone else laid down a solid amount of suppressing fire. This restricted the enemy machine gunners from firing accurately by forcing them to keep their heads down. Bravo's wings got around first, and we heard the unmistakable sound of several M79 Grenades exploding immediately followed by screaming and then silence on the left flank. We heard a spray of 5.56mm from a Commando's M4 Assault Rifle and then silence again. The suppressing fire had let up just a little, but it was enough for the Talibs to start the right flank Dushka Heavy Machine Gun up again.

Lead zipped through the leaves above us and splintered branches and trunks. The Commandos on the right had got in close using a slight dip in the ground leading to the high point where the enemy HMG was sited. The sound of four Fragment (Frag) Grenades thudded loudly shaking the earth beneath us and showering dirt and leaves metres into the sky. This time no rifle fire was needed to finish off the machine gunners. The two teams from each wing returned to formation. The Colonel gave the rise sign followed by the advance. We were off again. We had talked this through in the fine detail planning and it was decided to speed up the advance once there had been a contact so as not to give any Talibs time to evacuate the Ant Nest or get to any of those Quads before we destroyed them. The machine guns had slowed us down a little more than we had expected so we picked up the pace as much as we could.

The enemy roving patrols had been withdrawing ahead of us driven in front of our advance. They were running and then pulling up behind some tree or rock or dip in the ground to fire on us. Clearly, this was a planned and practised strategy designed to slow down an advancing force. They weren't hitting much but the AKs rate of fire was enough to be respected and it was successfully slowing us down. One of the Commandos beside me was hit in the shoulder, throwing him sideways. I opened up on the two Talibs that had fired. Emptying my magazine, I was rewarded by seeing one fall backwards and the other collapse like a bag of spuds. A Commando Sergeant took several bullets in his chest which drove him backwards into a crumpled mess up against a large Gum tree. Finally, we made it to the farmhouse clearing coming to the little raised area that had served me so well when I did my Recce.

As expected the stump at the Ant Nest was wide open and, just like the name suggested, soldiers in all stages of dress were pouring up the inside ladder and jumping down to the ground. These men had started firing as soon as they hit the ground. They were aware they had little or no cover, so they ran towards the house and cattle yards across the dirt turn-around surrounding the stump. Just as we expected, a quick look at the Quad Bike Shed showed ten or twelve Talibs had run to their Quads and were on them trying to start them.

Captain Thompson who was responsible for setting off the charges withdrew the remote control from his left breast pocket. Just as he was about to push the remote's button he was thrown on his back, a large red stain appearing on the front of his chest, his heart and lungs torn apart. I dived on his shattered body grabbing the remote control from his lifeless hand and in the same motion pushed the button to detonate the charges I had laid the night before. There was a fraction of a second when nothing happened. I thought: *oh no, why aren't the charges firing.* Then there was one explosion followed by another and then the other eight charges went off in unison. Quads and bodies and other farm equipment were thrown in every direction, some straight up to be driven into the iron roof only to fall immediately to the ground.

The debris from the Quad Shed had sprayed like shrapnel all over the surrounding area forcing the Taliban Soldiers who had been firing from under the cattle yards and a nearby shed to stumble into the open, stunned by the explosion. However, the Commandos showed no mercy mowing them down in a single burst. Not one soldier or Quad survived the explosion. We had no confirmed enemy numbers. They had already taken some casualties. I had been so busy with the remote control that I hadn't noticed a group of at least ten Taliban fighters had formed a defensive perimeter around the stump. Now while this was brave, and normally it would have been the right thing to do as they had little or no cover where they were, it was a mistake.

The Commandos, firing in a highly disciplined manner from slightly higher ground and from cover, decimated this resistance in a matter of minutes. There were three Talibs shooting from behind the stump which was now peppered by the Commando's hurricane of bullets. As another enemy soldier fell with a scream there was a break in the firing coming from behind the stump.

They must have had a quick committee meeting because the three-remaining enemy threw up their arms in surrender dropping their AKs, good choice. This was great as we now had at least three prisoners to question at a later stage.

We still had no idea how many enemy there were so all we could do was continue to advance, search and destroy as needed. As previously arranged, Colonel Black's radio operator called for Air Support as soon as the first shots were fired.

They were to patrol the property looking for stray Talibs trying to hide or escape and had been given the grid reference of our best guess for the location of the Ant Nest Back Door. They had orders to fire on any targets as they presented, being careful not to approach the cordon where Alpha Platoon was hidden along the property boundary.

With the three surrendering near the stump, there was a lull in the noisy proceedings and I could just hear the wop of the Helo's rotors heading towards us. The stump door to the Ant Nest was still wide open, I suggested to the Colonel that I take the assigned Section down into the cavern to see what we could find. He nodded in agreement, turning to a big NCO who had blood showing on his left bicep. "Corporal Farrell, take your men over to the stump with the Major here. Search whatever is down there, and be careful, we still don't know how many are left".

Still, on the alert, we moved over to the stump. I dug out the small ladder as I had seen the Talibs do, it was hidden in the sand, set it against the stump and scaled it. When I got to the top I turned, grabbed the internal ladder and slid down into the unknown. I remained at the base of the ladder, my gun at the ready covering the section as they came down the ladder just as I had. Section Commander, Corporal Farrell, came down last. He moved very lightly for such a big guy. I took command of the search but was happy for him to manage his men. “Now we have to get going; we're not sure where this goes or what we might find. Be careful keep an eye out for side passages, stragglers and for booby traps, especially trip wires”. With that, the shortest of briefings, off we went. I had been in a lot worse tunnels. At least the air was nearly OK if you were a camel, and there were lights, an absolute luxury.

We had gone about twenty-five metres, including two right-hand bends, when someone opened fire with an AK from a doorway off to our left. The Forward Scout, the first man in our single file search patrol had caught a bullet in his right shoulder.

It had spun him around to his right and that probably saved his life as the rest of the magazine peppered the wall directly behind where he had been standing. Corporal Farrell moved quickly against the wall and tossed a Frag grenade at the doorway on instinct. It was a great shot with fragments cutting the Talib down with wounds to his head and neck. I applied a First Aid Field Dressing to the Private's shoulder and strapped it up as best I could.

I knew I could pull rank, but the Corporal was obviously a class soldier. “Corporal, what do you think about leaving lucky here to guard our rear?”

The young NCO grinned. “Terrific idea Sir, he'll be right here, and he can start working on a good story for the girls while he keeps our butts covered."

With that we propped the wounded Commando up, so he was pointing towards where we had just come from and set up his rifle on his left side, so he could shoot if he had to. We continued in the other direction feeling a little better knowing that no Taliban was going to sneak up behind us. It is hard to judge distance in a tunnel, but it seemed to go on forever.

We came across two trip wires attached to Claymore Mines which we quickly disarmed, an evil contraption when pointed your way. These were SAS Troopers favourite toy, 700 grams of explosive in a directional curved casing full of ball bearings, a real crowd pleaser carving a swath through anything in its path. I had been thinking about how we had rushed through the barracks and other areas. I tried to put myself in the shoes of the person who had set up this incredible underground facility. As we turned another bend I decided if it had been up to me I would have built everything close to the front of the living quarters including the entrance to the Back Door.

The boys probably thought I had lost it when I stopped them and said. "I think we have got it all wrong. I want us to go back to the beginning and search every nook and cranny. Look for whatever they may have hidden, weapons, troops, who knows maybe even this back door everyone keeps wondering about."

I took off with them following. It was quicker going back, we made sure we made a bit of noise, so our wounded comrade knew it was us coming back. We picked him up and kept moving back to the main chamber. Once we arrived I asked the Corporal to assign his troops to the various rooms to search. He did this quickly and without any fuss. The men spread out and began thoroughly searching each part of the barracks and other rooms. Within ten minutes the Section had worked their way through each assigned area without finding any back door. However, they dumped what they had found on the floor of the dining room. There were eight

AKs, twenty or so Mags for them. My heart sank when I saw two boxes of RPG ammo.

You wouldn't have ammo if you didn't have the RPG Launchers to fire them. Somewhere outside the boys would eventually come under fire from these very lethal weapons. RPGs in some form or another have been around a long time. A good friend of mine ended up with a steel plate in his skull courtesy of one of the things detonating in the canopy above his fire pit in Vietnam. They're highly successful in environments where you can't see your targets. You simply aim above their suspected location. When the rocket detonates by hitting a wall or a tree it explodes in all directions including down on the targets hiding behind cover.

About the only downside to these RPGs is they require a straight-on hit to detonate. They must hit directly on the Grenade's nose. I have seen Talibs fire them in Afghanistan and not get that angle right, the rocket just bouncing off the roof of a Patrol Vehicle or the ground without exploding. I figured they should know before they came under fire from the lethal launcher.

"Corporal Farrell send a man up to HQ, advise them that RPGs are confirmed. It won't make it any better when they're under fire, but it may just help to be forewarned".

"Rodger that Sir".

Turning to a Private with tatts and a shaved head. "Donkey, scurry up and tell the boss the rag heads have RPGs confirmed".

With that, a Private whose nickname was obviously Donkey, flew up the ladder disappearing from our sight.

"Now Corp I want everything re-checked this time move everything, lift beds, move cupboards pull-down charts or shelves. My gut tells me we are not wrong in thinking this friggin back door is close by".

With that Corporal Farrell turned to his Section. "Will do Sir, you heard the Major wreck this rat hole".

I remained in the dining room rotating around each time I heard furniture being thrown around or a soldier swearing at something.

The boys were getting into it when I heard one of them yell. "Here, here it is!". Everyone stopped what they were doing and rushed into what must have been a prayer room.

There was a small Qibla on the wall to the right. I had seen these before, it showed the believers the direction of Mecca. However, our Commando was standing about halfway down the room leaning on the wall on the left side. There was a sort of carpet or mat hanging on the wall. It depicted the view looking out of a Mosque somewhere into a garden with a water fountain in the centre. It was perhaps two metres across and hung down from the ceiling to the floor. The Private was proudly holding up one corner of the wall hanging. A heavy wooden door could be seen behind the carpet. He had found the elusive back door.

I was over the moon at this discovery. "Great work Private, you two help him pull that thing down but whatever you do, don't touch that door until I get a look at it".

Once the carpet had been removed I studied the door for booby traps. I had a thought there would be none so escaping soldiers could quickly open it and go, or, if the door was booby-trapped, it would be a quick and easy disarming process, like a switch of some sort and not very sophisticated either. I had a look and there it was, a simple ring hanging on a line that went through the door to the other side. I gingerly pulled the ring; the line came back through the door without resistance and at the end when it did finally catch there was a small click. I was hoping that small click signified it was safe to open the wooden door and go into the secret passage.

It was my theory, so I figured it was up to me to test it. I turned the door handle and with a little creaking sound the lock opened, and the heavy door swung away from me on its rusty hinges.

We were in, turning to the Section. "Now boys, same as before, I doubt that they would have trips in here because Talibs bugging out along this tunnel would set them off for sure, but please still be careful hey?" I felt like I had done my bit down here, so I handed it over to Corporal Farrell.

"Follow this to the end and when it comes out throw some smoke so that the fly boys can see it and it'll stain the grass. You guys will have flushed out anyone in the escape tunnel so either you'll catch them, or the Helos will. I'm going topside to see how they're going. Catch up for a beer after we get back".

Corporal Farrell stepped forward. "Roger that Sir and thanks. You saved our arses on those Claymores."

I climbed the inside ladder up to the surface. When I reached the top, I looked out carefully to see how the raid was progressing. I could see our boys pinned down by several Talibs sheltering behind the burning wreckage of the Quads and other tractors and equipment. I was off to the side, so the enemy soldiers were unable to see me climb out of the stump and crawl around to their right flank. With no comms, I hoped the Commandos could see me and realise who I was and what I was doing.

There were five brave Talibs fighting it out with about fifty or so Commandos. Somehow the baddies had found another Dushka Machine Gun that was multiplying their firepower. Heavy Machine Guns are not that easy to carry ready to fire and throw around aiming at random or moving targets.

They are best resting on their built-in by-pods or mounted on a vehicle. I was relying on this when I stood up twenty or so metres at the side of the flattened shed. Aiming and moving my barrel I emptied my clip into the group. Not one of them even had time to think about trying to swing their Dushka in my direction before dying in that red dirt. Feeling a bit exposed I shoved a fresh Mag into my M4 and moved behind the same cover the dead Talibs were lying behind. They didn't need it anymore. Finding cover is just an old habit but when the lead is flying everywhere, it's a good habit.

The Colonel and a Section of ten or so Commandos joined me. Their uniforms had well and truly been christened. Each man including the Colonel was filthy, and to varying degrees covered in blood, someone else's hopefully, but in some cases their own. The Colonel looked around making sure the other Commandos were deployed in a defensive pattern around the farmhouse and truck turning area.

"Thanks, Steve those guys were pretty hot on that HMG. I think things are going pretty well now. Of course, until it goes quiet we still don't know how many Talibs were here to start with or how many are left. So far, no sign of the Rabbit or the others either. We've surrounded the house, it's a bit tricky but we don't want to flatten it because we're hoping to get those Leaders alive. Who knows what Intel they might have, either in their heads or inside the house?"

As they say, be careful what you wish for. Just as he was speaking a figure burst out of the house and stood on the verandah. He was holding the easily identified shape of an RPG up to his right shoulder and aiming straight at us. As he fired the tell-tale exhaust smoke hid him from sight. It didn't matter. As soon as I had seen him in the aiming stance I had reacted without thinking. I crash tackled Colonel Black, driving him behind some Quad wreckage. The explosion knocked the damaged Quad onto both of us, but it had taken the brunt of the concussive power and the shrapnel. Dazed and bloodied from a cut over my left eye I staggered to my feet. Thankfully Black had made it. He was beside me leaning on some twisted steel that he was using to climb to his feet.

Two of the Commandos who had been beside us had not been as lucky. They were dismembered and the smell of burnt flesh filled my nostrils and I gagged. Damn these pricks in the house! Once again, an RPG had caused me grief just like in my recurring flashback dream. We couldn't respond in kind because, as the Colonel had just said, we wanted them alive if at all possible. As I looked through the haze and smoke I saw the same man run onto the verandah again. He had rushed inside the house and had reloaded the RPG which was now aimed at the main body of Commandos. Nine years earlier standing over the shattered bodies of that SAS Patrol I had made myself a promise. What had happened that day in Afghanistan because of a slight hesitation on my part in allowing the Talib to get his RPG shot away, would never happen again. Time is a spectacular thing. Sometimes in battle, it can seem like time slows nearly to a full stop, this was such an instance. I aimed my M4 Assault Rifle at the man who was now raising the RPG to his shoulder. Allowing for the distance and the fact that when a weapon is on full auto the barrel usually climbs to the right, I squeezed the trigger sending off eight or ten rounds. I was rewarded by the appearance of a red zipper of bullet holes from the man's left hip up to his right shoulder. The knock-down force of these super-fast 5.56mm rounds meant he fell where he stood, the unfired RPG clattering to the hardwood verandah floor.

I didn't know it at the time, but I had just ended Commander Zahir's life. He had come such a long way to die on a dusty farmhouse verandah, but he had died bravely.

CHAPTER 29

Meanwhile, Corporal Farrell and his Section had been following the escape tunnel without any enemy contact or other incident. They had been moving along the compressed dirt floor for nearly half an hour when they saw a glimmer of light up ahead signalling that they were getting close to the end of the passage. The Section had been in either partial darkness or low artificial light for some hours now. To restore the men's vision, the Corporal wisely held up his hand signalling to stop before going outside into the harsh western Queensland sun. Once their eyes had adjusted to the light, they moved carefully through the opening which was like that of an abandoned mine.

They were too well trained to bunch up and have a meeting once outside. All the soldiers knew there could be enemy soldiers anywhere on this property, especially around the exit of the escape tunnel. Once outside Corporal Farrell remembered my suggestion and pulled out his coloured smoke grenade used to signal choppers and to assist them to read wind speed and direction for landing. This time it was to pinpoint Objective Back Door, so the fly boys could sweep the area and pick up any stray Talibs before they hit the cordon set up by Alpha Platoon. Farrell pulled the pin on the smoke grenade and tossed the canister. It twirled and cartwheeled until it hit the ground spewing out yellow smoke and creating a yellow stain on the branches and grass around its final resting place. After hours of being underground and with the strain of searching and expecting to be shot at or blown up easing, the Commandos were enjoying being in the sun again. It would be unfair to say they were switched off, but they had slowed down a gear or two.

Their minor relaxation resulted in all the Sections being caught watching the grenade being thrown. If they hadn't been distracted, one of them may have seen the group of four Cadre Staff off to their right. Unbeknown to them, as predicted, some of the baddies had fled using the Back Door and tunnel. However, they had escaped before anyone knew where the exit was. The Commandos must have been just behind the escaping Cadre staff. Too late for any defensive reaction the sounds of the bush were destroyed by the distinctive sound of several AKs firing on full automatic. When the smoke cleared only three Commandos remained able to return fire.

This was a classic case of relaxing near the perceived end of a patrol. The Vietcong had discovered that the American soldiers were alert while moving through the jungle on Patrol. However, when they got to a few Klicks from their camp they switched off. The Vietcong would set their ambushes and booby traps to capitalise on this. It is for this same reason that a lot of road accidents occur close to home. Drivers relax and begin to think about dinner or that first cold drink and sadly pay the price.

These young Commandos who had done such an outstanding job right up to that point sadly paid the ultimate price. The remaining soldiers looked around for guidance. But they soon discovered they were without their leader Corporal Farrell. He had caught a round in the neck and lay nearby in an ever-growing puddle of blood forming around his crumpled body. They had screwed up big time. However, that time had passed, and their training kicked in. They regrouped and commenced returning fire in the direction the onslaught had originated.

They did not realise that the Ex-SAS Cadre Staff, having successfully ambushed them, had already left, standard SAS ambush tactics. The small group of Commandos now led by a young blond Corporal were surprised to hear motorbike engines start up. As one they ran toward the engine noise. Together they crested a small rise just in time to see the four Cadre Staff race away in a cloud of dust. They were gone, it was too late.

The Corporal swore and said to his three-man squad. "They must have had the Quads hidden under camo nets for just a situation like today."

The Black Hawks had been scouring the property from boundary to boundary and so far, had not fired a single shot. These were highly trained Officers flying a $5.9 million Helo capable of unleashing hell in an incredibly short amount of time. The second pilot, a Captain named Paul Goodwin, saw a flash of red off to the east, then some blue and then another two more of red.

His red moustache twitched as he spoke to his mate. "Four Quads at our nine o'clock, B.J. Head over and we'll see whether they are goodies or baddies hey?"

BJ answered and laughed. "Roger that Paul, finally we might get a chance to get loud".

The Helo's nose lowered a little as it banked hard left levelling off three hundred feet above the short vegetation that blurred with the increased speed as the Black Hawk accelerated towards the rapidly disappearing coloured shapes. It was impossible to tell whether the Quads realised they had been spotted or not. But all four seemed to speed up and away from the Helos. The bikes slipped out of sight down a hillside and then turning sharply, headed up a thickly vegetated gully that lead out to the main highway. The four escaping Cadre Staff hadn't heard the Helos over the sound of the Quads. They were just being over cautious as was their normal approach to everything, but especially bugging out under attack. Each member knew the property well having spent hours riding around it doing a bit of hunting on their downtime.

The Helos simply gained altitude and eliminated the dead ground by getting above the gully the Quads had been hiding in.

The Co-Pilot exclaimed. "BJ, those uniforms aren't Commando and the other confirmation is them running so hard away from the farmhouse towards the highway".

BJ was a highly experienced Pilot who loved his job. "Paul, I say we are a GO. Let's nail them before they either get away or do some more harm." As BJ said this he thought: *what's that up ahead.*

The Helos crew could see two Commandos standing near a gate that lead through to the highway. The men manning the cordon were standing to, alert and ready for anyone coming their way. The pilots were pleased to see the two Commandos had the brains to be behind the little bit of cover that was available.

"BJ, our Rules of Engagement cover this exact scenario, which means we can blast these pricks into oblivion. What do you say?"

"I say let's rock and roll Boss." The Co-Pilot shouted.

With that he reached down selecting the General Electric M134 7.62mm Mini-gun, he was tempted to choose the 2.76" Folding Fin Air Rockets (FFAR) but wanted to make sure he eliminated them all. If he had attacked them with rockets he would not have been sure that all four Tangos (Targets) were down for keeps. He fired; the cyclic rate of the Mini-gun absolutely obliterated the four Quads and their riders as six thousand rounds a minute passed through man and machine in a blur of metal and bloody body parts.

The two Commandos on the cordon had heard the Helos approach but had not seen or heard the Quads until the Black Hawk rained down its deathly fire upon the four fleeing Cadre Staff. Neither Commando had ever seen anything so devastating nor so fast. The scream of the Mini-gun was mixed with four small explosions as the Quad's fuel tanks exploded. When the silence settled it was like a solid mass after the incredible cacophony of the air attack. It was as though they had each lost their hearing at precisely the same moment.

As we watched the farmhouse I knew there was no time to celebrate as the other two occupants could be seen making their way into the scrub at the rear of the old home. As it had been too dark to be 100% sure who the RPG shooter was that I had killed, I jumped up onto the verandah praying that the house was now empty. I turned over the body of the RPG soldier and saw a man perhaps in his mid-thirties. I now knew who the two runners were. They had to be the Rabbit and Fitzpatrick. All I knew was one way or another I was going to chase the pair down.

As fast as I could move I made my way to where I had last seen the two men. This was a bonus for me because if Fitzy had taken off by himself he would have used all the tricks in our SAS Handbook. However, dragging along an older man, Head Terrorist or not, would have to slow him down and make tracking them easier. Surprisingly it didn't slow him at all probably due to the Rabbit's endurance gained in a harsh life in Afghanistan. I respected SAS training too much for me to assume anything less of Fitzpatrick's skills. This would have been a big mistake. I knew that a trained and experienced Ex-SAS Captain who was on the run would still be highly aggressive.

Fitzy may have even prepared this exit route so there was no way I was going to rush on into one of his surprises. It has always been a balancing act between caution and speed when you are chasing someone. Now I was faced with that decision. I tracked them as quickly as I dared and although I hadn't seen them since they left the house I was sure I wasn't too far behind them. Coming to a thick stand of Brigalow trees it struck me that their silver leaves seemed out of place in amongst the green and browns of much of the surrounding vegetation. It crossed my mind that I had no choice but to avoid the Brigalows which meant I would be exactly where Fitzpatrick knew I would end up. It wasn't a pleasant thought at all. Just as I rounded the part of the thicket that lead back onto some sort of trail I saw the smallest reflection of something across the track, a trip wire. Any other time of the day it may well have been invisible lying across the path in the shade, but the growing light had exposed it. I wanted to make Fitzpatrick think he had got me, maybe this would cause him to slow down a little. Looking at the trip wire there was no way it set a swinging spear trap or something similar. I now knew what he had left for me. I moved down the trail to what I figured would be out of the kill zone.

Picking up a solid-looking broken branch a bit less than a metre long I threw the stick. It landed squarely on the trip wire and immediately the quiet of this part of the bush was shattered by three simultaneous explosions. The sounds were just separated enough to discern the booby trap consisted of three Claymore Mines. Their thirst for blood not being quenched on this occasion.

Aziz was used to long arduous treks back in Afghanistan, but he was totally exhausted, not from the escape or the walking and running. Following this Australian traitor, he felt absolutely gutted by the realisation that all he had conceived was gone. All that he had worked for, all that convincing of others the Operation should proceed, had come to nothing, a total failure in anyone's terms. Aziz was under no delusions that Major Smith saving him and helping him to escape was through loyalty to the cause or even to him. It was as usual purely and simply the money. Without Aziz, Major Smith would not get paid. Smith couldn't care less about what had happened. He knew for sure that any break in security hadn't come from him or his men, and although he respected and got on well with Zahir, losing him, well that was a pity but that was the business they were all in.

As he ran along the Major assumed his men, the four Cadre Staff, were either dead or captured. He thought: *so, what, I will have to take their share as well.* It might appear to be a disaster but within any chaos, there is always a pattern and all going well he would soon be home scot-free and very well paid, thank you very much. When this old rag head puffing along behind him paid him, if he had any extra money with him Fitzpatrick would simply kill Aziz and take the lot, a sort of performance bonus. Fitzpatrick's thoughts of wealth and freedom were interrupted by three explosions behind them. Aziz heard the explosion too and smiled thinking: *whoever was pursuing them had not made it past the booby trap* as Major Smith called it. The Major had guided Aziz safely around the trap and had quickly explained what it was. Fitzpatrick smiled too, hoping the Claymores had got all his pursuers. Of course, he still didn't know that he was being chased by his old friend and fellow SAS Officer, Steve Wallace.

I thanked God that the little bit of sunlight filtering through had saved me and I hoped that my quarry had now relaxed a little. One thing for sure was that Fitzpatrick had already had the foresight to have an escape route planned and to have set booby-traps along the way. What worried me most was, if he was this organised where was he heading and what did he have ready to escape in? I started working through the possibilities; a vehicle, a plane, I knew at least there was not enough water for a boat, so it was either road or air. I noticed my quarry had suddenly picked up the pace. Fitzpatrick was doing the opposite of what most Soldiers would do, He was not relaxing because the booby trap had been sprung. He had increased the pace since the Claymores went off. We had come out of the wooded ridges area and now the country opened to cleared grasslands. Now for all of us, there was nowhere to hide.

I visited this property years ago when this used to be a beautiful forest full of deer hidden in the thickets of the bush. However, the cattle farmer had cleared the entire paddock and now it resembled a motley-coloured undulating billiard table. There was not even a fallen log to hide behind. My only consolation was both Fitzpatrick and Aziz as well as myself had the same problem. Neither hunter nor quarry had anywhere to hide, except for the odd natural gully or small hill. Looking ahead as I ran it was from such a gully that the shape of the two men appeared. One moment I was in this massive paddock by myself and then all of sudden they appeared out of this gully. They were still a good kilometre ahead of me. I thought: *man, where is my Barrett 50 Cal Sniper Rifle when I needed it?*

The cleared paddock ended about six hundred metres in front of them. There was a three-strand barb wire fence and then more scrub. They hadn't slowed their pace at all. Where were they going in such a rush?

I could see they were both dressed in camos and I could also tell which one was Fitzpatrick because he was striding ahead of the older man. Fitzpatrick reached the barbed wire fence and although he was a long way off I could tell by the movement of his body he was cutting the wires. He stood up after cutting the bottom wire and the two men walked into the adjacent paddock. As they did so Fitzpatrick turned to Aziz possibly to say something. I threw myself to the ground hoping that from that distance I would blend in with the ground and grass.

I must have been a fraction slow and with someone like Fitzpatrick, a little slow was plenty of time for him to see me. He turned his shoulders towards me and I realised he was actually sighting on me, lucky for me he was armed the same way as the rest of the Talibs with an AK74. The modern AK is a fine weapon but only at shorter distances. Three hundred metres on full auto and maybe four hundred metres when set on single shot. Thankfully, I was a good seven hundred metres back. Now on a range from a prone position with plenty of time he still might have been lucky enough to hit me.

That is if I was stupid enough to stand still for him. But no way was I standing at attention waiting for him to figure out where to aim to put a bullet in me. I started running and rolling with him firing from the offhand position just standing there with no rest or support to keep the rifle still enough for an accurate shot. After five shots he gave up.

I was really pleased because I was worn out jumping around and I figured if he kept it up that eventually, he might get lucky. A saying that I have always liked is: 'even a broken clock gets it right twice a day'. Aziz had kept going all this time, so when Fitzy stopped shooting he ran after Aziz. I jumped up and took off after them while trying hard to get my breath back.

I was nearly at the barbed wire fence when I saw a flash of something about halfway up the next ridge. I wasn't sure what had made the reflection, but it was something big not like a binocular or telescopic sight on a rifle. I then heard a rumbling sound, I knew straight away. It was a sound I was very familiar with, but I just couldn't peg what it was. Suddenly with the sound of cracking saplings and the deep roar of a big V8 motor, a camouflaged Humvee broke from cover. Like a startled Gazelle the big American Military Vehicle literally leapt out of its hiding place and careened down the hillside. I then realised the reflection that I had seen must have been Fitzpatrick clearing branches or a camo net off the vehicle's windscreen. As the vehicle completed the sliding bouncing descent of the ridge, Fitzpatrick threw the vehicle sideways to orientate the Humvee towards the direction he wanted to take. There was the faintest hint of a track he had made months before. It would not have been obvious or indeed even continuous from above, certainly not from satellite height.

I stood there in a different predicament to the one Fitzpatrick had been in a short time ago when trying to stretch his weapon out to a longer range than its optimum. My M4 had a maximum range of three thousand six hundred metres and the Humvee was less than a thousand metres away at present. However, I was still thinking about all that Intel Aziz held under his turban and how many lives could be saved if that information was in our hands. I held my fire there was no point in chasing them harder. All I could hope for was that Alpha Platoon would pick them up. Or if by some chance they slipped through, the A.F.P. would get them on the road somewhere. I turned to make the long walk back to the Terrorist Camp when I heard the wop of a Helo. The sound was echoing off the ridge-line and I was having trouble working out where it was coming from.

As I started back, the Black Hawk was getting louder and louder and I estimated it was a lot closer to me than I had originally guessed. I was about two hundred metres into the cleared paddock when the chopper broke cover from behind a large rocky outcrop over to my east. The thought crossed my mind that I was very pleased they were on my side as I was caught out in the open like the proverbial dog's balls. The chopper passed me as I waved over my shoulder not even bothering to turn. The big black Helo banked, hovered and landed just in front of me showering me with dirt and small sticks. The door slid open and Colonel Black's face appeared. He had received some medical treatment and his head wound was now covered by a large white bandage.

Colonel Black's screamed. "Well, get in we haven't got all friggin day" he shouted over the Helo. What could I do but obey, I jumped in and slammed the door shut."The Rabbit and Fitzpatrick are in a Humvee going South along that dry creek bed." I shouted.

The Commando Officer was obviously pumped and alert from the past hours of combat. "Good work Steve. I didn't know if you got a chance to nail them but in a big way, I'm glad you didn't. Aziz will be like a Taliban Google if we can get him talking." Looking through the windscreen he pointed. "We should be getting pretty close to the cordon". As we swung around a bend in the creek the Colonel's speech was interrupted by what we could now see out of the side windows. There were two lifeless bodies thrown on either side of the track. It was hard to tell exactly what had occurred, but it looked like the two young Commandos had attempted to stand on the track to stop Fitzpatrick's Humvee. From the way, the bodies were twisted and their placement, one on each side of the track, I figured that the mongrel traitor had probably accelerated through them mowing the Soldiers down without looking back. The cruelty of what we saw and assessed was not lost on the pilots. I wasn't wearing a Flight Helmet with comms, but I saw the Colonel was listening. His voice was filled with anger and sadness as he spoke. "I am now very sorry we can't blast these pricks into little pieces, they sure deserve it."

We caught up to the Humvee just after it made it onto the highway. They turned towards Roma perhaps thinking they were home free having burst through our cordon. They had no way of knowing there was a second perimeter in place. I could hear the Colonel trying to get patched through to the A.F.P Radio Frequency, and it wasn't going well. We had decided to use this Freq as it was a strong possibility that Fitzpatrick would have used a scanner to monitor the local Police radio activity.

Fitzpatrick was very aware he was being tailed by the Black Hawk and knew full well that at any time they could have unleashed hell on the Humvee vaporising its escaping occupants. He signalled toward the Helo. "Aziz, I think they must have plans to capture us otherwise we'd be dead now."

He didn't realise how right he was. The decision had been made to attempt capture first and eliminate only as a last resort. We still couldn't get comms with either of the AFP boys manning the roadblocks and as the Humvee sped towards the checkpoint we wondered how to play this out. With the memory of the two young Commandos from Alpha Platoon fresh in our minds, we didn't want the Humvee to arrive at the checkpoint and wreak havoc without giving them ample warning. The pilot knew exactly where the roadblocks were and told us because the Helo was a lot faster than a Humvee, he had time to get us there and land giving us an opportunity to warn the Police at the Checkpoint.

The Colonel didn't hesitate to agree to the plan adding it might be best to land out of sight behind the roadblock. The pilot hit the go pedal and the Helo rose and bucked like a horse that just got the spurs. In less than seven minutes we could see the assortment of law enforcement vehicles parked across the highway, blue and red lights on flash.

We must have made a scary sight climbing out of the chopper filthy dirty, covered in all manner of other things and all carrying rifles. There was no time for pleasantries, so we quickly explained the situation. Between us, we worked out where we would be and what we would do when Fitzpatrick arrived with the Rabbit.

It was decided that Fitzpatrick was totally expendable and was driving when I last saw them, so if push came to shove I was to shoot Fitzpatrick in the driver's seat and hopefully that would end the chase. The Humvee was to be stopped routinely as though no one manning the roadblock knew they were the targets.

CHAPTER 30

If we could take them without a fire-fight well and good, but they had proven themselves extremely dangerous, so the Police were encouraged to show extreme caution. Fitzpatrick knew me so if he saw me he would immediately smell a rat and probably attempt to drive through. I hid from view behind one of the Police cars, I was able to see them but shielded from their view. Colonel Black kept his mike open, so I could hear the conversation that was about to take place. The Rabbit and Fitzpatrick took what seemed to be an eternity but was in fact only four minutes. The Humvee flew around a corner and then crossed a small bridge over a dry creek. Presumably, on seeing the roadblock, the aggressive war wagon slowed, the driver then accelerated gently towards the barriers. As they got closer our plan went out the window.

Through my scope, I could see Fitzpatrick had changed sides with Aziz who was now driving the Humvee. He drove a little closer to the barrier of cars and Police signs and then came to a complete halt. I couldn't believe my eyes. Fitzpatrick was in full SAS uniform including a peak cap with badge as he opened the passenger side door. Lifting an AK off the seat he pointed the muzzle to the ground and put one foot on the bitumen road.

Fitzpatrick then attempted a huge but creative bluff. "Oh, am I glad to see you guys I have Aziz in custody. I let him drive so I could keep control of him. I'll need one of you to accompany us to the airport where we can fly him to Canberra for questioning".

He delivered this speech with such confidence and sincerity I was glad we had got here first. I reckon he may have conned them into helping him onto a plane and escape. Colonel Black's sidearm was held loosely but decisively in his right hand as he stepped forward.

Black appeared to be playing along with the traitorous Captain. "Good work............." cleverly, his words trailed off like a question as in who are you?

"Major Smith SAS at your service Sir". The Colonel was thinking; *this man has more hide than a frigging rhino,* but his face never revealed such thoughts.

Meanwhile, the Colonel had gotten within good pistol range. I had learned to like and respect this no fooling around Colonel. But man, he had some guts to walk up to a known fugitive, SAS trained and holding a loaded AK74. Colonel Black had had enough of this traitor's theatrics. Perhaps he was starting to think about all the young faces he would never forget that had died today due largely to this prick of a traitor arrogantly standing in front of him.

Benefitting the traitor's created role he made a request. "Major Smith you have done exceptionally well as I have grown to expect from you SAS Officers. I think it best if your hand over the prisoner to me and head back to your unit".

Fitzpatrick must have figured this was it. He wasn't going to change a Colonel's mind, especially one who looked like he'd been in battle all day and had had enough.

With one smooth action Fitzpatrick swung the AK up to his shoulder and sighting on a target in the middle of the roadblock shouted. "Open that frigging road up and let us through or I'll blow that bitch's head off as pretty as it is, and she won't be the last I get."

Hearing his threat, I quickly looked through the side windows of the Police car I was sheltered behind to see who his target was. To my shock, it was Constable Chris Jackson. She was just plain unlucky I guess. Jackson seemed to have a knack for being in the wrong place at the wrong time. Show Time I guess. I wanted to distract Fitzpatrick and stall him until we were ready to act.

I stood up from behind the Police car. "Fitzy you haven't got a chance. Give it up and I'll see they look after you as best as possible, all considering".

"Well am I dreaming, is that you Steve what are you doing way out here I heard you were retired keeping Jack Daniels in business".

Coldly I asked, "Very funny, how could you be such a friggin traitor Fitzy?"

His perfect teeth showed as he went on. "Just got sick of getting jerked around by fools and paid nothing for it. Steve, it's nothing personal, it's just business and a truck load of money mate, an absolute ton."

Fitzpatrick seemed to think he could buy his way through this. "Tell you what mate how about you stop aiming that M4 at me and come over to the dark side. I have a truckload of Yankee bucks I would be happy to share with an old SAS mate like yourself. What do you say?"

I knew he was playing for time. I had shown more than enough patience seeing I was flat out stopping myself from ending him the other night. What I had seen him do to those young fellas on the track hadn't changed my mind. He had to go for everyone's sake.

"OK, Fitzy I suppose I........", I purposely left my words unfinished, so he would think I was still talking.

My sights were steady as a rock on his forehead. My finger took up most of the pressure on the M4's trigger, letting out some breath I held the rest as I caressed the last of the trigger. Fitzpatrick's cap flew off his head as his brain vaporised coating the interior of the vehicle with blood, bone and brain matter. He fell to the hard-black tar and twitched once never to move again. With the threat of Fitzpatrick eliminated Colonel Black took this opportunity to take several steps closer to the open passenger door of the dusty Humvee.

Aziz had been amazed by what Major Smith had tried and for a while had appeared to be succeeding. He had been lulled by the

Major's convincing tones. He listened intently to the conversation he struck up with some unseen voice owned by someone the Major had known from the past. The entire incident was just like a scene from a dream. And dreams nearly always had a way of suddenly having a twist or a shocking surprise at the end. This one was no different. Aziz was covered in sticky warm blood and brain matter courtesy of the Major. All his plans were now destroyed.

After years of evasion, he was about to be captured. He was sure that he would be interrogated, although he didn't know if Australians tortured people. However, he was certain the CIA would end up 'talking' to him as well. Aziz had never experienced such a strong feeling of being a crushed defeated man. He knew for certain there was nothing to go home to but humiliation, not to mention a highly probable beheading. His days as a Leader were over, those slimy ambitious young bucks had won. With those thoughts, Aziz picked up the automatic pistol from the seat beside him and attempted to place it beneath his chin and fire. Colonel Black was not in any state of confusion or a distracted daze by the spectacular violent events of the last fifteen seconds. He was focused on one thing and one thing only, the Rabbit Aziz.

All the harm this one man had caused around the world. All the hatred he distributed and all horrendous acts of terrorism that Aziz had brought to Black's beautiful country Australia. Even today he was responsible for the deaths of so many good young men on both sides. Black thought: *Aziz deserved to die more than once, more than most people he could think of, amongst some terrible people.* Colonel Black was standing near the open passenger door straddling Fitzpatrick's lifeless body and could see the fear and abject defeat on the face of the once brave and powerful Taliban warrior. Black anticipated the final act of such a desperate man. The very instant Aziz placed the gun under his chin the Colonel fired his pistol blowing Aziz's hand from his wrist whilst he was still clenching the gun. Aziz screamed like a wounded animal and maybe that was fitting. The Rabbit had been caught.

CHAPTER 31

NATIONAL SECURITY CENTRE
CANBERRA, AUSTRALIA
13th JUNE 2014

Twenty-four hours later I found myself sitting next to Colonel Goodrich looking over the huge boardroom table at the MAJGEN and Brigadier Dodds. The Commando Officer Captain Black was immediately to my left followed by A.F.P Commissioner Doug Wilson, Intel Section Head Clive Millard was next and the PM's rep Felix Norman. You would never say the room had a party atmosphere, but it was certainly lighter than that first meeting that seemed so long ago.

Major General Watson commenced proceedings. "Welcome back gentlemen, I trust that you've had time to eat and receive any medical assistance you required? I cannot say how happy we all are at the outcome of our operation. We are all painfully aware that we lost thirteen good men including Captain Thompson and have twenty-seven wounded but thank God I'm told they will all make a full recovery. The Rabbit, I suppose we can now call him Aziz, is secreted away and is being *interviewed* as we meet. I would assume that process will take some time given the seniority of the man and perhaps his reluctance to share. I will not waste your time making a long speech about how grateful your Nation is but let me assure every member at this table that is the case. I will hand over to Brigadier Dodds to touch on some detail now".

Brigadier Dodds nodded and without any introduction, in a calm quiet voice commenced. "Together you averted a terrible plague on the Australian public. Innocent men, women and children were the targets. Intel collected in that farmhouse showed twelve heavily populated target areas such as shopping malls and train stations across the eastern seaboard. From the Intel, in the farmhouse and the specially built training facilities, we know these soldiers had been specifically trained to attack twelve identified civilian targets and wreak havoc with automatic weapons and possibly RPGs. I thank God we got there in time. Most of you would be aware we recovered documents confirming this Cell coordinated by Aziz was responsible for those bombings all around Australia on ANZAC Day. This testifies to their ruthlessness and dedication to their cause. It appears to have been a second-wave attack that was to be launched from the Terror Farm. Once again coordinated if not designed by our friend Aziz. He really is a nasty piece of work. A glance at those dead eyes of his reveals his hatred of us and probably the motivation behind these attacks, both an official and a personal Jihad I suppose you could say. Just like the bombings, no Military Targets were chosen. These attacks would have been pure Terrorism, creating nationwide fear and uncertainty, possibly even causing civil unrest and pressure on Governments at every level".

The Brigadier took a deep breath through his teeth as he straightened himself in his chair. I wondered if it was to cover his emotions at the thought of the potential devastation to civilians. "Once again targeting civilians, innocents of every age; men, women and children going about their normal lives and just like the bombings a theme of symbolism attacking the very culture of Australian society at its grassroots. These mongrels had charts and maps pinned to the farmhouse walls of the chosen targets."

He hesitated and then continued. "Truly gentlemen the way they had selected these locations and the accompanying notes were nothing less than sickening and horrific." The Brigadier while an experienced and tough campaigner hesitated slightly. The fellow warriors sitting around the table were unsure whether the emotion displayed on his face and in his voice was anger or real compassion for the civilians these terrorists had planned to kill and maim. The Brig continued. "The Australian public must not know, must never know this information. Now gentlemen I am unsure if all of you were informed of the Terrorist's scheduled time frame, but we only just made it with a couple of days to spare. It was a dead-set miracle that their Leadership had decided to hold back deploying the Kill Squads until the very last minute. The Terrorists planned to attack those twelve civvy targets on the 14th, tomorrow in fact, an interesting choice of dates. You are all aware of the importance of symbolism in any Terrorist attack the best or worst example being the bombings all around Australia on ANZAC Day. However, Aziz went the other way and was launching this assault on the first day of Ramadan, this time symbolic to them rather than their intended targets".

The Brigadier paused for a moment. Pouring himself some water from the jug in front of him, he took a deep draught from his glass, clearly preferring for it to be scotch, and then continued. "There is a ton of detail around the operation that most of you saw first-hand if you went inside that farmhouse. Between some other Intel found at the scene and what we hope Mr Aziz will *volunteer* I wouldn't be surprised if we will be amazed at just how well connected this group was. We are also attempting to discover how so many military men with all that equipment could come into Australia without being detected. No one is interested in apportioning any blame, but we must employ a systemic approach to this and plug what appears to be a significant hole in our Border Security."He was enjoying sharing all this good news for a change. "Going back to connections both in Australia and OS, we are also exploring how this crowd can buy a cattle property and operate for what appears to be close on a year. We need to know who fronted them buying the place and carrying out all the day-to-day operations so normally that no one noticed anything. The other biggy is where did the money come from? And gentlemen it seems money was no object, the property, vehicles and the relatively High-Tech training facility plus the employment of captain Fitzpatrick and at least four other rankers as contract trainers all speak big bucks. And just as an example when those four Talibs went to Court in Roma, the local magistrate thought he had them by setting a ridiculously high bail, but no, it was paid in a blink, some six hundred grand."

The group around the table were men of action and this speech was very interesting but painfully long. The Brig droned on. "We also have five Talib prisoners, Privates, I suppose we would call them. While they may not be privy to the upper echelon information and plans we are sure that we can weave together their Intel to come up with some sound data. Then we can use this to target or cross-check our questions put to Aziz. Of course, it's still early days and the good thing is they're terrified, and we are actively keeping them that way. Separated, they are not getting a lot of sleep and a couple have already approached the guards wanting to deal. One interesting example of the type of information so far is that these Kill Squads were not expected to blend in. None of the five speaks English. We found no civvy clothes so one must assume they were going to execute this attack dressed in their ex-Russian camos. That would mean the plan was they were to be deployed and transported to the target site in their camos and kit at the mission location.

We couldn't find a single reference to any retrieval plan, RV plan or travel arrangements. They were simply going to be dropped off outside the mission site. There they would carry out their assignment and it would appear that most of these guys expected to be killed and receive their rewards in Jannah (Moslem Heaven). In the notes we found, the Talib Soldiers had been ordered not to try and escape. They were to fight it out killing as many as possible of the first responders and then die a glorious death. As I said, none of them can speak much English, if any. At present, due to language barriers, we are struggling with one item. Two of them keep raving on about, at least we think they are talking about, a giant crocodile. So, you see we are hoping the pieces will eventually come together as a clear picture of where they came from and how they entered Australia".

The Brigadier continued to speak a little longer, and although I was trying to concentrate, between fatigue and boredom, my thoughts had already turned to sit in front of a fire with Jake, my dog my best mate and Jack Daniels, my counsellor. Don't get me wrong this meeting was worthwhile. It brought all parties up to speed and closed off the operation, but I was tired, and I missed my solitude and the bush. I know it's a bit selfish, but I just hoped that all this action across the road hadn't ruined my little piece of paradise for me. Returning to my simple camp was the only way I would know that, and the sooner the better.

Interrupting my daydream, in the middle of Brigadier Dodd's speech, the Australian Federal Police Commissioner, Doug Wilson sidled up to him and whispered something to him. The Brigadier seemed to go a little pale. You could see the Brigadier considering whatever information he had received.

Brigadier Dodds gathered himself. "Now gentlemen I'm sorry to say there is some interesting and highly disturbing news from Commissioner Wilson. Doug, will you please share your report with the group?"

"Yes Sir, as Brigadier Dodds said, this is a frightening revelation. Once all the excitement calmed down after the camp was raided and escapees either terminated or captured, we all headed back home to regroup and debrief. Back at A.F.P HQ, we talked it all through, Wilson continued. "As you know gentlemen, as wonderful as it is to stop an attack such as we have just done it is always better to head it off as early as possible before any harm is done, or anyone can escape. Anyway, we were working through Major Wallace's reports again. Especially his information regarding the initial contacts he had experienced that was in a way not obvious Terrorist actions although in hindsight they involved Terrorists. Although by itself the altercation in sunny Roma involving that female Police Officer appears on the surface to be simply a criminal matter, we wondered what we could learn from it." The AFP Commissioner stated.

The AFP Commissioner continued. "We started to explore the questions Major Wallace had so efficiently included in his report. Questions he had put to that local Officer wondering if she had seen the perpetrators before and whether she saw a lot of Middle Eastern men around town? Now her answers were not that informative or startling. However, Major Wallace's local questioning provided us with an idea. Now with the benefit of 20/20 hindsight post identifying this Terrorist Camp and now knowing it was a training base, we figured out that if we had answers to just those two questions we would have enough to justify or cause further investigation now knowing what we do. An A.F.P team was assigned to develop a workable checklist of indicators to identify in any location. It included items such as; if there was an increase in day-to-day activities involving either Military types e.g. Ex-SAS Cadre Staff or Single Men or Groups of Men of Middle Eastern appearance. Now I know all the do-gooders will bitch about that being racial profiling and they would be right it is, but bad luck." The celebratory atmosphere had turned frigid in expectation of what was to come.

"Although this all sounds a bit basic if we started with a baseline of a sort of *normal* farm family maybe plus a few workers we could identify the existence of any large groups. This could be done through informal discussion identifying large resupply purchases. For example, a cattle farm that buys dozens of loaves of bread or packets of tobacco, toilet paper whatever, we are going to request that the local Police submit the questionnaire checklist. They can collect the data formally within their own systems and informally from local businesses. If there is nothing to report that's fine but this is an incredibly simple yet effective tool. I'll let you all know how it goes." He then sat down and poured himself some water. The AFP Commissioner concluded.

Brigadier Dodds stood and with a look that betrayed his reluctance to give the next speaker the floor.

The Brigadier turned to the Prime Minister's representative. "I will now hand over to Felix for some brief words. After he finishes we would like everyone to join us on the back deck for a celebratory drink, or by the sound of it, before we all get back to work".

When a Senior Officer invites Subordinate Officers in that way you know attendance is not optional so I mentally swapped Jake for all this crew and started concentrating on my immediate surroundings.

Felix Norman was and sounded like a politician in the making. "The Prime Minister has asked me to pass on his sincere appreciation for what this team achieved. To avoid such a calamity is exceptional work gentlemen, outstanding. The capture of such a high-profile Terrorist and hopefully the Intel we should gather from him is a huge bonus. The other rewarding feature was the high level of inter-service cooperation. I am sure you all understand that your bravery and expertise saved all those civilian lives. It also enabled Australia to avoid the aftermath of fear of further attacks that would have swept this wonderful country. If these planned attacks on the heartland had been executed and if the Australian public became aware of their existence it may well have triggered the worst racial riots in the history of Australia. In a sentence, the success of this operation will benefit all Australians for a very long time. That's why gentlemen I must say, with sincere regret, that the details, the courageous action taken, and any resulting repercussions can never become public knowledge. This operation has of right now been sealed shut."

Especially after the ANZAC Day bombings. The PM's spokesman stated.

The Public Servant continued. "Those negative reactions may still become a reality but if the public became aware of just how close we got as a Nation to being attacked in our homes and who the Terrorists were, we could have mass panic. So, gentlemen indeed your country once again thanks to you for your exceptional service."

With that the meeting wound up, no surprises there, it was a pity in one aspect because there were several Commandos that in a normal situation would have been up for a medal or similar. But that's how it all works. None of us in the Military looks for a medal. We all figured the things we did were simply just doing what we get paid for, and in most cases, anything past that was usually just looking after our mates.

As one we stood and headed out to the deck where there was a nice array of nibblies and, *'you little beauty'*, a bottle of Jack. I had a driver and a jet pilot before I had to drive myself back to my camp, so this looked mighty good.

As I was pouring my first drink a voice behind me caught my attention. "That Fitzpatrick fellow knew you well, hey Steve?" Colonel Black asked with a big smile on his face.

"Yeah, we were close once, but to answer your question, no, he only thought he knew me."

Holding the bottle above a glass I asked, "Can I pour you one, Sir?"

"Thank you, Steve, like all of us I sure could do with a drink" the Commando Colonel replied.

I poured the Colonel a good slug of the smoky brown liquor and we moved off to one side. This was the last time anything could be mentioned about the operation. These were the men that had made it happen and it was good to unload a little with fellow warriors you had kicked the door in with.

Black cornered me away from the group. "Steve I just wanted to say thanks for everything. I fully realise you are a Soldier first and foremost but your involvement at so many levels of this Op was a big part of the success of this mission. On a personal note I know I wouldn't be standing here today if you hadn't pushed me aside from that RPG, so that's one I owe you."

I wasn't sure what to say, just about any answer would either be arrogant or patronising. "Sir, not peeing in your pocket, but you're one of the best leaders I've had the pleasure of working with and certainly one of the bravest men I've known. But when I pushed you out of the way of that RPG it was only because you were in my way".

Colonel Black laughed so loudly that the entire deck turned to see who was making all the noise.

I didn't want to take away from the success of the OP and the need to let off a little steam, but I felt obligated to say, "I'm very sorry for all your losses. Captain Thompson was top class. From the little, I knew of him he was a good bloke and a quick decisive thinker an exceptional leader of troops. The way he overcame some of those obstacles, moving troops around under that Dushka fire was absolutely copybook stuff. He probably deserves a couple of medals for what he did out there, but I guess that will never happen".

Black's face saddened before my eyes. "Yeah, he was a terrific Adjutant. The men would follow him anywhere and, as you say, a bloody good bloke to boot." He lowered his voice, "As far as recognition, the Unit will erect a small memorial to him noting his bravery and his qualities without of course the operational details.

The men wouldn't have it any other way". I raised my glass, "Captain Tim Thompson" the Colonel did likewise. "Captain Thompson".

Everyone on the deck joined in with the toast. The Colonel looked around to see who was within earshot before continuing. After that solemn toast, he came back to my original compliments regarding the Colonel and smiled. "No good flattering me now Steve, it won't do your renewed career any good, I'm thinking of pulling the pin and retiring. There are fish to catch somewhere I am sure".

Smiling back, I said. "Yeah well, Colonel if you do retire, hide a lot better than I did and don't bump into any Taliban when you're out fishing". With that, we both laughed and went back to the bar to refill our glasses.

Thinking how nice it would be back there, I continued. "After everything that's happened I doubt if you'll want to visit Roma in your retirement. But if you do, come and look me up and we'll find a creek somewhere we can throw a line in together".

It was Black's turn to smile this time. "That sounds like a really good idea, Steve. I might do just that."

I could tell Colonel Goodrich was trying to catch my eye, so I farewelled Colonel Black and headed over to where he was standing by himself, looking out over the perfectly manicured lawns of the NSC precinct.

Colonel Goodrich, never one to beat around the bush, came straight to the point, just the way I like it. "Steve I won't make a big speech but thank you for everything you did from go to woe. I have been talking to the Brigadier and the Major General and we all share one opinion, that you're far too useful to let go. I was wondering what you thought about this?" He went on to offer me a contractor's job with the NSC. I would be placed on the Reserve of Officers, meaning I was in but I wouldn't have to attend a unit every day. I would be on call as needed.

If I was to accept this offer, I would operate more independently and covertly. I would be brought in when the NSC had a job that suited my background or skill set. They gave me a week to think it over but emphasised it was my choice. If I said no I was free to fully retire again or, if I wanted to continue to serve, I would be posted to a unit somewhere.

When the word retirement was mentioned I said, "I retire? It's too damned dangerous. I'm safer back in the field." This caused both of us to share a good laugh. Goodrich was like a dog with a bone. "Well that would suit us, Steve, but I am just being single-minded I suppose. We could use a thinker who backed it up with the action when needed, let me know hey?"

The get-together started to close down. It was noticeable that Felix Norman had the one obligatory soft drink and then took off with a politician's wave to the group. We were all too tired and this wasn't the venue for a lot of drinks. We had lost good men and while it's good to celebrate a win, sadly we all knew this was probably only the beginning, not the end. So, after a little while, people started to leave. There were plenty of handshakes, shoulder slapping and promises to keep in touch. I made a point of approaching the MAJGEN, the Brigadier, and Colonel Goodrich, shaking their hands and thanking them for everything.

Brigadier Dodds' nose had turned a little darker red than normal with a couple of Johnny Walkers in him and he couldn't help himself. "Steve, give some serious thought to the idea Colonel Goodrich spoke to you about. A lot of us think you'd be an asset and you're too bloody young to hang up your spurs anyway. You'd only get bored and make some more trouble somewhere", he said with a fatherly smile beaming under his glowing nose and regulation moustache.

Laughing quietly, I said my goodbyes to everyone, grabbed my gear and was in the car on the way to the Airport twenty minutes later. On my way to the airport, sitting in the NSC car I was thinking how I had enjoyed the few drinks on the deck. I had learned very early in my Military career the importance of mess life. Having a drink with those you work with sometimes smoothed out a problem, but mostly it just built trust and understanding. This meant that in a training or real situation you did know the Officers above and below you on the totem pole.

Innocent to what had happened nearby just a few days ago, Roma didn't look any different as the Citation Jet CJ1 flew over the town to set up for the final approach. Except for the local Police, all the people living in town and the surrounding cattle properties and gas pipeline assembly camps had lived and slept through the entire operation. They were oblivious to the potential havoc that had been germinated so close to their day-to-day existence. The memory of a few annoying roadblocks was probably already forgotten by most of them.

There would have been plenty of speculation and rumours discussed over a few Queensland local favourite XXXX beers, at the local pub, but no one would take any of that seriously. I was sure we'd kept a lid on it. The farmer that allowed the Helos to land on his place would believe it was some sort of training exercise and all the loud stuff was out of sight at the Terror Camp. Any neighbours who heard any explosions would have been surprised at how many they had heard. However, they would have put them down to a few stumps being blown as part of clearing a paddock, a common occurrence in these parts. The small arms fire would have been swept away by the winds into the hillsides and gullies before anyone even heard them.

CHAPTER 32

I was so pleased to be back I nearly ran to my old battered Ute parked alongside all those new gleaming Gas Pipeline Utes just like those we had used to transport the boys into our Forming Up Place. My Ute wouldn't start, it's something to do with the starter motor. I hit the starter twice with a hammer and it roared into life. Toby Keith started singing Clancy's Tavern and I felt like things were back to normal. I had three things to do before heading back out to my camp. First, off to the mate's place to pick up Jake who always forgives me for dumping him. He makes me feel loved and wanted by going crazy when he sees me come back on occasions like this. Second, you guessed it, two sausage rolls with lots of tomato sauce later and life would be good, no life would be bloody excellent. Third, on my list of things I must do, I know you thought I was heading to the bottle shop to buy some Jack Daniels. Well, you're wrong, this time anyway. Although thinking about it, I did just add a fourth thing to my mental shopping list, yeah alright a few bottles of JD. I give in.

I parked in Queens Street right outside the white weatherboard Police Station. It was a converted Queensland-type farmhouse with a beautiful wide verandah surrounded by a well-kept low water need garden, bordered by white pool-type fencing. I opened the wrought iron and wire entrance gate and walked through. A few steps later I reached the end of the concrete path and started to climb the wooden stairs, two at a time to the front door. For about the hundredth time I asked myself 'Did *this make sense? Was I being stupid, acting like some dumb teenager'? Yeah, probably but I still wanted to try.*

Inside looked like pretty much every Police Station anywhere in Queensland starting with the cluttered counter, the grubby walls over-crowded with Missing Person Bulletins and anti-Domestic

Violence Posters. On hearing heavy footsteps, I looked up to see an overweight, over-tired-looking civilian clerk walk behind the counter. With some difficulty, she climbed up onto the office stool. Looking up through a mess of blonde curls and red-framed glasses she asked, "How you goin? What can I do for you?"

"Good morning, can I speak to Constable Chris Jackson please?" I smiled after my request.

"May I ask your name please?" the Admin girl enquired.

"Sure. Steve Wallace, hopefully, she'll remember me". Smile again.

With that, the blond leaned forward and placed her weight on the counter to enable her to dismount the stool. A big sigh to compensate for the expended effort, and she slowly walked to the left of the counter disappearing through an open doorway and behind a wall. I kept reading all the Missing Person Bulletins thinking: *are these people dead, do they want to be found? Most of them look like they are on drugs, or sell them, are they in jail somewhere under different names.*

It always amazed me a little how I could look at a sad picture of some missing man or woman and create an entire story around him or her in the minute I was filling in reading old posters. Did everyone judge people this way? Thankfully my deep and meaningful, probably fuelled by fatigue, was interrupted by a gentle cough.

Looking up from the poster I saw Constable Chris Jackson looking a lot better than when we had first met, or even the second time.

The Admin. Officer hovered behind the counter looking like she was busy, but I could tell she was interested in our conversation. I am sure that women working together in a country Police Station would be sharing breaks and talking about men.

Chris smiled. "Steve, I'm so glad you came in. After the roadblock and what happened, you just disappeared."

Being mindful of the security covering that roadblock and its casualties, I gently took the Constable's elbow and ushered her out onto the top step away from friendly but still prying ears. Not answering her question. “It’s good to see you again too, you’re well?”

Nodding and smiling Chris understood moving outside where she picked up where she had left off inside. “And then later they told me you saved my life *again* you seem to be there when I need you most. Thank you for that. Words seem so little compared to what you have done for me.”

Putting on a slightly hurt tone I agreed. “After all that I think you would probably owe me what, two dinners at least and at a venue of your choice, either your favourite restaurant or your place if you can cook.” I laughed seeing the look on her face unsure whether I was serious or not.

Her face lit up with a smile joining in the game. “Well, what can I say to that other than we must remedy the situation immediately. Let's start with Tapas at The Tasting Co down there in Hawthorne Street tonight. Then tomorrow night, Chinese at the Golden Dragon, that is if you like Chinese food? And then you might be ready for a BBQ at my place because I can't cook at all. Frozen dinners and take-away otherwise I would starve.”

Laughing and feeling happier than I had for a very long time it all sounded wonderful to me and it wasn't just the idea of restaurant food. Every word this girl spoke seemed to be like a little bell ringing. What?????? I am starting to have thoughts like a Mills and Boon novel. Not that I would know what they sound like. Where did that rubbish about tinkling bells come from? I knew I was in trouble, I could feel it. But I wasn't going to run this time and I wasn't going to rush anything either. Suddenly Roma seemed a lot better place to be than out at my lonely camp talking to Jake. Feeling like that awkward teenager I used to be, I’d made a date with Chris to pick her up for dinner later that night. She returned to work and I was heading over to a men's clothing shop to buy a new outfit when my phone rang.

It was Colonel Goodrich. On seeing who it was on my screen I was initially annoyed. They had given me a week so why couldn't he leave me alone for that time? I would make my decision by then. Reluctantly, I answered the phone but immediately regretted my anger when I heard the concern in the Colonel's voice.

"Sorry to phone you so soon, Steve."

"Good afternoon Sir, what can I do for you?"

Goodrich continued. "Steve, I'll come straight to the point. We had no idea what sort of a Pandora's Box Doug Wilson's mob was opening with that Indicator Check-list. You won't believe what's happened. I'm sorry I couldn't leave you alone for the week. I'm phoning you purely to keep you in the loop just in case you agree to help, or if we need you again. You'll understand when I explain further. I am 100% sincere Steve. We see your role as operating singly, maybe collecting Intel overseas, eliminating a target.

Not and I say again, *not* being part of another attack force every time one is required. Recent events required you to act in that role as part of a Military Unit but only because you owned the Intel and, as you know, in the role of a local expert guide. The Colonel stated.

Goodrich continued. "So, this Intel I am giving you is just that. At this time, I don't see you involved in any actions resulting from this new info. Well at least at the moment anyway".

He was a good man. I could still hear the anxiety in his voice. "Thank you, Sir, so what's bothering you enough to phone me so soon?"

"No less than seventeen different Police Stations contacted us within five hours of receiving the Indicator Check-list. Steve, we certainly hope they are all false alarms of some sort but being realistic that would be a dream. That means there are probably a dozen live ones out there, potential Terror Camps all over Australia. It's our worst-case scenario come true. Until we have fully assessed each report we won't know what we have or what response is required. But it is not beyond possibility there are another twelve to seventeen established Terror Camps similar to the rats-nest we just torched."

"I saw no point in attempting to minimise this terrible news. So, the obvious question is whether these other camps are at that same point. We can only pray they aren't."

Colonel Goodrich continued. "I can see 2 Commando being very busy from now on. We have requested a Squadron of SAS to be on standby to be deployed in Western Australia and South Australia as targets are identified. Another SAS Squadron is to be based here to cover the Eastern States on a rotational basis. The Northern Territory will be covered by the United States Marine Corps Detachment out of Robertson Barracks Darwin, supported by a few SAS Officers for local input. Steve, it might sound like we're organised but, in reality, we don't have a clue what's going to happen, what we're up against. All we know for sure is that this once safe and innocent Nation of ours is no longer safe and no longer innocent. The enemy has breached our walls."

The Colonel's concerns about where Australia found itself were palpable. "Except for the bombing in Darwin in WW2 and those Jap subs in Sydney, Australia, unlike most places in the world has never seen war within its shores. But we have now, and it appears to only be the beginning. It has arrived on our shores. Australia is going to have to grow up rapidly and painfully". The Colonel concluded.

Sadly, as he spoke, a deep sadness came over me as I realised three things. The Australia we had known was no longer. The relaxed life we were all so used to was never going to be the same again. And although there seem to be more and more people set to give it away, freedom doesn't ever come without a price.

ANY NATION THAT FAILS TO LEARN FROM HISTORY IS DOOMED TO REPEAT THAT HISTORY.

THE END

TO MY READERS.

Thank you for reading Terror In Our Homeland, the first book in the Steve Wallace Series of Action Thrillers. I hope you enjoyed it.

Reviews help other readers find books they may like and assist me to strive for excellence in my writing. I really appreciate reviews, whether positive or negative. Please take a couple of minutes to post your review, thanks.

Thanks

Dave.

MY NEXT STEVE WALLACE ADVENTURE, TERROR IN PARADISE

IS OUT NOW

ISIS are funding their evil plans to dominate the world by selling stolen ancient artefacts. The CIA need Australian Agent Steve Wallace to go undercover to collect Intelligence so the organisation can be destroyed. The money gained from these illicit sales is being used to buy missiles, guns, and ammunition as well as fund cells and terrorist attacks including 911. Steve Wallace is ex SAS and one of the best, but this undercover job calls for a James Bond or Jason Bourne. This time he's way out of his depth. Can he succeed out of his comfort zone? Tracking the smugglers all over the world while racking up a body count he sends shock waves through the sophisticated organisation, all the way up to the third generation New York Antique Dealer.

Steve Wallace comes up against Smugglers, Hitmen, Bedouins and ISIS, and they all want him dead. Will his luck run out this time? This mission becomes a real Terror in Paradise when it takes him to exotic places all over the world climaxing aboard a luxury Cruise Liner travelling to New York.

Based on the true story of ISIS funding its operations by selling stolen ancient artefacts. Hawala is an Islamic banking system employing trust between members not requiring the transfer of funds. It was developed over two thousand years ago and thrives to this day.

Don't miss out!

Visit the website below and you can sign up to receive emails whenever David Adams publishes a new book. There's no charge and no obligation.

https://books2read.com/r/B-A-MAZP-QMHZB

BOOKS 2 READ

Connecting independent readers to independent writers.

About the Author

David Adams served as an Officer in the Australian Army Reserve, trained alongside United States Marines Corps and Special Air Services SAS personnel, and served in the A.D.F as a **Platoon Commander of Military Police**. He has worked alongside **Queensland Police** Officers and held investigative roles with **The Commission for Children and Child Safety.**